Experience the grand dame of "first-rate romance!"
(*New York Daily News*)

TEMPTATION'S DARLING

"A fun, light romance . . . full of witty banter, drama, action, mystery, humor, and unexpected twists."

—*Harlequin Junkie*

MARRY ME BY SUNDOWN

"With humor, a lively pace, appealing characters, a dash of danger, and solid historical detail, Lindsey's latest provides a compelling picture of the Old West, in the author's inimitable style."

—*Library Journal*

BEAUTIFUL TEMPEST
A Malory Novel

"With its lively, bantering dialogue and sharp-edged repartee between hero and heroine, along with the rising sexual tension, readers know they are in for a fast-paced treat. It's marvelous to see how a grand mistress of the genre lures readers into her story while having them believe in the power of love and the wonder of family."

—*RT Book Reviews* (Top Pick, 4½ stars)

MAKE ME LOVE YOU

"[Lindsey] never disappoints, writing love stories that get to the heart of what love can and should be. . . . Compassionate, powerful, and filled with surprises, this latest novel makes readers believe dreams do come true."

—*RT Book Reviews* (Top Pick, 4½ stars)

WILDFIRE IN HIS ARMS

"If readers need to remember why they are Lindsey fans, she delivers every reason in this spin-off of *One Heart to Win*. She incorporates her signature captive/captor plotline with sassy dialogue, plenty of verbal sparring, lots of heat, and a bit of humor, all in perfect proportions."

—*RT Book Reviews* (4½ stars)

STORMY PERSUASION
A Malory Novel

"This is the story Malory pirate fans have been waiting for. . . . There's adventure, sensuality, battles, storms, family high jinks, and rapier wit . . . [with] a slew of Malory family members to satisfy everyone who wants to see their old friends in new adventures as a new generation makes waves. Lindsey delivers!"

—*RT Book Reviews*

ONE HEART TO WIN

"A character-rich, action-packed Western . . . Lively, entertaining . . . Simmered in vengeance and shot through with humor."

—*Library Journal*

LET LOVE FIND YOU

"Filled with Lindsey's trademark humor, sensuality, and emotional intensity . . . Lindsey knows what readers want and makes us believe in love."

—*RT Book Reviews* (Top Pick, 4½ stars)

WHEN PASSION RULES

"A whimsical, magical tale . . . perfect for a lazy summer afternoon."

—*Library Journal*

ALSO BY JOHANNA LINDSEY

Marry Me by Sundown

Beautiful Tempest

Make Me Love You

Wildfire in His Arms

Stormy Persuasion

One Heart to Win

Let Love Find You

When Passion Rules

That Perfect Someone

A Rogue of My Own

No Choice but Seduction

The Devil Who Tamed Her

Captive of My Desires

Marriage Most Scandalous

A Loving Scoundrel

A Man to Call My Own

JOHANNA LINDSEY

Temptation's Darling

Pocket Books

New York   London   Toronto   Sydney   New Delhi

Pocket Books
An Imprint of Simon & Schuster, Inc.
1230 Avenue of the Americas
New York, NY 10020

This book is a work of fiction. Any references to historical events, real people, or real places are used fictitiously. Other names, characters, places, and events are products of the author's imagination, and any resemblance to actual events or places or persons, living or dead, is entirely coincidental.

First Pocket Books paperback edition February 2020

POCKET and colophon are registered trademarks of Simon & Schuster, Inc.

For information about special discounts for bulk purchases, please contact Simon & Schuster Special Sales at 1-866-506-1949 or business@simonandschuster.com.

The Simon & Schuster Speakers Bureau can bring authors to your live event. For more information or to book an event, contact the Simon & Schuster Speakers Bureau at 1-866-248-3049 or visit our website at www.simonspeakers.com.

Manufactured in the United States of America

10 9 8 7 6 5 4 3 2 1

ISBN 978-1-9821-1081-9
ISBN 978-1-9821-1082-6 (ebook)

Temptation's
Darling

Prologue

THE TWO COACHES FOLLOWED the rider out of London to a secluded glade where shots wouldn't disturb anyone. The length of the ride was meant to give the duelists time to change their minds. That rarely happened.

William Blackburn was maintaining silence on that ride, though his friend Peter wouldn't stop listing all the reasons why the duel was a mistake, mentioning more than once that the Rathbans were too powerful to suffer any sort of challenge, a duel wouldn't be the end of it for them.

"Just strike Henry Rathban and claim satisfaction," Peter counseled. "As long as no blood is spilled, you can both walk away without further consequences."

"Perhaps you should be riding in the Rathban coach instead of mine."

"I'm here to help you see reason, Will."

"No, you're here to assure all the rules are followed," William countered. "Are you ready to hear why I've challenged Henry Rathban?"

"Don't say it. I'm to remain impartial. If the insult was too great, I'd want to shoot him m'self, so it's better I don't know."

"Yet you aren't being impartial a'tall when you sound like their bloody arbiter."

"I just want you to be able to walk away from this without further consequence."

"Assuming I won't be the one dead, the consequences are already upon me," William said. "This duel just deals with my rage. Nothing will fix what brought it about. That I will have to live with."

"I'm not asking why! Stop tempting me."

"Then a little silence might be helpful, since we've arrived."

William stepped out of his coach first. Peter followed with the small box that held the matched pair of dueling pistols. William would offer one to Henry Rathban if Henry hadn't brought his own, or accept one of Henry's if offered; he didn't care which pistol he used. It wasn't as if he had a favorite weapon or had ever dueled before.

Henry hadn't brought an impartial second with him, he'd brought both of his brothers instead. Highly irregular, but again, William simply didn't care. The rider who had led them here was apparently a physician who had come to this spot before.

Henry's eldest brother, Albert Rathban, wanted a word with him, another irregularity, but William stepped aside to listen to the older man. "This shouldn't have gone this far. You were asked to recant the challenge. You will shoot at the ground and be satisfied this matter is settled, or I promise you will regret it. Don't cross me on this, Blackburn. I'm not willing to lose a brother over this sordid business."

"Then you should have kept a better leash on your younger brother, or at least warned him not to cuckold other men," William said before he turned away to assume his position for the duel.

It was there again in his mind, the image of his wife naked in their bed, and Henry Rathban just as naked, crawling into it with her. He never would have known of their affair if he hadn't decided to surprise her by joining her in London. She went there occasionally without him, while he stayed in Cheshire with the children. She loved spending a few weeks socializing with her friends during a high Season. He preferred the country. Not once did he ever suspect she was carrying on illicitly while away from him.

Of course he'd recognized Henry that night. The man had been one of Kathleen's other suitors the year William had won her hand. But apparently Henry hadn't lost after all. He'd still gotten the spoils, just without the ring.

William had run to fetch his pistol that night, so blinded by rage he would have killed Henry on the spot. But by the time he loaded it and returned to the bedroom,

Henry was gone and Kathleen was in tears. She swore she was innocent. She swore Henry had blackmailed her into compliance. Then why hadn't she brought the matter to him so he could deal with it? He believed nothing except what his eyes had seen.

He'd felt so betrayed, so utterly furious, it was a wonder he didn't point the pistol at her that night. He kicked her out of the house instead while he drafted the challenge to Henry Rathban. And there had indeed been two missives from Henry's brothers that week demanding he desist from pursuing an innocent man. Calling that blackguard innocent had added fuel to the fire. He'd sent back a note explaining exactly why he couldn't recant and had heard no more from the brothers after that.

Henry did look afraid when they faced each other on the grassy field, turned, walked the requisite paces, and turned again before they both fired their weapons. William didn't aim at the dirt. Henry collapsed where he stood. The physician ran over to examine him and with a shake of his head pronounced Henry dead. William bent down to confirm it, hearing the physician's gasp of shock that he would do that. Henry was indeed dead, it just didn't ease William's rage or his pain.

Peter tried to pull him back to their coach so they could leave quickly, the remaining Rathbans looking furious now. Albert suddenly pulled him in a different direction. William put up a staying hand toward his friend, who seemed ready to fight to free him. But Albert wasn't dragging him to the Rathbans' coach, just out of anyone else's hearing.

The eldest Rathban was in such a rage now, William thought he might issue a challenge of his own. But Albert kept his voice low as he hissed, "You made up an excuse to kill my brother!"

"I caught your brother in bed with my wife!"

"Then maybe you should have dueled with your whore of a wife instead of our innocent brother. You don't get to walk away from this smiling, Blackburn. You will leave England, permanently, never to return, or we will ruin your family with this sordid affair."

"And ruin your own in the process?"

"Hardly. Henry was innocent in all this, and you knew he wasn't a marksman of any distinction."

"I knew nothing of the sort—!"

Albert cut in. "But you still forced this duel, thinking you could get away with murder, when all he did was succumb to your wife's seduction. That wasn't worth dying for, and you don't get to kill him and not suffer for it. You were even warned, given every opportunity to recant your challenge, and yet you still killed him. So absolute exile from England, Blackburn, or your family will pay the price for what you did here today."

William didn't need to think about it. He nodded. What did it matter, after all? His heart was already broken, his marriage was over, so it made no difference to him where he nursed his wounds.

As he got into his coach, Peter asked, "What did he want?"

"To discuss those consequences you mentioned, and no, it's too late to ask what that duel was about. It's just as well you don't know."

Chapter One

Vanessa Blackburn sat on the edge of the cliff overlooking the North Sea. It was a chill spring day in the Scottish Highlands, but she was bundled in her fur-lined winter coat as well as a thick tartan that she could use as a hood if the wind picked up. She wasn't Scottish—well, she was a little. Her great-grandfather Angus MacCabe had been a Scotsman, but his youngest daughter had married an English earl, a Blackburn. Vanessa's father, William, was their only surviving son.

There was an old campfire pit nearby, which she and her father lit in the winter on clear nights when they would sit out here to watch the most bizarre display of lights that filled the sky to the north. She was going to miss that amazing spectacle. She was also going to miss riding across the hills and dales, fishing, helping her father with the cattle and horses, all the things she could only do here. She would be leaving soon.

She didn't want to go. The freedom she'd enjoyed here

was addictive. She didn't want to give it up, but she knew she would have to, at least for a little while when she visited her mother, Kathleen. She was already dreading the arguments and rows they would have when she reached Dawton Manor in Cheshire. She hadn't forgotten for a minute how adamant and determined her mother was about serving up three absolutely perfect daughters to the *ton*. Her mother had already put her and her twin sisters through a grueling regimen of the do's and don'ts of a lady's proper decorum. Her father called it being turned into a puppet, and it had felt that way to her more often than not. He had taken a different approach to educating her when they arrived in Scotland, hiring all sorts of tutors for her and not one of them had mentioned etiquette to her.

She would never forget the traumatic day their lives had changed when she was thirteen. There had been yelling. Her parents had gone outside to do it so no one would hear them, but even from a distance it was obvious they were yelling. She'd watched from an upstairs window with her sisters, the twins in tears. None of them had ever seen their parents fight.

Later that day she was surprised to find her father in his room packing, gathering up everything in the room that was his.

"Where are you going?" she asked.

"Away."

"For how long?"

"Forever."

"Why?"

"Ask your mother." His tone had been angry, but he'd glanced at her then, seen her tears, and held out his arms. She ran into them, refusing to believe it might be the last time he would hug her, but he confirmed it when he added softly, "I'm sorry, darling girl, but I can never come back here."

She ran out of the room to confront her mother, who was in tears, too, but they were angry ones. Still, Vanessa asked, "Why is Papa leaving?"

"Because he has to. There's no choice, and that's all you need to know."

"He said to ask you!"

"Yes, of course he would. And I answered. Now go away. I'm too angry to deal with you girls today."

Vanessa cried for the rest of the day until she decided to sneak away with her father. She even left her mother a note: *You drove Papa away. I hate you, you'll never see me again!*

William was leaving that night in a coach with his belongings piled high on top of it. She left with nothing. She jumped up on the back of the vehicle and climbed carefully to the top, putting a finger to her lips when the driver saw her up there. She revealed herself to her father the next night, only when she got too hungry to hide any longer. Papa was going to take her back immediately. She promised she'd run away again. She swore she wouldn't live at Dawton Manor without him, that she hated Mama for fighting with him and forcing him to leave. He tried to tell her it was nothing like that, that it wasn't Kathleen's fault, yet from his tone and his expression she knew it was a lie. He finally agreed she could stay with him until he got settled, but then he'd have someone take her back. He even arranged that night for a letter to be delivered to Kathleen informing her that Vanessa was safe with him. Her father's plan hadn't come to pass, though every six months he asked her if she was ready to return home. Her answer was always an emphatic no.

He couldn't go back himself. For the longest time he wouldn't tell her why, and she'd asked often, but his answer was always the same: that she wouldn't understand because she was too young. The only thing he would tell her was that before he'd left home he and her mother had come up with a story to account for his departure from England—he'd gone to the West Indies to oversee some of their investments and was in no hurry to come home to dreary, damp England.

When she turned seventeen, she pointed out she wasn't too young anymore. He sat her down to tell her the sordid tale, and that was when she started hating the Rathbans, the odious family who had threatened her father's life and split up her family. An indiscretion led to a duel, which he'd won, with a nobleman named Henry Rathban. His opponent's family had been enraged over the outcome and had promised to ruin him and his family in scandal if he wasn't punished. They'd lost a member of their family that day; his family had to lose a member, too. Him.

"Exile from England was the Rathbans' choice," her father explained. "It was more lenient than 'an eye for an eye.' It could have been much worse. They accused me of deliberately committing murder. Albert Rathban, the eldest, is an earl, but the family is descended from dukes. They are powerful enough to have filed those murder charges against me or just killed me themselves and gotten away with it. You and your sisters would never make good matches if that scandal broke. And my marriage was over anyway, so I didn't mind leaving to protect our good name."

"It wasn't your indiscretion, was it?"

It didn't look as if her father would answer that. A few minutes passed while she waited, but then he said, "No."

Well, that said it all, and she was so glad that she'd never chosen to go home. She had been missing her sisters—and occasionally even her mother—but not anymore. But she and her father had always agreed that once she was of age, she would return to England.

But she loved living with her father in the Highlands. He bred stock, both horses and red-haired cattle, just to keep busy here. It kept her busy, too, since he let her help. The two shire horses he'd taken north with them, he'd mixed with Scottish mares from Clydesdale. Most of the offspring didn't end up as tall as the shires, but one white albino did. Vanessa claimed that one for herself and named him Snow King. At least Snow would be leaving with her. But maybe she didn't have to leave. . . .

She ran her fingers through her copper locks, which she'd cut short for the journey because she refused to ride in a dress and didn't want people staring at her in disapproval when they saw her in britches. She saw the shadow approaching. It had to be her father. The two servants who lived with them, a married couple, never came near the cliffs. She turned and saw him, his dark red hair, which had grown long in recent months, whipping in the breeze. There was a merry glint in his pale blue eyes, the same color as hers.

"It's Thursday," William said. "Do we fish today—one last time, Nessi?"

Yet another thing she was going to miss, hearing him call her by that nickname. He'd given it to her during their first month here when they'd traveled around the Highlands looking for horses and cattle to buy for breeding and two servants who would be willing to live so far from any towns. One of the towns they stopped in was near Loch Ness. There they heard the legend about a monster that lived in the lake, fondly referred to by the locals as Nessi. They even camped out on the water's edge for one night to see if they could spot the water dragon so many people swore they'd seen.

They laughed about it in the morning because the beast hadn't made an appearance for them, but William teased her with the nickname Nessi after that because she could be as fierce as a dragon at times.

As for fishing, she answered with a resounding, "Of course! If the boat survived the tides."

She grinned as she jumped to her feet. Every week, except in the freezing months of winter, they would take that little boat into deep waters and bring home fish for dinner. They often joked that the little rowboat would get smashed against the cliffs, but it never did because her father staked it down so well. But they did always have to empty it of seawater before they took it out.

"Let's go fishing now while the sun is still bright." As she walked toward the path that led down to the rocky shore, she glanced at her father beside her. "I don't have to leave this year just because I turned nineteen."

He sighed. "I let you get away with that reasoning last year only because the twins will be having their official come-out this spring, and if that's something you feel like doing, you'll probably feel more comfortable doing it with them. D'you really want to hide up here any longer when so many adventures await you in the south? You were eager to spread your wings right up until last spring when it was time for you to go. If I didn't know better, I'd think you are afraid."

She stopped to hug him. "The only thing I'm afraid of is my heart breaking when I have to leave you here alone. It's been six years, Papa. Maybe the Rathbans have forgotten about you and you can finally return to England."

"They lost a brother. That's not something people ever forget. Even after you girls are safely married, a scandal like that will still hurt you and your new families. I'm not willing to take that chance."

"But it was a legitimate duel!"

"The Rathbans can make it appear otherwise. Besides, I agreed to this."

She loathed that family, especially the eldest, Albert, the one who had set the terms of their revenge against her father. There had to be something she could do to get them to agree that her father had suffered enough after six years of exile. Of course, she couldn't do that until she actually went to England.

"And besides," he added with a grin. "If you do end up deciding that you want a husband and children, you don't want to be labeled an old maid and be ignored by all the best catches."

She laughed. "You know that won't happen. How many times have you told me I'm beautiful? Or were you only teasing? Perhaps I am ugly and that's why you don't keep mirrors in the house."

He snorted. "You think I didn't see you admiring yourself in the mirror in that shop in Fraserburgh last month? You know exactly how pretty you turned out."

"I was admiring the new britches I just bought."

"Ha!"

She tsked. "Beauty is in the eye of the beholder, so your opinion is biased by love." She held up a staying finger when it looked like he would argue. "It doesn't matter, and besides, I'm not interested in marrying now or when I become an old maid."

"Probably not ever. You're too independent."

She could tell he was teasing, but she was serious when she said, "The only way I would wed a man is if there were a signed contract that stipulates my intended can't tell me what to do, or touch my money. It would be a rare man who would agree to that."

"True, darling daughter, but you would be surprised what a man will do for love."

He smiled wistfully, making Vanessa wonder if he was thinking of her mother. He'd loved Kathleen, Countess of Dawton, enough to defer to her wishes and live in her home instead of moving her into his. He hadn't made the concession because her father's title, Marquis of Dawton, was more lofty than his. He was the Earl of Ketterham, after all, and richer than his wife.

"And you're an exceptional young woman, well educated and a natural at handling horses and pistols," he added proudly. "You also know I was only teasing with that 'probably not ever.' When you fall in love—and I wouldn't want you to marry without it—I don't doubt the man will agree to anything just to have you by his side. But I've prepared you for more than the circumscribed life of a lady. I wish I could have done the same for your sisters, but your mother refused to budge when it came to the social rules she herself was raised by. Now that you've come of age, you have a substantial income, enough money to start that horse-breeding stable you've always dreamed of, though that will be much easier after you marry. So reunite with your mother and sisters and go with them to London to break a few hearts first."

She laughed. Her father made it seem as if all her dreams could come true. While she still had her doubts, she couldn't deny it might be fun to be twirled around a ballroom by a few dashing lords. And once she reentered fashionable society she would undoubtedly cross paths with the Rathbans. She had to figure out a way to make them end the vendetta against her father so he could go home, too.

When they reached the shore, they stopped short, staring at the pieces of the rowboat scattered about. Vanessa started to laugh. William soon joined her.

"It was old, it was bound to happen eventually," he said.

"I'm glad it succumbed. I would have worried about you taking it out by yourself. Promise you won't replace it, at least not until I come to visit."

"If you'll promise you won't cry when you leave."

"I don't cry," she said, but added with a grin, "What do I look like, a girl?"

Chapter Two

CARLTON HOUSE, THE PRINCE Regent's London residence, was as large and opulent as a palace. Montgomery Townsend followed his usual path into the grand mansion, through the foyer and into the well-lit two-story entrance hall decorated with marble columns. Beyond that hall was an octagonal room flanked on one side by the grand staircase and on the other by a courtyard. Besides the magnificent French decor and furniture, Carlton House boasted a superb collection of artworks, most of which were displayed in George's private rooms.

Continuing straight ahead, he entered the main anteroom, where many of the Regent's cronies were clustered, waiting for George to make an appearance, if he deigned to. The door on the left, which led to the Regent's private rooms, was closed.

Montgomery approached a man he recognized whose name he thought was Henry, but he wasn't sure and couldn't be bothered to make sure. He didn't like this group of toadies and didn't pretend to. The only reason they were here was to share in the Regent's extravagances and dissipated lifestyle. But they could still supply useful information.

"What is the mood today?" he asked the fellow. "Money, women, or politics?"

"Prinny isn't saying. He did ask for you, though. You do seem to be his favorite savior."

The jealous tone was noted. Montgomery didn't doubt every man in the anteroom wished to be in his position. Did they even consider that failure could lead to an immediate ousting? George could be that fickle. And where would they be without the Prince Regent's favor? Back with their families or wives or running again from their debtors. The difference between him and them was he didn't care if he was ousted from the Prince's inner circle, though the bigger difference was that he wasn't there with ulterior motives and needed no favor from the future king.

He liked living on the edge. He could blame his brief stint in the army, he supposed. But lately the danger was getting out of hand, with thugs breaking into his rooms and chasing him down the streets brandishing axes. Lord Chanders didn't have the nerve to challenge him to a duel, Lord Halstead was all too eager to, yet he hadn't done anything to provoke either man, although he'd led them to think so. That was the point, after all. He wasn't fed up yet with being the Regent's personal scapegoat, but shifting

Prinny's scandals onto his own shoulders came with a steep price that tarnished his reputation.

Still, Montgomery viewed his clandestine royal service as another way of serving his country now that he was off the battlefield. It was exhilarating. And there wasn't much difference between dealing with his own scandals or those handed to him by George. Dodging bullets on the front lines did something to a man, catching bullets and surviving could have turned him toward a more cautious way of life, but it didn't. The second bullet that had struck him had sent him home to recover for six months, and his father made him promise not to return to the Peninsular War where he'd been stationed or anywhere else on the continent where British troops were advancing or defending. That was two years ago. But his father couldn't get him to promise to stop courting scandal.

He'd enjoyed a new woman every week, losing interest before any one of them could be called his mistress. But he'd developed a reputation for being something of a rake, which was what had led George to him. George admired prowess of all sorts, including the less valiant kind. But at least Montgomery steered clear of married women. He wished George would do the same. It wasn't as if the Prince didn't have a number of longtime mistresses he could visit instead.

Montgomery moved to the Regent's door, knocked once, and entered without waiting for a response. "George?"

It had been established that formalities weren't his forte the very night they were introduced with Montgomery saying, "Pleasure to meet you, George. You can call me Monty." Granted, he'd been a little foxed at the time or he might have thought better of insulting the Prince Regent with anything less than "Highness."

But while a number of gasps were heard that night and someone would have gotten around to admonishing him as soon as the shock wore off, the Prince Regent had laughed and said, "I think we'll be friends, Monty."

And so they were, after a fashion. Montgomery didn't join George's entourage and follow him around like that group in the anteroom, but he did come when summoned. He'd come the first time because he was curious, but all George had wanted was a private game of chess with him and someone new to talk to about his love of art, his excitement that he was working with John Nash to redesign and grandly extend his Brighton Pavilion, where he took his holidays by the sea, and his worry that a scandal might be descending on his head over a foolish mistake he'd made in dallying with the wrong woman.

Montgomery had been amused. Scandals didn't worry him, but obviously a royal couldn't be so cavalier when the entire country kept their eyes on him, and those who advised him on all matters social and political would be outraged. He'd decided that night to fix the problem that was worrying the Regent if he could, and he did. But the first time he got George out of a pickle, as it were, without being asked to, had established a precedent. George started asking for discreet favors after that, and the man was getting himself into one pickle after another.

"In here!"

Montgomery followed the voice to the lavish drawing room. George was in the large, well-padded chair he favored, however he was too wide of girth for it and would probably have trouble getting out of it on his own. That might be why there were two footmen standing nearby whom George dismissed as Montgomery approached.

The Prince Regent was aging badly. Only in his early fifties, he had too many vices he didn't try to curb. A bottle of laudanum stood on the table beside him, along with a decanter of brandy and a basket of pastries more than half-empty.

Even though it was the middle of the day, George wasn't dressed to leave his rooms, merely wearing trousers and a white linen shirt. Even his feet were bare. While the Prince of Wales had ended his long friendship with Beau Brummell when he became Prince Regent after his father's madness took a turn for the worse, he still favored the long trousers that Brummell had single-handedly made fashionable.

Bets had actually been made that George would return to the knee-length britches and stockings of the last decades because of that rift, but he didn't. He'd confided to Montgomery that he'd been forced to cut all ties with his old Whig friends, including Brummell, when he became

Regent four years ago. Just one of the trials and tribulations of being the Prince Regent.

"I received your summons, George," Montgomery said as he took a seat on the sofa.

"That was three days ago, you're late," George complained, though mildly.

"Your servant might not have been able to find me in a timely manner. I've been hiding rather unsuccessfully from the last lord you cuckolded. Chanders sent thugs after me, the bloody sod. Not to mention, Lord Halstead continues to send me challenges to a duel, four of them to date."

"So just duel with the chap already. You were in the army. You ought to be an excellent shot."

"I am, which is why I won't duel." It was stated flatly but with absolute conviction.

"You prefer to be labeled a coward?"

"I prefer not to kill a man just because I'm accepting blame that's not rightfully mine."

Montgomery was well aware that statement could be considered an insult to the Prince, but George merely raised a brow at him before reaching for another pastry.

"Did you find somewhere else to hide?"

"I'm staying at my father's town house for a few days until I can find another flat. Those thugs won't try breaking into a house filled with servants. But unfortunately, one of my brothers is also in residence, in town this week on business. And he's heard the rumors that I'm cavorting with married women. I believe he sent for my father, but I expect to be out of there before the earl arrives to berate me."

"I knew your father in my youth. Liked him then, don't want to be yelled at by him now. I hope you said nothing to your brother."

"Of course not. I don't mind the yelling."

George laughed. But Montgomery wasn't having a pleasant reunion with his brother, whom he hadn't seen since the last time he'd gone home to visit his parents last year. And with the point being to save George from a scandal by turning it on himself, he didn't want to tell even his favorite brother, Andrew, about it. His family wouldn't condone what he'd gotten himself into, even for the sake of the next king of England. So he'd had to listen to Andrew's long diatribe about what he ought *not* to be doing in London.

"You know, George, this sudden fancy you've taken to married women is turning into a bad habit, don't you think? It's not as if there aren't hundreds of attractive un-married women, even young ones, who would swoon in delight to share a royal's bed. You do realize, don't you, that a woman can't keep a secret? She may say she will, but she rarely does. And a dalliance with the next king of En-gland is too big a secret not to brag about to her friends. From there it goes everywhere, eventually to her husband. On the other hand, no one begrudges you a mistress or two when you are estranged from your wife, they just in-sist the lady not be encumbered with a husband."

"I am well aware of social, royal, and political protocol. As I said before, it was a mistake, that first time. There have actually been only a few women I've been smitten with over the years who were already taken. I have resisted all these years pursuing them, but then I saw Lady Chanders recently and was quite overcome with temptation. I thought that would be my only faux pas, but I think you might have enabled me by cleaning up the aftermath of that delightful affair."

Montgomery laughed. "So it's my fault?"

"No, no, it was simply my taking advantage of your kind and brilliant resolution to the problem, for which I do apologize and promise there will be no more after this," George said, and tossed a note to the sofa where Montgomery was sitting. "And now that you'll be out of town for a while—"

Montgomery cut in. "I will?"

"Won't you? At least until Lord Chanders stops sending thugs after you? It's not as if you are socially active in this town and will miss anything of note. By the by, why is that? By choice?"

"Indeed by choice," Montgomery replied. "The only women at these events are chaperones, debutantes, and wives. Not my cup of tea."

"Yet you were at Lady Mitchell's soiree when we met," George reminded him.

"A rare happenstance. She's my eldest brother, Weston's,

mother-in-law. It was coercion at its best. She wouldn't leave my bloody flat until I agreed to make an appearance at her party."

"Well, you are a prime specimen, dear boy. The only one of three brothers who hasn't been leg-shackled—strapping and with a face to make the ladies swoon pleasantly— you are a hostess's dream come true, I would imagine."

Montgomery grinned. "I prefer to remain my father's bane. He got the rest of his brood married off. He's bound to give up on me eventually."

Montgomery hadn't yet picked up the note that had been tossed to him, but George was now staring at it pointedly. Recalling the Prince's promise that there would be no more indiscretions with married women *after this*, he didn't need to be brilliant at deduction to know what was coming.

"Lady Tyler will be at that address tonight with some of her friends," George said, nodding at the note. "If you should happen to make it obvious that you're the object of her interest, it will get back to her husband. Problem solved. He was overheard accusing her of infidelity, demanding to know the culprit's name, and several of her servants saw me calling on her a few days ago. So the scandal will soon be upon me if not deflected elsewhere."

"So once again you want me to take the proverbial bullet for you?"

George wouldn't say yes—he never explicitly requested

these favors. Instead, he stated facts. "Lord Tyler has the temperament of a lunatic, he doesn't care that he'll be tossed in prison if he comes here to kill the next king of England. You'll be saving his life by turning his suspicions on you instead. And I'll be saving your life by getting you out of town for a few months. I'd already arranged it when I heard about that ridiculous race through the streets with a band of ax wielders. I found you a secluded estate where even your family won't find you—in case you are worried about your father's imminent arrival. I had an immediate reply from the lady of the house that you will be welcome in her home for as long as you like. A stint in the country will do you good, don't you think? At the very least, you can stop worrying about Chanders sending the dregs after you."

Montgomery picked up the note with two addresses on it, one in town, one in the country. "Who will my hostess be in the country?"

"Countess of Dawton."

"A widow I hope?"

"No, but she might be lonely, since her husband has been in the West Indies for so many years it's being assumed he prefers the climate there. But she may be a little old for you."

Montgomery was amused, since all of George's ladies had been old enough to be his mother. But seeking confirmation, he asked, "And this will be the last time?"

"That I trespass where I ought not? Yes. But I do have

a greater favor to ask of you, one of national importance that lines up well with your own departure from London. Considering secrecy will be involved and patience will be needed, well, let's just say for your service to the future crown, I will be giving you a parcel of land that currently has twelve rented cottages on it and a small manor house available for your use. The documents will be delivered after the scandals have subsided and the favor is completed."

"I never asked you for anything, George," Montgomery reminded him.

"I know, that's why I'm being generous. Don't think for a moment, Monty, that I'm not immensely grateful for your handy solutions to my waywardness. But there may be more danger than dealing with irate husbands involved with my final request. The package that will be under your sole charge and protection has become quite a nuisance, at least to me. He seems to think because we are both from esteemed bloodlines that we should be best of chums. He won't feel that way about you. In fact, I warrant he'll be suitably afraid of you."

"Why would he be?"

"Because I've quite embellished your credentials. Needed to make him feel he would be safe with you, after all. He will be, won't he?"

The Prince sounded worried, which made Montgomery ask, "Who exactly is this package, and why do I get the feeling someone wants him dead?"

"Because there are factions that do, even my own detractors would like to see me embarrassed by his demise because I offered him my protection. But Carlton House is too open to visitors, all of the royal residences are. It was a mistake to try to keep him here."

"A squadron of your royal guards couldn't keep him safe?"

"Too obvious and just what his enemies are expecting. Better that he be hidden away for a while—like you."

George was taking it for granted that he would agree to this request. Maybe he would. It was something new, possibly interesting, possibly dangerous. And while he hadn't thought of leaving town to escape the repercussions of the scandals, this would save him from having to look for a new residence. It would also get him out of town before his father arrived.

"Who is this package I'm to protect?"

"It's better that you not know. Be warned, he's a liar, so believe nothing he says. I'm providing both of you with false identities, the names of the guests your host is expecting. Use them. Any and all precautions, dear boy, shall be your motto. And do practice patience. As I said, he can be an incessant nuisance."

Montgomery raised an auburn brow. "If I didn't know better, I might think you're trying to talk me out of this, George, before I can agree."

"Not a'tall. Forewarned is forearmed, a bit of advice from my advisers. But you wouldn't really refuse, would you?"

George actually appeared to be taken aback. He wasn't used to being told no—except by the government that controlled his purse strings. Montgomery was glad no one controlled his, otherwise his father would have cut him off long ago. Instead of giving him an annual allowance when he'd left home, each of his parents had given him a small property that supported him, nothing grand, but more than enough for his simple needs: nice clothes, nice pistols, a good horse, and enough money to rent decent lodgings. An extravagant house would be forthcoming on his wedding day, but what did he need with extravagance— or a wife? Wives nagged, wives curtailed, wives heaped guilt on you if you strayed. And since he was in the habit of straying . . .

Without waiting for an answer, obviously not wanting to hear one that wouldn't please him, George said, "I will send him to you early tomorrow morning in a nondescript coach for your journey. And Lady Tyler tonight . . . ?"

Montgomery stood, pocketed the note, picked up a pastry, and nodded. Before he walked out the door, he tossed back, "Absolutely no more contretemps?"

"I wouldn't dare," George called after him. "My dear Maria has forgiven me. I had a note from her yesterday."

Maria Fitzherbert? George's longtime mistress with whom he'd caused quite a scandal when he'd illegally married her all those years ago? Thank God for small favors.

Chapter Three

"I FOUND OUT TODAY THESE women are *old*. What the deuce, Monty? How can anyone believe you're pursuing them, let alone gossip about it?"

Montgomery turned to glance at Andrew filling the doorway to his room. The vexed expression on his brother's face amused him. He supposed he'd be just as perplexed over the age difference and really wished he could explain the situation to his favorite brother, but that would defeat the purpose of the whole charade.

They both took after their parents, but not the same one. Montgomery was as tall as their father at a little over six feet, and had the same auburn hair. But he had their mother's emerald eyes. Andrew got his shorter stature and brown hair from her side of the family but had the same lighter green eyes, the color of fresh limes, as their father.

Andrew was the brother he'd been closest to growing up in Suffolk. Weston, their eldest brother, had had different tutors and responsibilities befitting the heir. Six years their senior, he couldn't be bothered by the brats, as he called them, and their more rambunctious predilections. Weston had even called their sisters, Evelyn and Claire, brats, because they were the only ones who got away with teasing and otherwise annoying him at every opportunity.

All of Monty's older siblings were married but not very happily. Weston's wife was a nag; Evelyn wasn't speaking to her husband; Claire had returned home to live with their parents because she wanted a divorce but couldn't get one. Only Andrew had no complaints about his spouse, but then he often traveled—without her. A good strategy if it was a strategy, Montgomery thought, because didn't absence make the heart grow fonder? There was enough evidence in his own family to convince him that marriage wasn't for him. Even his parents had argued a little too often for his liking during his last years at home.

He finished tying his cravat before answering evasively. "The *ton* is bored; they'll gossip about anything, even a polite kiss on the hand."

"So you didn't bed them? Why the deuce didn't you say so sooner?"

He grinned at Andrew, his senior by only eleven months. "And ruin your diatribe?"

"We'll put a stop to this outrageous gossip immediately. You know how serious scandals can be. People die from them in crimes of passion, suicides, or duels, and entire families can be ostracized, which is utterly ruining. So I'll help to defuse this while I'm here."

"You'll do nothing of the sort, dear brother. I rather like the notoriety, and if it warns off the debutantes, all the better. I assure you, no one is dying over any silly rumors circulating about me."

"When do you even run into debutantes?"

"Our family has too many mothers-in-law who live in London."

"Ah, point taken."

"I usually ignore their invitations, but sometimes I can't. But now I should receive fewer of them."

"You still don't want to marry? Ever?"

"When I don't need to? Our parents have six grandchildren already, and there are bound to be many more, which is more'n enough to assure the family line will continue long into the future. There are benefits to being the youngest of five, Andy. Why the deuce wouldn't I take advantage of that?"

"Maybe because Father still wants you to marry?"

"Father doesn't need to always get what he wants. Besides, dragging all his offspring to the altar has just become a bloody habit for him. Why don't you point that out to him the next time you see him?"

"He'll probably be here tomorrow, you can brave that conversation yourself."

"Then it's a good thing I'll be leaving in the morning to find new lodgings."

"Whatever for? I don't understand why you aren't living here permanently. This house is huge and usually unoccupied except for the servants."

"I'm used to smaller accommodations and no servants underfoot."

"If you tell me you can't afford—"

"Not a'tall, I just prefer to do for m'self, a habit from my days in the army. I can even cook, you know."

"Gads, Mother would be appalled, so we'll keep that tidbit to ourselves. But Father will be angry if you aren't here when he arrives."

Montgomery chuckled. "And whose fault will that be, traitor? You shouldn't have sent for him, so it's only fair you deal with him. Now I'm off for an evening of revelry. I'd invite you to join me, but your wife would probably object. Don't wait up, Brother. I expect to be late."

"You will send us your new address when you get one?" Andrew said as he followed him downstairs.

"Not bloody likely. But I'll keep in touch."

He didn't like leaving his brother frustrated, but since he was leaving London specifically to not be found, he could provide no further explanation. Perhaps someday, when George was king and his brief courtship with scandal was long forgotten, he could at least share his misadventures with Andrew—or not. It wasn't as if scandals, true or mere rumor, stayed very long in the gossip mill when so many new ones arrived to supplant them.

Before he reached the front door, it opened and their

sister Claire swept in. The younger and more petite of his two sisters, Claire took after him with her auburn hair and dark green eyes.

"Monty!" she exclaimed as soon as she noticed him, and opened her arms for a hug. "Is this where you hide? Father will be so pleased to know."

"Sorry to disappoint, but it's just a brief visit."

"And where's my hug?" Andrew asked Claire.

"I saw you just last week, but I haven't seen the scamp for months."

"What are you doing here?" Andrew queried.

"Escaping Father's nagging about my marital state," she replied as she removed her fancy bonnet.

"I thought you were separated—"

"Yes," she cut in. "That state."

But Andrew continued. "—from the cheater, as you're now fond of calling your husband."

"There's no fond left where *he's* concerned."

"He swears he's innocent, Claire."

She humphed. "He swears to lots of things that aren't true. He's very good at that—or thinks he is."

"Well, you've come to the wrong place to escape," Montgomery warned. "Andy sent for Father and expects him in the morning to chew on my ear."

She grinned. "Better you than me, darling brother!"

He grinned back. "Ah, but I won't be here to receive the tirade, so you're welcome to it."

"How unchivalrous of you—chew on you, why?"

"No time to explain," he replied, kissing her brow before heading to the door. "Andy can tell you if he must, but it's all lies and will have a quick demise if left alone, so leave it alone."

He quickly got into his waiting carriage but still heard his sister yell through the open door, "Gossip! No, no, there can be no gossip!"

Montgomery rolled his eyes but wasn't going to worry about his siblings undoing his sacrifice. There had been eyewitnesses, as he'd intended, so the gossip about him wasn't going to be easily dismissed until something new took its place, especially since he would be adding to it tonight. . . .

The address he had been given actually led to a wedding reception. He had no trouble getting in the door, which made him laugh to himself. George had no doubt paved his way. There were musicians and a space cleared for dancing. The bride and groom had apparently already had their twirl on the floor. Should he dance with his target or just get her alone for a few private words? He had to find her first, and that required asking someone to point her out to him. That problem got solved when Anne Beddows suddenly put her arm through his.

"It's been too long, darling, I've missed you."

He was surprised. He hadn't seen the young widow since last year, when they'd ended their brief affair amicably. Of all his dalliances, he'd liked Lady Anne best. No strings, no false protestation of love, just laughter and sex.

He would have extended the relationship, had enjoyed her that much, but it was better to stay the course, so he broke it off before she started thinking of something more permanent.

"And you are as beautiful as ever, Anne. I trust you still follow your whims?"

"If you mean have I replaced you, of course I have. And you?"

"I pine for you when I allow myself to."

She blushed slightly but then tapped her fan against his arm to scold, "Ever the charmer, dear boy. But what brings you here?"

"I'm looking for Lady Tyler," he replied. "D'you know her?"

"Another wager?"

"Wager?"

"Surely that's what's behind the recent gossip about you?" she asked.

Trust Anne, knowing him so well, to come up with that excuse, but he replied, "A gentleman never tells."

She smiled. "I'd forgotten how gallant you are."

He grinned. "No, you didn't."

"No, I didn't," she agreed, and pointed to his target.

He guessed Anne would be avidly watching, and he hoped so, since one of Anne's whims was to gossip. He was disappointed to see that his target was yet another lady closer to George's age than his, but then the Prince did admit these women were old infatuations of his, decades old apparently. He sighed. One more ridiculous endeavor, but for once he was going to try to avoid provoking an insane husband to chop off his head.

Putting on his best smile, he approached Lady Tyler's table. She was sitting with four friends, all finely garbed. They hadn't been served food yet, but a servant stood by to refill their glasses. They looked bored with the party and likely wouldn't get a chance to dance, since they were there without their husbands. They might see him as a boon.

He greeted all of them, gave his name, but his eyes were on Lady Tyler as he asked her to dance. She declined, but her friends, a couple of them giggling, urged her to stand up with him. He smiled charmingly and asked again. Grudgingly, she agreed. Half the battle was won, and there were four avid witnesses to the show.

He wasted no time getting to the point, whispering, "I'm here to do you a service, madam, to deflect any brewing scandal onto myself rather than you and our overzealous friend. You must interrupt this dance with a slap to my face and tell your friends I have been pursuing you all week and you have finally made your rebuff more forceful."

"I'm old enough to be your mother. No one is going to believe you are seriously pursuing me."

"Nonsense. You're still a handsome woman, and I'm a rake, which I'm sure someone of your acquaintance can verify. But truly, only your husband needs to believe it. If he has doubts, tell him I made an effort to seduce you on a bet with my friends. Tell him whatever you like, but assure him I was unsuccessful. I would prefer not to be chased after by yet another husband. I am here merely to enable you to claim innocence. I tried to seduce you, you rebuffed my advances, your virtue and faithfulness remain unharmed. A very simple tactic, one I wish I'd thought of sooner."

"George was seen at my door," she whispered.

"Well, other than firing all your servants, can you claim he came by to personally apologize for my horrid behavior? He's a friend of my father's, after all."

"There is still a problem with your strategy, Lord Townsend. I am enceinte."

Said with an utter blush and adding an infuriating wrinkle to the situation that he hadn't counted on. In defense of his indulgent friend, he said coldly, "Not by George you aren't. I know for a fact he visited you too recently for you to know one way or the other."

Lady Tyler's blush deepened. "It's not his."

"But not your husband's, either?" he guessed.

"No, he's been away several months and only just returned to London."

"Then I would suggest you seduce your husband immediately."

"Yes, I have decided on that course, but he's not exactly enamored of me anymore. However, you might be a boon after all. He is a jealous man. If he thinks someone as handsome as you has pursued me, indeed, that might work very well to get him back in my bed, however briefly, and have it be his idea, rather than mine."

"All good luck with that, my lady. Now, the very loud slap? And do huff off afterward. I will look suitably chagrined."

Chapter Four

M ONTGOMERY WASN'T EXACTLY EXPECTING dawn
to be George's definition of early morning, yet the sky was
just turning gray when he was woken by a male servant and
told his coach had arrived. He'd prepared ahead, though, in
case he overslept, having packed his trunk before he left the
house last night. Now he made quick work of dressing. The
long strip of linen for his cravat he merely draped over
his shoulders for now, and he didn't take the time to club his
hair back because he always had extra ties for that in his
coat pockets.

The driver outside was standing by to secure his trunk
to the top of the coach, but there were already so many
trunks up there, he wondered if his would fit. "More'n
one package?" he asked the young man.

"What package, m'lord?"

With a frown, Montgomery opened the door to see for
himself how many people warranted that much baggage.
One lantern was lit inside, not very bright, but bright

enough for him to see just one body was present, huddled in the corner under a furry cloak, apparently still asleep. He thought about slamming the door shut to awaken it, whatever it was, but decided against it. He'd prefer a bit more sleep himself before the sun rose.

He tried, using one of the lap robes on the opposite seat as a cushion so he could lean his head against the side of the coach. One blaring question in his mind kept his eyes open. What sort of "he" could be termed a nuisance? Someone too young, too old, deranged like King George? Was he to be a bodyguard or a bloody nursemaid?

The driver failed to avoid a nasty pothole, which was not surprising when the sun hadn't quite cleared the horizon yet. But the bounce nearly unseated the package.

Golden hair appeared first, a lot of it, then the untied cloak slipped back and the child sat up straight. Fine clothes, exceedingly fine, jewels dotting the starched high collar. Very slim fingers adorned with an excessive number of rings. A large medallion hanging from a very thick gold chain around his neck. The package was a walking bank of wealth. Smooth ivory cheeks, dark blue eyes, dimples that appeared now with a smile of greeting.

"That's a pretty face," Montgomery said suspiciously. "If you're female I'm taking you right back to London."

"Do you need to see my manly credentials?"

That was so unexpected Montgomery burst out laughing. "When we're relieving ourselves on the same rock will be soon enough. George didn't warn me the package would be this young. Is there a good reason he didn't want me to know who or what you are?"

"Why would you add a 'what'?"

"More precisely, are you one of his bastards?" Montgomery demanded.

The boy leapt to his feet in outrage but was a tad too tall to pull it off with aplomb, banging his head on the coach roof. The driver started to slow down, apparently thinking he was being directed to stop the vehicle. Montgomery growled before yelling out the window, "Keep going!" then snatched the boy's arm, pulling him back onto the padded seat.

"You're lucky you didn't concuss yourself," he said. "If you're going to get angry, stay in your seat to do it. If you're going to get angry at *me*, be warned I might shake you out of your temper tantrum. So you're not a bastard? I suppose I shall apologize for that errant thought. But you're a child. George bloody well should have warned me."

"I'm seventeen, no longer considered a child," the boy replied with markedly arrogant disdain.

"Is that so? Well, I'm Montgomery Townsend. You can call me Lord Townsend. And you—?"

"Can call me Highness," the boy said stiffly.

"Not bloody likely. So this is what George meant about your predilection for lies. But if I'm protecting an urchin who happens to be wearing fancy clothes, maybe I won't be very diligent about it. Out with it, who are you really?"

"Charles Maximilian Pachaly, the seventh Pachaly to inherit the throne of Feldland."

"Never heard of it."

"We're a small kingdom near Austria."

"Still never heard of it, but I was warned that you lie, so let's agree at least not to tell such grandiose whoppers. I'll call you Charley."

The boy gasped. "I could have you beheaded for such insolence! My father certainly would have."

Montgomery wasn't impressed. "Want to take after him, do you? I suppose he's a king, too?"

A curt, albeit sad nod. "He was killed in the rebellion. I was secreted out of the country to take refuge here. My father was an old friend of your Regent's father, though the king is too ill to remember."

"Just so you know, I'm not believing any of this and an in-depth explanation is bound to trip you up, so let's hear it. I'll give you a few minutes to convince me."

"You realize I am not required to do any such thing?" Charles said.

"You realize you ought to make the effort?" Montgomery countered. "King or not, boy, you have twice taken umbrage for no good reason, which needs to stop. King or not, you can't bloody well act like one if you want to remain hidden. So spit it out. This is the only opportunity I'll offer you to make your case for kingship."

"Because you think I will 'trip up'?"

"Exactly."

The boy smiled. "Truth might be forgotten, truth might be embellished, but the essential truth will remain. My country is rich in resources, which is why Napoleon didn't ignore us. He demanded we join his Grande Armée when he marched deep into Europe. My father refused to support the upstart, but our people were afraid the little French emperor would bring his war to our land so they revolted against us. Father died when the palace was stormed, while I was secreted out of the country. But I still have many supporters at home, which is why these rebels think their new republic will fail if I remain alive. They are determined to kill me and have tried numerous times when I was on the way to England and even in this country."

"You know that Napoleon was defeated last year?" Montgomery mentioned.

"Yes, and exiled to Elba, only to escape early this year to take up arms again. I was making arrangements to go home when he took control of France once more."

"I doubt the new war will last out the year. He simply doesn't have the support he had when he tried to conquer all of Europe."

"I agree, and the rebels in Feldland are once again fearful of losing power because your Regent sent them a warning that he expects the monarchy to be restored. It was worded nicely, without threats, but still provided powerful incentive for them to kill me. I think he sent the missive out of desperation. I suppose I overstayed my welcome with him."

Mentioning something George would likely do without approval from his ministers was a nice touch. He could definitely see why George had issued the warning, not that he gave credit to anything the boy had said so far. He was proud of himself for not laughing. But Charley could be a foreigner. His slight accent suggested he hadn't been born in England or at least not raised here. And his clothes and manner suggested lofty social status. George had mentioned factions and esteemed bloodlines, after all, oh, and national importance, though Montgomery took that with a grain of salt. No doubt it was merely an embellishment the Regent had added to convince him to do the favor.

Still the threat to the boy's life could well be true, so he felt a little sorry for him for having to endure such travails at his tender age.

Which had him saying, "Buck up. Even a polite request from England can yield amazing results, so we just need to keep you alive until the new war ends."

"Then you believe me?"

Montgomery gave the boy a hard look before he answered, "It doesn't matter if I do or don't. I was curious and you spun an interesting tale to satisfy my curiosity, but it's a tale that shouldn't be mentioned again—to anyone. There's obviously a good reason why I wasn't told who you are, Charley. You obviously know what it is, so you shouldn't have told me that preposterous tale, which is bloody well much worse than the truth could possibly be. A tale like that will not deflect attention from you, it will just enlarge the target on your back. *Do* you understand me?"

"You asked," Charley grumbled.

Montgomery gave the boy a narrow look. "Yes, I did, but what should your answer have been?"

The boy's cheeks suddenly turned red. "That I'm nobody?"

Montgomery shook his head, waving a hand at Charley's garb. "Unless we find some rags for you to wear, you're obviously not a nobody. You should have just used the false identity the Prince gave you."

"I wasn't told about any false identity. But one of the servants at Carlton House handed Arlo a note when we left."

"Who's Arlo?"

"He's driving us."

"Well, I'll ask him for the new names we're to use when we stop."

Charley sighed dramatically. "This effort to safeguard me seems too hastily planned."

"Possibly, but *secretive* is the operative word and one you need to take to heart, so consider it your motto henceforth. I've been charged with taking us to a safe location where neither of us can be found, and that I will do."

"I was told you were a soldier."

"I was."

"And a master duelist."

"That's . . . possible."

"Then you can protect me no matter what?"

"Boy, how do you envision that happening if a dozen ruffians overtake us because you sound off about being someone worth abducting?"

"Are you referring to the men who are after me?"

"No, nor the ones after me. I'm talking about criminals who will see you as a prize."

"I think I get your point."

"About bloody time."

Chapter Five

THERE WAS A RAP on the top of the coach. Montgomery stuck his head out the window.

"What is it?"

"Two riders following us."

They were barely thirty minutes out of London, and while dawn had arrived with the sun making an appearance behind them, it still wasn't all that bright on the road yet with trees on both sides of it.

He told the driver, "Pick up the pace to see if they keep up."

"I've heard your country suffers from highwaymen," Charley said with a curious look.

"We could wish that's all it is, but it's doubtful considering we both have enemies. Besides, it's a bit early in the day for robbers, with so few travelers on the road for them to prey upon."

"Why would the Prince Regent appoint you as my guard if you have enemies?" Charley asked.

"Because I'm so good at eluding irate husbands."

Charley's eyes lit up. "You're a rake! We have that in common—I'm a rake, too. The ladies can't stay away from me."

Monty chuckled. "Are you sure they aren't attracted to all those jewels you wear?"

Charley turned away in a snit.

Five minutes later, Arlo rapped again to say, "They are keeping up exactly, m'lord."

"Then stop so we can find out why."

He sighed as he glanced at Charley to explain, "Whether they want you or me, or just our purses, they still don't get to tag along with us to find out where we're going. Stay put, do *not* look outside, and put that cloak back over your head."

He took one pistol from his belt and stepped out of the coach before he drew the other and pointed both at the two riders approaching them. There wasn't much to distinguish them in their black clothes and short capes, except their clothing appeared to be identical, bringing to mind regimental uniforms, but he knew of no soldiers who dressed all in black. Both men had very long hair, and they'd made no effort to contain it.

"If you're thinking of robbing me, you'll need to work hard at it," he told the two men who had reined in their horses.

The answer was gibberish to him, spoken in some foreign tongue—which answered to his satisfaction the question of who they were after. They must have been watching Carlton House day and night and following any coach that looked unusual. And while George had of course supplied his unwanted guest with a plain, unadorned coach, it had departed from the Regent's residence before the crack of dawn carrying an inordinate amount of baggage.

One of the men fired at him, ending any further speculation. The shot missed, but Montgomery got behind the open coach door before firing back. His first shot struck the man who hadn't fired yet but was yelling more gibberish after he fell off his horse. This gave Montgomery plenty of time to pull his other pistol and aim it at the other man, who was desperately trying to reload his flintlock.

But they were both distracted by a third fellow, a short one in a hooded cloak, charging out of the trees on the right side of the road, brandishing a flintlock in each hand and snarling, "You knocked me off my horse with your bloody racket. Drop your weapons or you'll be knocked off yours!"

Montgomery didn't wait to find out how that would play out. He aimed, fired, and the chap who was still reloading tumbled backward off his horse and lay still on the ground.

"I didn't think you were going to kill them," the short one accused.

"Well, if that had been my goal, it would have been done, but more's the pity, I only shot to wound so they won't be able to bother me again. Be a good chap and unsaddle their horses, I'll tie them up with the saddle straps."

He saw just a bit of smooth ivory cheeks above a yellow plaid scarf tied around the fellow's neck and lower face, holding the hood of his cloak in place. This was no short man after all, just another boy. And this one come to their rescue? He was beginning to wonder if George was playing an elaborate joke on him. But the boy had already turned aside to do as he'd been asked, while Montgomery approached the first assailant who had fallen. There was some blood, not a lot, on one leg of the man's trousers, and he was still angrily spouting words in some foreign language.

"Do I need to gag you?" Montgomery asked pointedly as he dragged the fellow off the road—and came up short. His eyes widened when he spotted the great white beast hiding in the trees, its lower legs feathered with hair that was likely as long as the animal's mane.

"That's a bloody hairy horse you've got there, boy," he said, unable to take his eyes off such an unusually large animal.

"He's magnificent, isn't he? I named him Snow King, but pretty much just call him Snow."

"I'm glad you didn't end up calling him King or I might feel insulted."

Montgomery swung around incredulously to glare at his charge, who hadn't done as he'd been told. "I warned you to stay inside the coach. I did, didn't I? I remember it, so why didn't you?"

"Because the danger is gone and I need to stretch my legs."

"Well, now you can stretch them by getting my trunk off the coach, retrieve two more flintlocks from it, and come finish off these fellows."

Charley's eyes turned owlishly wide. "Point taken." He scrambled back to the coach.

"Too bloody late, boy," Montgomery called after him for good measure.

The gibberish was coming louder and faster from the assailant on the ground. Montgomery turned and saw the man trying to sit up, his eyes avidly following Charley's departure. With a frown, Montgomery took one of the ties for his hair out of his pocket and gagged the man.

The boy in the cloak tossed a saddle by his feet. "I thought you said you were tying them up."

"I am, and I expect to be in Portsmouth by the time either of these miscreants is capable of remounting a horse."

"If that's where you're going, you've taken the wrong road out of London."

Montgomery rolled his eyes. Two children, both know-it-alls. He wasn't going to explain that he was misdirecting the two attackers instead of killing them. They hadn't spoken English, but that didn't mean they couldn't, or wouldn't recognize the name of an English port on the south coast. They might even have entered the country from that very port.

But while he worked to get the straps off the saddle, he could see the boy out of the corner of his eye waiting for an answer, so he merely offered, "I've other stops to make before turning south."

"Why would the boy with you be insulted by a horse that is named King?"

Montgomery gritted his teeth, trying to keep in mind that boys were naturally inquisitive. Still he had to stop the lad from asking more questions.

"My ward is delusional, imagines all sorts of ridiculous things about himself. I simply ignore it. Now I'm curious. How did those pistol shots knock you off your horse?"

"I was sleeping on his back, which is much warmer than the hard ground."

"Another one for tall tales, are you?" He laughed as he started binding the feet of the noisy miscreant.

"Look at Snow. He has a very wide back, and I'm skinny."

"Why'd you sleep so close to the road if you didn't want to be disturbed?"

"It was quiet in the middle of the night, but I didn't want to oversleep, so I was counting on the early-morning traffic to wake me. Though I wasn't expecting pistol shots."

"If you are on your way to London, it's less than an hour from here."

"I know. I went, didn't like it, and left."

Montgomery finally looked up from his task. "What's not to like about a grand city like London?"

"Too many people, too much smoke and soot, and everyone gawked at me as if they'd never seen a horse before. And it took me nigh two hours to brush all that soot off Snow last night."

"If you were riding that giant shire into town, it's no wonder people stared at you. Horses that big and hairy are usually only seen pulling large loads."

"He's only half shire. His dam was a Scottish mare from Clydesdale county, but yes, she was very tall as well."

Montgomery took another look at the boy when he dropped the other saddle near his feet. The lad's garb was expensive, a finely tailored coat, polished boots under long trousers, and the dark brown hooded cloak pushed back over his shoulders with the hood pulled forward to cover most of his face. No cravat, though, just a fine linen shirt likely fastened to the neck beneath the bulky plaid scarf. He'd used proper diction so he must have had some education, but his voice shifted in pitch, occasionally sounding rather gruff. At the age when it changed from boyish to mannish?

"You don't look like a ragamuffin," he pointed out. "What's a boy from money doing traveling alone? Or did you steal those clothes?"

"I'm not actually alone, and don't ask me to explain."

Montgomery had purposely asked a goading question that should have offended the lad and made him ride off in high dudgeon, which would have prevented any more questions. But while the boy had turned away from him so he couldn't see if he looked angry, not that he could see much of his face with that hood he was wearing, he had answered in a neutral tone.

"You count your horse as company? Or do you have an imaginary friend? My sister Claire had one, made us all sit down to tea with it. Even Father indulged her. Two months later, she patched up the little rift she had with my other sister, Evelyn, and never mentioned the invisible friend again."

Now why the deuce did he volunteer that? Something silly to make amends for the insult? But the boy didn't comment, he was busy saddling his great beast of a horse and attaching his belongings to it. It suddenly occurred to him that an extra boy in tow, even one around the same age as his ward, might be good camouflage for his little group. And the lad was heading away from London as they were, so he might agree to join them if asked—if Montgomery stopped trying to drive him away with insults.

He went over to the quieter miscreant, who must have hit his head when he fell off his horse because Montgomery could see now that he was unconscious. The shot had grazed his left shoulder where his jacket was torn. After Montgomery trussed him up, he dragged him off the road to where his partner was struggling to free himself. He considered leaving the noisy one gagged to delay their rescue even longer, but, in the end, removed the ribbon, letting loose more angry gibberish. He would take their horses instead and have a look inside the saddlebags later. Either way, they wouldn't be catching up to him.

He headed back to the road, but paused when he saw the boy was about to mount, curious to see how he would accomplish it on a horse that size. Shires were reputed to be the tallest horses in the world, and this one certainly aspired to match that record. But the lad, even as short as he was, accomplished it with ease, hopping up to grasp the pommel and lifting himself high enough to reach the stirrup, then the rest was a normal mount.

"Considering you're not done growing, I'd think you'd want a horse more your size," Montgomery said when he reached the boy sitting atop the white beast.

"I like the view from up here."

Montgomery choked back a laugh, since the boy was looking down on him when he said it. There was probably a grin on his face, but with the light from the road behind the boy leaving his entire figure darkly shadowed, Montgomery couldn't tell for sure.

"He's a good extra weapon, too, if I need one," the boy added. "He would think nothing about charging into another horse to unseat its rider. He would have made a magnificent warhorse in olden days."

"Know your history, do you?"

"I know a lot of things."

The boy walked Snow King out to the road. Even light steps like that fluttered the hair on the horse's legs.

Montgomery followed, remarking, "I should just turn those two over to a magistrate in the first town we reach since they attempted to rob us. They'd have a devilish time trying to defend themselves when they can't speak English." He stared at the top of the coach with no room on it for trussed-up bodies and amended, "Too much trouble and time wasted. And where are you going now that you've snubbed your nose at London?"

"Anywhere else."

Montgomery raised a brow at the boy's disagreeable tone. He didn't try to change the boy's mind about his fair city. Besides, riding a giant horse and brandishing pistols, the boy might prove to be entertaining, whereas the lad he had to protect had been nothing but annoying so far.

"Since you don't have a particular destination in mind and appear to be going in our direction, you're welcome to join us. Safety in numbers, as it were."

"I've no desire to go south."

"So anywhere except south? Well, as it happens, we're not going to Portsmouth. That was just misdirection for the benefit of the robbers, so the offer stands. We'll be riding north most of the week, and it's possible more highwaymen might try to delay us along the way." And for good measure he added, "They'll stop lone riders, too."

"They'll be surprised if they do."

"Oh?"

The boy ignored his query and actually yelled, "Joining you is an excellent idea!"

"Keep your bloody voice down," Montgomery growled. "If the gunshots didn't wake the countryside, you just did."

"I was letting my imaginary friend know I'm in safe company."

"Were you now?" Montgomery looked into the woods, but seeing nothing, he snorted. "You can ride in the coach with us."

"I'll ride Snow alongside you. The appearance of a guard will deter other robbers."

Guards didn't come in such small packages, but he merely said, "Suit yourself, but it's likely to rain sometime today. This is England, after all."

Chapter Six

IT WAS A MISTAKE. Vanessa knew it even as she agreed to ride north with the handsome man whose coach had been attacked. Her guards would be annoyed because she'd refused to allow them to ride alongside her. But the man and his ward were interesting and had supplied the first little bit of excitement to what had been an uneventful journey so far.

Besides, by yelling her reply to the man's invitation, she'd let her guards know that it was her decision to follow the coach and its occupants. It might be a silly way of communicating, but she was sure it had worked.

She had been surprised when the two huge Highlanders, brothers who looked like a pair of mean bears, arrived the day before she was to leave for England. She rarely argued with her father, but this time she did. He'd hired them to accompany her to her mother's house in Cheshire. She was certain she could protect herself and didn't need them. But William was adamant, saying, "I'll never sleep a wink again for worry if I don't know you have protection in case you need it."

She'd finally agreed, but with her own stipulation that the Highlanders keep their distance from her during the day and guard her discreetly at night.

As the coach started off down the road and she urged Snow to follow it, she glanced at the trees on the right, looking for a flash of bright-colored plaid. Nothing, not a single movement as far as she could see. Then she remembered the two guards were no longer wearing their usual tartan garb. It wasn't her idea that they not wear their kilts into England, not a'tall. She'd admired the fine muscular bodies of many a young Highlander while she'd lived in Scotland. It was William who didn't want the guards drawing extra attention to themselves. She probably would have enjoyed their company, but she wanted to make this journey on her own. It would be her last taste of freedom and independence for a while. The guards certainly were abiding by her wishes, and she would have only the occupants of the coach as traveling companions until she turned off the north road to ride west to Cheshire.

She wondered about the duo in the coach. The boy's hair was unusually long and not only curly but such a bright gold, women might be envious of it. Nor was it tied back as hers was. His clothes were ridiculously gaudy. It would be preposterous to think the gems he wore were real, obviously they weren't. The man was dressed like a gentleman or a lord, wearing a dark gray greatcoat over a blue jacket, but oddly no cravat. She'd caught a glimpse of a scarf or a length of linen around his neck that had flapped in the breeze and could be made into a cravat. She might be wearing male garb of good quality herself, but she drew the line at wearing a cravat, even though most gentlemen wouldn't be seen without one.

The man's hair was dark auburn. She'd noticed reddish streaks in it when he stood in the sun. It was longer than hers, which she had a devilish time tying back at its current length, but he hadn't clubbed his, leaving it to float about his wide shoulders. He had a strong chin, a narrow nose, dark emerald eyes. She found his face fascinating and had let her eyes linger on it more than once, blushing when she'd caught herself staring at him too long. She could blame her sheltered existence in the Highlands, and yet she and her father had both traveled, going often to Fraserburgh. But the simple fact was, she'd never come across a man so attractive that she wondered if he might be the rare one who would sign a contract so she could bed him, well, marry him . . . She laughed aloud, what fanciful nonsense was that?

She'd been alone too long, that's what. She missed having someone to talk to. She should have just ridden in the coach with them. Acting on that thought, she rode closer to the open window to start a conversation but heard one in progress. . . .

"The names we've been assigned in this note aren't that bad," the man was saying. "Lord Montague Hook for me, not one I would have picked, but calling me Monty will get a quick response. And you are Lord Charley Bates, so a Charley, after all, which you seem to be answering to just fine— Oh, I get it, hook and bait, George was trying to be amusing, apparently. While it isn't necessary to tell our hosts a single thing about ourselves—"

"Why not?"

"Because our sojourn is to be a secret. They are aware of that and are accepting us as guests as a favor to the Regent, and everyone loves to do favors for George, whether they've met our next king or not." A deep laugh. "Even me—well, I didn't love it, but I didn't mind it. However, because of your grand wardrobe—"

Vanessa was surprised that they knew the Prince Regent and wondered why they weren't using their real names. What had she stumbled upon—two men involved in a secret mission for the Crown? Her boring journey had just turned exciting!

"—we might need to drop at least one falsehood to explain your extravagant clothing," the man continued. "Compensation for your parents' absence? They lived in Vienna enamored of the social whirl, while you were stuck in the country with servants? Missed birthdays, et cetera, lots of guilt on their part, so they lavished you with coin, and being furious with them, you squandered it all on a ridiculous wardrobe. How's that sound? Too close to the truth?"

"Suit yourself," the boy said in a petulant tone. "I don't like telling lies."

"Sure you do. I did m'self at your age, so did my brothers, so did my sisters."

"You are lucky to have siblings."

"You have none a'tall?"

"Three died young, only I survived."

"Well, I wouldn't say I was lucky to have so many. As the youngest, I bloody well was rarely heard, if you know what I mean."

"I don't."

"Runt of the litter? Surely you can grasp that concept, the little one gets ignored or pushed around, never wins? By the by, I suppose I should have asked, are you pleased to have a playmate for this journey?"

"Kings don't get to play," Charley said in a tone that sounded indignant yet also like a complaint.

The man taking the name of Monty replied harshly, "We might be alone for the moment, but that nonsense about being a king ends here, and don't make me say it again. You need to get yourself in line, boy. For the duration, consider yourself an actor in training, one who has no delusions of grandeur. And no more bloody snits, either!"

Silence followed, but she imagined the two in the coach were glaring hotly at each other. And she wondered who was telling the truth, the boy who claimed to be a king, or the man who claimed the boy was delusional. She sided with delusional, because it was insane for a king to travel with only a single guard, no matter what country he was from.

Vanessa pulled up to let the coach get ahead of her again. She couldn't try to talk to them now when they would think she'd been eavesdropping, and rightly so. And although she was smarting a little at having been called a "playmate" for the conceited boy, which she most certainly wouldn't be, she was amazed at her luck at running into acquaintances of the Regent who were obviously on some clandestine mission. She might just have an adventure to recount to her sisters when she got home.

Maybe going to London hadn't been such a bad idea after all. If she hadn't gotten so nervous about reuniting with her mother and turned away from Cheshire in favor of a visit to her father's house in London, she wouldn't have encountered the odd duo. But London had disappointed her. She wondered why anyone would go there for a Season. It was so smoggy her eyes had burned, and the streets had grown more and more congested with each block she passed. Every vehicle imaginable seemed to be leaving the city at that time of day. By the time she and her guards had managed to ride out of the daunting city, it had been dark and too late to look for an inn, so they'd slept outdoors—the first time they'd done that since crossing the border.

Maybe now, with the amusing distraction of her new traveling companions, she wouldn't feel so nervous about going home. She would veer northwest to Cheshire when the time came. Better to get the unpleasant reunion over with soonest. Her anger would surface; her mother's rage would also rise because Vanessa had chosen Papa instead of her and had run away to be with him. That was the truth, and she'd own up to it. She knew the other truth, too, and Kathleen Blackburn wouldn't be able to deny that she was to blame for breaking up their family.

Chapter Seven

"WHAT DO WE CALL you, boy?" Monty asked her as he stepped out of the coach.

Vanessa had already slid off Snow and led him into the grass for his lunch. She glanced at the man and was dazzled by the array of reddish tints glinting in his hair before he stepped out of the sun and into the shade. Which could explain why, without thinking, she said, "Nessi," and then quickly amended, "Er, well, it's short for Nestor."

"Not much shorter, by just one letter," he pointed out.

She watched him club back his auburn hair before he sat on the blanket the driver had just spread out on the grass.

"If you have a problem with my name, don't use it," she replied a trifle stiffly.

"Not a'tall, but I'll go with Ness, which is shorter than Nestor, if that's all right with you."

She had a feeling he didn't care if it was all right with her, he'd call her Ness anyway. "Suit yourself. And you and the boy? What are your names?"

"The boy is Charley," he said. "My friends and family call me Monty."

She knew that was a lie. She'd overheard him and the boy talking about the new names they'd been given. She hoped to learn in the next half hour why they couldn't use their real names on the journey and wherever they were going.

They had stopped beside the road to eat and rest the horses. There was just one old oak tree there with meadows all around it and a few farms in the distance. The last stand of trees they'd passed was far behind them. Her guards wouldn't like being so far from her, but they might have to get used to it. There weren't many forests on the way to Cheshire, and that might become a problem for her, too, she realized.

She'd pulled aside into that last stand of trees to relieve herself, then galloped Snow to catch up with the coach. The pair inside it wouldn't have noticed, but the driver did glance back at her, no doubt wondering why she was being missish.

She sat on the other side of the large basket the driver had set down on the blanket, across from Monty, and crossed her legs comfortably. Charley had gone off and hadn't returned yet. And Monty was staring at her. It was a bold stare, which made her quite uncomfortable. Even though they were sitting under the oak, the shaded area was still quite bright with the sunshine all around them— and he might be seeing something she didn't want him to see despite the hood she was wearing. She'd taken off the scarf earlier because the spring day had warmed up considerably, but now she wished she hadn't.

She glanced back to see what was keeping Charley but didn't see him. "Your ward is missing."

"No, he's not."

She turned back to see Monty nodding toward the field to her right. When she looked in that direction she saw the boy walking about briskly for a little exercise. That was a good idea, and it would seem quite normal if she wanted to join someone her age rather than endure the scrutiny of Monty's inquisitive emerald eyes any longer.

She started to get up to do that, but then he added, "I take my guardianship seriously. The boy will never be out of my sight."

When he'd just been staring at her instead? But she wasn't about to point that out and have him tell her what he found so interesting about her. She redirected whatever thoughts he was having by asking, "Why did you steal the horses?"

"Steal from robbers who meant to steal from us? More like justice, wouldn't you say?"

"I suppose, when you put it like that."

"And yet there was a more prudent reason. I simply didn't want them finding their mounts too quickly and deciding their wounds could wait to be tended until after they'd caught up with us again. Besides, we can alternate those mounts with our horses, although that huge brute of yours could probably pull this coach on his own and get us there in half the time."

"He was bred to be a workhorse, but he's never been one, has been a friend instead, so I decline the suggestion. Get us where?"

"Oh, somewhere up north, on the coast I think, an estate where we've been invited to sojourn for a month or two. I'm sure they won't mind if I bring you as another guest."

"And Arlo," Charley said as he sat down and reached into the basket.

"Arlo can take himself back to London once we get where we're going," Monty replied.

"No, he can't," Charley insisted.

Vanessa noticed the boy's jewelry was gone, well, most of it, and likely at Monty's request. Getting rid of the gems adorning his clothing would require a change of clothes, but that beautiful golden hair would probably be the first thing anyone noticed about him.

"He's not that pretty," she heard Monty say when she'd stared a little too long at the boy. Charley immediately gave Monty an aggrieved though haughty glare for that remark.

Vanessa couldn't help chuckling. "But his hair is."

"Excellent point," Monty concurred, and said to Charley, "We need a hood for you, boy. If you have one buried in one of those trunks, fetch it out. Otherwise Arlo can stop in the next town to buy one for you before we go on. As for Arlo staying, explain."

"You assumed he's just a driver but he's not. Arlo is with me, groomed to be my manservant from the day I was born."

Monty sighed. "So much for thinking he would know if we'll reach an inn before dark."

"No, he's never been out of London before, so he wouldn't know."

"What the deuce was George thinking not to give us a real driver?"

"Arlo has a map."

Monty growled in his throat. Vanessa managed not to laugh but remarked on what was becoming obvious. "It doesn't sound as if you've been Charley's guardian for very long."

"Merely an absentee guardian until now," Monty said evasively.

She decided not to press and got back to what he considered a dilemma, saying, "It's hard to get lost in England if you're on a road. Roads lead to people, and people can be asked for directions."

"Thank you very much, Nestor, for information I am aware of, which doesn't help a bloody bit if we don't encounter any people to ask before—or perhaps you know if we'll reach an inn before dark?"

She was offended by his sarcastic tone. If she wasn't hungry and tempted by the aromas coming from that basket, she might have gotten up and left. Impatience like his could be dangerous—or just amusing. Actually, it was another thing she found interesting about him. Was he really so used to getting what he wanted immediately that he became snide and sarcastic if it was withheld? But this was so silly! Had he really not noticed the many travelers they'd passed coming from the direction in which they were headed? Inside the coach, he might not have seen them.

And then she heard a rider coming their way. "You could ask him," she said a little smugly, and cast her thumb at the road. "But as it happens, if you don't tarry here too long, you'll reach a hostelry before dark."

He raised a brow at her. "You came from the north, did you?"

"I did."

"And you couldn't just say so?"

She grinned. "I just did. I had no trouble finding a bed to sleep in each night. But I didn't need to stay at the next hostelry we'll be coming to," she added. "I make better time riding alone on Snow."

He glanced over her head at her pet. "Then you're not in a hurry to get home, since you're plodding along with us?"

He was assuming that's where she was going. Or he figured the question would make her reveal her destination, which she wasn't about to do, so she simply replied, "You're an interesting pair of traveling companions who will break the monotony of a long trip."

"I don't think I've ever been called interesting before,"

Charley remarked a bit snobbishly before tossing a napkin onto her lap.

"I know I haven't," Monty added with a laugh, but then he added as he looked at Charley, "But I assure you we aren't interesting a'tall, just ordinary people undertaking a long journey."

Another lie, Vanessa thought, but then he didn't know she'd overheard him remind Charley in the coach that they were being accepted as guests wherever they were going as a favor to the Prince Regent. And that wasn't interesting? They were definitely hiding something, but then so was she.

The boy started passing her the food. There was a lot of it, and it was incredibly fancy food, too, fit for a king or at the very least a couple of noblemen, but she wasn't complaining. There were several different cheeses, fruit she couldn't name because she'd never seen it before, a pile of sandwiches, each tied with ribbons on all sides so the filling wouldn't fall out, and pieces of roasted chicken, the skin so crisp it crackled when she bit into it.

Wherever this strange duo was from, she guessed the fancy food basket had come from the Prince Regent's own kitchen. So without appearing too curious, she remarked, "Did one of you prepare this sumptuous feast?" Charley gave her such an incredulous look, she laughed. "Well, obviously I meant one of your chefs."

"This is hardly sumptuous if you're used to ten-course meals of the finest meats and sauces," Charley said loftily.

"English cuisine pales in comparison to the cuisine of—"

Monty cut in, "We get the point, boy. You miss your own chef. Next time bring him along. I'm sure he can produce wondrous meals over a campfire."

Charley scrunched his lips at the mild rebuke, but a moment later he glanced at Vanessa and asked, "Are you English, boy?"

She found it incredible that a boy likely younger than herself was addressing her that way, but she merely replied, "Don't I sound English?"

"I sound English, but I'm not," he replied.

"Oh?"

Charley ducked his head, and she noticed why. Monty was giving him a very pointed look. So she amended, "Actually, you've got a bit of an accent."

"So do you," Monty remarked. "Scottish?"

She chuckled. "Just a tad by blood, but I'm English born and bred—mostly. I've just spent the last six years in Scotland, so I suppose I picked up a bit of the brogue."

"What were you doing up there?" Monty asked casually.

"Visiting family," she said before taking a large bite of her sandwich so she wouldn't have to say any more.

She would have liked to savor that amazing lunch, but Monty was staring at her again as she ate. It was starting to annoy her because she'd like to gaze at him but couldn't if she'd end up meeting his fascinating green eyes. So she wolfed down the meal, then left their little picnic to give Snow some fruit while her companions finished eating.

But she was only there a moment before an arm slipped around her shoulders and Monty said in a conspiratorial tone, "We're not going to mention it to my ward unless he guesses, but if you were intentionally trying to look like a boy, you probably should have padded your shoulders and mucked up your cheeks, wench."

Vanessa growled low, turned, and slammed her fist into his gut. She ignored the pain spreading up her wrist from giving it all she had and hitting what felt like a wall. She was too satisfied by the whoosh of air she heard him exhale and seeing him half bent over.

For good measure she snarled, "What sort of daft idiot are you? Calling me a wench? Get some spectacles, you bloody sod!"

He straightened. "It's not the first time I've been mistaken, and in fact I thought the same thing about my ward when I first saw his pretty face, but he offered to show me his manly credentials."

"I knew I should've grabbed my pistol instead of clenching my fist. *Wench!* Some insults cannot be suffered. This is where we'll be parting—"

"Hold on," he said, and stopped her as she leapt up to mount Snow. The sensation of his hands on her waist startled her, but he removed them as soon as her feet were on the ground again. "I'll apologize if I must, but surely I'm not the first to make that assumption—considering."

"Considering *what*?" she growled.

"Your narrow shoulders and waist, your smooth ivory

cheeks, which I caught a glimpse of, and that hood you obviously hide under. I suppose you're too young to grow a beard, but at least do what I suggested and muck up your face with some dirt so you can take off that hood."

"I'm not hiding. The hood protects me from the wind when I'm riding."

"You aren't riding now!" he replied, his tone turning jocular. "Well, if you're just afraid of being recognized by someone we cross paths with, then by all means continue as you are, *boy*, and accept my profuse apology. I'm learning something about hiding m'self, so who am I to complain about other people's behavior, eh? You're still welcome to stay with us. There's safety in numbers, and you know how to use those pistols you tote. And don't forget you find me interesting."

Was he joking now? "You *and* the boy!" she yelled after him.

She stared at Monty's back as he returned to Charley to finish his lunch. He'd conceded she was a boy, hadn't he? This was the first time on her journey anyone had challenged her about her sex. But until now she hadn't met anyone she'd wanted to converse with at length or share a meal with. She suddenly realized it didn't matter if Monty and his ward eventually figured out she was a female. Well, it was scandalous behavior to pass herself off as a boy, but they would never find out who she really was, and in a few days they would part ways and she'd never see them again.

She would still prefer to maintain her male persona

because it made traveling so much easier. Besides, why should she volunteer any information about herself when they were concealing their own true identities? But she did concede that Monty had a point. She had to be more careful not to let anyone get a good look at her face, which clearly proclaimed her a female!

She looked at the grass and frowned as she bent down to sift through it until she reached some dirt. Then she quickly straightened and brushed off her hands, laughing. She wouldn't go that far to convince anyone she was a boy. She'd put her scarf back on instead.

Chapter Eight

THEY REACHED THE FLYING Coach inn by dusk that night. Arlo had stopped briefly that afternoon in a small town and purchased a hooded cloak for Charley. It was a very plain brown woolen one but it covered his pretty golden locks and concealed his jeweled collar. The servant was also wearing one now. *In solidarity with his master?* Vanessa wondered. In any case, she felt better about wearing her hood inside the inn because with the three of them hooded she was much less conspicuous.

She had stayed at several of the inns operated by the Flying Coach company on her way south. Based in Manchester, Flying Coach had built numerous inns along the route to London to accommodate the passengers in their vehicles and to honor their claim of comfortably transporting their customers from Manchester to London in three and a half days. But one of those coaches had just passed through and dropped off a number of passengers for the night, leaving only two rooms available for anyone else.

Of course Monty took both of them, but Vanessa didn't like it when she heard him tell Charley, "You and Arlo can share a room, Nestor will bunk with me in the other."

"I thought you said your ward was never going to be out of your sight," Vanessa reminded him.

"Charley and I discussed the matter in the coach. He expressed a strong preference for sharing a room with his longtime servant, and since I'll be next door and the inn-keeper confirmed the doors have locks, I decided to grant his wish—amends, as it were."

"For?"

"If you'd heard his tirade about having to wear a woolen cloak and hood, you wouldn't ask. The boy thinks wool belongs on sheep and nowhere else."

She might have laughed, but for the second time that day she wondered if he still suspected she was a female and was testing her for a show of maidenly outrage. Earlier, when his coach had pulled over for a relief stop, he'd called to her, "Over here, Ness," as if he expected her to join him and the boy as they faced the same tree.

She had already intended to use a copse of trees, which she'd spotted before the coach stopped, so she said simply, "I'll find my own tree, thank you."

"Embarrassed by size?"

She was glad she'd read the anatomy book one of her tutors had given her and didn't have to ask what he meant. "Yes, if you must know."

"All right, then!" he yelled, but he also laughed, confirming her initial impression that he was only teasing.

But sharing a room with her wasn't a tease. Either he no longer suspected that she was female and saw nothing wrong with the arrangement—or just the opposite. In which case, he probably expected her to go back outside and sleep on Snow again instead of rooming with him for the night. Or maybe he was trying to force her to admit she was female and demand the room for herself. She did neither—yet.

Her heart raced with indecision. She knew it was scandalous to share a room with a man, but this man had no idea who she was. She decided to accept his dare—if that's truly what it was. After all, she wasn't sure if he still suspected she was female, so why give up her male identity before she had to? Besides, she was intrigued with him. Why couldn't she have a little fun and observe him up close? She wouldn't let anything truly improper happen.

"I'm going to go check on Snow to make sure he's settled properly for the night," she told her companions.

"Or hie off on him without a goodbye?"

With only a glance over her shoulder on the way out of the inn, she told Monty, "Not a'tall. If we're eating, order me whatever you're having, I'll be only a few minutes."

In the stable she saw that Snow had been unsaddled and his stall was full of hay. She wondered if she should just sleep on his back again. Logically, Monty should be sharing a room with Charley and she should be sharing one with Arlo. Were the current sleeping arrangements really Monty's way of making amends to Charley?

"Ye're with those people by choice?"

Vanessa started. She was amazed that such a giant man could move so silently. Barrel-chested, well over six feet tall, Donnan MacCabe stood beside her, arms crossed, his face expressionless. Donnan and his brother, Calum, were related to her great-grandfather, and therefore distantly to her.

"Yes, they're traveling north, too, and I'll likely be with them until I turn west toward my mother's house." And then recalling the crowded inn, she added, "There aren't any more rooms available here for you and your brother."

"Calum rode ahead tae get one for us," he said, then warned, "If yer accosted on the road again, lass, we will intervene."

"Suit yourself, just don't tell my traveling companions that you're with me."

"Yer no longer alone, so why not?"

"Because I still don't need guards to protect me, and I don't want anyone to think I do."

Donnan still didn't look happy. "Yer father might think ye especially need tae be guarded when yer traveling with three male strangers."

At the mention of her father, she relented. "We can say you're my servants and we got separated, but you've caught up to me. But can you try to look a little less lethal?"

His laugh was a bass rumble. "If ye've an idea how, I'm listening."

She tsked. "At least wait until midmorning tomorrow. I'm too tired to explain tonight."

Returning to the inn, she found the odd pair sitting at one of the tables with Arlo, which was a surprise. Servants usually didn't sit with their masters, but since Arlo had been with Charley since the day he was born, he was obviously more than a servant to the boy. And besides, there were only a few tables in the dining room, and all of them were occupied by other travelers.

"There wasn't much to order," Monty said as she sat down across from him. "Normal stew or stew with extra meat, and you look like you could use more muscle, so extra meat you shall have."

She looked down at the large bowl in front of her and saw chunks of meat but no vegetables. Charley, who was seated next to her, had the same, so she said, "Yes, we boys are sadly lacking in those."

Charley shoved his cloak to the side, lifted his arm, and flexed it. She was annoyed to see a slight bulge rise in his upper arm beneath his jacket, disproving her remark. But then he looked at her, obviously waiting for her to show off her muscles.

She snorted. "This isn't a bloody competition."

Charley laughed, apparently deciding he'd won. He was also drinking wine with the two men, and Monty picked up the bottle on the table to pour some in her empty glass. She quickly put her hand over it, shaking her head. He raised a brow, but she dropped her eyes to her bowl of stew. She wasn't going to explain why she wanted all of her senses highly alert tonight and not befuddled, when it wasn't something a boy would say.

She found the meat tender and the gravy tasty, and yet Charley, half-done with his meal, complained loudly in Monty's direction, "This is horrible food."

"George spoiled you, did he, with his lavish meals?" Monty rejoined.

"Who's George?" she snuck in. If he meant the Prince Regent, she wished he would just say so.

Monty merely replied, "A friend."

But Charley wasn't done complaining. "I hope you will do better tomorrow, Monty."

Vanessa saw other people in the dining room looking over at their table.

"Keep your voice down. The stew is hearty fare, does the bloody job of filling the stomach—and beggars can't be—"

The gasp from Charley and the appalled expression on his face made Monty pause before he amended, albeit a little harshly, "We don't get to be picky on the road, boy. Our hosts will no doubt offer finer fare at their table, but we aren't there yet. So in the meantime, we suffer in silence and make do."

"I—"

"Have said enough," Monty cut in.

The boy still finished his thought in high indignation. "—should have brought my own chef."

Vanessa had to choke back her laughter. Charley really was a spoiled child—a rich, spoiled child. And Monty didn't appear to have any patience for his tantrums, even mild ones, or perhaps he didn't like what Charley's haughty manner and disdainful remarks had revealed to everyone in the dining room—that he was wealthy. It was a good thing the boy had taken off his jewelry. Thieves would come pouring out of every nook and cranny, not realizing they were fake gems.

Who the devil were these two? She wished she knew. Nobles, obviously, and high up the proverbial ladder if they knew the Prince Regent. And while she had thought they might be on a secret mission for the Prince, she was beginning to suspect they might be in danger instead. Why else were they traveling so modestly and concealing their identities?

They made quick work of finishing the meal, and soon the group of four was heading upstairs for the night. Vanessa began to feel a little nervous about sleeping in a room with Monty—or was it anticipation? But she could do this. They were only going to sleep, after all.

She hadn't noticed Donnan entering the inn after she'd spoken to him, but when she reached the second floor she saw another staircase leading down to the back of the inn. She was glad that the brothers had a room nearby, not that she thought she'd need them, but she couldn't deny she always went right to sleep when she knew they were close. For all her bravado about being able to defend herself—and she didn't doubt she could— it was still comforting to know she didn't really have to.

"Two blokes and the bed is big enough for two," Monty noted as they entered the room where two lamps were already lit.

He was right, two blokes would indeed share the bed and think nothing of it. And it did look inviting—but she wasn't getting in it.

"I snore," she said.

"I'll punch you if you do."

She narrowed her eyes on his back as he went to the bedside table and unloaded the sack he was carrying. "You would, wouldn't you?" she said churlishly.

"Don't I owe you one, boy?"

"The hell you do. You're lucky I didn't challenge you to a duel for your insult today."

"No, *you're* lucky you didn't," he returned. "But by all means, suit yourself. You're welcome to sleep on the floor."

She swiped the quilt and one of the pillows off the bed, then tossed them against the wall on the other side of the room. When she looked back his way, she noticed that he'd put at least a half dozen pistols on the table.

"What are those for?" she asked.

He didn't turn around as he said, "Just in case."

"In case of what?"

"An ax pounding at the door."

She snorted. "If you don't want to say, just tell me to mind my own business."

"So why don't you do that?"

Had she really found him interesting? He was a bloody rude gentleman, probably a lord, condescending, curt, quarrelsome when impatient. And then with his back still to her, he started to undress.

Her eyes got wider and wider as she watched him. He tossed his jacket aside, then his shirt. Made of such fine linen, it floated for a moment before it landed on the floor. But her eyes veered away from it, going right back to the wide expanse of sinewy brawn. She noticed a scar, round and dark like a bullet hole, on the upper left side of his back. Had he been shot in the back? Or had it gone straight through his chest? Obviously it had missed his heart, but not by much.

She wanted to ask him about the scar but didn't want to own up to looking at him long enough to have noticed it. He sat on the edge of the bed to remove his boots, then stood to remove his trousers, leaving only his short small clothes. Her eyes flared even wider and she choked back a soft gasp. That much bare skin was simply too much for her senses to experience all at once. Heat flushed up her cheeks, her belly fluttered, and she felt the oddest desire to touch him and feel those muscles ripple under her fingertips. Last summer in Fraserburgh she'd seen bare-chested Scotsmen lifting and throwing massive larch poles while competing at a Tossing the Caber event, but never before had she seen such a handsome man with such a magnificent body up close like this.

Fascinated, she wondered aloud, "How'd you get that bullet wound?"

He turned toward her. Not what she wanted! She bent her head quickly, enough to conceal her face in shadow but still able to peek up under the edge of her hood. Standing as far across the room as she was, she probably could have met his eyes, but hers rose no higher than his shoulders. She really couldn't help it. Now she had a perfect view of his wide chest, thickly muscled arms and legs. She was getting exactly what she'd wanted when she'd decided not to protest sharing a room with him—a chance to satisfy her curiosity about what a magnificent male body looked like.

Instead of answering her, he said, "Why are you still wearing that cloak?"

"It's drafty in here."

"No, it's not."

"Well, it will be for me. You've never slept on a floor to notice how cold it can get down there?"

"I just gave up my quilt, you'll be warm enough."

"Take it back if you want and stop procrastinating. Or does talking about your wound bring back painful memories you don't want to recount?"

"Does stubbornness run in your family?"

"No, I think I got all of it."

He finally chuckled, giving up. "My regiment was sent to the Peninsular War, tasked with taking that territory back from the French and then defending it. I'd been shot before, a minor wound that hadn't fully healed when I was shot again. But the second shot went clean through and laid me low for several weeks. My condition wasn't improving, so they finally sent me home to recover—or die. I don't think the army surgeons were sure which would happen. But I convalesced with my family, and my father got me to promise I wouldn't go back. I think he did it when I was delirious with fever, because I really don't remember making that promise, but he swears I did."

"Does it still hurt?"

"Occasionally."

He stretched his arms above his head, twisting his torso from side to side perhaps to see if this was one of those occasions, and he did actually gasp. She cringed for him. "So it does hurt?"

"Just on my back, never on my chest, deuced odd," he replied. "A bit of rubbing usually helps, but I can't reach it."

She sucked in her breath. He wasn't suggesting she massage his back, was he? She wouldn't mind! But she didn't dare give in to a temptation that could lead to a lot more than rubbing his back if she got that close to him.

"Or you can let me sleep on the floor," he added. "Hard surfaces tend to help when this old wound acts up. If you wouldn't mind taking the bed instead?"

She nodded and headed toward the comfortable-looking bed while he picked up two of his pistols and went over to where the quilt had landed on the floor. But he was going to wonder why she slept in her clothes after he'd stripped down almost completely, so she bundled up fast under the covers so he wouldn't notice and faced the side of the room away from him.

She guessed he was looking her way again when he asked, "Are you asleep yet, Ness?"

Of course she wasn't, only moments had passed since she lay down, but she still said, "I am, and we're leaving early in the morn, so you should be, too."

"Tell me about yourself. I'm beginning to think your secrets are more interesting than mine."

"Was I not clear enough that I'm asleep?"

He laughed. "Most definitely. Very well, we'll resume this conversation in the morning when you're not asleep."

But about a half hour later, he mumbled, "I should have drunk more of that cheap wine."

A short while later he added, "Bloody hell, I'm calling a truce."

Vanessa didn't respond, but wondered what the deuce he meant by that. He wasn't the only one having trouble getting to sleep tonight.

Chapter Nine

As Montgomery lay on the floor, he thought about the very pretty wench in the bed nearby. Who did she think she was fooling?

He'd been unable to stop staring at her from the moment he'd guessed he was a she when she'd turned to look for Charley after they'd stopped for lunch and he'd gotten a glimpse of her face. He'd been bowled over. The audacity of her trying to pass herself off as a boy when her waist was so narrow, her hands so delicate, her face so feminine and pretty. Why was she disguising herself? Or maybe it wasn't a disguise. She could have been raised without any of the feminine frills, might never have worn a dress or coiffed her hair or batted her eyes. Good God, she would be devastating if she did. But why had she continued the pretense after she'd been found out?

Her denying it was silly, didn't matter a jot. It just made him determined to get her to fess up so they could enjoy traveling together in other ways. But he let her think her ruse was still working because he didn't want her to ride away. However, trying to tempt the wench into revealing herself or force her to scream at him in outrage for disrobing in front of her proved that the idea of enjoying an amorous night with her had turned him into a bloody fool. There would be no more silliness like that. For whatever reason she wanted the world to see a boy standing in her boots, he had to go along with it and give up the notion of her in his bed. As soon as that was settled in his mind he got right to sleep.

A loud noise at the door jolted him awake. It was much louder than a normal knock. Having left one lamp burning for the night, he immediately saw why. There was an ax blade stuck in the door. It hadn't been pulled out yet for another whack. Grabbing a pistol, he ran to the door before that happened.

A bloody ax. How the devil had Chanders's thugs found him?

But the ax didn't get pulled out of the door. Before he could unlock the door, he heard a loud thud in the corridor, then some other noise that wasn't very loud. When he flung the door open, ready to shoot, no one was there. He peeked into the hall and saw a body being dragged around the corner to the stairs, only the boots of the downed man were visible for a moment before they disappeared.

A head suddenly poked under the arm he had braced against the doorframe, followed by a hand gripping a flintlock. He was arrested by the sight of copper-colored hair.

Copper? What a lovely color! No wonder she hid that, too, until now. And she probably didn't know the hood of the cloak she was still wearing had slid back enough to reveal it. But she was trying to get past him and into the corridor.

He shifted his hips so she couldn't squeeze through before saying, "I suppose one of the other guests didn't like the noise, either, and put a stop to it. You can go back to bed, Ness."

"I will, after I make sure there's no one who needs shooting."

He almost laughed but had a feeling she was serious. "I'll do that. You'll get back in bed."

"Don't be absurd. I'm dressed, you aren't. There could be more thugs downstairs."

This argument was getting silly, but there was no way he was letting her run downstairs and possibly straight into more of Chanders's thugs. He lowered his arm and hooked it around her waist then hefted her horizontally against his hip and carried her back to the bed.

She immediately started to squirm. "Let me go!"

But he kept his tone reasonable as he explained, "We'd hear more noise if there were more thugs downstairs, so there's no reason for both of us to lose more sleep over this. And you've delayed me from checking on Charley long enough. Go back to sleep."

"But—"

"Stop arguing. You won't like how I win," he said, and tossed her into the bed.

Not another word. He waited to see if she would roll off the other side of the bed and run back to the door, but she didn't. She pulled the blanket over her head instead and made some snarling noises underneath it and what sounded like a muffled scream of frustration. Aggressive, stubborn—and a temper. Their mysterious companion really was a delightful surprise.

He donned his pants, slipped on his greatcoat, picked up a second pistol, then went back to the damaged door. Glancing back at the bed, he saw no movement under the blanket, but he still said, "I'll find out who I should thank for ridding this ax of its wielder. I'll be back in a moment."

There had been only the one loud whack, so he wasn't worried about Charley's safety, but he still needed to check on the boy. His knock wasn't answered immediately, and the door was locked, as it should be, so he just knocked harder. Then it was yanked open and a pistol came very close to his face, although Arlo's hand was trembling.

The servant backed away immediately and pointed the weapon at the floor. "Apologies, my lord!"

"Don't be ridiculous. I hope you would have used that if necessary."

"Of course, he is also mine to protect."

He was sitting up in bed wearing a ridiculously luxurious nightshirt. And yawning. Charley had to have been awakened by the disturbance, but Montgomery guessed he was too arrogant to be afraid, confident that his people would protect him. But another glance at that silly nightshirt had him rolling his eyes. So much for the boy trying to blend in as an ordinary fellow.

"You two can get back to sleep. That particular miscreant was after me, not you."

"Do try to keep these disturbances to a minimum!"

Montgomery just snorted and left the room, but paused long enough to hear the door being locked again. He headed downstairs barefoot and bare-chested under the greatcoat, one pistol still in his hand, another tucked in his pants. The ax wielder had been deposited in front of the innkeeper's desk. The gash on the man's head was bleeding a little, but he was still breathing.

The innkeeper cringed when he saw Montgomery. "Profuse apologies, m'lord. My boys have gone to fetch rope and hitch a wagon to take this criminal to the magistrate."

"Did he ask for me?"

"Not by name. He said he had something for the lord staying here, so I told him which room you are in since you're the only guest who resembles a lord. Utterly my mistake, but we're not used to having noblemen under our roof."

"What he had for me was the ax. He's a bloody maniac. Make sure your boys tell the magistrate that."

The only other person in the common room was a big fellow sitting at one of the tables with a tall mug of ale before him. Montgomery caught his eye and nodded toward the body. "Did you do that?"

He didn't really expect an answer. The man could have been involved in the attack and was just sitting there trying to figure out how to get his friend out of there.

Yet he got an "Aye."

Montgomery approached him but gripped his weapon a little tighter when what he'd thought was just a shadow on the man's back appeared to be an ax blade. And the big fellow had a distinctly unfriendly demeanor, was actually glowering at him.

Cautiously, he said, "I'm not sure whether to thank you or ask if you arrived with the man who attacked my door. You do appear to be carrying the same weapon."

"The ax is an easy weapon, doesna need tae be reloaded and causes a guid fright."

The man's size alone would cause a good fright. Chanders's London thugs had been big brutes, but this chap far surpassed them in size.

But before Montgomery's suspicions got out of hand, the big fellow yelled at the man behind the desk, "Innkeep, who was it brought the miscreant tae ye?"

"You did!"

Montgomery smiled at that point. "Well, I'm glad you were disturbed sooner than I and put an end to the noise for me. Much appreciated. I didn't relish sleeping with blood spilled in my room.

"I'm going to check the stable." He nodded to the big Scotsman and headed to the front door, grabbing one of the lanterns.

"Ye expect more?"

Montgomery paused to admit, "Merely a precaution. I want to assure m'self there are no other suspicious chaps lurking about."

He didn't think there would be or they would have come upstairs en masse to take his head off, but his duty to his ward demanded he make sure. Chanders certainly was determined to avenge himself. No doubt he'd had the Townsend family home in London watched when Montgomery didn't return to his flat. The watcher could have seen him leave in the coach with Charley and followed the coach as it left London on the northwest road. Even if the man had kept his distance, all he'd needed to do was check all the inns on that road until he found him.

Quite a parade following him and the boy out of London this morning, he thought. It was a good time to look into those saddlebags he'd taken from the foreigners. Something in there might shed light on why those miscreants had been willing to shoot to kill in order to capture the boy. Or did they just want Charley dead?

Stepping outside, he saw a lone horse tethered there, then he was startled to hear, "Ye can be at ease, mon, there'll be no muir attacks. My brother will be standing guard oot here for the rest o' the night."

Montgomery glanced to his side, then up, bloody hell, quite a bit up. He certainly wasn't used to standing next to a man who was taller than himself. Nor had he heard the Highlander come out to join him on the porch.

"Then once again, much appreciated, but I still want to have a look around the stable."

As he entered the stable, he was puzzled by the man's vigilance and his and his brother's willingness to go to such trouble. No doubt a purse was involved. The innkeeper could have hired them after the disturbance, at least until there was no longer a lord under his roof. Nobles traveled in their own coaches, after all, and didn't usually stay in coaching houses specifically built for stage passengers.

He found the two saddlebags where Arlo had tucked them between Charley's trunks. The first one revealed no clues of any sort, was just stuffed with clothes. The second bag appeared to be the same, but rummaging on the bottom of it, he felt something hard and pulled out a silver inlaid locket. He opened it and saw a small portrait of a young child with short ash-blond hair and a silken jacket—and jewels. A very young Charley? And if the foreigners had carried it with them, did that mean they didn't know what Charley looked like now?

Monty began to think he'd put himself into the middle of a high-stakes, dangerous game, safeguarding a boy with perhaps an inheritance so grand that there were other claimants willing to kill for it. No wonder George was giving him a parcel of land and a manor house for taking this problem off his hands.

When he got back to the inn, he double-checked that the door to the boy's room was locked. Back in his own room, he was pleased to see that the ax had been removed from the door and the wench appeared to be asleep. He removed his greatcoat, lay down on the floor, and was soon asleep.

But when he awoke in the morning, Nessi was gone. She might even have slipped away last night, for all he knew. And if she had, he wouldn't be able to say he was surprised. Traveling with his entourage was turning out to be a little more dangerous than she might have anticipated. More dangerous than he'd anticipated, too. But her defection still annoyed him, a lot, so his rap on Charley's door was a little too loud.

"Let's go, boy! A quick breakfast then we're back on the road."

He didn't wait for a response, and a good thing, since he found the lot of them at one of the tables downstairs already eating. Including Nessi. Well, he'd misjudged her. While he felt inordinately happy that she hadn't left, he wasn't going to allow the wench to distract him from what was important, keeping his mysterious ward alive.

To that end, he held Arlo back when everyone left the table and handed the servant the locket. "Is that your young lord when he was a lot younger?" At Arlo's nod, he added, "So his pursuers don't know what he currently looks like?"

"His face, probably not. He lived in seclusion. But his hair—"

"Yes," Montgomery cut in dryly, "it's no doubt legendary. Then it needs to be dyed or kept out of sight. And you need to tell me the real reason he's a target."

"He said he told you."

Montgomery's eyes narrowed. "Are you really going to keep his secret when his life depends on my knowing?"

"You know he is important enough for the Prince Regent to ask you to keep him safe. Act accordingly," Arlo said, and followed the others outside.

Had he just been put in his place by a servant?

Chapter Ten

Vanessa stood with snow outside the inn, waiting for her traveling companions to congregate and for the coach to arrive. It was barely dawn, cold enough for her to have put her scarf on, which provided the additional advantages of holding her hood in place and covering more of her face. She'd ignored the tub in the common bathing room, wouldn't have used it even if there had been time, but she'd taken a few minutes to splash water on her face and arms, so she did feel somewhat refreshed. And she was excited to continue her journey with her unusual traveling companions for a few more days. She'd already forgiven Monty for being so high-handed last night when she'd wanted to help. It had been bad enough when he'd thought her a girl, but now he apparently thought she was too young to be useful in a dangerous situation.

She felt her cheeks grow warm at the memory of the way he'd slipped his arm around her waist last night. She'd thought something else had been about to happen, and her stomach had actually fluttered, but he'd rudely toted her back to the bed.

He hadn't known he was carrying a girl, obviously, but she'd still been furious at his strong-arm tactics and might have bitten the knee in front of her face if she weren't deeply unsettled by being in close proximity to that magnificent body she'd admired earlier that night, even in that absurd position.

She understood now what he'd meant about "calling a truce." He'd obviously been testing her to see if she was a girl, but she had passed his test and could comfortably continue to travel as a boy in his company.

"So you're staying with us despite the mayhem?"

She glanced covertly to the side and saw Monty in his greatcoat stepping out of the inn. And lo, he'd even tied a cravat after leaving the dining table. If he hadn't left his auburn hair loose about his shoulders, he would have been the epitome of a dashing, well-dressed nobleman.

As for his question, having seen him practically naked last night—and what a delightful show that had been—she had no desire to part company with this bunch until she had to. They were still proving to be far too interesting as companions.

"We still seem to be going in the same direction," she answered.

"I was surprised to find you asleep last night when I

returned to the room. Not a bit of curiosity over how an ax got embedded in our door?"

"I was curious last night, but *someone* kept me from investigating."

He chuckled. "The disturbance was over, so you didn't miss anything exciting, Ness."

"I've already concluded that. Inns that serve spirits, like this one, can get as rowdy as any tavern."

"You've been in that many to know? Even at your tender age?"

She wasn't going to tell him she had come of age, but she could say, "My father and I used to stop for lunch in a tavern when we went to town for supplies. More'n once we had to pick up our plates and take them outside to finish eating before our table got smashed to bits."

"Is that really true?"

She chuckled at the skepticism in his tone. "You're a very suspicious fellow, Monty, but I'm not making up stories for your amusement."

"Well, whether you want to hear it or not, I'm obligated to warn you that it might be dangerous for you to travel with us. We've already been singled out twice on this trip. Rowdiness wasn't the problem last night. The boy is in the middle of a power struggle. One side wants him dead, the other wants to keep him alive, and his enemies could be searching for him. I tried to get him out of London with no one the wiser, but I'm not used to this sort of shenanigan.

So we will not be staying at any more inns. That was a huge mistake on my part. And while we will still stop for food baskets, Charley and I will remain in the coach, out of sight, if other people are around. It didn't occur to me until last night that any Tom, Dick, or Harry could point out the direction in which we depart. So the fewer people who see us on the road, the fewer who can tell our enemies which way we went."

Vanessa was incensed on Charley's behalf. "You're saying the point of that disturbance last night was to kill the boy?"

"Actually, that one was likely for me."

Now she had to wonder who was lying. "Are you in the middle of a power struggle, too?"

"Not a'tall, that was just recompense for dallying where I ought not to have dallied. But I've learned my lesson and am taking m'self away from temptation to a quiet spell in the country where neither the boy nor I will be found."

"So the men who shot at you yesterday morning weren't highwaymen?"

"Likely not."

"And you've crossed me off your list of pursuers?"

That drew a snort from him. "You're too young and brave to be in the employ of a coward like Lord Chanders."

"And too rich to need employment."

"Is that so?" he asked. "And how is it so?"

"Maybe what I consider rich, you'd consider humble. Stop being so bloody nosy."

"Ah, said something you shouldn't, eh? So what difference does it make if I know you have money? You're not wearing rags, Ness. It was already obvious. What's your real name?"

"What's yours?"

He laughed. "Touché."

"I could've sworn you called a truce."

"Aha!" he exclaimed. "I knew bloody well you weren't asleep."

"No you didn't, and I was," she lied. "You just kept waking me with your silly remarks."

"Well, I meant what I said about a truce," he assured her. "But now I need to ask if you even want to continue with us?"

"A little danger just sounds like an adventure to me. Tell me you wouldn't have felt the same at my age."

"Well, if I knew your age—"

She cut in with a chuckle. "I'll let you know if or when I've had enough adventure."

She leapt up to mount Snow so Monty would know she was done discussing the subject. A woman carrying a basket rushed out of the inn and handed it to Arlo, who had just driven the coach to the entrance. She guessed it was for lunch and hoped it contained enough food for dinner, too, if Monty really intended to forgo any more inns.

When it was nearing noon, Arlo stopped the coach by a tree where they could eat. By then she was wondering what was keeping the two Scotsmen from joining them. She had been watching for them since midmorning.

Charley was first out of the coach and was stretching his arms and legs. He might be a mere boy, but he had long legs and was as tall as most men. She chuckled as she watched him. He even walked imperiously.

"What's so funny?" Monty asked.

She didn't turn around, lowered her head a little instead before admitting, "The airs your ward puts on."

"Utterly silly, I agree, but let's not tell him I think so." He suddenly put an arm around her shoulders, causing her to stiffen, remembering that he'd done the same thing yesterday. But today he was merely turning her toward Snow before he let go of her and asked, "I don't suppose you packed another hood in your bag that I could borrow for m'self? I'm wary of eating out in the open like this where any passerby can ogle me."

"Then eat inside the coach. You don't need to keep me company out here."

"Nonsense. We will be spending all too much time in that vehicle, and besides, the least we can do is provide you with excellent company at mealtimes when you're willing to risk life and limb for our protection."

She managed not to laugh. He'd done all the life-risking so far. "Sorry, I traveled light, with only a few sets of togs, and didn't think an extra cloak would be needed."

The moment he sat down on the blanket Arlo had spread on the ground, she headed off to find a tree.

Returning a few minutes later, she slowed her step, since Charley still wasn't there. She located him in the field to the north walking around. Arlo had joined him, and the two appeared to be talking, not thinking about food yet. Before she reached Monty, he suddenly stood, a pistol in each hand. But he wasn't pointing them at her.

She followed his threatening gaze to the road they had just traveled and saw her tardy guards finally approaching.

"Put your weapons away!" she yelled at Monty. "They're with me."

Chapter Eleven

"WITH YOU? HOW CAN they suddenly be with you when they weren't?"

Vanessa ignored Monty's question and hurried over to the Scots. "Why are you so late?"

Donnan dismounted. "Calum stood guard last night, so he needed a few hours' sleep—"

"I was volunteered, and those few hours were a pittance," Calum cut in with a grumble.

"—or we would've been here sooner, lass," Donnan finished.

She heard Monty laughing behind her. "About bloody time that was settled."

"Bloody hell, Donnan," she snarled. "Didn't you see him approaching?"

But Monty was still gloating behind her. "I knew it! My instincts about women never fail me."

She swung around to glare at him. "Nothing, and I

mean absolutely nothing, has changed, so keep your 'I told you so' to yourself!"

"Ah, but this"—he pushed back her hood—"you don't need anymore." And then with some surprise as he stared at her face, he added, "This beautiful spring day doesn't hold a candle to you—Nestor."

He laughed again, infuriating her so much she swung her fist at him. She got in one blow because he was too busy staring at her face, but then he put his hands on her upper arms to stave off another.

That's when Donnan stepped in. "Get yer hands off her or ye will be feeling mine."

Monty didn't look worried, despite the Scot's size, but he did remove his hands from her person. He even sounded amused when he pointed out, "The wench put her hands on me first, and rather roughly, too."

"She's not a wench, she's—"

"Donnan MacCabe, not another word!" Vanessa cut in sharply.

Looking at Donnan for a moment, Monty remarked, "And this explains who you were actually guarding last night." And then his eyes dropped to Vanessa. "Brothers you neglected to mention?"

"Brothers, yes, but not mine," she said. "We're distantly related, though, on my father's side. We were separated—"

But Donnan interrupted, "The wee lass objects tae our protection, threatened tae lose us if we didna stay oot o' sight, but we've always been close enough tae hear her call oot."

That was the last straw! Monty had no business intruding on her conversation with her guards—who kept saying too much.

Glaring at Monty, she said rather sharply, "Do you mind? This is a private conversation."

"I'm feeling decidedly accommodating," Monty said with a grin. "So I don't mind a'tall—Nessi." He chuckled as he walked back to the food basket.

Vanessa hated how amused he was by this discovery that she was a lass, but she swung back around to Donnan. "We do *not* need to explain every bloody little thing to that man."

Donnan shrugged. "I met the mon last night and now he kens we were with ye. Ye trust him enough tae guard his back, ye can trust him with the truth."

"You were supposed to join me earlier this morning when we would've had time to talk before he noticed you," she reminded him, still furious that the Scot had revealed so much about her.

"I was nearby," Donnan assured her. "I was just waiting on Calum tae catch up before we joined ye."

Calum spoke up. "I asked the bonny maid tae wake me after a few hours. I think she thought I wanted something else from her, so she didna show up tae get me oot o' bed. A disturbance ootside woke me, or I would've slept the rest o' the day away—which is what I still feel like doing."

He headed toward the coach, climbed to the top of it, and started pushing the trunks around before lying down between a few. She stared at him incredulously until Donnan said, "Dinna begrudge him a wee bit muir sleep when he was awake all night guarding ye. At least he isna asking the haughty lowlander for a seat in his coach for the nap. Getting a nay would add hot spice tae the pot."

That remark gave her pause. "You're both annoyed with me, aren't you?"

"Aye. Ye be playing a dangerous game, sleeping in a mon's room and accompanying lowlanders who've clearly been marked by every thief 'tween here and London. Yer father certainly wouldna approve."

"There was nothing untoward when he thought I was a boy—until you just informed him otherwise."

She thought about telling him that it wasn't robbers who were after her traveling companions, but that would just make the situation worse. Besides, the brothers would be alert to any kind of threat.

Instead, she said, "This is my last chance to be myself before my mother starts ordering me around for my debut. And after what happened last night, my companions are going to take the precaution of not stopping at any more inns to eat or sleep, which will lessen the chances of their being attacked at night, but I still want to help protect them during the day."

"Championing them, are ye?"

"If you didn't notice, one of them is just a boy. Pompous and haughty, but still a boy who won't be a bit of help in a fight. Yes, I'm going to help them until their path diverges from mine."

"Does the laddie need lessons in firing a pistol?" he asked.

She chuckled, trying to picture Charley holding one. "Undoubtedly, but you won't like his response if you offer to teach him, so maybe you shouldn't offer. The boy acts like he's a bloody royal, so protecting himself would be beneath him."

She was still utterly frustrated that the choice of revealing her true sex had been taken out of her hands, but she reminded herself that she'd already concluded it didn't matter if Monty and the boy knew she was a girl, they just couldn't know that a *Lady* came before her name.

She looked over at the blanket and the basket of food. "Can you join us for lunch without spilling any more secrets?"

"I've eaten already."

That wasn't the answer she wanted. "Donnan, they can't ever know my real name, is that clear? It would cause a scandal if it were to get out. That sort of tidbit could hurt my sisters—and me—if it made its way to London before our debut this Season. Absolutely no scandal can be attached to my family's name."

"A thought that should've took guid hold before the disguise, aye?" he countered.

"No one was supposed to see through it, and Monty didn't until you called me a lass."

"Is he blind, then?"

"No, he guessed, but I convinced him he was wrong." And she yanked her hood up, adding, "How much can you really tell about me when I wear this—if you didn't know?"

"It mun be hot under there."

She laughed at the evasion. But she had to agree it was hot on such a beautiful spring day and she had nothing to hide any longer. No one approaching from a distance could distinguish that she was female, and she would have enough time to pull up her hood before she spoke to any strangers.

She pushed the hood off her head before saying, "Well, I'm hungry if you aren't—and glad you can ride beside me now. So even if I'm presently annoyed with you, I'm still glad you've joined us."

He chuckled as he took his and Calum's horses over to the grass alongside the road. She headed to the blanket where Monty was sitting by himself. She looked around for Charley and spotted him and Arlo. They'd stopped strolling and appeared to be having an argument.

"D'you need to break that up?" she said, gesturing toward the pair.

"His manservant from the day he was born was how Charley referred to Arlo. I think not. Perhaps Arlo is try-ing to talk some sense into the boy."

"It's difficult to believe Arlo has been Charley's manservant for that long when he doesn't look much older than him."

"No doubt it was Charley's bombastic way of saying they grew up together. Then again, who knows how things are done in their country?"

She might have been relieved that she could now look directly at Monty. Having to avoid eye contact with him had been very frustrating for her. But the amused expression she saw on his face now rubbed her the wrong way. The man was gloating and making no bones about it.

He proved it when he asked, "Are you going to tell me why you are trying to disguise yourself as a boy?"

She narrowed her eyes at him. Just because he knew she was a female didn't mean he had a right to know anything else about her. "No, I'm not, and if you pry into my personal affairs any further, Monty-whoever-you-are, you're going to end up with another hole in your chest to match the one you got in the war. I promise you that. Who will protect your ward then?"

She thought that was a pretty good threat, yet all he said in reply was, "That implies you're not deserting us?"

She raised a brow at him. "Just because you've been an arse?"

Monty laughed. She ignored him and reached into the basket for a sandwich. He was already done eating, and she had the feeling he was still watching her. A glance back at him confirmed it, and she felt a delicious warmth spread through her. His gaze wasn't just admiring, it was ardent! And like a moth to a flame, she was drawn to him, unable to look away from his emerald eyes, feeling suddenly breathless and most certainly stirred.

Even though she no longer had to fight the urge to look at him directly, maybe she should still refrain. There was far too much heat in his eyes now. Very annoying! And yet she still liked the man. He was witty and humorous, sometimes even charming, incredibly handsome, and certainly heroic in his diligence in protecting his ward. She didn't want him to get hurt on her account.

"You have to stop looking at me like that," she cautioned. "If the Scots notice, they won't care if you're a lord, they'll knock you on your arse. And don't look so bloody pleased about what you now know about me."

"Do I need to apologize again? I had thought I could let it go, that suspicion I had that you're a female. I truly did intend to. But now that it's out of the bag, as it were, sweetheart, I am a man and you're a beautiful young woman in close proximity. It's my bloody nature to entice—"

Her laugh cut him off. "This changes nothing, so no more seductive looks."

"What about you? You fessed up to seeing my wound, so you must have seen a lot more. You couldn't take your eyes off me last night, could you?"

For the first time she blushed in his presence, not just

from his teasing—and she was sure he was just teasing—but because she'd been unable to push the image of his magnificent body out of her mind. And he was close enough to see her blush, so hoping he'd attribute her reddened cheeks to anger, she sharpened her tone. "You weren't facing me when you started to undress, so you don't know if I was gazing at you or I was mortified and turned away. It's not wise to assume things about me."

"I would never—well, only occasionally . . ." Then a sigh. "Very well, this is becoming a dreadfully bad habit, but I apologize again."

It sounded grudging yet sincere, so she allowed: "I've a bit of a temper, not that you would've noticed." She smiled to indicate she was teasing, because of course he'd noticed by now. "But I suppose I should apologize, too, for being snappish. I would've preferred to finish off our journey with you thinking I was a boy. We won't be traveling together much longer, but I'd just as soon you not tell your ward. Unlike you, he hasn't suspected anything amiss."

"Unlike me, he lives in a world that apparently revolves around himself. And for the record, I most certainly did notice your temper."

She tsked with a slight roll of her eyes. "Not so much the gentleman, are you?"

He grinned. "A rake through and through."

"Really?"

"A discreet one, yes—except when I'm warding off scandals."

She laughed. "What a contradictory remark! Did you say that backward by mistake?"

"What I said shouldn't have been said, so do forget it and eat your lunch." And then he bellowed, "Charley, we're about to leave, and you've yet to eat!"

"Shh," she hissed. "One of the brothers is sleeping atop your coach."

He glanced up at it. "He'll fall off when we leave."

"No, he's rooted himself."

"Who are they to you really?"

"As I said, blood relatives. I'd never met them before this trip. My father hired them to guard me."

"And your father is?"

"My father."

He laughed at the evasion. Did he really think he could get names out of her that easily?

Chapter Twelve

"I PROMISE YOU, YOU WON'T starve. But no one expects a lady to have a hearty appetite, darlings. So you are going to practice merely picking at the food on your plates and leaving most of it untouched."

Kathleen Blackburn glanced from one to the other of her beautiful twin daughters sitting on either side of her at the dining table. With their perfect blond hair, light blue eyes, and identical delicate features, they were going to make superb matches this year, she had no doubt of it. She was so proud of them. They were ready for their Season, they just needed a few reminders about the small things that could enhance or detract from a successful debut.

"This food isn't going to go to waste, is it, when I'm so hungry?" Emily complained, but at least in low tones. She knew better than to raise her voice. "You could have warned us ahead of time that we were to have a lesson in starving."

Emily could be as willful as her older sister, Vanessa, but her twin, Layla, was completely malleable, always eager to please. Emily might start the fight, since she was the more aggressive of the two, but Layla was the peace-maker, able to defuse it. They complemented each other so well, her adorable twins.

But to Emily's complaint she replied, "Normally you can eat something beforehand so you aren't hungry when a lavish meal is served, which is what I was taught to do, and if that doesn't suffice, you can eat more afterward when you are alone. Tonight we practice restraint in case you don't arrive at your hostess's table replete."

"Or we just make sure that never happens?" Emily said.

"What if you've been invited to someone's house for a weekend party? You can't very well get underfoot in their kitchen, can you?"

"I would," Emily said assuredly.

"I wouldn't," Layla promised.

Kathleen stared at Emily long enough for the girl to amend her answer a little petulantly. "At least I'd send our maid to the kitchen."

"Much better and allowed," Kathleen said. "Now practice restraint. I'll have plates sent up to your room in a few hours."

But after a few minutes of merely moving food around on their plates without eating, Emily's stomach growled noisily, making her laugh. "I think that would be more embarrassing than eating most of the food on my plate, wouldn't you agree, Mother?"

Kathleen sighed. "By all means, if you are that hungry, eat enough to avoid making that embarrassing noise, but keep in mind, there is always dessert. I hope you haven't forgotten any other lessons I taught you."

Layla grinned, Emily giggled, before they said nearly in unison, "Not one."

Kathleen rolled her eyes. "Do refrain from exasperating your mother and simply prove how perfect you both—"

Loud noises were suddenly coming from the central hallway. She stood up without finishing her sentence and moved to the doorway. Just as curious, the girls crowded behind her in time to see a second large trunk being set down in the foyer. The butler was there, still holding the front door open for two of their own footmen who were coming in with a third trunk.

Kathleen approached the butler. "Did our expected guests arrive early?"

"No, mum, just these trunks."

"Ask the driver who they belong to."

"To Lady Vanessa."

The twins squealed in delight at hearing their sister's name, but Kathleen was shocked rather than thrilled. If Vanessa was going to come home, why the deuce couldn't she have done so last spring, when Kathleen had expected her to return to make her debut? She'd assumed as much. William had promised he would send their eldest daughter back when he'd let her know that Vanessa was with him, he just hadn't specified when. And he had never written to her again. He wrote to the twins, though, but those letters were filled with nonsense about plantation life, when he wasn't on a plantation at all!

That had just been his suggestion for what she could tell their friends and acquaintances about where he and Vanessa had gone. To this day she still didn't know where her husband and her eldest daughter were. Nor did Peter Wright, William's longtime friend. Only William's solicitor knew. All correspondence between William and the twins went through him. But that exasperating man had refused to speak to her when she'd gone to London and tried to get the address from him.

The twins were so excited about Vanessa's imminent arrival that they began opening the trunks and rummaging through them. But after a few minutes, Emily looked up, nearly in tears. "There's nothing of Papa's in them."

Of course there wasn't, Kathleen thought. But she was hopeful he would be coming home soon, now that Vanessa was apparently on her way.

"Did you know Nessa was coming?" Layla asked quietly.

"Yes," Kathleen lied. "I had a letter from your father earlier in the year. I was leaving it to be a surprise. But your father still hasn't finished his business in the West Indies, so we must all be patient a little longer in awaiting his return."

Sending men to search for William had proven to be a frustrating waste of time and money, and yet even this year, she'd sent more out to do so. But she did get an unexpected boon several years back, rife with stipulations, but still a possible way of putting her family back together again.

If everything worked out as she hoped it would, William would finally be able to come home to England. Even if he would never return to her, at least she would have assisted in bringing him back to his homeland and all his daughters, not just Vanessa. If Vanessa knew how to find her father, if she would ever volunteer that information, if she had turned out more like Layla than Emily and could be managed, and didn't indulge in theatrics, if, if, if! Kathleen hated uncertainty, hated when her domain wasn't exactly as it should be. All because of a harmless flirtation that had gone terribly wrong.

It was a shame Henry Rathban had died because of it. None of this would have happened if not for that duel. And she hadn't just lost her husband and eldest daughter because of that duel, she'd had to give up her social life in London, which she loved so much! Even though no one knew of Henry's blackmail and the ensuing duel because Albert Rathban had let it be known that his brother died in an accident, Kathleen had stopped going to London. Constantly being asked when William would return and having to make up so many lies to explain why he was still away had become intolerable.

The twins were directing the servants to take the trunks to Vanessa's old room and excitedly talking about Vanessa's being home in time to have her Season with them. But Kathleen was worried it might be too late—a year too late.

She hurried to her study. She had to write a letter to find out if the bargain she'd agreed to was still on the table.

Chapter Thirteen

AFTER ONE NIGHT OF sleeping in the blanket Donnan had tossed her, with the MacCabe brothers on either side of her and one of them snoring most of the night, Vanessa was wishing she could sleep in a bed again. She found out that Charley was, too, when he pulled her aside to join him for a walk, which seemed to have become part of his daily routine. She was surprised to see him wearing the luxurious fur cloak she'd seen him in the day she'd met him and Monty.

"Arlo isn't usually such a worrier," Charley said, "but he actually agrees with Monty that I should try to blend in better, and he was quite emphatic about it yesterday. Do you think you could teach me how to be a commoner?"

"Does insulting people come naturally to you?" she rejoined.

"No, I didn't mean to imply you are a commoner when it's obvious from your clothes that you come from money and possibly rank. And I make this request for two reasons. I want to improve my ability to disguise myself not only for security purposes but so we can go back to sleeping at inns. I can't bear the indignity and discomfort of sleeping in the coach! I just thought you might have had more dealings with the common man than I have had, and you could impart some needed advice." Then in a whisper, "Monty wants me to play a role I have no knowledge of."

She realized the boy must like the older man if he trusted his advice and wanted to please him by being an "actor in training," as she'd overheard Monty counsel him, so she relented to say, "Just as you made assumptions about my background from the clothes I wear, people do the same to you, Charley. But it's also your expression. You seem to have the habit of looking down a very long nose at others. And why are you wearing that fur cloak again? What happened to the brown woolen one with the hood that Arlo bought you the other day?"

Charley sniffed disdainfully. "I find wool too scratchy for my delicate skin. Besides, I needed fur to stay warm when I was sleeping in the coach."

Vanessa pointed out, "But if people see you wearing a cloak that fancy, they will think you're wealthy, a nobleman, maybe even a royal."

She added the last to see if he would try to convince her that he was a king, just as she'd overheard him doing with Monty. And he did smile as if she had guessed right, but then he frowned, apparently having remembered that he wasn't supposed to announce any grand credentials.

So she continued. "As for the rest of your person, you really ought to cover up your beautiful hair, or at least tie it back—better yet, cut it." He looked so shocked she amended, "Or you could borrow a cap from Arlo if you don't want to wear a hood, as well as some of Arlo's less grand attire."

"He's taller than I, if you didn't notice," he replied.

"Wearing clothes that don't fit you properly would actually be a good touch because people will think you can't afford better. But if you'd rather not, at least get rid of the cravat and the fancy cloak, maybe scuff up your shoes, and take off the jacket if weather permits."

"So the less I wear the better?"

She grinned. "I think what Monty is really concerned about is your air of superiority, but yes, clothes still do make the man as you pointed out. Perhaps if you change your clothes and your snobbish attitude we can both broach the subject with your guardian and he'll agree we've removed the risks involved in stopping at inns. You may need to promise not to say a word when strangers are near, but your new appearance will prove you've taken to heart his warning about not drawing attention to yourself."

Monty agreed rather quickly to using inns again, making her wonder if he wasn't just as pampered and used to comforts as his ward. But the group got into the routine of traveling hard during the day and sleeping comfortably at night with Vanessa staying in a room next to the one her guards occupied. And finally, with complete privacy, she was able to bathe again!

She figured she still had two or three days left with her amusing, although mysterious, traveling companions, unless Arlo turned off the main road before she needed to. She asked Arlo where they were going, since he had the map marked with the location, but he turned terse and merely mumbled something about secrecy. She asked Monty, too, but he countered by asking where she was going, which made her laugh because they were both still keeping secrets and making no bones about it. So she decided to just enjoy what little time she had left with them and possibly test her feminine wiles, if she got a chance, while traveling with such a handsome man.

Monty hadn't taken advantage of the knowledge that she was female other than to behave a little more courteously to her. Charley hadn't remarked on it at all, might not even have noticed, he was so self-absorbed. But with the weather warming up she'd started taking off her hooded cloak when they stopped for lunch. One day she even stretched a little after tossing the cloak on the picnic blanket, aware that she was drawing attention to her figure and Monty was watching her.

But gazing at the long meadow beside the road that looked like so many others they'd passed, she realized she wasn't sure where they were because she hadn't paid attention to which town they'd entered yesterday at dusk to spend the night in. Monty probably knew. The Mac-Cabe brothers, who were having their lunch across the road, must know, because Donnan had told her he'd gotten directions to the town of Dawton from an innkeeper. But she was feeling a little playful, enjoying her last few days of freedom, so she didn't bother to ask. She came up with a more amusing way of figuring out if a town or natural landmark she might recognize lay ahead.

"I don't know where we are, but I bet I can spot the next town from that tree," she said.

Monty looked in the direction of the tall black poplar she was pointing to. It wasn't as thickly leafed as the oak nearby, so it would afford her a better view from up high. She started to run toward it before Monty could tell her exactly where they were, which would deprive her of an excuse to get a little exercise—and tempt him to follow.

She heard him yell for her to wait, but she didn't. Her plan was working. She knew he was running after her because she clearly heard him right behind her. "You're not climbing that tree, Nessi. If you really want to know what lies ahead, I'll climb it for you."

"Want to bet!" she yelled back with a laugh.

She was almost there, too, racing hard, trying to stay in front of him, but also imagining him pulling her off the tree and right into his arms . . .

She tripped on an old fallen branch hidden in the

grass, gasping as she fell, but then she started laughing at herself for too much imagining and not enough paying attention—until she felt Monty fall nearly on top of her. He'd been so close he'd ended up tripping over her, which just made her start laughing again, especially when she heard him laughing, too, over their clumsiness. She leaned up on her elbows and was startled when her back rubbed against his chest.

She turned over to face him and saw just how close he was to her, his green eyes looking down into hers. He had a knee over her legs, a hand braced on one side of her, an elbow braced on the other, leaving his chest half-pressed to hers. They both stopped laughing when they suddenly became all too aware of each other.

Vanessa saw the hot flicker of desire in Monty's eyes before his mouth covered hers and he kissed her passionately as if it were long overdue, and maybe it was. She couldn't deny she'd thought about kissing him more than once. She'd thought about his arms around her, feeling his body pressed to hers. Not something a woman of her station should be thinking, and yet she didn't doubt any proper lady would do the same thing when she crossed paths with a man like Monty. Attraction like this was just too strong to resist and led to all sorts of improper thoughts and feelings. . . .

She ran her fingers through his auburn hair, releasing his queue. He slipped his arm under her neck to brace her head when he lowered his chest fully to hers. The closeness was exquisite, stirring all sorts of urgent new feelings in her. And the kiss got even more exciting when he explored with his tongue, sucked on hers when she tried to do the same. A moan escaped her. She luxuriated in the amazing sensations that overwhelmed her as she lay on the grass in the sunshine and this handsome man kissed her so exquisitely. He seemed as strongly attracted to her as she was to him. This was all too thrilling, her first taste of passion, him, touching him, a whirl of sensations inside her making her weak and yet wanting more . . . What the devil was she doing?!

"Stealing the moment. Don't worry, your Scots haven't noticed."

He said that as his lips moved hotly to her neck. Had she spoken aloud? She didn't really care, groaning again as delicious shivers spread out from where his lips touched her skin. She didn't want to stop what she was doing! But someone would see them if they tarried any longer, and embarrassment at being so daring was starting to sneak up on her.

She put a hand to his cheek to guide his mouth off her. She didn't want to scold him when she'd instigated that kiss as much as he had, so with a grin she said, "You've been too bold, sir."

"You've been too fetching, wench. D'you think I haven't noticed how well you fill out those britches?"

She chuckled, because she could say the same about him! But she pushed lightly against his chest to indicate she wanted to get up. She heard his sigh as she got to her feet. Not wanting this magical moment to end on a note of contrition or embarrassment for either of them, she glanced down at him still spread out on the grass and said, "I'll race you." And she started running before he got up. "I think you know I'll win."

"Only if I let you win again!"

They were laughing again and laughed even harder when he easily passed her. Good grief, she felt so giddy!

Charley, with his long golden hair queued back and wearing ill-fitting trousers and a homespun shirt he'd borrowed from Arlo, was already eating when Vanessa and Monty joined him. He merely remarked, "I hadn't thought of running for exercise, never have, actually. Doesn't it make you sweat?"

"Would a commoner object to a little sweat?" Monty countered.

"Right you are."

Although Vanessa was a little embarrassed that she'd let Monty kiss her—and that she'd kissed him back so fervently—Monty didn't gloat over what had happened. His behavior toward her didn't change as they continued on their journey that week, although she caught him looking at her rather intently whenever they stopped for lunch or were eating together at an inn.

One day, Monty even rode beside her on one of the extra horses, possibly because she still wouldn't ride in the coach with them. He didn't seem to notice the disparity in their heights, with Snow a good three hands taller than his mount. She thought he might want to talk and hoped it wouldn't be about that kiss, because her guards had only dropped back a little and still might be within hearing distance.

But Monty only said casually, "Another beautiful day. I am frankly amazed it hasn't rained yet."

"It probably will now that you've mentioned it!"

"Bite your tongue. This is going to be a delightful journey—in all ways."

Monty's grin turned into a smile. His green eyes seemed to sparkle in the sunshine, too. She blushed only a little, wondering if he was referring to her company. He looked especially handsome today, less formal than usual without his cravat, and his lawn shirt was open at the neck. But then it was a warm spring day, which was why she'd left off her cloak and hood, though they were within easy reach if they encountered any other travelers.

This was also the first time she was seeing him mounted, and since he didn't seem at all nervous about it, she couldn't help asking, "Did you learn to ride so well while you were in the army?"

"My unit wasn't cavalry. As an officer, I had a horse, but none of my men did. No, I grew up riding in Suffolk."

"I wish I had."

He snorted before he scoffed, "You control that brute very well, so don't tell me you haven't been riding since you were an infant."

"Don't exaggerate, and no, my mother wouldn't allow me to ride," she said a bit bitterly.

"Had no stable?"

She didn't want to talk about herself. But maybe he wouldn't mind talking about himself. "So you grew up in Suffolk?"

"I did, near the coast. My siblings and I once tried to swim in the Channel, but it was too bloody cold and we never attempted it again. My sisters talked Father into having a pond dug for us near the manor. Even though it took several years to finish it and for it to fill with rainwater, it was worth the wait. We spent many a summer cavorting there."

"Even your sisters?" she asked, surprised.

"Of course. You don't know how to swim?"

She didn't. That was another thing her mother wouldn't allow her and her sisters to do. She shook her head.

"I could teach you."

"I'm a bit old to learn."

"Nonsense. The next body of water we pass—"

"No," she cut in. "But thank you."

"I might just toss you in when you least expect it," he warned.

"I'm not going near water, and besides, my guards wouldn't allow it."

"I could throw you in when they aren't looking."

"Snow wouldn't allow it."

"Well, that's different, I concede to the brute. But if you change your mind, just let me know."

When? After they'd already gone their own ways? But he suddenly steered his horse a little closer to hers and she felt something on her head. When she glanced at him she saw that he'd stood up in his stirrups to reach her. Had he just caressed her hair with the Scots right behind them?

"What are you doing?" she asked, a little alarmed.

"It was a butterfly about to land on your head, attracted by that lovely bright copper color no doubt. I brushed it away for you."

She glanced up and around her before saying, "I don't see any butterfly."

He laughed and said, "That's a shame. It was beautiful."

Another double entendre? Vanessa's mood turned a little gloomy when she realized how much she was going to miss this man once their paths diverged. She'd also be parting with her two guards soon, not that she'd gotten to know them well enough to miss them.

But when she followed the two brothers into the stable next to the inn where they were staying that night, she did say to Donnan, "So you'll return to Scotland after we reach Dawton Manor?"

"Nay, we're with ye, lass, till ye marry."

"But I thought—"

"Yer faither was specific. I dinna think he trusts his estranged wife tae keep ye safe."

She was incredulous. Her father had encouraged her to return to Kathleen, so she'd assumed—wrongly, apparently—that he considered Kathleen's care all the protection she needed here in England. But the more she thought about it, the more it made sense to her that he didn't trust her mother even for that. She recalled what her father had said when she'd asked him a few years ago if he had forgiven her mother: "For my exile, which she is indirectly responsible for, I might forgive her one day. But I'll never forgive her for betraying me and our marriage vows. That sort of pain can dim but will never be forgotten."

Now her mother was on her mind to the exclusion of all else. There would be no hugs or kisses for her. For her sisters, Layla and Emily, yes, she was eager to see them. But she was afraid that the moment she saw Kathleen, she would revile her quite loudly, which would lead to a terrible fight. She didn't want that to happen. It would make her stay at Dawton Manor intolerable.

Somehow, she was going to have to restrain herself from throwing down the gauntlet. She would have to pretend she didn't hate her mother, pretend that Kathleen hadn't single-handedly split their family apart. What, after all, could her mother say for herself if Vanessa did end up making the accusation?

With thoughts like that, she didn't get much sleep that night and woke to rain blowing in the window she'd left open. At breakfast she gave Monty a smug smile and said, "I told you so," blaming him for the downpour because she'd warned him that his gloating about the fine weather would bring rain.

She wouldn't object to riding in the coach with him and Charley until it stopped, although he must have thought she would because as they left the inn, he reminded her, "I did warn you we would see rain, and I'm bloody well amazed it didn't happen sooner, so no complaints. You'll travel dry or you better have a very good reason why you won't."

"Did I say, 'No, thank you'?"

"You were about to."

She laughed. "No, I wasn't."

In the coach, Monty opened a deck of cards and told her, "I've been teaching Charley how to play whist, not that it's a game he really needs to learn when we won't be attending any parties where it might be played, but he expressed an interest in it. D'you play?"

"I know how, yes," she replied. "My father taught me over a long winter, though we preferred chess, a game for two."

"Yes, Charley is having a hard time grasping that whist is played with a partner to whom he can't talk or hint about his hand."

Vanessa nodded. "That would be cheating, Charley."

The boy gave Monty a pointed look. "You could have said that instead of making me think some skill must be involved. I don't cheat. If I cheated inadvertently, someone would need to be punished."

Vanessa choked back a laugh, guessing, "Your teacher?"

"At least he didn't say my head would roll," Monty said bearishly.

She enjoyed watching them and listening to their bickering, which was much milder than it had been earlier in the week. She imagined Monty was growing fond of his charge. She'd grown fond of both of them. That she'd never see either of them again once they parted was a dismal thought.

The rain continued, so they ate lunch in the coach. Vanessa fell asleep afterward, having not gotten enough sleep last night. But she awoke when she heard Donnan's loud voice outside. He was shouting something to Arlo, who seemed to be having difficulty hearing him over the pounding rain.

She straightened and realized she'd been resting her head on Monty's shoulder, but she felt his hand gently guiding her head back to where it had been as he said, "I don't mind. Go back to sleep, Nessi. You're not the only one fatigued by all this rain."

Before she closed her eyes she saw Charley bundled in his fur cloak, asleep on the seat across from them. She must have slept again because a gust of damp air woke her this time and Monty was sternly saying to Arlo, who'd just opened the coach door for them, "Get the butler to open the front door so we can make a mad dash for it."

She looked out the window next to the open coach door. It was still pouring rain, but she could see two rosebushes on either side of the wide double doors just like the ones she and her sisters had planted at their house, the mullioned windows above the entrance, the tan stone walls that rose for three stories, the two-story additions that jutted out on either side. It looked so much like her house. Could two houses really be identical?

Vanessa backed herself into the corner opposite the open door. She wasn't getting out of that coach.

Chapter Fourteen

"WHY ARE YOU BACKING away?"

Vanessa stared at the hand Monty had extended to help her to the ground. Charley had already run for the house. She met Monty's eyes now but was pretty much frozen with indecision and panic, so she didn't move. She couldn't go in there with him! He'd find out who she really was, which could ruin her and her family after he'd witnessed her scandalous behavior on this trip.

But when she didn't answer him, Monty guessed, "If you're that eager to part ways and continue your journey rather than wait for the rain to stop, I understand. You can use the coach and return it after you reach your destination. But be assured, you're welcome to remain with us for a while. My hosts won't mind another guest."

But Donnan chose that moment to stick his head inside the coach to say, "That haity butler says yer trunks arrived, lass, and I'm no' pleased that yer traveling companions appear tae have reached their destination, too." He ended that with a distrustful glower at Monty.

"She needs a moment to compose herself, man. Big re-union and all that," Monty told the Scot. But the moment Donnan moved away, he glanced back at Vanessa. "Well, this is a delightful surprise. So you're either an earl's daughter or your parents are servants. I'm leaning toward the former."

She didn't confirm it. Her panic was rising that a scandal would erupt if people found out she'd been traveling with his group—dressed as a boy. She evaded. "I haven't been here for six years. They won't recognize me."

His eyes moved over her attire. "Or they won't recog-nize you like *that*. D'you really have cold feet to find out whether they will or won't?"

What she needed was time to figure out how to handle her homecoming. "Not a'tall," she lied, even as she pulled her hood back up over her head. "But I'm not ready to re-veal myself to them."

Monty shook his head. "And here I thought we were done with that. Suit yourself—*boy*. I can keep your secret."

Her heart leapt. "Really?"

"Depends for how long. I just don't think you'll be able to pull it off for very long, not with family. If it's been only six years, they'll recognize your face." And then he chuck-led. "It's rude to wear a hood in a grand house like yours, you know."

Annoyed that he could tease her at a time like this, she said rather sharply, "No one will notice me hiding behind your back when they have you to look at. There are a lot of women in that house. I'll probably be overlooked and the housekeeper won't even offer me a bloody room!"

He burst out laughing. "Who are you mad at, me, or yourself for turning coward?"

Ignoring his hand, she got out of the coach on her own and quickly followed him into the house. Only the butler was standing in the foyer. She didn't recognize him, but the previous one had been old and must have retired. Still she stayed behind Monty's back. Charley, who had changed into his brown wool cloak, was looking at a painting on the wall. The Scots were helping Arlo bring in some of the trunks, which formed a puddle just inside the door, so Monty moved into the adjoining hall to get out of the way. She and Charley followed him.

She heard footsteps on the grand stairs and looked in that direction. Her heart started pounding. She quickly tugged her hood down to hide more of her face and stepped behind Monty, using him as a shield. Her mother was coming down the stairs, dressed regally for the day. The cloak-like robe, made of a light white-and-blue material, mimicked a pelisse coat, opening to reveal the stylish dark blue empire dress underneath it. But then Kathleen was never taken unaware by visitors, was always at her best and always gracious no matter who she was greeting.

Vanessa carefully peeked out from behind Monty's back to steal another glimpse of Kathleen. God, her mother appeared not to have changed at all! She was still beautiful with fashionable blond hair artfully arranged and adorned with jeweled pins, and pale blue eyes, which were identical to those of all three of her children. Tears welled up in Vanessa's eyes. She used to love that woman—before Kathleen single-handedly tore their family apart.

When Monty lifted one arm, she stole another quick peek at her mother, who was holding out a hand in the usual manner, to be kissed or very lightly touched by whoever she was greeting.

"I presume Lord Mont—?"

Vanessa's shield cut in. "Monty will do, and no titles please. My ward is Charley," he said, and lightly slapped the boy on the back. "And the shy one behind me is Nestor."

"I am Kathleen Blackburn, Countess of Dawton. You are most welcome in my home, gentlemen. I'm surprised Prince George remembered me, it was so long ago that we met in Brighton, where he took his holidays. But of course I was delighted by his request."

"You understand our visit is to be clandestine?" Monty asked.

"Certainly. I will not be introducing you to my neighbors, and I will try to keep visitors to a minimum. My only worry is that you may get bored. We live quietly here."

"Exactly what we need," he assured his hostess with a slight bow.

The bow panicked Vanessa and made her turn about so Kathleen could only see the back of her hood. But that allowed her to see the housekeeper approaching, and she definitely recognized Mary Edwards. Anytime she and her sisters got a little rambunctious when their mother wasn't around, Mrs. Edwards always caught them at it. And while she didn't reveal their antics to their mother, she certainly did her share of scolding.

Turning to face Monty's back again, she heard Kathleen say, "We weren't sure when you would arrive. My daughters went to visit friends in Dawton town early this morning before this storm blew in. They may be waiting for it to end before they return, but they will be here for dinner, rain or no, so you will meet them then. How many extra settings for the table?"

"Three—" Monty started.

Vanessa jabbed his back and whispered, "Two."

So he amended, "Actually, only two. It's been a dreadful trip. One of my companions will need time to recover from it."

"Certainly," Kathleen replied. "But perhaps you would like some tea before you rest?"

"I don't know about the boys, but I've been craving a proper bath. As I said, it's been a dreadful, rushed trip."

"Of course! Mrs. Edwards will show you to your rooms.

I've opened the west wing for you, which was otherwise not in use and will give you more privacy."

"Thank you, dear lady."

Mrs. Edwards waved an arm toward the stairs while saying, "There's a large room the boys can share—"

"That won't do," Monty quickly cut in. "They don't get along, fistfights that could damage furniture and break windows. Well, boys will be boys, you know."

Kathleen chuckled. "We've never had young boys living in this house, so we wouldn't know about their behavior. Just show them to three rooms," she added to the housekeeper.

"There are three servants, too," Monty mentioned. "One is our manservant who will need to be close to us. The two big brutes, on the other hand, can stay anywhere."

Monty was no doubt making sure there would be no complaints from Charley about Arlo's not having a room close to his. She might have laughed at the reference to the MacCabe brothers, though, if she weren't so nervous.

"Of course, everyone will be accommodated."

Upstairs, when the housekeeper turned left toward the long corridor of the west wing, Vanessa was struck with a bit of nostalgia. She knew this wing well. It was the one place in the house she and her sisters could hide from their mother and her etiquette regimen, where they could play, get into arguments, delight in unrestrained laughter, and simply be children, at least until Kathleen summoned them to attend some type of lesson. The servants knew they liked to play there and kept one bed-room at the end of the long hall cleaned for them.

She and her sisters had hidden themselves away in this wing right up until her last year at home, though there was less playing by then and more talking about boys and debuts and their eagerness to join the adult world they were still too young for. Had her hopes and dreams really mirrored her sisters' so closely, all leading to love with the perfect man and marriage? She supposed they had, but back then there had been no other options for any of them—or so they'd thought.

Monty was shown to the first room on the right, which faced the extensive back lawns and would afford him a view of the setting sun. Charley got the room across the hall, and Vanessa was given the next room on the right. She thought about requesting the room at the end of the hall, but Mrs. Edwards knew it had been a playroom for her and the twins and might find the request odd and sus-pect she wasn't a stranger to the house. She didn't pursue it—being here again was bringing her close to tears—but she couldn't help wondering if the twins still used it as a sanctuary from their mother.

It took a long time for the servants to deliver hot water for her bath, but she'd anticipated the delay, since she'd been the last guest shown to a room. Nonetheless, she was impatient for the stream of servants to end so she could have some uninterrupted time to think. Her valise was delivered by a footman, but the clean clothes inside it would probably still be damp because they'd been washed last night at the inn and delivered back to her at dawn.

After her bath, which didn't relax her but did leave her feeling cleaner than she'd been since beginning her journey, she crinkled her nose at the idea of donning damp clothes. She knew very well she could have had a wonderfully dry dress to wear if she had just greeted her mother normally. But there would be nothing normal about that reunion. And she certainly didn't want it to happen in front of Monty and Charley. It was bound to be ugly—and loud with all the repressed anger that had built up over the years spilling out. William hadn't forgiven Kathleen, and she wasn't about to, either.

She wrapped herself in a sheet and hung the damp clothes on the furniture, hoping at least a pair of trousers and a shirt would dry quickly. She considered taking a nap, considered a ride with Snow, damp clothes or no, if the rain had let up. She went to a window to check if it was still raining and found it was. But she was arrested by the sight of the lawns she and her sisters had played on, could almost envision their games of croquet and tag, diving into large piles of autumn leaves before the gardeners could haul the piles away, building snowmen in the winter. The tears arrived, overflowed her eyes, and wouldn't stop. She'd missed her sisters more than she'd admitted to herself. The late-childhood years they might have shared were lost forever. Six years was a very long time, all three of them were adults now. Would Emily and Layla even want her back after so long?

"I know how difficult homecomings can be. When I got carried home from the war wounded, my mother and siblings wouldn't leave my bedside. Even if you love them dearly, family can be a bloody nuisance sometimes. They wouldn't let me sleep for all their fussing!"

She didn't smile at Monty's anecdote. She was a bit outraged that he had just entered her room without knocking and had come to stand right next to her. But she was also cognizant that she was naked under the sheet and how beyond the pale this was.

She turned slightly away from him, giving him mostly her back, and tightened the sheet at her breasts before she said emphatically, "You shouldn't be in here."

"Nor would I be if I hadn't heard your crying from downstairs."

He was trying to tease away her tears. It wasn't going to work. But then he added, "Has the dam been plugged yet? I could go search for a beaver to help, but alas, they are extinct here, so I won't lie, you'll have to do the plugging yourself."

That did provoke a laugh from her, but she immediately cut it off. She ought to be reprimanding him, but she just didn't want to. She was still a little incredulous that he was even in her home, that they'd been heading to the same destination all along while they'd been so determined to keep secrets from each other. But considering all that had happened on that trip, she wondered if he was simply treating her as the boy he'd first thought her to be and really didn't think there was anything untoward about being in her room. But he couldn't do that anymore.

Then she felt his hands on her shoulders, massaging them, drawing forth the most exquisite sensations. "I'm sure I can take your mind off the dilemma you face, Nessi," he whispered by her ear.

Wrong! He wasn't treating her as a boy. She shrugged away from his hands. "Behave like a gentleman for once and go."

He tsked. "I'm always a gentleman, I just have more fun than others. But until you're dressed as a lady, I'm not inclined to be the gentleman for you—nor have you wanted me to be."

Chapter Fifteen

VANESSA GASPED AT HIS blatant reminder of the kiss they'd shared in that meadow. She swung around to glare at Monty, but he was already holding up his hands in a conciliatory manner and quickly said, "I was going to add, go borrow some of your sisters' clothes. I'll even stand watch for you while you do. My sisters always stole each other's clothes, though I think they only did it to have an excuse to fight with each other—they did so love to do that. And then dressed as you ought to be, you can present yourself to your mother on an even footing, so to speak. It's much better to face your fears right away, Nessi."

"I'm not afraid of my mother, I'm afraid of what I'm going to do when I see her," she said, turning her back on him again. "But in either case, it's not going to be pleasant once she knows I'm back, so I would like to reunite with my sisters first."

"Well, then! That's a different thing altogether. So I'll get you some clean men's clothes if you insist on continuing your disguise, not my clothes, but Charley's, which will fit you better—and he won't mind a'tall now that he's wearing hand-me-downs."

"No, thank you. My clothes will be dry before long."

"And yet the dinner hour approaches, such a perfect time for you to greet your mother—without the hood, of course—with me by your side," he rejoined.

She swung around incredulously. "Are you mad? It will be so much worse if Mother finds out you knew I'm a girl while I traveled with you. She can't learn that. You said you would keep my secret."

"So I did, and so I will."

"Thank you."

"But the cat appears to be quite out of the bag, as it were, at least for me. So, it's Lady . . . Nestor?"

She almost laughed over the way he'd paused before teasing her, but grumbled, "Not by choice."

He chuckled. "No, of course not, newborns don't get choices. Then may I know your real name? It's going to come out anyway once you are officially reunited."

"Vanessa Blackburn."

"And you chose to live with your father in Scotland instead of here in this beautiful manor? Why did you do that? Deuced cold up there in the north, I've heard."

"That's none of your business," she retorted.

"Family squabbles, obviously, that separated your parents? I'm good at guessing, don't you know."

"You're good at being annoying," she countered. "Go eat. Charley will have no complaints about the food tonight. Dawton Manor has an excellent cook. Just make sure a servant brings a plate up to me. Once you enter a room, little things tend to get overlooked."

He grinned. "That's twice now you've alluded to me as a dazzler. D'you really think so?"

"I think you're full of yourself," she replied, and pointed a finger at the door.

Instead, he touched her hair briefly, which was still a little damp from her bath, and then chucked her chin. "I wish I could say the same of you, but you aren't the least bit. You cleaned up amazingly, Nessi. Are you aware of how beautiful you are?"

She felt the blush rising, so she stabbed her finger even more forcefully at the door. He chuckled but went toward it now, though he did pause and turn to say, "Last chance, sweetheart. Are you sure you won't join us downstairs?"

"I'm not ready for that. I thought I was, but—not yet. I warned you it wouldn't be pleasant, but not on Mother's end, on mine. I hate her. I don't intend to hide it. Which is why I want to reunite with my sisters first, before she turns them against me."

He'd opened the door, but now he closed it again. "You can't leave me with remarks like that. Tell me more."

"No, and it truly is no concern of yours. I was just

letting you know where most of the rage will come from, if you witness any of it. But she'll make sure you don't witness it. She's like that. Appearances matter most to her."

"All the more reason why tonight would be the perfect time for you to tell her you're home," he pointed out.

Possibly . . . no. She was still afraid she'd get so overwrought from the confrontation with Kathleen that she would storm out in a rage and not return, losing her chance to have the reunion she wanted. She had to see her sisters first, then she wouldn't hesitate to find her mother and deal with the *unwanted* reunion.

She pointed at the door once more in answer, and this time he left. But she also locked it behind him and heard him laughing in the hall because of it.

She wasn't tempted to deviate from her current plan, but she was very tempted to sneak downstairs and eavesdrop on that dinner. The problem was there would be too many servants about at that time of the evening, and one might inform Kathleen she was out there. Then Kathleen would come out and insist she join them at the table, and she really couldn't do that wearing a hood. But temptation won out the moment she remembered that the formal dining room abutted the conservatory and in the spring and summer months, the doors that led to all that greenery and flowers were usually left open.

It was tricky getting there without being noticed. She hid in the study until she heard the family and their guests moving from the drawing room, where they had gathered, to the dining room across the way. For a few minutes the wide hall was empty and she was able to run across it and slip into the conservatory.

The room was dark, only the light from the dining room left a narrow lit path through the open door. It was a perfect room to eavesdrop from. There was even a potted tree near the door that she could stand behind.

She saw Charley first, her eyes caught by all the glitter. He certainly wasn't wearing the hand-me-downs anymore, was back in his full regalia. A concession on Monty's part, now that they were safely ensconced in their hiding place? Monty was even in the middle of that explanation she'd overheard him making up about Charley's neglectful parents to account for his extravagant clothes. She hoped her sisters didn't think all those gems were real! Monty was more formally dressed tonight, too, wearing a very fancy cravat. His hair was queued back, and he looked so damn handsome, she had to force herself to move around the tree until she could get a full view of her sisters.

And then she just stood there transfixed, staring at her beloved sisters, happy tears already in her eyes. They'd grown so much! She'd left behind two girls with chubby cheeks and returned to two exquisitely beautiful young women she almost didn't recognize. But they were still identical. While growing up they'd always differentiated themselves with colors, white for Layla, pink for Emily, wearing ribbons around their necks or in their hair and white or pink nightgowns at night. Apparently, they still wore the ribbons in their hair.

"So this will be your first Season in London?" Monty was saying. "I almost pity the young lords. Once they clap eyes on you two, not just identical, but stunning, they will be bowled over."

That was quite a compliment. Emily giggled. "It feels like we've waited forever."

"It's going to be so exciting," Layla added.

"How many sisters do you have?" Emily queried.

Kathleen, sitting at the head of the table with her back to the conservatory, scolded mildly, "Now, now, you promised no questions."

Both girls blushed as if they'd made the worst sort of blunder, but Vanessa was sure it was simply because they'd just displeased their mother and they abhorred doing that. And Monty didn't make it any easier for them by not answering the innocent question. She would have kicked him under the table if she were sitting there.

And then Charley remarked, "Where is the third daughter in that portrait?"

Vanessa couldn't see the wall he was staring at, but she knew which portrait he was referring to. It had been painted the year before she left. It depicted her seated on a chair with a twin on either side of her, sitting on an arm of the chair. They had laughed so much that week while they'd had to sit for it because none of them could stay still for very long and the artist got so annoyed with them.

But then Charley added, "She looks familiar somehow, but how can that be?"

"Because aside from the hair, she closely resembled her sisters when she was young," Kathleen replied.

"We expect she will be home from the West Indies soon, because her trunks have already arrived," Layla said excitedly.

Vanessa panicked at the mention of the West Indies. Monty would realize she'd been keeping secrets from her own family! She held her breath, praying he wouldn't mention something about Scotland. But he looked only a little confused, might even be thinking that she'd lied to him about living in Scotland these last years.

And Kathleen was explaining, "She traveled with her father and has been gone for several years."

"Six years is more than several, Mother," Emily said almost angrily.

"Emily!"

For once, Emily didn't back down from one of Kathleen's rebukes. "She never even said goodbye to us! And not one letter from her in all that time!"

"She added notes to Papa's letters," Layla reminded her.

"Did she really? When those notes were penned in his handwriting?"

In that particular quiet tone that all her daughters recognized as the one that masked her fury, Kathleen said, "Perhaps you are not ready for London, after all. Apologize, darling."

"That isn't necessary," Monty said, trying to intervene.

Vanessa was crying by then and slipped out of the room to run back upstairs. She had wanted to write! But every time she started to she ended up crying because she missed her sisters so much. And what could she really say about life on a Caribbean island, where her sisters thought she'd been living, when she'd never been to one?

But while she ate her own solitary dinner, which a servant had left outside her door, she was determined to come up with a good explanation for Emily—if she could without telling her the truth. She was going to sneak into her sisters' room that very night. She just had to wait until everyone was asleep.

Chapter Sixteen

V ANESSA LEANED AGAINST THE wall by the parlor doors, her head bent very low to make sure her hood was hiding her face. She imagined the servants who passed her were giving her odd looks, but she didn't budge, because in that spot she could hear her sisters' voices in the parlor. But, annoyingly, they were speaking softly, so she couldn't make out most of what they were saying. She was also straining to hear if Kathleen was in there with them.

She was so angry at herself for falling asleep last night before the house had gone quiet. She planned to take a long nap today so that wouldn't happen again, and a long ride first to tire herself out. She remained in the hall in case the girls were alone in the parlor. If they were, she could grab them as they walked out, run them up to their old playroom, and have her reunion right now.

Listening to her sisters, she couldn't help thinking they giggled too much, then she cringed, remembering she used to giggle as well. When had that stopped? Of course she knew—the very day she'd run away with her father and embraced a different style of life that had been exciting and wonderfully unrestrictive. What if her sisters would be appalled by the life she had been living away from here? It looked as if Kathleen had turned them into perfect young debutantes. She might not have anything in common with them anymore!

"Is there something wrong with your face, Nestor, that requires you to wear a hood in the house?"

Bloody hell, she'd missed her chance to catch her sisters alone! Kathleen wasn't in the parlor, she was standing right beside her.

"Yes, ma'am," she said in a very low tone. "Plagued by unsightly blemishes, ma'am."

"The bane of some children, I suppose. Our cook, Mrs. Griggs, might know of a remedy. Why don't you run along and ask her?"

Vanessa bolted down the hall to the back of the house. But she couldn't talk to the cook. She knew Mrs. Griggs well from all the times she and the twins had run into the kitchen for a sweet treat. They'd all three been daring back then, ignoring their mother's litany that "Ladies do not go in the kitchen, do not make friends with the servants, do not, do not, do not . . ." As children, that list of "do nots" had seemed endless.

She did pass through the kitchen, but quickly, to go straight outside to the stable. She'd take that ride now.

One of the stable boys helped her saddle Snow quickly, but Donnan arrived before she left.

"Did you get settled for the duration?" she asked. "Any complaints?"

He didn't answer and was frowning at her. "Why are ye still wearing those clothes?"

"Because my mother doesn't know I'm home yet, and I didn't mean that sort of complaint."

"And why doesna she know?"

"Because I haven't told her," she replied. "I want to talk to my sisters first, but I'm having a deuced hard time getting them alone."

"So yer not trying tae escape?" he said, staring at her horse.

She laughed. "No, just going out for my last ride before I'll need an escort."

"Ye still need an escort. I'll join ye."

"No, you won't, not this time. This is my very last day of freedom. Tomorrow I'll be back in a dress and you can escort me then, but not today. Besides, my mother's property is huge. If I see anyone a'tall, I'll race back home. Now where are you off to?"

"Tae visit the town nearby tae see if they've any good taverns worth a second look."

She grinned. "At least two as I recall, maybe more by now. Dawton town is rather big. But by all means, see for yourself, and you can save me the trip if you'll post this for me?" She handed him a letter she'd written to her father to let him know she'd arrived safely.

"Ye dinna put the address on it," he said as he glanced at the envelope.

"Because it needs to go to your father's house and I haven't dug into my trunks yet to find the address. Your father knows to send it on to mine."

"Ye Blackburns act like bluidy spies," he mumbled.

She grinned. "Not really, just protecting my father's privacy. Father did warn you that no one can know where we've been."

"Aye."

She gave him a wave as she mounted and went around the house and started riding southeast toward the lake a few miles away. But she soon noticed Monty had the same idea. She ought to avoid him. The man was trouble—for her senses. But she was too curious to find out how the rest of the dinner with her family had gone after she'd quit spying last night. So she whistled loudly, as her father had taught her to do, and he reined in to wait for her.

"You're not worried about being spotted out here?" she asked when she was abreast of him.

"The point of coming this far north was to find safety in a remote area, which this corner of Cheshire certainly is. And your mother appears to have extensive lands with nary a forest in sight! You can see someone coming for miles."

"Not that far, but I get the idea."

"I'm not worried a'tall. Dawton Manor is far from the

main roads. But if you're worried about your family's safety, don't be. We lost our pursuers days ago. I assure you I was keeping a close watch on our journey, if you didn't notice. And your servants have been warned not to mention houseguests to anyone outside the house, and Charley and I shall avoid Dawton town. By the by, I did tell your mother that she didn't need to entertain us. We can ride, and I was shown to the extensive library. And there are a number of pretty maids in the house . . ."

She narrowed her eyes at him. "Is that so? My mother will never allow such shenanigans under her roof. Did you fail to notice how utterly proper she is?"

"Ah, but ladies have been known to turn a blind eye if circumstances demand it, and she's not going to want to annoy George when she is so delighted that he remembered her well enough to ask for a favor. But I do find it curious that you knew what I meant."

The grin on his face made her think he might only be teasing, but she didn't really think so. Besides, what he did was really no concern of hers. Still it rankled for some reason. She turned the conversation to a different topic.

"Did you enjoy dinner last night?"

"You didn't come down to eavesdrop?"

A blush rose to her cheeks, making her wish she hadn't let her hood fall back. But she lied, "Of course not."

"Would you admit it if you did?"

She gritted her teeth. "I'll admit I wanted to and thought better of it."

"Well, if you're curious, your sisters were delightful. Beautiful twins! You should have mentioned that. London will love them this Season—and you, too, now that you're home from the West Indies."

She cringed. "I would appreciate your not mentioning that I was in Scotland."

He grinned. "Of course. I rather like being your confidant, after all. It's so—intimate."

She wasn't even sure if he was teasing this time, but she got back to the subject of last night's dinner. "Were my sisters perfect ladies?"

"You mean unlike you? Don't answer! Gads, what a bloody cad I am. It appears I got in the habit, a little too quickly, of not watching my tongue with you. Yes, perfect young debutantes—mostly. Emily lost her composure when she spoke of you, something about a lack of correspondence on your part, and that you didn't even say goodbye to them, but I'm sure you'll patch that up once you speak with her. From your clothes I assume you still haven't?"

She shook her head, so he continued.

"But Charley was certainly fascinated by the pair. I don't think he's ever seen twins before."

"Did he behave to your satisfaction?"

He rolled his eyes. "No, and I'm beginning to think he never will. I don't have the heart to make him continue playing the role of a commoner when he so obviously abhorred it, so I've given him leave to return to his atrocious finery."

"You trust Charley to stay out of trouble while you are out of the house?"

"Arlo knows to keep him in line. But they are currently engaged in swordplay on the back lawn, evidently a sport that is still popular on the continent, and surprisingly they looked as if they knew what they were doing!"

"If England weren't so civilized, you gentlemen would still be wearing swords, too. Pistols are so limited in use, when you spend more time loading them than you do firing them."

"I suppose that's why you carried two?"

"And had two more in my saddlebags!"

He chuckled as they continued on, with her directing Snow toward the lake and him following her lead. It felt almost like summer rather than late April, the day was so hot and cloudless, so she hoped it would be cooler there next to the water. When they reached the lake, they stopped the horses and he dismounted. He came around to help her down, but she slid off Snow on her own and left her cloak and jacket hooked on the saddle before she found a spot to sit for a few minutes. Lone trees set far apart dotted the grassy landscape they'd ridden past, just as they did the back lawn at Dawton Manor. But there were quite a few trees surrounding the lake and an abundance of spring flowers.

"Pretty, this time of year," he commented as he sat next to her.

A little amazed, she said, "I wasn't sure it would be. I've

never been here before in spring or summer. Mother was a strong believer in a lady's staying out of the sun. But on cloudy days in the winter our parents used to bring us here to ice skate, even joined us on the ice. It was an idyllic time in our youth." When everything was as it should have been and her parents still loved each other.

That thought made her sad, which might have been why Monty's hand reached toward her cheek. She leapt to her feet immediately and moved away to pick a few flowers. He stood up but didn't follow her.

"I'll wager you didn't avoid the sun in Scotland?"

"You would win."

"But you've come home for a Season in London, haven't you? Are you prepared for it, after being away from your mother all these years?"

"Probably not."

"I could give you some lessons."

She glanced back and was struck again by how handsome he was. His hair wasn't queued today, was loose about his wide shoulders. She had kept the tie she'd taken out of his hair when they'd kissed in that meadow, a memento of her very first kiss that she was going to keep. He'd slipped out of his jacket after he'd dismounted, and without the cravat, his white shirt opened at the neck, he looked like a country lord, reminding her of the casual way her father dressed when he was at home.

They hadn't parted ways as she'd thought they would,

and his pull was very strong when they were alone like this. And he'd done a good job of distracting her from the sadness he'd caught a glimpse of with that attempted caress.

As for lessons from him, she might enjoy that too much, so she said, "And deny my mother that pleasure? Believe me, she thrives on cracking that whip."

She bent to pick another flower, then heard, "How about a moonlit ride tonight? Sounds rather romantic, doesn't it?"

It did indeed, but she had to decline. "It might be with the right man—which you are not."

"And why not me?" he said indignantly.

She laughed and threw a flower at him. "Don't pretend you're wounded. You admitted you're a rake. If I do end up considering marriage and all of my stipulations are met, I certainly won't be marrying a rake. So I will wait until I find that perfect chap before I agree to a romantic rendezvous."

"Then you wouldn't marry a rake even if you happened to fall in love with one? Not that I'm asking you to consider marriage, mind you, gads no—but what if I were? That's a rather rigid restriction to impose on yourself, don't you think?"

"Ha! What if I end up shooting you when you stray and I get hung for it? No, thank you."

He laughed. "Appreciate the warning, but—what stipulations were you referring to?"

She started to say "None of your business," but stopped when she realized this was a good opportunity to get another man's opinion of her conditions for marriage when all she currently had was her father's biased view. "I intend for my fiancé to sign a contract prior to our marriage, whereby he agrees that as my husband he will not attempt to govern my behavior, will not touch my money, will not sell any businesses I might acquire—"

"You intend to become a shopkeeper?"

He looked so appalled she couldn't help laughing.

"Goodness, no, but if I find any businesses that look promising and it appears they could use financial assistance, I might send my solicitor round to offer an investment from a potential silent partner. They'd never have to meet me or know the investment comes from a woman. However, I might be more active in a horse-breeding farm I hope to start. I wouldn't mind breeding Snow again. He produced some very sturdy foals in the last few years before I left Scotland. My father and I both enjoyed working with the horses there."

"Why not breed racehorses here? Much more lucrative, which is exactly why so many nobles dabble in it."

"But I've no interest in that. And consider how limited the uses are for racehorses. Would you hitch one to your coach, or wagon, or plow? But a strong, sturdy horse from Snow's line would be useful for everything except racing— not that he's not fast, too."

He approached her, but only to give back the daisy

she'd tossed at him. "I'm curious. With both of your parents alive, how is it you have so much money to waste? An inheritance from grandparents?"

"No, Father just wanted to make sure I have options to do whatever I want, and not to have to depend on my mother, who is very, very good at saying no."

"So let me get this straight. Your husband will have to sign off on never touching or promising away your money, but you can still empty his pockets?"

She grinned. "No, I'll agree to the same terms. There won't be an endless stream of creditors banging on his door on my account."

"Sounds rather fair, then."

She looked at him in utter amazement. "You're joking, right?"

"Why would you think so? I wouldn't mind a wife who paid the bills."

She snorted. "I didn't say I would do that."

"Afraid you will need to offer some sort of incentive, sweetheart, if you are serious about such a contract. Without giving up something on your end, you'll never find a man who will sign it."

She frowned. She'd known it would be very difficult to get a man to agree when most men married for money or property or, at the very least, a lucrative dowry. But she wasn't going to give a husband carte blanche on running up endless bills, either.

But then she narrowed her eyes on Monty, reminding

him, "Don't nitpick. I already said I'd be offering myself as a wife who doesn't require any upkeep. And besides, my mother will no doubt supply a dowry. Getting her daughters well married seems to be the only bloody goal she's got."

"Don't you think you're being a little harsh on your mother, who's been nothing but gracious since we arrived?"

"Not harsh enough and *don't* ask."

"I'll find out eventually," he predicted. "Might as well fess up."

"No, and you won't."

She moved back to Snow, annoyed by his negative opinion of her stipulations for marriage and his certainty that he'd find out why she hated her mother. He couldn't really find out about the scandal that loomed over her family, could he? No, not unless she foolishly mentioned it. But his confidence still irked her.

Before she reached Snow, she was suddenly lifted off her feet and Monty was carrying her toward the edge of the lake.

"What are you doing? Put me down!" she demanded.

He grinned at her. "I'm going to toss you in the lake."

"Don't you dare!" She squirmed in an effort to free herself, but he wouldn't let her go.

"It's time you had a swimming lesson. Since I'm apparently never going to get you into my bed—remember, you're not in a dress yet—I need to impart something useful to this delightful relationship. Swimming is a life lesson everyone should learn."

"I refused this lesson the first time you offered it. Besides, you'll ruin my boots and will have to buy me a new pair."

"Can they be female boots?"

"No, I've got lots of those. You'll have ruined my only pair that's manly."

"Sweetheart, there's nothing manly about you. And you realize, of course, you could remove the boots before the lesson. Besides, it would be worth the price of a new pair of men's boots. I'll take any excuse to put my hands on you."

She should have gasped, but instead she laughed and wiggled harder to get out of his arms, finally succeeding. "You're incorrigible—and I'm going home to put on a dress."

"Not on my account!" he yelled after her as she returned to Snow.

She leapt and pulled herself into the saddle, then glanced down at him. "A race?"

He grinned. "Really? A kiss if I win?"

"How about never mentioning kissing again if I win?"

He laughed and pointed to a lone oak in the distance. "There's the finish line."

She knew he'd win if they raced only that far, but she was fairly certain he'd lose a longer-distance race. So she said, "Back to the stable and I'll agree."

"Wager accepted!"

She didn't cheat; she let him mount his horse before

she turned Snow back toward Dawton Manor. And he got far in front of her rather quickly, but the horse he'd borrowed from the stable wasn't a thoroughbred, and it soon tired, letting Snow catch up and take the lead. She left a trail of laughter behind her.

Chapter Seventeen

CARRYING THE LAMP FROM her room, Vanessa walked silently down the corridor in her bare feet. She'd taken a nap, was surprised she'd fallen asleep when she'd been gloating so much over winning that race with Monty today. She'd awakened to the knock on her door when her dinner arrived. And after that had come the excruciating wait for the house to become utterly silent. But finally it had, and now she was on her way to her sisters' room.

She knew which room her sisters would be in, the same one they'd shared as children. She'd had her own room across from theirs in the family section of the main house, on the east side, but the twins didn't want to be parted even for a night, so they shared one. And the door wasn't locked. She didn't think it would be.

She set her lamp on the night table and removed her cloak. She'd taken off her pants and was wearing only a clean linen shirt and knee-length drawers. That was the best she could do not to look mannish for them. She didn't want them to start screaming because they thought a man was in their room, especially since their mother's room wasn't far down the hall.

She stood there staring at her sisters for a long while. She was so pleased that they had turned out so pretty, that they still had things they could giggle about, that Kathleen hadn't turned them into mindless puppets.

She wasn't sure how to wake them without causing any loud exclamations, worried that she might not be able to contain her own. She couldn't exactly cover their mouths at the same time. One would wake before she reached the other and she was afraid they'd think they were being attacked and start screaming. She decided on a very quiet approach and sat on the floor, leaning her back against the side of their bed.

"I'm home and you're going to greet me quietly. Layla, it's Vanessa. Em, wake up and see for yourself, I'm really here. You aren't dreaming, my sweets. Your big sister has returned to you."

She repeated the greeting in a soft voice that wasn't much louder than a whisper and winced with each word, hoping she wouldn't elicit any squeals in response.

A few minutes later she heard, "Really?"

And the second voice finished, "You expect us to be quiet about it?"

"Yes, please," Vanessa said with a wide grin and tipped her head back to look up at the two wide-eyed faces peering over the edge of the bed at her.

And then there were the squeals, somehow quiet ones, as the twins tumbled out of bed and onto the floor with her, one on each side, and smothered her in hugs. She laughed because she couldn't get her arms around either one of them, so she finally leapt to her feet and pulled Emily up with her.

"I want to do some hugging, too," she said, wrapping her arms around Emily, then held out a hand to Layla.

She wasn't sure how long the three of them stood there in a circle with their arms around one another. She kept pulling one closer, then the other, then the other again. She was so relieved she'd returned to the same loving relationship she'd had with her sisters when she'd left. Despite Emily and Layla's sharing a special bond because they were twins, they'd never, ever excluded her. She was their big sister, well, only by a year, but they'd still deferred to her because of it. Would they still?

She finally stood back to really look at them and noted with surprise and the complaint, "How did you grow taller than me when I'm the oldest?"

"Not by much!" Layla exclaimed, then gasped, "Nessa, where's your hair?!"

Vanessa cautioned, "Shhh, we can't be discovered, well, I can't be discovered, not yet." But then she grinned and flicked a lock of hair on her shoulder. "It's still long enough to coif or tie back."

"Barely," Emily said with slight disapproval, but went on to ask, "Is Father with you?"

"No."

"Why not?"

"Because there's still too much work for him to do."

But Layla asked, "What did you mean, you can't be discovered yet? We've been expecting you ever since your trunks were delivered earlier in the week, but did you actually arrive in the middle of the night?"

"No one does that," Emily remarked in a scolding tone.

"And neither did I," Vanessa said. "I've been here a couple of days, I've just been hiding."

"Why?" they both asked in unison.

Vanessa was beginning to realize that Kathleen hadn't told them the truth, of course not the whole sordid truth, but not even that she had snuck away with their father without telling Kathleen. She could tell them that, but not much else without revealing where William was and why. Maybe they ought to know that, too. If it was to be a family secret, the whole family should know it. And it was time Kathleen paid the price for her transgressions, even if it was just scorn from her daughters. But for tonight, she would continue with the lies no matter how distasteful she found it—at least until she spoke with her mother.

But in answering her sisters, she told a little of the truth. "Mother is going to be very displeased with me. I wasn't supposed to go with Father. I snuck onto the roof of his coach without his knowing."

Layla gasped. "What an adventure! Mother didn't tell

us that. Did she know? She said Father chose you, the eldest, to accompany him."

"No, it was all my doing. That's why I didn't say goodbye to you. Father tried to send me back when he found
out I was on the coach, but I refused to leave him all
alone. Before we left England he wrote to Mother, informing her that I was with him. I'll let Mother know I'm here
tomorrow and face her wrath then. Don't tell her first."

"It's not fair you got to go and we didn't," Emily complained.

"She didn't get to go," Layla reminded her. "She snuck
off."

"We could have snuck off, too! We should have all
gone with him."

"I agree that would have been exciting," Layla said.
"But from his letters, it didn't sound like he was having
any enjoyment of the place."

"No, it was all work," Vanessa said, expanding the lie.
"One disaster after another."

"We could have helped," Emily pointed out.

"Then we wouldn't have been separated," Layla said.

"Even if it meant working in the fields," Emily added.

Layla grimaced. "I wouldn't go *that* far."

Vanessa smiled, almost laughing. The twins still finished each other's thoughts. Though it used to exasperate
her, it was yet another thing she'd missed about them.

"And you never wrote, not once!"

That loud complaint was from Emily, who had always

been the more determined twin, occasionally reminding Vanessa of herself. While Layla was the soother, quick to try to calm tempers or end an argument by distracting the opponents with a bit of news or a humorous comment. Vanessa used to try to emulate her but never quite managed it because she was even more determined than Emily.

But from what she'd overheard last night, she'd been expecting Emily's question. "Every time I started a letter, I ended up crying instead of writing it." That much was true, but then she lied, "I didn't want you to know how miserable I was over there. You would have felt bad about my situation, and my letters would have been filled with nothing but complaints."

"Then it's not a nice place?" Layla asked with a frown.

Vanessa didn't know if it was or wasn't! But she guessed, "The sea and the beaches are quite beautiful, but the weather is always too hot to enjoy being outdoors for very long."

"You should have come home sooner!" Layla exclaimed.

"I wanted to. I missed you both so much. But I couldn't bear the thought of leaving Father all alone."

"But now you have," Emily noted. "Why did you come home now?"

"Father grudgingly let me remain with him this past year, but only if I promised I wouldn't miss my debut a second time. However, I planted a kernel before I left, that he ought to just give up and sell the place, so he could come home, too. He did say he'd think about it." And if she could figure out a way to get the Rathbans to relent, then all of that wouldn't be a lie.

"That would be wonderful!"

"Yes, it would," Vanessa agreed.

Emily suddenly exclaimed, "You arrived with our visiting nobles, didn't you?"

"Yes, though I joined them only a few days ago. I don't know them very well."

"But—they're men and handsome at that, maybe a little too handsome," Layla said. "Em has already decided she wouldn't mind marrying that Monty fellow."

"I did not!"

"You did, too."

"He's a rake," Vanessa put in, then groaned to herself.

Why the deuce did she mention that? Both twins looked shocked. But it was Emily who asked, "How do you know that?"

Vanessa shrugged. "Men talk freely among men. I heard it mentioned."

"Well, Lay was teasing, I didn't say anything about marrying him."

"Your eyes did." Layla giggled. "But it doesn't matter. We're not picking husbands until we've seen all the Season has to offer."

"And you've changed the subject, Lay," Emily scolded, then glanced back at Vanessa. "If you traveled with those men, who was your chaperone?"

"Father sent me off with two very big guards who

would raise an ax if any man even looked my way, but of course none did. I traveled disguised as a man."

"No, you didn't." Layla giggled again.

"I really did."

Emily gasped. "But that's scandalous!"

"When no one found out?"

Layla glanced at Emily to ask, "Doesn't that count?"

But Vanessa jumped in, "Of course it does."

Emily disagreed, "It might have, except *those* two noblemen are our guests now and will soon find out you were disguising yourself as a boy when you reveal yourself to Mother and the rest of the household."

"I didn't know they were going to be guests here because they're keeping secrets of their own, which is why they won't embarrass any of us by revealing mine. And remember, Mother is doing them a favor by letting them stay here." But for good measure Vanessa added, "Father allowed me to travel that way."

"But did you browbeat him into allowing it?" Emily guessed. "You always could wrap him around your little finger. Layla and I were still trying to figure out how you did that when you hied off with him—for six years! I can't forgive you for that!"

"Emily!" Layla gasped.

Vanessa didn't like it that Emily was making her feel defensive—when she couldn't share the bloody truth! But she did manage to say quietly, "Did you really want Father to be alone?"

"I wanted us all to go!"

"As the months turned into years, we did start asking Mother to take us to join you and Father," Layla confessed.

"She always said no. Her excuse was either that she gets seasick or that the tropics have endless sunshine, which would harm our complexions," Emily grumbled. "But she eventually got angry when we kept broaching the subject, so we stopped asking."

"And we really don't like it when she's angry," Layla added.

No, they wouldn't. For all of Emily's boldness, even she was prone to backing down to a higher authority like their mother.

So Vanessa said, "Well, I'm here now, and it's not my habit to avoid confrontation. I'm not the least bit afraid of Mother's anger."

No, she'd welcome it, was looking forward to it, so she could express her own. Just enough anger to show Kathleen that she wouldn't be cowed, not so much that she'd have to abandon her sisters—and she really needed to prove to herself that she could handle anything, even her feelings about Kathleen.

Chapter Eighteen

V ANESSA WASN'T SURPRISED THAT the twins came to her room the next morning, even though they'd spent hours together catching up last night. Well, at least she'd caught up with what had happened in their lives over the past six years. When she'd mentioned fishing with their father and Emily had quickly shown her disapproval, just as their mother would, she'd decided not to tell them about any of the other kinds of freedom she had enjoyed in Scotland. Her sisters really had become perfect young ladies, adhering to, even embracing, all of the do's and don'ts their mother had taught them. Vanessa thought that Kathleen must be very proud of her twins but would be equally appalled by her, the daughter who had escaped her regimen.

But she didn't mind at all when the twins followed the maid in with her breakfast. She was already dressed and never opened the door unless she was wearing her cloak and with the hood firmly in place.

"So that's how you did it," Emily said as soon as the maid left.

And Layla finished with a laugh, "Well, of course you'd have to when there's nothing mannish about your face, Nessa."

But the moment she shrugged out of her cloak they both laughed when they saw how she was dressed for the day. "Very dashing, Nessa." Layla giggled.

But Emily asked, "You're going to show yourself to Mother like *that*? Let me get you a dress."

"That isn't necessary. I'll find my clothes later. I wasn't sure if my trunks had been put in the attic or in my old room."

"They're in the attic."

"But empty. We unpacked them for you."

"Thank you. But I'm still going to greet Mother like this. It's not just a disguise, it's actually how I've enjoyed living these last six years. I'd rather she know that because it speaks volumes about how I've changed. And besides, you would be amazed how a pair of pants can bolster one's courage. I don't intend to be intimidated by our formidable mother."

"But she's missed you, Nessa," Layla said.

"We hear her crying a lot," Emily added.

Vanessa was surprised, but immediately discounted Kathleen's crying over her. If she'd shed any tears, they were more likely over her dead lover, or even more likely over having been caught with Rathban, which had ended the affair.

But Layla insisted, "She will be ever so pleased that you're home where you belong, just as we are. You'll see. You've no need for courage."

Easy for them to say. Her own anger and expressing too much of it when she faced her mother was making her queasy with dread over the meeting. Vanessa really, really didn't want to start out that way with Kathleen when she would be her ticket to the *ton* and all its social events. That's where she would have the best chance of finding Albert Rathban and approaching him for a deal or simply to plead with him to let her father come home. She hadn't come up with a plan yet but she still had a month or so to figure it out.

Or maybe she wouldn't have to. She needed to find out why Kathleen had diligently written to William over the years even though they were estranged. He'd never read any of those letters, of course, had tossed them straight into the fire and stood there to watch them burn. But why had her mother continued to write? Did she hope for a reconciliation? Or had Kathleen somehow gotten the threat over their heads removed? Or maybe the Rathbans had accommodated her family by simply dying off? It was possible that all three Rathban brothers who had been at the duel were now resting in peace, leaving no one in that family who was willing or able to carry out the threat. And she and William could have come home sooner! That

TEMPTATION'S DARLING   181

might be wishful thinking, but she wouldn't know until she asked her mother.

A half hour later the twins followed her downstairs and went off to the dining room for their own breakfast, while she slipped into her father's old study, which the twins had mentioned was now Kathleen's. She didn't expect to find Kathleen in it yet. It had been their mother's habit to eat all of her meals with the girls, then deal with any correspondence between breakfast and luncheon, and even when William had been there, she'd used his study for that. So Vanessa didn't think she'd have to wait too long. . . . She didn't have to wait at all.

She paused inside the study door. Kathleen was sitting at her desk, head slightly bent as she read the letter in her hand. She looked so serene, so similar in appearance to the mother she'd left six years ago. This unobstructed, unhurried view of Kathleen was stirring long-forgotten feelings in her, the love she'd felt before the hate had pushed it away. Kathleen might have been rigid with her rules, but there had never been any doubt that she loved her family—even William. Why had she strayed?

Kathleen finally glanced up. "Nestor? Do you need something?"

"No," Vanessa said, and turned to close the door.

She removed her cloak before she turned back to the desk. It wasn't instant recognition. The trousers, vest, linen shirt, and cravat all delayed it. Then there was shock before

Kathleen's expression turned bland and she remarked, "I see your face has cleared up."

"Don't pretend you don't know me, Mother."

"Of course I know you, but your sudden appearance like *that* has resulted in too many questions clamoring in my mind, and if I address them, I won't get to say first that I've missed you, Vanessa."

Vanessa was caught off guard and even more startled when Kathleen came around the desk and hugged her. Last night she'd happily hugged her sisters. There was nothing happy about this embrace from her mother. She even felt like crying!

"Give me a moment to digest that you've really returned to us," Kathleen added, not letting go of her.

Vanessa didn't mind, she closed her eyes to absorb the warmth of the moment, but she didn't hug her mother back. This wasn't the reception she'd expected. Her mother had disarmed her anger, the only defense she had against these feelings.

She stepped away to regain control of her emotions. Addressing the thought she'd had earlier that morning would help. "Why did you write to Father?"

"He wrote to me first to let me know you were with him. Even though he was furious, he didn't want me to worry. He just didn't say where you both were. Where did he take you?"

"Somewhere very remote."

"He cautioned you not to say?"

"No, he didn't have to. He knows I wouldn't betray him to you."

"Vanessa!"

"Don't look offended, Mother. It's far too late for that. Is it safe for him to come home?"

"It's— No, not yet."

So much for hoping the threat had ended. But her hostility was rising and she wasn't sure how to curb it. A little would be helpful in defending herself, but too much would ruin her plans.

Kathleen was looking her up and down. "Why are you dressed like that?"

Finally something Vanessa could shield herself with, her own preferences, and proof that Kathleen hadn't gotten to turn her into the perfect debutante. Vanessa spread her arms wide. "It's how I dress."

"Don't be absurd."

"Truly, it's how I prefer to dress."

Kathleen frowned. "Did anyone we know see you like this? Have you been using your name across England dressed like *that*?"

"You don't like the way I tie my cravat?"

"You think this is a joking matter?"

"Not a'tall, but is this really all you have to say to me, Mother? No, and no, to answer your questions, and before you think to ask about my traveling companions, Lord Montague Hook didn't know, but now he does, and soon his ward, Charley, will know. However, he assured me he can keep secrets because he has a few of his own, so you needn't worry on their account."

"But you traveled with them without a chaperone— dressed like that! Your behavior—"

Vanessa cut in. "I had chaperones, two very big, very mean-looking guards Father sent with me who threatened anyone who even looked at me too long. I was protected. I was anonymous. I even used a male name. But I guess we have nothing else to say if you only want to discuss apparel, so I won't take up any more of your time."

"Sit down!"

Vanessa had only turned toward the door. She had no intention of leaving, because her own questions hadn't been answered yet. But she didn't move to a chair. She struck a male pose instead, leaning back against the door, crossing her arms, even lifting one knee and pressing the sole of her boot against the door. There would be no concessions she hadn't already decided to make. No buckling to this parent's rules. But the defiant pose didn't appear to increase Kathleen's anger.

"How is he?"

Caught off guard again, Vanessa was surprised that question didn't spark more flames. But her mother's concerned expression appeared sincere.

Without rancor she said, "He's fine. Healthy, robust, and probably missing me too much."

"Does he—?"

"Still hate you?" Vanessa cut in sharply, but regretted

it immediately when Kathleen began to pace and wring her hands.

"He wouldn't believe the truth, and I suppose he's turned you so much against me that you won't listen to it, either?" Kathleen asked.

"He didn't turn me against you," Vanessa replied, trying to sound neutral but not quite managing it. "He wouldn't even tell me what you did—"

"Good."

"Until I turned seventeen and then he told me all of it. Because of you he was forced to leave. Or will you deny you are—were, ultimately responsible for that?"

"There was no choice!"

"There's always a choice, Mother. That's the one thing I've learned living away from you and your rigid rules. Father will never forgive you for what you did. He wouldn't even read your letters, just burned them without opening them. But he gained a measure of peace once he stopped loving you."

"Did you only come here to wound me?"

Good God, were those tears on her mother's cheeks? She wasn't prepared for tears! Utterly disarmed, she tried to think of something consoling to say but gave up in a moment. How the deuce did one console someone one hated?

But Kathleen wasn't finished. "The only mistake I made was not taking the Rathban matter to your father, but even then the results would have been the same. He still would have challenged Henry Rathban to a duel and still would have had to deal with Albert Rathban's wrath. But at least he wouldn't hate me now."

"I didn't say that he does," Vanessa said. "He fell out of love with you. That's what gave him peace, so do *not* begrudge him that."

"I don't," Kathleen said. "I've never wished any ill on him. My heart broke when he had to leave me—that he wanted to leave me."

Vanessa didn't believe any of that. "I don't like lying to my sisters. I don't know how long I can keep it up without slipping and saying something about where I've really been. They are grown women now and deserve the truth."

"No one deserves that kind of truth. It was your father's idea to claim he had business to take care of in the Caribbean to explain his absence."

"But I don't think either of you thought far enough ahead. It's already been six years. What happens in another five years when a business trip will no longer suffice as an excuse? Or when the twins are married and they want to visit him, what then?"

"That's a bridge that doesn't need to be crossed yet."

"Bloody hell, Mother, that bridge is sinking."

Kathleen stiffened. "What exactly did your father tell you?"

"Everything. You betrayed him with another man!"

"I swear I didn't."

"But you would have," Vanessa accused. "You were in the very process of doing so when Father caught you."

"Good God, he had no right to tell you that!"

"Hardly the point. Too much time has passed. The twins don't understand why he's still not home. It's not as if we're going to become paupers with the loss of a plantation in the West Indies. Layla and Emily aren't stupid, Mother. So at least tell them something about why Father can't return to England, or I will."

She left the room with that ultimatum, bolstered by anger once again and proud that she had it somewhat under control. She wasn't sure what to make of Kathleen's swearing that she hadn't betrayed her husband. Why did her mother think she could lie when she'd been caught in the act? William hadn't believed her denial with that sort of evidence. Why should she?

Chapter Nineteen

KATHLEEN STARED AT THE door Vanessa had just closed and let her tears flow freely now. She was so utterly pleased to have her firstborn home again, but so conflicted because of it. Six years! She had begun to fear she might never see Vanessa again and there would be nothing she could do about it.

But she was finally home. It just wasn't *their* Vanessa who had returned to them. The young woman who had stood there so defiantly was nothing like the thirteen-year-old child she remembered. The child had never been so bold or ever expressed so much anger. She was nothing like her sisters. She didn't even look like the lady she was, or apparently think like one. Good Lord, what had William done? Turned Vanessa into a son just to spite her? Bold, daring—defiant, just as a boy would be. And how could she tell Vanessa about what she'd done when the girl was already so angry over the past? She couldn't, not immediately. She had to disarm Vanessa's anger first but wasn't sure if the truth would suffice. It hadn't with William.

Once again, her hatred of the Rathbans for destroying her family rose up to choke her. The rest of them weren't as despicable as Henry, but Albert Rathban, the eldest, was a close second and still held the cards.

After the debacle, she'd still had hope that the ultimatum Albert had given William when he'd been grief-stricken could be rescinded. She'd intended to appeal to him after some time had passed and would have done so if she hadn't heard that his remaining brother, John, had died barely a year after Henry's death. She'd had to wait again until Albert's grief over the loss of his last brother had ebbed and wouldn't cloud his judgment so much that he wouldn't listen to the truth about what had transpired between her and Henry, as William had done.

So nearly two years passed before she'd dared to visit Albert to appeal to any sense of decency and fairness he might have. She'd struck a deal with him, although it wasn't what she had hoped for. And the interview had been an utterly debasing experience for her.

Too many bad memories were returning all at once. She thrust them away and joined the twins for breakfast, hoping they could distract her. But all they did was give her expectant looks, and she didn't doubt they were waiting to hear what she had to say about Vanessa's return—and her ridiculous appearance. Vanessa was going to be a bad influence on them. She had to make peace with her eldest daughter before that happened. But how?

She was too distraught to eat and left the dining room to seek out Vanessa. She found her in the room she'd been given in the west wing. She didn't even think to knock and realized too late that she couldn't treat Vanessa as a child any longer. But she didn't apologize. She had caught Vanessa in a pose before the mirror of an empty wardrobe, examining herself in a lovely aqua frock, not one of the twins' colors.

Vanessa merely glanced over her shoulder and, seeing her mother, looked down at the ratty-looking boots she was also wearing. She casually said, "I forgot to fetch shoes when I grabbed the dress."

"You don't need to fetch anything. Your room was prepared for you the day your trunks arrived. Why didn't you arrive with them?"

Vanessa shrugged nonchalantly. "I thought to see a bit of London first, since Father gave me full access to his house there."

"I bought another house in London. I didn't feel comfortable going back to that one."

"I'm not surprised."

Kathleen drew in her breath at her daughter's disparaging tone. So much for keeping their discourse neutral. Or making peace, for that matter. That wouldn't happen unless Vanessa would listen to the truth. William had refused to listen, but she really had no choice but to try with her daughter.

"Have you told the twins anything yet?" Kathleen asked.

"Have you? But when d'you think I had the opportunity? You think I sat down at the dining table dressed as I was? I came up here instead to change my appearance. I decided not to rub in my preference in clothes any further."

"Thank you for that, but they can't hear your version of why their father went away, Nessa. It simply isn't the truth."

"So Father didn't find you in bed with another man?"

Kathleen's face felt as if it were exploding with heat, but she couldn't avoid this. At least Vanessa, who had it all wrong, had to understand that she'd had no choice.

"You're being naive," Kathleen said sharply. "But I should have known you were too young to understand that sometimes a woman has to take extreme measures to protect her family and all she holds dear."

"And?"

"There is no *and*. I did nothing wrong!"

"Other than split our family apart? If that's the rubbish you tried to feed Father, I'm not surprised he didn't listen. But I know too much to listen to platitudes at this point, Mother. Save them for the twins. Maybe they won't mind that you aren't offering an actual defense for your indiscretion. You know, I think I would rather have heard the oldest excuse there is, that you fell in love with Henry Rathban and just couldn't help yourself."

Kathleen sighed. "No, that wasn't it a'tall. Henry and I were old friends. He'd even competed with your father to win my hand all those years ago, though there was never any chance of that happening. I loved your father then, and I still do. But Henry and I became reacquainted when he came to London in the spring when I was visiting my friends as I usually did for a few weeks each year. Your father didn't always join me, and that time I was there without him and was flattered by Henry's attention. His family is old wealth, powerful, and held in high regard by the *ton*. And he was amusing. There might have been some harmless flirtation but not the sort that would lead to anything."

"Yet it did," Vanessa said.

"No, it didn't. He came to the London house and tried to kiss me, but I rebuffed him strongly and told him to get out. He was actually amused! And he told me, 'Everyone will think we are lovers, I'll make sure of that—unless we do actually become lovers, then I'll keep it secret. Your reputation will remain sterling, our spouses won't get hurt, and we can enjoy ourselves. I'm making it easy for you, Kathy. You know you want to.' He was so confident. I think he really believed there was something more between us, when there wasn't. But I was too shocked at the time to answer him and he left. But I realized because our acquaintances thought we were already friends, and we had been seen laughing together, dancing together, that if he did actually spread that rumor, it would cause a full-blown scandal because no one would doubt it was true. Henry had very cleverly set the trap for me by showing up at the events I attended and spending so much time at my side, almost as if we'd gone to those events together."

"So you gave in?"

"No, I wasn't going to! I left the house to go to his elder brother Albert, who I hoped would convince Henry to call off the threat. But Henry was waiting outside for me on the step. He'd guessed exactly what I'd intended to do. He laughed at me and said, 'D'you think my brother will care? He'll consider this such a trifle I'll only get a slap on the wrist, but before you even reach Albert to tattle on me, the rumor about our affair will have been spread all over White's. I'm going there now. You'll be shunned by the *ton*, Kathy. And you might want to think about your daughters and what a scandal like that will do to them.'"

"So you were going to engage in scandalous behavior to defuse a fake scandal?"

"The moment he mentioned you girls I knew I had no choice. Even if a scandal like that died down, it would rise up the moment you went to London for your come-out and ruin your chances for a good match, then the same thing would happen to your sisters. I could *not* let that happen. Your father accepted his exile for the exact same reason, to protect you girls from scandal."

"You could have denied all of it!"

"It doesn't work that way, Vanessa. Once gossip like

that spreads, it never really goes away. My friends might believe me, but no one else would. There would always have been whispers. And I would have lost your father anyway because he would still have challenged Henry. No matter what I did, nothing would be any different than it is right now. So I chose to protect you girls from that scandal."

"And Father showed up instead?"

"Yes, but he didn't give me a chance to explain. He kicked me out of the London house. When I returned the next day to explain, the servants wouldn't let me in. I waited, but when William came home, he walked right past me without a word as if I were invisible. He was still too angry. So I went home to Dawton Manor and waited for him to come for an explanation."

"Did you ever tell him what you just told me?"

"He never gave me a chance to in London. So I didn't know he'd challenged Henry to a duel or the results of it until William came to Cheshire to gather his belongings and leave the country. But yes, I told him everything then, I just don't think he heard a word of it he was so enraged. He kept saying I'd ruined his life. He didn't consider that mine was also ruined by that duel. I even offered to leave the country with him, but he said he never wanted to see me again."

"Because you betrayed him. No matter how you look at it, Mother, whether you did it or not, you *would* have slept with another man instead of letting Father know about Rathban's threat to ruin you in a scandal."

"Vanessa, think about it! Do you really think the results would have been any different if I'd taken the matter to William? There would still have been a duel, but one based on supposition that Henry would have certainly denied, so it could have been much worse."

"You don't know that! You never gave Father a chance to fix it! *You* should have fixed it. I would have shot the bastard the moment he got near my bed—where he didn't belong."

Kathleen was taken aback. "Don't be ridiculous."

"I'm not. If he really did promise to ruin you and your daughters if you didn't let him have his way with you, he would have deserved it. At the very least you could have given him a minor wound to prove you would kill him if he went through with his plan."

Kathleen was amazed. Why couldn't she have had this sort of courage in the face of Henry's threats? It had never occurred to her to resort to physical violence. She thought she'd been courageous in going to Albert Rathban to appeal for mercy, but truly, she'd only been desperate. And it had all been for naught.

She began to pace, frustrated by Vanessa's lack of understanding—so like her father's. Even after she'd made a full confession, Vanessa was still blaming her for everything. Would this nightmare never end? Dare she tell Vanessa about her meeting with Albert Rathban? It had been so humiliating, how could she repeat any of it to her daughter? Yet her memory of that horrible meeting was still so vivid in her mind. She'd gone to Albert with such hope in her heart. She'd wanted her family back!

She'd been able to tell him that his brother had promised to create a false scandal to ruin her family if she didn't crawl willingly into his bed. Not in those exact words, she'd been more circumspect, but she'd pleaded with him to let her husband come home safely without their family being ruined.

She'd managed to get that much out before his nasty response, "If you're here to offer yourself to me, I'm not interested. I have no brothers left, thanks to you. John fell off his bloody horse and died the year after Henry did."

"You can't blame me for that," she said.

"No, but I'd still have one brother left if you weren't so damn pretty Henry lost his head over you."

"I never encouraged him! He blackmailed—"

"Enough!" Albert cut in furiously. "Henry told a different story, that he was the innocent in that sordid affair, you the seducer. You led him to expect a certain outcome. You can't dangle a carrot in front of a man and never hand it over. If you knew him at all, and I assume you did, you knew he wasn't a man with a great deal of patience. You taxed him to the limit and he lost his life because of it."

"It was a harmless flirtation with an old friend!"

"One who didn't consider it harmless at all. You made him fall in love with you again. You can't play the sophisticated game you do and not reap unpleasant results occasionally. You courted scandal."

"You don't blackmail someone you love. You can't defend that."

"I condemn you for bringing it to that point—because you stupidly let your husband find out."

"That isn't what happened," she said stiffly.

"No? I'm to believe you instead of my brother? But even if what you claim was true, it would have been no more than a bluff on Henry's part, because he wouldn't intentionally create a scandal that would have touched his own family. Which makes you a bloody fool, madam, not to have realized that."

"I have three daughters! I don't gamble with what a man might or might not do when *their* futures are at stake."

She started to leave, too insulted to try to reason with him further or point out that a scandal of that sort didn't hurt a man nearly as much as it did a woman. But he snapped, "Sit down, I'm not done with you. I need a moment to think."

He took more than a moment before he gave her a calculated look. "To satisfy both sides of the argument, and to pay for my loss, which is greater than yours, give me one of your daughters for my son, he'll never get a wife otherwise. Your heir will do, since other than your holding the honorary title of Countess in the interim, your father's title, the Marquis of Dawton, will pass to your firstborn's son—my grandson. I find that an acceptable trade for all the pain you've caused the Rathban family."

"And that will be the end of it? There will be no more talk of ruining my family?"

"Would I ruin the family my son has married into? But I want the girl and the marriage first, and I warn you it will be difficult. Daniel is determined to never marry. I've brought him five young ladies, any one of whom he could have taken to the altar, and he refused to marry any of them! The marriage will need to be his idea, so your gel will have to seduce him. If she takes after you and dangles the carrot, perhaps she can succeed where others have failed."

She'd left the Rathbans' London mansion that day with a firm agreement. It wasn't an ideal solution, but it was a solution. And she kept telling herself that one bad apple like Henry didn't rot the whole basket. But then Vanessa didn't come home last year when she should have to seal the bargain. But how could she offer the Rathbans *this* Vanessa even if the bargain was still available? The Rathbans wouldn't want a girl this intractable—even if she could manage to get such an angry, aggressive hoyden to the altar.

Kathleen stopped pacing, shook her head in frustration, and inadvertently said aloud, "Not that any of that matters now, when Rathban hasn't answered my—"

"What?"

Kathleen turned with a gasp, then blanched. "You weren't supposed to hear that."

Vanessa's eyes narrowed. "I could have sworn you were

about to make a clean breast of it, Mother. What exactly have you left out?"

"I struck a deal with the eldest Rathban a few years back, but it expired last year because your father foolishly didn't open my letters to learn about it. So it's not worth discussing at this point."

"I disagree. I'm interested in anything to do with the Rathbans, particularly if you had an agreement with them. What sort of deal did you make?"

"I approached Albert to appeal for mercy. It was two years after your father had left. I'd hoped he would consider that long enough. But he'd lost yet another brother since then, so he wasn't amenable to relinquishing his revenge— not without receiving something in return."

"He wants more? Wasn't Father's exile enough for him?"

"It was but, apparently, he has a dilemma of his own that he believes we can fix for him. He made us an offer," Kathleen said. "But the time has expired."

"What did he want in exchange for Father's freedom?"

"I wrote to him the day your trunks arrived, but he hasn't answered, so it's likely too late. The opportunity has been lost. We will say no more—"

"You are incredible," Vanessa said scathingly. "D'you mistake me for one of the twins? I will go to Rathban m'self to find out what he offered—"

"No, you will not!" Kathleen cut in.

"Watch me! I'll ride to London right away," Vanessa

said, and began to remove the dress to put her pants back on.

Kathleen sighed. "His son—in marriage. That is what he offered. He had the gall to say he wouldn't ruin us if his son was a member of our family."

"Did Father divorce you without telling me?"

"Divorce! Of course not. He left to save us from scandal, not to cause one. Rathban wasn't talking about me. He wants my heir for his son."

"And I'm your heir?"

Chapter Twenty

"YOU KNOW YOU ARE."

Kathleen said more, lamenting that William's lack of curiosity had cost them dearly, that he could have been home by now if he'd just read her letters. Vanessa had stopped listening. She was stunned—and alarmed that she might have to marry a member of the ruthless Rathban family to win her father's freedom to come home. It was ironic that she'd have to give up her freedom and independence to attain what she'd wanted most these past six years—her father back at home and her family reunited. As awful as it sounded, she reminded herself it would be a solution to her biggest problem, and she hadn't come up with another solution. But still . . .

"You can't give them the sordid details," Kathleen said, wrapping up her long list of complaints. "Unlike you—apparently—they are too delicate for that."

Vanessa focused on her mother again, though it took a moment to catch up to what she was saying and to realize

Kathleen was talking about the twins now and comparing them to her. Disparagement and concern in the same breath?

And then Kathleen added, "This is the most exciting year of their lives. Don't ruin that for them, Vanessa, just because you don't like telling a few minor lies to spare them, especially when you could simply avoid saying very much about where you've been."

She hadn't considered that, so she said, "I'll think about it."

"Good. Now return to your old room. You can't stay in this wing any longer with strangers."

There was the disapproval again, but she pointed out, "They aren't strangers."

"But they are men. And while they are welcome guests, we are due a private family meal. Join your sisters and me in my suite for luncheon."

Vanessa hadn't said yes to any of that, but Kathleen left her room with the assumption that she had agreed to all of it. Her mother ought not to assume anything where she was concerned.

With the room to herself again, Vanessa fell back on the bed with a frown. She had been prepared to bargain with Albert Rathban herself, but marriage certainly wouldn't have been on the table when she wouldn't have known that he was shopping for a wife for his son. But with Kathleen making that bargain for her, would he even be open to an alternative—if she could think of one? But this arrangement was the exact opposite of what she'd hoped for in a marriage. She would be giving up her dreams of romance and the perfect husband who would agree she could retain her independence. How could she do that? And why would Albert Rathban even need to arrange a marriage for his son, a wealthy nobleman from a powerful, prestigious family? Was there something wrong with the boy that he couldn't find his own wife? Perhaps a hideous deformity? That would be unfortunate. She'd been so stunned she didn't get a chance to ask her mother. What if the boy would actually sign her contract? She ought to at least find out before she weighed all her options.

When she vacated the guest room with her valise repacked and in hand, Monty walked out of his room as well and was suddenly blocking her way. Had he been listening for her? Surely not, but it still felt like an ambush. But she paused—and he approached.

"I may miss the pants," he remarked, his eyes moving over the pretty dress she was wearing. "Then again, probably not."

He'd added that when he was close enough to look down at the low cut of the bodice. She had the urge to laugh, but he was being too risqué, and her protective instincts rose instead—for her sisters. Was he like this only with her? It better only be with her.

"Still no blushes, sweetheart?"

"Why would I? You're a professed rake. I anticipate

rakish nonsense to come out of your mouth. But if you try to make my sisters blush . . ."

"I won't. I don't misbehave with ladies," he assured her as he moved forward enough to maneuver her back against the wall. "But I'll make an exception for you because you've worn pants from the moment we met. It's going to be very difficult to forget that you're incredibly bold and resourceful. Please don't punch me again."

She did laugh this time. "Should I thank you for the reminder?"

"No! But yes, I did say I would behave once you were dressed like a lady, however—you're still wearing boots, not quite transformed yet."

His hand caressed her cheek, then moved up through her hair, then down to the back of her neck, making her tingle with anticipation and tilt her head back so his mouth could more easily reach hers. But he hesitated when his mouth was a breath away. What a tease! She boldly bridged the gulf herself and was enraptured to taste him again, to hear his groan at her acquiescence. If there weren't a loveless marriage looming in her future she would have protested— or would she? But the firm decision she'd made to wait for the right man and stop kissing the wrong one might be quite irrelevant now that marriage to the Rathban scion could turn out to be her father's salvation.

Utterly unconcerned about the risk of discovery there in the corridor, she dropped the valise to put her arm around Monty's neck, but he heard it drop and leaned back to look down by her feet, then met her eyes to accuse, "You were abandoning us without saying goodbye?"

"No, just moving to my old room," she replied. "You didn't actually think Mother would let me remain in this wing with male guests, did you?"

"What a shame."

He feigned a sigh and braced his hands on the wall, one on either side of her head. She didn't find his physical proximity threatening. In fact, she found it thrilling and deliciously improper because his leg was touching hers.

But he continued, "I thought about sneaking in on you one night for a little more of that activity, which my losing the bet yesterday forbids me to mention, but now I won't be able to."

She chuckled. "No you didn't."

" 'Course I did. The bet didn't say I couldn't do it, only that I couldn't mention it."

"Ah, but it sounds to me like you did just mention it," she said, and ducked under his arm to back slowly away from him down the corridor.

He didn't pursue her, instead leaned a shoulder against the wall and asked, "So you completed all your reunions? How did it go with your mother?"

She paused for a moment to reply, "Not exactly how I expected."

"Do I need to hide from the theatrics?"

"She's not angry. Not pleased about some things, but not angry."

"Splendid. I missed you at our meals."

She wouldn't admit she'd missed him, too. With a wave, she turned to continue on her way to the east wing.

The man still fascinated her in too many ways. And she enjoyed his banter—and his kisses. But she ought to start thinking of herself as affianced since she might be headed for an arranged marriage. Then again, would a man let a little thing like an engagement stop him from flirting and kissing elsewhere? Maybe if he loved his intended. However, she would be consigning herself to a marriage of convenience with a Rathban *if* she agreed to the match. But she wasn't married yet . . .

Chapter Twenty-one

HER OLD ROOM WAS being cleaned again, which was hardly necessary, but Vanessa entered it anyway, telling the two maids working there to just ignore her. It had been a little jarring when she'd come here earlier to get her dress and she had seen that the room appeared the same as when she'd left it. But she hadn't paused to look at everything, all the things she hadn't taken with her the night she'd run away to be with her father. Now she did. All her dolls, which she had stopped playing with but had been too sentimental to get rid of, still sat on the mantel. Her ice skates were still at the bottom of the wardrobe. But at least all the clothes she'd left behind had been removed to make room for her new clothes. Only one of her trunks from Scotland was still there.

She didn't notice when the maids left because being in her old bedroom was bringing back so many childhood memories. When she opened the first drawer of the bureau, she realized the twins hadn't unpacked the last trunk because they hadn't wanted to empty the bureau when it might contain things she wanted to keep. And she most certainly wanted to keep all the ribbons that filled the drawer. She'd picked them out one day when Kathleen had taken her and the twins shopping in Dawton town, every white ribbon in the shop for Layla, all the pinks for Emily, but Vanessa got to have one of every color.

In the next drawer she found the rack of parasols her mother had bought for each of her daughters because they couldn't leave the house without one, along with the wide-brimmed hats with netting they'd had to wear when they were allowed to garden. Kathleen didn't object to floral gardening, a genteel hobby, as long as her daughters were outfitted in accoutrements that would protect them from the sun. But she adamantly objected to her girls riding, being rambunctious, swimming, fishing, or doing anything that kept them out in the sun too long.

At least she'd gotten to enjoy all that and more in Scotland. And she supposed the twins' not having had the same fun experiences hadn't hurt them. What they didn't know, they wouldn't miss.

And then in another drawer she saw a few items from Scotland that the twins had unpacked, including the box in which she'd packed her father's portrait. It wasn't a miniature, though it wasn't large, about the size of a dinner plate, but it was such a good likeness of him she hadn't wanted to risk its getting damaged on the trip and had wrapped it in linen before putting it in the wooden box.

Had the twins peeked when they'd unpacked for her and stuck it in a drawer? Wouldn't they have mentioned it if they had?

She opened the box, unwrapped the portrait, and held it in her hands. And the tears fell silently as she gazed at William's likeness. She missed him so much! With all her heart she wished he could be home, too—and he could. She'd known, deep down, that she was willing to do whatever it would take to bring her father home, even marry a man she didn't love. And Albert Rathban himself was handing the solution to her—if it wasn't too late. It better not be too late.

A little while later, there was a knock on the door and she was surprised to find her sisters there. They'd never knocked on each other's doors when they'd been children, but the twins were proper ladies now, so of course they wouldn't barge in on her as they used to do.

"So here you are," Layla said as she took one of Vanessa's arms.

"Weren't you told we're having lunch with Mother in her rooms?" Emily asked, taking her other arm.

"We're already late, so do come along."

They were merely dragging her across the corridor. Vanessa didn't laugh when she realized they might have thought she had no intention of joining them. They knocked on Kathleen's door, too. A footman opened it. Two others were in the large room as well, having brought in the first course already placed on the table that would seat four.

"I've sent for our seamstress," Kathleen said as the girls took their seats.

Since she didn't doubt the seamstress was for her, Vanessa replied, "Inspect my wardrobe, Mother, if you must. It's perfectly—"

"More of those ridiculous pants?" Kathleen cut in.

Vanessa laughed. "No, what you would consider appropriate—and just a few pair of pants."

"The twins said you have only two ball gowns. Hardly sufficient."

"Why ever not? They can be worn more'n once."

"No, Nessa," Layla said.

"Unheard of," Emily added.

"And not necessary," Kathleen said. "You will be fitted for at least four more, and you can pick the colors and fabrics, if you like. The twins will guide you if you aren't sure what is appropriate."

Vanessa shrugged. "Do as you like."

"No 'thank you'?" Kathleen asked. "Have you even forgotten common courtesies?"

"Not a'tall. But I didn't ask for more clothes, because I already have a very nice new wardrobe. It feels as if you're forcing this on me."

"Your father should have known that you would need more than two ball gowns. Six may not be necessary, but there is no reason you shouldn't be prepared for more than a few balls."

Faulting William for her supposedly inadequate wardrobe rubbed Vanessa wrong and brought out the lie, "I hadn't even decided on having a Season, if you must know."

Everyone gasped at that point—except Vanessa. But she regretted the lie immediately. She just couldn't help getting contrary with her mother. How was she going to deal with Kathleen if she couldn't shake off this defensiveness? And she was being provoked. Kathleen's stiff hauteur, the disparagement. Was this how she was with the twins? Was she this way now because they were present? Or did she somehow think that Vanessa would "behave" with them listening to every word?

It was the twins who both said in unison, "But you must have your Season!"

"Of course she will, darlings," Kathleen assured the girls. "Our Vanessa is merely being difficult because she didn't prepare sufficiently for the Season, but it's an oversight that can be easily rectified."

Must she really? Now, when she already had a husband lined up? Before she could mention that, Kathleen asked, "Did your father at least teach you how to dance?"

Hearing yet another disparagement of William, Vanessa stood up abruptly. "This was a mistake. When you can act like a mother instead of a bloody taskmaster, perhaps we can try this again."

"Wait," Kathleen said quickly. "I apologize, Nessa. I've let my disappointment get out of hand, but it was such a surprise that William sent you home alone. I thought surely he would return with you for your Season, but I understand why he can't."

Well, Kathleen certainly had no trouble keeping up the lies. But she did sound sincere in the apology, making Vanessa realize she was being far too antagonistic, especially after she'd heard a new version of what happened six years ago. Both parents determined to stave off scandals? Ironic if that was so. But the trouble was, she wasn't sure if she could believe Kathleen's excuse. After all, she'd just heard how guilelessly her mother could lie.

But she nodded and sat back down, then amazingly, Kathleen went right back to complaining. "There's no time to get a dancing instructor here to teach Vanessa."

"We can teach her," Layla quickly offered.

"You don't know how to lead, which is what a gentleman does," Emily pointed out, though she added, "But we've got two presently in residence."

"So we do," Kathleen agreed. "If they won't mind."

"We'll ask!" the twins said in unison again.

Which brought Kathleen's censure. "You certainly will not. Ladies are never that bold."

"But I am," Vanessa said, and was proud that she managed not to smirk.

"No, you will not!"

Vanessa rolled her eyes. "It's a little late for comportment lessons, Mother. I won't embarrass you in public, but I won't pretend to be someone I'm not in private.

Besides, I know them well enough for it not to be the least bit bold to ask for something as harmless as dancing lessons."

Kathleen actually conceded. Even the twins seemed surprised by it. But they got through the rest of the lunch without any more combat, so Vanessa waited until dessert was set before her to mention, "By the by, Mother, I agree to your arranged marriage for me."

Layla gasped. "Arranged?"

And Emily exclaimed, "You said we could pick our husbands as long as you approved!"

"And so you shall," Kathleen replied. "This particular match for Vanessa was merely too good to turn down when it was offered years ago. Leave us. I need to speak to your sister alone about it."

Layla immediately stood up to depart, but Emily stayed in her seat and her expression had turned mulish. Vanessa almost laughed. This twin had definitely gained some courage over the years.

But there was no doubt that Kathleen was angry when she repeated, "I said, leave us."

Emily instantly rose with a loud huff and headed for the door. She still wouldn't confront Kathleen's anger, but apparently she didn't mind displaying some of her own these days.

Once they were alone, Vanessa said, "That wasn't necessary. You could have waited to speak to me alone after they were on their way out the door."

"And you could have waited until then to make that incredible announcement, but you didn't. What do you mean you agree? I told you, I haven't heard back from Albert Rathban yet and found out if the offer is still available. His boy doesn't want to marry, ever."

"Why not?"

"He didn't say, only that he had arranged for five other brides before you and they were all rejected. It might just be his son's shyness."

"What else can you tell me about him?"

"I met the boy only briefly years ago at a horse race. He's not especially good-looking, but certainly not ugly. However, his shyness makes him appear socially awkward, perhaps even a little dull, but I still thought he was a nice boy. I'm not trying to put you off by having nothing wonderful to say about him."

Vanessa was actually pleased by Kathleen's description because marriage to such a compliant fellow might not be all bad. He might sign her contract, and she might even gain the upper hand in the marriage. But she wasn't going to mention that to Kathleen.

"You haven't put me off," she assured her mother. "Is he Albert's only son?"

"Indeed, which is why this has been a dilemma for Albert and is the reason why he made the offer. Yet his son might have finally married this last year for all we know. And Albert was angry when you didn't come for your Season last year to try to win him. I was forced to tell him you weren't here, that you went into exile with your father. I didn't hear back from him after that."

"It's going to allow Father to come home, isn't it?" Vanessa asked.

"Yes, it would have. And it had seemed like the perfect solution at the time, but that was before I knew how willful you turned out."

"Not about this. I'll do anything to break Father's chains. He never deserved any of this. So write to Rathban again. If he's just making you stew because the marriage didn't happen on his time schedule, assure him that I'm willing to do whatever it takes to bring his son to the altar—if the boy is still available."

Chapter Twenty-two

THE TWINS WERE WAITING for Vanessa in her room across the corridor, the door left open so they could see when she left Kathleen's room. Such forbearance! She would have eavesdropped, but they probably didn't even consider it, Kathleen had trained them so well.

But both girls were impatient and didn't even wait until she was fully in the room before asking, "Why are you already affianced?"

"Did you know?"

"And didn't mention it to us?"

"How could you agree?"

Vanessa almost laughed, having to glance back and forth between the twins. It so reminded her of their childhood. But she closed the door, then turned to give them a wry smile.

"It was—unexpected," she said.

"Then why did you agree?" Emily asked.

"Wouldn't you?"

"No, we were promised choices."

"Ah, but I wasn't here for that conversation," Vanessa pointed out. "But in either case, why would I refuse before I even meet Lord Rathban? I'd be very annoyed with m'self if I end up liking him."

"Then you will decline if you don't like him?" Layla guessed.

She just shrugged. Of course she wouldn't, but the less said, the better. Because on one issue she did agree with her mother—this most exciting year of the twins' lives shouldn't be ruined by the revelation of unsavory truths they were presently unaware of. So her real reason for wanting the match couldn't be mentioned.

But Emily was still confounded by her easy compliance and wouldn't let the subject go. "Why was such a marriage arranged at all? There's always a particular reason for something that antiquated."

Yes, a recalcitrant boy who didn't consider it his duty to continue his family's line, but Vanessa wasn't about to tell the twins that or mention her other reasons for agreeing to the match. But she was still able to answer Emily's question without revealing too much by making a logical guess based on something her father had told her about the Rathbans.

"The eldest Rathban is an earl," she said. "But they have much higher ranks in their ancestry, including a duke. They are an old and very highly esteemed family, which is why Mother couldn't refuse such an offer when it was made."

"But what do they want if they are already so well-connected?" Emily asked. "Money?"

It was Layla who answered that. "Don't be a goose, Em. Have you forgotten about grandfather's title that's still unclaimed? Nessa's firstborn son will become the Marquis of Dawton, more'n enough reason for an earl, however rich and highly esteemed he already is, to suggest the match for one of his sons." But then she gasped and stared wide-eyed at Vanessa. "It is with a son, yes? Not a doddering old earl?"

"Yes," Vanessa said with a chuckle, then decided to change the subject by offering her sisters a treat. "Let's go for a ride. I'll find you some horses, even teach you how—"

Emily cut in. "We have our own horses."

Vanessa was amazed. Other ladies rode, but not Kathleen's daughters—except now they did? "How did that come about?"

"Mother was just waiting until we were old enough," Layla said.

Emily added, "She was afraid that when we were children we wouldn't be able to handle a horse that might get out of hand or spooked; she made us wait until our fifteenth birthday."

"Why the devil couldn't she just tell us that instead of always saying no?" Vanessa complained.

"Mother has never really explained herself, Nessa, surely you realize that by now," Layla said. "She is a firm believer in the old 'Because I said so!' instead of explaining what she considers obvious, even when we were too young to find anything obvious."

Considering how disappointed she'd been, year after year, that she couldn't ride here at Dawton and didn't think she would ever be able to, Vanessa grumbled, "I suppose."

"And I'm pretty sure you weren't bold enough back then to demand answers."

That came from Emily with marked disapproval, which raised Vanessa's brow. "Is there something about me that you object to, Em?"

Emily sighed. "I'm sorry, I'm disconcerted by how much you've changed."

"She was with Father too long," Layla pointed out. "We can't expect him to have taught her any of the female virtues Mother taught us."

"Mother taught me about those before I left," Vanessa said. "I just missed the comportment lessons."

"Then how did you become so bold?"

"I could ask the same of you, Em," Vanessa countered with a stare. That made Emily blush, which had her amend, "I'm sorry, it's simply that I've been away long enough to have forgotten how intimidating Mother can be, and since I'll be married soon, I don't feel a need to buckle under, as it were."

It wasn't the whole truth. Yes, six years of freedom from Kathleen's motherly oppression and restrictions had indeed changed her. But it was more than that. Unlike the twins who wanted to please their mother, Vanessa didn't. She used to, but anger and resentment had gotten in the way of that. And despite what Kathleen had told her about Henry Rathban's despicable efforts to blackmail her and the scandal that would have ensued if she hadn't given in, Vanessa couldn't seem to shake off those feelings yet.

Chapter Twenty-three

THE SISTERS RUSHED INTO the house laughing, having only just missed, by seconds, the downpour now pattering outside the front door. But having avoided getting wet, they all three composed themselves and comported themselves properly now, just in case Kathleen was nearby. But Vanessa was still grinning when she noticed that neither her mother nor any servants were in sight, although Monty was. He was coming down the grand staircase.

Once again, her breath caught for a moment. Fashion did not make this man. No matter what he wore, he was a feast for the eyes. Today his blue jacket was open, his dark auburn hair loose, a crop was in hand. He must not have noticed the rain approaching.

She whispered to Emily, "I'll meet you in the parlor for tea. Give me a few moments to arrange for those dancing lessons."

Emily followed her gaze and gave Monty a brilliant

smile before she whispered back, "Only if you bring him with you for tea."

"I'll certainly try," she replied, and removed her riding hat.

Monty had reached the bottom of the stairs but paused there as she walked toward him. He bowed in an exaggerated manner, then held his hand out to her, palm up. When she just stared, he said, "You're supposed to offer your fingertips to be kissed."

She tsked. "I'm aware of that, but you're a houseguest. We can dispense with that amenity every time we cross paths here, and you know it."

"Ah, but this is the first time I'm meeting the complete lady. Humor me—Lady Nestor."

She burst out laughing. "I will not, and you'll stop calling me that. You didn't really want to kiss my gloves anyway." She raised her arm to wiggle her gloved fingers at him.

"I disagree," he said, and snatched her hand to plant his lips on her knuckles. "I will take my kisses where I can get them."

She snatched her hand back. "Don't think you'll get away with that again."

"I can wait until you are . . . gloveless."

Why the pause? It was such an innocuous word, and yet he somehow made it seem naughty. Or was it the sensual expression in his eyes? She still felt her breath catch, feeling a distinct rise in temperature, and she couldn't even remember why she'd approached— Oh!

"How do you feel about dancing?" she blurted out, still a little breathless.

"An excuse to hold a pretty lady in my arms."

"So you know how?"

"Of course," he said indignantly.

"Then you wouldn't mind teaching me?"

He grinned. "I'll find us a secluded spot—"

She laughed before saying, "You won't. We'll need music, and my sisters have agreed to play their favorite instruments for us tonight after dinner."

He sighed dramatically. "So we'll have an audience? Not quite what I'd hoped for."

"Then you're declining?"

"Absolutely not!" he assured her. "Did I not just say any excuse?"

"Everything you say just proves you are incorrigible," she rejoined. "I could have sworn you said you would behave once I donned the persona of lady."

"Did I fail to mention 'in public'?"

She rolled her eyes. "Yes, you neglected to include that stipulation."

"But my rakishness amuses you, sweetheart," he teased. "Admit it."

"A lady would never admit that. But I do cordially invite you to tea with my sisters and me."

"Gads, you're going to drown me in proper, aren't you?" he complained. "Cordially? Really? How about a pact instead, that when we speak alone, we be ourselves?"

That finally made her blush because she had a feeling he was no longer teasing. So she said pointedly, "I bloody well need the practice in proper ladylike speech and behavior, and you are the perfect foil to wield my lessons against."

"Much better! By the by, navy blue is taboo for you. Your mother didn't tell you that pastels and more pastels and still more pastels are all you get to wear until you marry?"

"I believe you know I've been away with my father for a number of years, but I'm well aware of the silly restrictions placed on the wardrobes of young ladies. Riding habits are the exception—in case you didn't know."

He grinned. "And how magnificent you look in that one. I just enjoy watching you get all defensive. You're so adorable when you do."

So the teasing hadn't ended, after all. She snorted before stating, "Tea. Come or don't come." And she moved into the parlor without waiting to see if he would.

"Will the dragon be joining us?"

It was the first thing Monty said when he followed her into the room and, with a bow of greeting for the twins, sat in the chair beside the sofa. And Vanessa wasn't surprised he'd given Kathleen that nickname after her mother had gotten so sharp with Emily at dinner the other night. But both twins giggled, knowing exactly who he meant.

Vanessa joined them on the sofa before saying, "If she does, we give you leave to run from the fire."

Both girls kept up a running stream of conversation, Layla's quite proper, Emily's bordering on intrusive, but Monty evaded with aplomb. "In the east," was his answer to Emily's question about where he was from. "Youngest son," he replied when she asked how many siblings he had. If Emily tried to pin him down on particulars, and she did once when she asked if Montague was really his first name, he just gazed at her with a smile, making her blush.

Vanessa decided to stay out of it. She wasn't about to assume her mother's role and censure Emily, not when Monty didn't seem to mind the questions. And she even knew why Emily was persisting after she'd been warned not to. It wasn't to piece together information so she could figure out his real identity. She simply liked Monty as Layla had said and thus, wanted to know everything about him. Vanessa knew the feeling.

The tea tray arrived precisely at four o'clock as it did every day regardless whether anyone was in the parlor, which was one thing that hadn't changed at Dawton Manor. Kathleen didn't join them, but Charley did, arriving in a flourish of bouncing golden hair and a long satin coat that defied fashion, flaring at the hips, dark green on the outside, bright red on the inside. And the lace! It extended from both wrists and overflowed from his cravat. Wherever he was from, they were quite behind in fashion—or he was just so extravagant that he preferred to create his own.

He gave the ladies a very courtly bow, smiling at each twin, but when his dark blue eyes moved to Vanessa and he paused, she had the alarming thought that he was going to call her Nestor and ask what she was doing in female attire. But he didn't.

If he did recognize her, he didn't let on that he did, saying, "You must be Lady Vanessa, home from your travels? I am Charles, Max—"

"That's—" Monty started to cut in.

"And I've been told to call you Charley," Vanessa interrupted Monty, wanting to spare Charley from being scolded.

"Have you?" Charley glanced at Monty, but when his eyes came back to her, they were alight with, she wasn't sure what, until he said, "You are exquisite. You *must* marry me."

Layla giggled. "He's asked us to marry him, too."

Vanessa didn't laugh, but she did ask, "How many wives are you allowed where you come from, Charley?"

"One, though I'm sure an exception can be made for twins," he said, and winked at Layla.

With the boy so full of himself as usual, it was an amusing moment, until Emily said, "Vanessa must decline. She's already engaged."

Was Emily being catty? Vanessa wondered. Her tone didn't suggest it, but that was information that certainly didn't need to be dropped on the table.

"I am devastated," Charley said, but then flicked his

hand dismissively. "A minor inconvenience that can easily be broken when you know that I can make you a—"

"Bloody hell, Charley! D'you need a foot in your mouth? Mine will fit."

Vanessa wasn't sure why Monty was suddenly so angry, but she was sorry to see Charley blush and stood up to hook her arm through his, teasing, "D'you always state your wishes as if they were facts? You do know that you have to do some wooing before proposing?"

"Actually, I do not have to," he mumbled low.

"Well, I came home and found out I was engaged, but I'm not sure what I think about it yet."

"She needs to meet the fellow first," Layla put in.

"So wishes for your future happiness aren't in order yet?" Monty suddenly asked.

They would never be in order when she was prepared to commit herself to a loveless marriage, but she wasn't about to mention that and merely said, "A bit premature, when I've only found out about it today."

"Who is the lucky chap?"

She laughed a bit wryly. "I actually don't know his full name. It's Albert Rathban's boy. Do you know the Rathbans?"

"Lord Rathban has only one son. Daniel isn't a boy by any definition—and condolences might be more in order."

Chapter Twenty-four

CONDOLENCES? AND MONTY DIDN'T stick around to explain such an incredible remark. He'd very rudely left the parlor directly after saying it.

Layla was alarmed and asked Vanessa, "Do you know what he meant?"

Vanessa made light of it, replying, "Mother told me the Rathban son is rather quiet and shy. I suppose Monty might think he's a boring fellow."

"I'm sure we don't want boring," Emily put in.

"But if it's just a matter of shyness, won't that change after marriage?" Layla added.

Vanessa smiled at Layla's logic, but the fact was, the excuse she'd given didn't really explain Monty's remark, and she intended to find out what would.

She went in search of her mother after tea, but was frustrated to learn Kathleen had gone to Dawton town after lunch and wasn't back yet. She considered riding to the town her grandfather had founded, well, the marquis had founded the village of Dawton, which had since grown into a township, but she ended up breaking propriety and knocking on Monty's bedroom door instead. But that just increased her frustration because he wasn't in it—or wasn't answering.

She began to wonder if he hadn't meant to say what he'd said and was now embarrassed by it. He'd been angry with Charley, after all, and her engagement had been mentioned immediately after, so his condolences remark could have just been a churlish remnant of that anger—or from his surprise at hearing she was so suddenly engaged. Or he simply didn't want to be cornered to explain because he had no intention of explaining.

She stood at the top of the stairs, debating whether to look for him further, when Mrs. Edwards suddenly approached from the east wing with a wide smile and tears glistening in her eyes. "Welcome home, Lady Nessa! You have been sorely missed by the staff, you and the earl both. We look forward to his return very soon, too."

Vanessa was surprised by the housekeeper's warm greeting, but the mention of her father just made her miss him all the more and strengthened her conviction that she was doing the right thing in accepting the arranged marriage to end his exile—boring groom or no.

She gave up on her search for more answers and ended up taking a long bath before dinner. And then the maid arrived to do her hair, sent by the twins. When the girl was finished, Vanessa barely recognized herself. The hoyden was definitely gone. She'd never once tried to coif her hair in Scotland. She probably could have, but she was too active there to want to be bothered by slipping pins and unraveling locks, so she'd simply worn her hair clubbed, braided, or loose—one of the little freedoms she now had to give up.

She did find her mother before dinner, catching Kathleen's maid leaving her room and slipping inside before the door closed. Kathleen was still sitting at her vanity. "A private word, Mother?"

Kathleen turned, then smiled brilliantly. "Don't you look lovely tonight, darling. I knew you would once you shed the . . . boy."

Vanessa rolled her eyes. "You might not want to remind me that I'm giving up my preferred attire just to please you, Mother."

"Forgive me. I have so much on my mind that I am thoughtlessly blundering repeatedly, which you might remember, I never do. But I'm still upset that I was sharp with one of the twins the other night at dinner—in front of our guests."

Having eavesdropped on that dinner, Vanessa didn't need to ask about that and got right to the point of her intrusion. "Is there a reason someone might offer condolences for the match you arranged for me?"

"Who would dare be so, so—?"

"Accurate?" she cut in, then sighed. "Just tell me what you've failed to mention about Daniel Rathban."

"I told you I don't know much about him except that he's quiet and perhaps a little dull."

"You must know something," Vanessa persisted.

"Lord Albert mentioned those five potential brides that his boy refused to court to stress his dilemma to me. I gathered that the refusal had nothing to do with the brides, that the boy just won't marry, though I suppose it could be simply because his father picked those girls."

"Yet Lord Albert has picked me, too. So if the son is that determined not to marry, what made Lord Albert think a wedding to me would change his mind?"

"It won't if *he* suggests it to his son. He stated clearly that it would have to be his boy's idea, which puts the onus entirely on your shoulders, I'm afraid."

That was unexpected. "You're saying I will need to woo Daniel Rathban?"

"To the point of a proposal, yes. But again, let me repeat, it may be too late. As I said, I haven't heard back from Lord Rathban about whether he even needs the match to go forward now. And besides, it may be an impossible task to win a man who rejects the very idea of marriage. Some men do go through life as confirmed bachelors, you know."

"How old is Daniel now?"

"I'm not sure how old he was when I met him. Possibly midtwenties now, or at least younger than thirty."

"And you never saw him again on your many trips to London?" Vanessa asked.

Kathleen sighed before admitting, "I stopped going to London after that first year I went to let it be known your father was away from England on business. I miss it terribly, but I found it too tedious after that, always being asked if he'd returned yet—and why not. You'll probably find it ironic that I agreed to Henry's despicable terms to avoid a scandal and being shunned by society, then I ended up unable to participate in society anyway."

Vanessa found it just deserts but didn't say so. She was going to try, very hard, to keep peace with Kathleen while they both had the same goal of getting William home. "You must miss your friends."

"I do. Only a couple of them ever came to visit me here in Cheshire, though they all write. I've heard that the speculation now is that William likes the warm weather too much to want to come home. And his friend Peter has squashed the other rumor that he stays away because of another woman."

Vanessa rolled her eyes. "No, there has been no other woman."

"I didn't think so, not when you were with him. But speculation tends to run its course of all possibilities when the protagonists aren't around to say otherwise. I must say how happy I am that we'll be in London soon and my isolation from society will end."

"How soon? When exactly are we leaving?"

"No later than the end of next week. But that trip doesn't compare to my joy in having you home again, darling. And your willingness to consider the marriage bargain, if it's indeed still on the table, was a surprise but is very appreciated."

Next week! She didn't have much time left with Monty. Once again, she was faced with the prospect of never seeing him again, but she refused to become downhearted about it again as she had on the road.

And that wasn't why she gave her mother a sad smile. She was commiserating with her. "I want Father back, too, Mother, more than anything."

They went downstairs together to find that Charley was waiting in the parlor for them with the twins, but Monty wasn't with them. Nor did he arrive before they moved to the dining room or at any time during the meal.

Vanessa had completely lost her appetite by then and only picked at her dinner, certainly not intentionally, but she did get a nod of approval from her mother that almost made her force the food down, but she didn't. She was too frustrated and starting to get angry as well, afraid that Monty had information about the Rathbans that would ruin this golden opportunity to get her father home. And he wouldn't share it! He was hiding instead, leaving her to brood over all sorts of dire possibilities for his nasty condolences.

Kathleen politely asked Charley if something was amiss with his guardian. He apologized for not mentioning sooner that Monty was not at the manor. He'd ridden off to Dawton town after tea, despite the rain, because he had some business to take care of.

Kathleen smiled. "Assure him that Mrs. Griggs will be happy to serve him dinner whenever he returns."

"It's still raining, dear lady. He will likely want a bottle of brandy instead to warm up, if he makes it back tonight. If you wouldn't mind?"

Kathleen tsked but agreed to his request and asked one of the maids to bring him the brandy. However, the moment Charley left the room, she told the girls, "You will find that some men have a fondness for drink and indulge it to excess, which is fine on certain occasions, but not something you will want to live with, so make sure the men you pick for yourselves don't have such proclivities."

That was obviously not a warning for the already engaged daughter. But Vanessa wondered if the brandy was for Charley or Monty, or perhaps both of them. She was only slightly relieved that Monty wasn't hiding as she'd thought, but it was still annoying that he wasn't there to explain his condolences remark. And he'd forgotten the dancing lessons, or was his business more important? Maybe he really didn't know how to dance, after all. That thought eased some of her annoyance with him.

But by the time she went to bed that night, she wondered with some consternation if she'd gotten upset because she'd missed him this evening—his banter, his jocular manner that so easily made her laugh, his handsome face. She bloody well better not be forming that sort of attachment to a rake.

Chapter Twenty-five

By teatime the next day, Monty still hadn't appeared and Vanessa was ready to laugh at herself. She'd come down for breakfast feeling excited. The man had to eat, after all. At lunchtime she'd gotten to the dining room early, again, with that underlying excitement that she would be seeing him. But she'd pushed aside her disappointment and reasoned that unless he'd abandoned his charge, which wasn't likely, he was still in the house and she would see him eventually.

Kathleen had shrugged off his failing to join them for the midday meal with the sage remark, "The aftereffects of strong drink can turn an otherwise charming fellow into a growling bear. We shall be grateful he is sparing us a demonstration."

And perhaps that's all it was, so Vanessa didn't let herself look forward to seeing him that night before dinner, and yet when she came around the corner to go downstairs, there he was in the main hall heading to the parlor,

236 J OHANNA L INDSEY

and she felt a little fluttering in her belly and gripped the handrail tightly.

"Sneaking downstairs for another bottle of brandy?" she queried in the most casual tone she could muster.

He turned and waited for her to finish her descent. "Why would you think so?"

"Didn't you get foxed last night, which required you to sleep the day away?"

He laughed. "No to both charges. I did enjoy a single glass of brandy last night and wondered who I should thank for it."

"That would be Charley."

"The nuisance can be thoughtful? Imagine that."

"So you went to town again today?"

"No, just scouting around the property. Your family really does own an extensive amount of land here. An army could camp on it and go unnoticed."

"I thought you were certain no one followed us here."

"I was, but that doesn't mean people aren't still searching for me and the boy. At any rate, after doing my due diligence I found myself famished for the sight of you."

"Rubbish."

"Very well, merely eager," he said, then in a whisper when she stopped a foot away, "I apologize for missing your dancing lesson. I didn't think I could be in the same room with your mother and not lambaste her for arranging such a marriage for you."

Really? But it was a pretty good excuse—if it was true. "Such a marriage? There are different kinds?"

"Indeed, if one is to the younger Rathban. He's not for you, Nessi. He'll crush your spirit."

She supposed boredom might do that if the groom was still a shy fellow, but she could find other amusements. She smiled. "I think I can protect my spirit."

"So you don't even know what sort of chap he is?"

"Yes, a socially awkward introvert."

"This isn't an amusing subject, so don't treat it so lightly. He's a rake of the worst sort. I could have sworn you said you wouldn't marry one."

A rake? Had the boy outgrown his shyness and timidity? She supposed he could be paying for a lot of sex to get that designation, offering coin instead of personality—if it were true.

Monty seemed to think it was. There was such accusation in his tone and expression, but she couldn't exactly tell him what she would gain from the marriage, so she said, "Well, that explains why you would offer condolences. But what d'you mean by 'worst'?"

"Dissolute, without conscience—and what about your rule of not marrying a rake? There were exceptions you neglected to mention?"

"It doesn't matter what Rathban is, when other things might be more important to me."

"You confound me. You can't want his title when you're already a lady, and you appear not to need his money."

It was annoyingly apparent that he wasn't going to bury this bone, so she assured him, "Emily spoke out of turn. The engagement might have been arranged by our parents, but it's not a certainty yet when Albert's son doesn't even know about it."

"Then he hasn't agreed?"

"As far as I know, my name hasn't even been mentioned to him yet."

He smiled. "That's different. He'll never agree."

She wasn't sure if she wanted to hit him or let that bloody bone stay buried. Was the man so dense he didn't even realize how thoroughly he'd just insulted her? But she continued to the parlor to join her family. Monty could go back to his reconnaissance of the property for all she cared.

He didn't, nor was he questioned about his absence from so many recent meals when he joined her family in the parlor. The twins might have inquired if Kathleen weren't present, but she was and would consider it rude of them to do so. And the conversation stayed utterly neutral, which, as was typically the case, meant boring enough to ignore.

And so it continued through half the meal as well, after they'd adjourned to the dining room. Dancing was mentioned and Monty confirmed that he was still willing to give a few lessons. Vanessa kept her eyes off him as she pondered the challenge before her. Had Kathleen deceived her or did she just not know what sort of man the shy boy had turned into? And how did one woo a dissolute rake? With Monty it would have been easy, since he was mostly harmless in his rakishness, an outrageous flirt, but too amusing about it to ask him to desist. It wasn't going to be that easy with Daniel Rathban, yet she still had to try.

But she did hear Kathleen say her name. "Vanessa, you won't feel like dancing if you eat too much."

The twins giggled. Vanessa stared at her nearly empty plate. She could have simply agreed with her mother, though it was rather late to do that since she already felt full, but no matter how innocuously her mother had couched it, she'd still rebuked her, and Vanessa couldn't help reacting to it.

"I know very well I'm supposed to eat like a puny chicken, Mother—at formal gatherings. But here in the country we're among friends and family, and I have a normal appetite I'm not ashamed of."

Emily started to applaud. That drew such a cold look from Kathleen that Vanessa rescued her sister, adding, "But thank you for the reminder, Mother. I suppose I should get in the habit of eating more sparingly with the Season soon upon us."

Charley broke the tense moment with the question, "When is the commencement of this Season I keep hearing about?"

"It's already begun, though not officially yet," Layla said.

"It follows the sessions of Parliament because that is

when so many lords are in London with their families," Emily added.

"There is no exact date," Kathleen said. "Early in May can be considered the official start, but a few invitations have already trickled in, even here in the country, so we shall be leaving for London by the end of next week."

"I am devastated," Charley confessed.

The boy actually did look crestfallen, which had Kathleen assure him, "You can, of course, come to London with us. Or you can remain here in seclusion. Either of my houses will be at your disposal for however long you require them."

Vanessa stood up and feigned a light laugh. "I believe I've had enough food. I will await the rest of you in the music room."

She didn't like being reminded yet again that she would be parting company with Monty so soon. She should have known. Father had warned her that Kathleen favored London in May. It's why she had left Scotland in early April, so she would have plenty of time to get to Cheshire before Kathleen and the twins left. And hadn't she already expected to part with her companions while they were still on the road? But they hadn't parted. Monty and Charley had come here instead, and she somehow had thought that would give her a lot more time with her new friends.

She was feeling as downhearted as Charley, so it took a moment for her to grasp Monty's remark behind her. "I don't think George knew that our hostess would be deserting us when he arranged our sojourn here."

She turned, saw his half smile, and had the ridiculous urge to run to him and put her arms around him, but it was gone the instant her mother came into the music room behind him. Kathleen apparently hadn't heard him, because she moved to one of the padded chairs set up in front of the piano and harp without comment, and Charley joined her there.

When the twins came in, arm in arm, they moved to their favored instruments, the piano and the harp that were the focus of the room. There were a dozen chairs in the room, too, for musical entertainment after the dinner parties Kathleen often arranged for her neighbors and friends in town. The girls hadn't usually been invited to the table, young as they'd been, but their mother had often shown them off to her guests by asking them to play afterward.

Vanessa had favored the piano and hadn't realized that Layla did, too, because it was against Layla's nature to fight for a choice. She apparently got that choice after Vanessa had deserted them. Emily checked the strings of her harp, plucking a few of them. Monty moved to the empty space on the left side of the room and held out a hand to Vanessa for her to join him there.

She started to, but as soon as the twins started playing, she paused, tears came to her eyes, and she smiled widely at her sisters. They were playing her song!

Monty noticed her reaction and approached to lead her to the space that served as a small dance floor. "A favorite song?" he guessed.

She smiled. "I suppose it is, but this one I actually composed."

"An accomplishment I wouldn't have expected!"

"You don't have to look so bloody surprised," she admonished playfully. "But I didn't expect it, either. Composing music wasn't exactly part of our curriculum here. Our music teacher merely asked if any of us were interested in learning about composition. The twins didn't want to, but I thought it might be fun and gave it a try. Keep in mind, I was barely twelve at the time."

"Which makes it even more impressive."

She grinned. "There are many things about me that you don't know."

"What an intriguing remark. Your melody is lovely. Shall we put it to good use?"

But the music suddenly stopped, and she couldn't help laughing. "I'm afraid that's as far as I got. I never did finish the composition."

"Which doesn't mean you can't."

"Someday," she agreed.

He had moved her into position, placing her hands where they needed to be, one on his shoulder, one lightly touching his extended hand, then placed his other hand on her waist, which sent a tingle of excitement through her. "My sisters didn't learn the waltz for their come-outs," he said, "though I'm sure they have by now. The cotillion was still popular when they came of age, a much more lively country dance embraced by the *ton*. But the waltz is now quite fashionable, even if it still has detractors among the old guard. Close contact and all that rot, not that we're going to do that, mind you—more's the pity! However, George likes the waltz, and what George likes . . ."

She managed not to laugh over his "more's the pity," and asked, "Do many people call the Prince Regent by his first name?"

"You're assuming I'm referring to the Prince?"

"Don't pretend you aren't."

The twins started another song, and he said, "Follow me," and she concentrated on not stepping on one of his feet for a moment until she heard, "You've coiffed your hair and you're wearing proper shoes, I suppose I must ask for kisses first now that you've so perfectly donned the lady?" and she stepped on his foot.

She didn't apologize for the misstep, she instead gave him a coy look. "You're reneging on our bet not to mention kissing, but would you really want to risk a no?"

"Does that mean . . . ?"

She grinned. "You'll just have to find out."

"Tease! You're just looking for a reason to punch me again."

"Now that might be true—especially if you aren't taking this lesson seriously."

"I'll concede—for now."

She got the hang of it pretty quickly when he made it so easy to follow his lead, but she pretended not to and stepped on his feet a few more times. She simply didn't want the dance lesson to end. And she definitely got his point about the close contact being frowned upon by the old guard, not that their bodies touched, but being even a foot apart from Monty when he was holding her hand and had his other hand on her waist was quite titillating. How the devil could one man excite her so much when he wasn't even trying?

And then Charley insisted on taking a twirl with Layla, while Kathleen took over for her at the piano. Emily got a turn and was giggling at Charley's blandishments. The mood in the room had turned quite festive. Even Kathleen seemed to be having fun. Vanessa was happy dancing with Monty and seeing her sisters and mother so gay, but she still felt a bittersweet pang. The evening would have been perfect if her father were there.

Chapter Twenty-six

Montgomery tried to keep his thoughts from wandering hither and yon as he finished shaving, otherwise he'd end up slicing his throat. He was already dressed, had intended to go downstairs for breakfast with the Blackburn family, but then he'd thought about the end of next week, when the ladies would no longer be in residence, and he was struck with annoyance and something that might be melancholy.

Bloody hell. Charley's distress was contagious. And yet he did wonder what the devil he was going to do with himself when the lovely distractions marched out the door and he was left wondering what could possibly have induced Vanessa to agree to marry a man she hadn't met? The amazing wench who'd trotted across England in britches wouldn't have done that. She'd bloody well stand up for what she wanted. Not having an answer to that was going to drive him crazy. And would he even know if she ended up turning Rathban down in the end? Not stuck in the country he wouldn't.

He supposed he could stay foxed for the duration. He had initially thought that this particular favor for George was going to be a boring task and he'd been prepared to suffer through it—until Vanessa had arrived to liven it up considerably. But she'd very quickly become his focus and *too* much of a distraction. He couldn't seem to help himself, even after finding out that she was a lady.

That he couldn't get her out of his head wasn't helping a'tall. Logically, the women's departure was going to nip these unwanted feelings in the bud. He hoped. But what if it didn't? Ridiculously, he was already missing her when she hadn't even left yet!

Annoyed with himself, he went downstairs to see if anyone was left in the dining room. Charley must be, because Arlo, looking somewhat bored, was standing at attention outside the door in case he was needed. But then Montgomery paused when he heard the twins squealing in delight inside the room and one of them exclaiming, "A king in our house!"

He stepped into the doorway, noted that only the twins and Charley were in the room, caught the boy's eye, and directed him out of the room but didn't wait for compliance. He was already halfway to the front door when Charley complained, "Do wait up."

"We're going for a ride. If you don't know how, too bad, we're going anyway."

"Is there a reason we're going outdoors?"

"I might yell."

"Oh," Charley said, apparently guessing why. "Very well, but I have a good reason."

Montgomery didn't pause to hear it and his stride was long. He was angry, at Charley, at himself, at Vanessa for getting herself engaged to a rotter like Rathban. It was a bit much, and he didn't want to take it all out on Charley, so he ignored the boy until they were mounted, along with Arlo, who had insisted on accompanying them and had ridden out of view of anyone in the house, then reined in under a stately oak.

Charley had kept up with him, did indeed know how to ride, sat on the horse almost in a military fashion, which was a bit odd, though who knew what sort of teachers the lad had had growing up.

Montgomery didn't mince words, said with sharp censure, "Explain to me why you have utterly disregarded everything I warned you about?"

Charley wasn't cowed, was instead a little loud in his explanation. "They intend to abandon us tomorrow!"

"What happened to next week?"

"A letter was delivered this morning. I was there when the countess made the announcement that it changes their schedule. That won't do! These ladies are delightful. And I am in love with Vanessa. She cannot be removed from my entourage. I won't allow it."

"Boy, wake up. You're too young to be in love. You are

a target, so having women anywhere around you, other than in that house, puts them in danger as well. And you don't have a bloody entourage, you have *me*."

Charley sighed. "I had hoped they would remain here if they knew who I really am."

Montgomery snorted. "Nothing will keep newly turned eighteen-year-old ladies of the *ton* from their first Season in London."

"Vanessa missed hers."

So she did, and Montgomery wished he knew why, but the lady was as secretive as he was about certain things. He narrowed his eyes on Charley. "You will tell the sisters you were joking and you will make them believe it."

Feigned or not, Charley sighed again with unmistakable sadness. "I really am the last surviving king of Feldland, you know. I don't know why you don't want to believe it."

"I'll tell you why. Because it would scare the hell out of me if I thought for even a moment that I was the only hope for a country I've never even heard of, of keeping their monarch alive long enough to get back on the throne. You trying to scare me, boy?"

"Of course not. But I have every confidence in you. And if I must lie to the Blackburn ladies about who I really am, then we shall instead go to London when the ladies do to experience the Season, as they call it."

"No."

A full measure of haughtiness reared back up when Charley huffed, "Need I mention I outrank you?"

"Need I remind you we came to Cheshire to hide? You won't be safe in London."

"Yes, I will, if I wear a disguise."

"Who the deuce gave you that idea?"

"Arlo has nagged me from the beginning that I ought to change my appearance."

"Don't say I did the same. I don't nag."

"You did want me dressed in rags on the way here," Charley reminded.

"The devil I did. Putting on a cloak and removing your jewels was all I requested—and men in rags don't hobnob with ladies."

"But a simpler disguise would be possible, wouldn't it? To allow us to move about in your society without being found out? No one would be looking for us in such circles."

To hide in plain sight would indeed be possible. At least for the boy, but not for him when he had cuckolds looking for him in those circles. Yet damned if he wasn't struck by a moment of temptation anyway, until he realized it was because he abhorred the idea of Nessi's going off on her own to meet the cur she'd been promised to. But trotting the boy back into danger wasn't the deal he'd made with George.

So again he said, "No."

But he'd waited a moment too long in the second denial, which prompted Charley's guess, "You were thinking about it. Don't deny it. You must think more quickly. Their departure is imminent."

He gave the boy a nasty look, but Arlo interrupted the argument. "Look yonder." He was pointing to the south.

Montgomery turned to see a menacing group of mounted strangers approaching them. He didn't for a moment think that they might be locals returning home. And he hadn't brought his pistols, hadn't been wearing them inside the house and hadn't planned on the ride. Bloody hell.

"Do we return to the house?" Charley asked.

"No, we're not leading them there. We ride fast for Dawton town, where they won't dare attack."

Which is what they started to do, but the men behind them had superior horses and were gaining on them. And then a shot was fired, which changed Montgomery's mind. They were easy targets out in the open like this.

"Follow!" he yelled, and directed Charley and Arlo to a small copse of trees for cover.

He was furious at himself by then for not having a single weapon on him. He would have to yank the chasers off their horses and see if he could confiscate a few weapons to deal with the rest. But their pursuers reached them too quickly. No sooner did they get to the trees and dismount to take cover than the rebels were upon them.

Charley hurled a dagger at one man that struck true. Montgomery was a little incredulous, seeing that. What did Feldlanders teach their children? He grabbed the man's pistol as he fell to the ground. Another shot was fired, and he panicked until he saw Charley and Arlo running behind a tree. Then Monty fired the confiscated pistol and snarled when he found it empty. He flipped it over in his hand and bludgeoned another attacker with it as the man was dismounting. He took his fists to the next one, and out of the corner of his eye saw Charley doing the same to another rebel, which infuriated him. Why hadn't he remained behind the tree? With the boy not staying out of firing range, Montgomery was forced to get between him and the assailants.

But no more shots were fired in such close quarters and having to deal with the three men in front of him, he didn't immediately notice when another man grabbed Arlo from his cover and rode off with him. Charley noticed and immediately jumped on his horse to give chase. Montgomery growled, cracked the pistol against another head, then leapt toward his horse to go after Charley. He glanced back to see if the last two assailants were going to do likewise, only to see they'd mounted and were riding off in the opposite direction. To get more reinforcements? And the mount he and Charley were chasing was still faster than the nags they were riding. They weren't catching up to the abductor.

Chapter Twenty-seven

VANESSA WAS STILL A little dazed after her mother took her into her study to give her the good news—good news in Kathleen's opinion. Vanessa wasn't so sure. Albert Rathban had finally answered Kathleen's missive. He had concurred that the engagement could move forward and to that end, he was hosting a ball at his own residence in London so the affianced couple could meet. They had barely a week to arrive in time for it, which meant they had to depart in the morning.

Vanessa met that news with aplomb, though that certainly wasn't how she felt. It was one thing to accept this engagement to a man she didn't know, quite another for it to be this imminent. She would be giving up so much, her dreams of the perfect marriage that would include a signed contract, her independence, the freedoms she had become accustomed to. And she knew in her heart that her father would never approve—if he knew. He would never ask her to make this sacrifice for him, though

Kathleen had no such qualms. But she had to do this! She couldn't bear the thought of William living out the rest of his life alone and away from everyone he loved. But if there was still some other way to attain the same goal, she would pursue it with alacrity.

Bemoaning her limited options, she changed back into her trousers and hooded cloak and went for a long hard ride on Snow to work off her frustration. She wasn't ready to leave Monty this quickly, she wasn't ready to meet the man she had agreed she must marry this quickly, either.

She'd circled around the property to head south when she saw the rider galloping in her direction with someone tossed over his saddle, legs dangling. And it appeared two others were following—or chasing the rider, and one had bright golden hair. Charley? But when she heard Monty yelling in the distance, she squinted and could make out his large frame on one of the horses and realized in alarm what was happening.

The rider, trying to keep an eye on his pursuers behind him rather than what was in front of him, noticed her almost too late and tried to veer away. Vanessa didn't, and she was riding fast enough that she needed only to steer Snow in his direction then abruptly to the side for a collision to occur, Snow's shoulder slamming against the smaller mount. The other horse stumbled, losing its balance. Snow reared up to avoid the horse's flailing legs. Arlo pushed himself off the animal before it crashed to the ground. It all happened so quickly. Vanessa saw Arlo sprawled in the grass, but at least a few feet away from the fallen horse. The rider wasn't as lucky with one of his legs trapped beneath his horse.

Charley arrived almost immediately, jumped off his mount, and ran over to Arlo.

"Is he all right?" Vanessa asked, dismounting from Snow.

"Yes, just somewhat stunned," Charley said, helping Arlo to his feet. Then he beamed at Vanessa. "That was incredible, what magnificent bravery!"

"Indeed," Arlo agreed, rubbing his arm. "Many thanks, Lady Vanessa."

Monty dismounted next to her and scolded, "What is it about those clothes that makes you take such risks?"

She couldn't be daunted after such success and grinned. "It was Snow's idea. He deserves all the credit. I told you he has the strength and spirit of a warhorse." Monty gave her an admonishing look but before he could do more, she asked, "What happened? How did your enemies find you and why was one of them riding away with Arlo?"

"Those rebels are relentless!" Charley fumed. "Seven of them attacked us. Monty and I were fighting them off and when they couldn't apprehend me, one of them snatched my servant as a hostage and rode off."

"No more heroics, boy!" Monty walked over to the fallen horse. Vanessa joined him and together they helped the horse back to its feet. She saw the rider was unconscious no doubt due to the pain of his crushed leg. Monty hoisted the man over the now skittish mount before asking Charley, "All of those shots missed, correct? Or do I need to find a doctor when I take this fellow to town?"

"We're fine, but I think your horse got nicked, so you probably shouldn't ride him. And we'll go with you to town."

"No, you won't. The townsfolk can't get a gander at those golden locks of yours. Our hiding place might be compromised but Dawton Manor is still the safest place for you right now. I'll escort you back there. I need a few more horses to transport the miscreants we left behind to the constable."

"You can ride with me," Vanessa offered as she remounted her giant horse. "Snow could carry all of us if he had to."

He nodded and tied off the reins of the two other horses to her saddle, then mounted Snow, sitting behind her, while Charley and Arlo started off ahead of them, talking loudly, perhaps arguing, she couldn't tell which, they were so far ahead of her. Monty put his hands on her hips since she wasn't giving up Snow's reins for him to hold.

She was very cognizant of that touch and she couldn't stop herself from leaning back against him.

"That could have gone much worse than it did, if you hadn't come to the rescue." He pulled her closer to him. "But we might have caught up to that abductor if your mother didn't keep such a poorly stocked stable, not a thoroughbred in the lot."

"I'm sure you would have."

Monty laughed and tugged on her queued-back hair. "So brave, bold, and beautiful, yet self-effacing. Quite a tantalizing combination," he added close to her ear. Then more sternly, "But never do anything like that again, Nessi. You could have been hurt. And I would hate for anything to happen to this lovely neck."

Vanessa gasped when she felt his mouth on the side of her neck, kissing her, nibbling her there. Shivers of pure pleasure rippled through her, and she craned her neck to give him greater access. She'd never expected to experience this kind of passion on a horse! And then Monty's hands moved down from her hips to her upper thighs, and he began to stroke her there. Her breath caught in her throat, she was so startled by the heat suddenly flaring deep inside her.

"And now I am reminded that you're not a lady today in these pants," Monty murmured hotly in her ear.

She sucked in her breath as his hands started to slowly roam up and down her body, over her belly, over her breasts, then back down to her thighs. He was taking thrilling new liberties with her, and she let him because she knew they would be parting tomorrow. How could she pass up this once-in-a-lifetime opportunity for a passionate encounter with a man she truly liked and was so wildly attracted to?

"I could turn around," she suggested.

"God, wench, don't tempt me further."

"You're tempting *me*!" she said, leaning forward and sitting up straight.

"How nice that we can argue over who is tempting whom. But seriously, my only excuse is that I don't often have the pleasure of holding you in my arms. And it seemed a natural way of thanking you for all you did today. Now, back to the business of being a guardian," Monty said with a sigh, lowering his hands and resting them lightly on her hips.

The manor was in sight now. Vanessa sighed, too, wishing she hadn't started donning dresses as quickly as she had.

BACK AT THE HOUSE Charley went off to find the twins to tell them he'd been joking about his royal status while Montgomery fetched his pistols and some rope, then rode back to the scene of the battle. Four horses were still grazing there, but as he got closer, he saw that one of the assailants had regained consciousness and was kneeling by one of the others, trying to wake him. But the fellow must have heard him approaching and quickly abandoned his friends, riding off to the south. Montgomery didn't even consider giving chase when it was yet another fast horse racing away and he was riding yet another nag. And four culprits apprehended still put a big dent in that little army.

The town spread out before him, but he'd found out the other day that it was bigger than he'd hoped, which had kept him there longer than he'd planned. He'd asked around discreetly if any strangers had been seen in town and had received only negative replies. After what had happened today, however, it was obvious that Cheshire wasn't as safe as George had assured him it would be.

When he brought the four captured attackers to the constable, he warned the official that three more had gotten away and might be showing up in town today. But before Montgomery returned to Dawton Manor, he realized that the three men who escaped might already be in town, and now that they knew that their quarry was in the area, would be asking questions themselves, and where better to do that than in a tavern. So he rode to the southernmost tavern he'd noticed earlier and entered it, which those men would likely have done, too, if they'd just come from the Blackburn lands south of town. And it was a good guess. There did happen to be three men standing at the bar.

As he approached, he heard one of them say to the barkeep, "Golden locks? Fancy dresser?"

"Nay."

"Any other lords living in town they might sneak in to visit?"

The questions were being asked by a man who spoke perfect English, not what Montgomery had been expecting.

"Aye, a guidly number," the barkeep answered. "We've a quiet town the gentry fancy tae escape the crowds o' wicked London."

Montgomery knew that voice. He rolled his eyes when Donnan MacCabe turned around and set mugs of ale on the bar for the three men who then moved off to a table. He kept his face averted until he reached the bar.

"What the devil are *you* doing here?" he asked.

The Scot shrugged. "Calum and I thought it a guid idea, with ye staying in the same house with our wee lass, for one o' us tae keep an eye on the town. And where better tae do that than in a tavern. And rather than drink this place dry, which I would surely have done, I got a job instead."

"Did those three men ask anything else before I got here?" Montgomery queried.

"Nay, but it was surely funny listening tae the foreigners trying tae tell their hireling what tae ask aboot when they canna speak the English tongue themselves, least no' more'n a few words o' it."

"Damn, when I heard English being spoken I'd hoped I'd gotten it wrong and they were just thieves."

"Wishing for one trouble o'er another, I'm thinking ye have tae many and a guid thing the lass will be hieing off soon away from ye. Since they've hired a sassenach tae speak for them, I'm guessing these are the ones she said are after the wee laddie?"

"Yes."

Donnan raised a brow. "Ye kin if they dinna find what they look for here, they'll move off tae some other shire?"

"But I'll feel better if I at least bash their heads."

"Aye, but then ye'd need to kill them or they'll be waking and thinking they've come exactly tae the right place."

"They already know, just not where we're staying," Montgomery said, confident that the rebels wouldn't be here now with their interpreter if they knew Charley was staying at the manor. He explained about the encounter that had occurred on Blackburn lands, ending with, "And no, your lass wasn't part of that fight." Well, mostly she wasn't.

But Montgomery paused, then grinned. "These blokes weren't supposed to get this close," he continued. "So it appears we will be traveling with the ladies to London after all—and as you say, these three need a reason to waste their time around here."

"Dinna say *I* gave ye that excuse," the Scot growled low as he slammed a mug down in front of Montgomery.

Montgomery laughed. "No, Charley beat you to it."

Chapter Twenty-eight

"WELL, DON'T YOU LOOK—different!" Vanessa exclaimed.

Charley had come out to bid them farewell, and Vanessa didn't recognize him at first without his magnificent mane of golden locks. He'd dyed his hair black! It still cascaded down his shoulders and back but was certainly no longer the beacon it had been. She still couldn't believe it, considering how vain the boy was, so she tugged on a lock to see if it was a wig. It wasn't, but the tug made him laugh.

The twins had regaled her yesterday morning before she left for her ride with an account of Charley's announcement that he was a king, but then in the afternoon they brought her the disappointing news that he'd confessed that he'd been joking about it. Vanessa didn't mention that fib to him now, or ask which of his statements had actually been a fib, but she did wonder why he hadn't gone to this extreme to disguise himself before leaving London. "Why now?" she asked.

"Anything to remain near your side, dearest lady," he said with a wide smile. "Even if I weren't in love with you, which I most assuredly am, you also have my undying gratitude for your brave assistance yesterday."

Remain? She hadn't heard much after that. And then she saw his coach behind her mother's two coaches, already loaded with his many trunks, and her heart beat a little faster. She gasped, "You're traveling with us?"

"Did Monty not tell you?"

No, Monty did *not*. But she hadn't exactly seen much of him yesterday after he left to deal with the wounded men they'd left behind, only at dinner last night where they weren't alone. Charley hadn't attended that dinner, neither had Kathleen, but the twins had been with them and had talked excitedly about departing for London in the morning. Monty hadn't looked disappointed by that news. She had thought he must have already heard about it with the house bustling most of the day with so many preparations for their impending departure. But now she wondered if he had already decided he and Charley would travel with them. But why? Didn't that defeat his purpose in coming here? Or did he no longer think the manor was safe after the encounter yesterday?

Confused and yet still incredibly pleased by the unexpected arrangement, she warned Charley, "Dye doesn't last very long, so I hope you have more."

"Indeed, Monty brought me an ample supply when he returned from town yesterday. And I shall ride with you ladies to keep you entertained."

"No, you won't," Monty said as he rode forward, leading Snow with him. "A week of listening to your incessant chatter and Lady Kathleen will bar us from her London residence. Seeing the ladies at mealtime will suffice for you, boy."

Charley huffed and moved to his coach. Monty tossed Vanessa Snow's reins, saying, "I saw him saddled, so I assumed you are going to ride today."

"Just part of the way," she said. "He's not used to the sidesaddle yet."

"And neither are you?"

"I learned. My father made sure of it. I just don't like it any more than Snow does."

"But ladies must persevere."

He appeared to be waiting with some curiosity to see if she would jump up to mount as she usually did. Of course she couldn't do that now when she was wearing a riding habit, and he knew that, was already starting to dismount to help her when a footman ran forward with a stool she could use as a mounting block.

Once she was mounted, he asked, "Has your mother seen that horse?"

"No."

"You like annoying her, don't you?"

She grinned. "Is it that obvious?"

He laughed. "A little. Care to mention why?"

She didn't and said instead, "I'm more curious about why you didn't say something last night about your decision to return to London."

"Because it wasn't yet a foregone conclusion. I was still debating the merits of it."

"What made you decide to go?"

"I didn't think Charley would dye his hair." He gave her a half grin. "I couldn't tell him no after he made that sacrifice."

So it was Charley's idea, not his? Odd that Monty would give in on this when he usually ignored Charley's preferences. And they'd come to Dawton Manor to hide far away from London.

They moved to the front of the line of coaches to wait until everyone had boarded. Out of the shade of the house, she noticed the slight bruise on his cheek. She hadn't seen it last night possibly because the candelabras on the dining table had limited her view of him, but it was apparent now in the sunshine.

"Fell out of bed, did you?" she teased, pointing at his cheek.

"No, your Scots guard was annoyed with me." She gasped and stared beyond him at the MacCabe brothers, both already mounted and waiting for the coaches to depart. "They wouldn't hit you!"

"No, they probably wouldn't," he agreed. "But Donnan was annoyed enough not to help me when I dealt with the three remaining men who escaped the fight yesterday."

Her eyes widened. "So you confirmed that those men are Charley's enemies?"

"Yes, I found them in town asking questions about

him, well, their interpreter was. They'd hired an Englishman to speak for them. But he didn't understand their native tongue, either. Your Scot said they used pantomime to communicate to him the questions they wanted him to ask. But he ran off as soon as the scuffle started, yelling, "They didn't pay me to fight for them!"

"I assume you won against the two and they are now in jail?"

"No, I left them unconscious. I'd rather they waste their time searching all over Cheshire, and if there are more of them in England, these two can get word to them about where Charley has gone into hiding. They and their cohorts will know with certainty that we aren't in London, so chances of any of them looking there again are next to none."

Well, she obviously wasn't going to hear, "And I couldn't bear to part from you," so she said no more. And Kathleen finally came out of the house. She did not have to board her coach to find out that Vanessa wasn't in it with the twins when Snow caught her eye.

With a cringe, Vanessa wondered if her mother was going to walk over to her and insist she travel inside the vehicle as a lady ought to. It would be a long walk for Kathleen to reach her with both Blackburn coaches harnessed with four horses for greater speed. Kathleen did neither, but Vanessa didn't doubt she'd hear about it later when they stopped for lunch. If they stopped. This was going to be a very hurried trip. After all, they had an important ball to attend in a week's time.

Chapter Twenty-nine

Vanessa stood at the parlor window waiting for the horses to be brought around so she and her sisters could go riding in Hyde Park. Kathleen was on the sofa behind her, going through all the invitations that had already come in. Her mother seemed so happy, so vibrant now that she was back in London.

Suddenly the very proper, punctilious butler entered and, trying his best to hide his annoyance, said, "Lord Bates has requested that yet another armoire be brought up to his bedroom. Would that be acceptable, Lady Blackburn?"

Kathleen didn't even glance up from the invitations in her lap to say, "Of course, he can have the one in the empty bedroom on the third floor."

Vanessa smiled, amused that Charley and Arlo hadn't yet finished unpacking Charley's wardrobe even though they'd all arrived yesterday. Mr. Rickles looked aggrieved, had likely hoped for a different answer, but then he wasn't at all pleased with their houseguests after Monty had called him Pickles yesterday instead of Rickles, and Vanessa, at least, was sure Monty had done so deliberately because he couldn't resist ribbing the stiff, stuffy butler.

Kathleen rose a few minutes later to join Vanessa at the window and remarked, "There are so many social events to attend, we're all going to have a lovely time!" But then her expression turned aghast. "You can*not* ride that beast in the park!"

Vanessa raised a brow at her mother, but Kathleen was still staring out the parlor window that faced the street where the horses had just been led. The twins hadn't come downstairs yet to join them, which meant they could both, for the moment, speak their minds.

"Yes, I can," Vanessa stated simply.

Kathleen swung about, her expression rife with anger. "It's a draft horse!"

"This fine riding habit I'm wearing will suggest otherwise. And he's a magnificent beauty. I won't be surprised if I get a number of offers for him. He makes a fine placard for the breeding farm I intend to open one day."

Kathleen humphed. "The Rathbans will never allow something that common. You will need to undertake more genteel hobbies."

That was *not* what Vanessa wanted to hear! She was giving up everything else for this marriage, she wouldn't give up the stable she wanted, too. "Then I may have to do some bargaining with Albert Rathban myself. As a wedding gift, he can promise me that I'll have a place on his estate to further Snow's line."

"You're going to make that ridiculous demand and risk losing his agreement to allow your father to return home?"

Kathleen almost looked panicked, so Vanessa assured her, "You misunderstand. I would never make it an ultimatum, Mother, or risk your bargain. I would merely make the suggestion, and only after the engagement is secure. But if it will relieve your mind, I suppose I could wait until after the marriage to mention it."

Mollified, but still staring at Snow, Kathleen mentioned, "We have other, more suitable, horses."

"But I love that one, have raised him from birth."

Vanessa didn't add that she'd helped with that birth, which would appall her mother. But she resented that Kathleen was treating her like a child she could control and was so insistent on curtailing yet another of her freedoms.

Hoping to drop the subject, she added, "We'll be back in plenty of time to rest and prepare for the ball tonight."

"Are you being deliberately obtuse to think that might be of concern at this moment? You are among the *ton* now, the people whose opinions matter. Even you must know that riding a draft horse in Hyde Park would be scandalous. I could have sworn you promised you would not misbehave in public and embarrass this family."

Vanessa's cheeks bloomed with color. She had indeed said that, and she did indeed get Kathleen's point, but couldn't her mother have reminded her of that to begin with instead of saying no and expecting that to work as it did on the twins? She hated it, but she was going to have to concede on this one thing.

"As fond as I am of Snow, as uniquely beautiful as he is, and I might add, I've never viewed him as a draft horse, he has never been an embarrassment to me. But you are quite right, Mother. He isn't suitable for a lady's mount in town."

"Thank you for seeing reason."

Vanessa felt a little choked up at having another chunk of her independence whittled away. "Excuse me while I request a new horse."

She left the room and went outside to do that and also to give Snow a bit of petting. She whispered to him her apology and her promise to still visit him each day to attend to his grooming, then she told the groom holding Snow's reins, "I'll need a different mount, please."

"I honestly didn't think you would."

She hadn't actually looked at any of the three grooms but turned about now with a laugh, recognizing Monty's voice. "What the devil are you doing dressed like a groom?"

"Because I'm part of your escort."

"Why?"

"Why not? Charley isn't the only one who can make sacrifices in exchange for our new lodgings."

She laughed again. "So you're going to be a groom for our entire stay in London?"

"Bite your tongue, I'm not subservient enough for that.

And I was teasing. Your mother would never request payment for her kindness."

"A tweed cap and jacket is not much of a disguise," she pointed out.

"It's not meant to be other than for your mother who might object to me escorting you. Voilà, a mere change of clothes and I can steal more time with you. How could I resist? And as it happens, I'll be attending your ball tonight, too."

"Really?"

He grinned. "Surprised? I just won't be arriving with you, since that would point out to any interested parties where I'm abiding."

It was a delightful turn, but she still had to mention, "I thought you were still in hiding."

He shrugged. "Revealing myself might present a few personal pitfalls, but nothing I can't handle. It was imperative that Charley change his appearance before we came here, and he's done a fine job of it."

"I'm still surprised that you would want to go. As a rake, I didn't think you would favor balls and the like."

"To be honest I never have, but I feel compelled to attend this one so I can console you after you meet your fiancé."

She frowned at him. "That's not nice."

"Neither is he."

"Do stop disparaging him. I'm sure I will find something about him to like, and if not, I shall cry."

"Good," he said without any sympathy. "Now I'll find you a stodgy old mare to ride."

She choked back another laugh. "Don't you dare! She at least needs to be spry!"

The twins were coming down the stairs when she reentered the house, Layla in a white riding habit, Emily in a pink one, and both bubbling with excitement. This would be their first ride in a London park. Kathleen had never brought them to London with her, though as Kathleen had told her, she hadn't come here often herself after William left the country.

"We will be another moment," Vanessa said. "I've had to request a different horse."

"A shame," Layla said.

But Emily had the same thought as Kathleen. "I assumed you would know better than to ride the white one in London."

"Yes, I merely forgot," Vanessa replied, not wanting to acknowledge Emily's supercilious tone, at least not now, since it would undoubtedly put her and her sister at odds for their ride. But she intended to get Emily alone one of these days to find out why she had turned so disagreeable toward her. It wasn't constant, but from time to time she would make catty remarks to Vanessa for no reason—at least, no reason Vanessa could think of.

The twins didn't notice Monty when they came outside, though they weren't in the habit of paying attention to grooms. But on the short ride to the park, Vanessa laughed at herself when she recalled what she had originally thought of London, and what had turned her away from it—too much smoke and soot. This area of the town was utterly different, with beautiful, clean streets, not at all congested, exactly what she had imagined it would be like before she had turned away in disgust nearly three weeks ago. When her mother's coach had entered the city yesterday afternoon, she had closed her eyes for a few minutes. But by the time they'd reached Grosvenor Square in the area of Mayfair where Kathleen's new town house was located, she'd been utterly pleased with London—at least this part of it. Elegant homes, fancy carriages and coaches, well-dressed couples strolling the streets. No wonder Kathleen used to love coming here.

In the park, Monty surprised the twins with his presence and his attire. Emily was a little embarrassed that she hadn't noticed him sooner, but Layla did question his disguise, to which he rejoined, "I didn't want to scare away any young gentlemen who try to meet you today."

Yet he stopped behaving like a groom and rode between the twins instead of behind them with the other two grooms. He kept up a steady banter with them, provoking giggles, laughs, even a few blushes. Vanessa began to feel neglected, riding on Layla's other side, but it was just as well that he paid some attention to the twins. If he spoke with only her, they might wonder if there was more than friendship between her and Monty. There was; she just wasn't sure exactly what it was—flirting, a mutual attraction that sometimes ran out of control, letting herself be led astray by a charming rake? And she'd been a little too bold and daring with him, but no more. She had an arranged marriage to take care of now that she was in London. But he was definitely amusing the twins. She loved how easily he could make those around him laugh.

But he did fall back when the gentlemen in the park started catching up to the girls to introduce themselves. Vanessa was greeted almost as an afterthought, which made her want to laugh because she'd been expecting it. The twins were a novelty, after all, identical *and* beautiful. None of the young men stayed long, but all expressed hope that they would meet again. And the twins were thrilled. They hadn't even attended their first social event yet and they were already a success.

Chapter Thirty

VANESSA FELT EXCITED ABOUT her first ball in London, even if it would be at the home of people she despised. It was still a momentous event for her, one she should be sharing with both her parents, but that wasn't possible. At least she could share it with her sisters. But her nervousness mounted as the hour to depart approached and now it was overshadowing the excitement. She would be meeting her future husband tonight. She would have to speak with Albert Rathban at some point in the evening, too, and not revile him as she'd like to do. She would have to be on her best behavior—she would have to be a lady.

She certainly looked the part. Her ball gown was exquisite, such a pale aquamarine it might be mistaken for white in sunlight, but it would never be worn during the day. The trimming was a complementary shade of turquoise, but very thin so the bold color couldn't be objected to. And then Kathleen arrived in her room, carrying her jewelry box, which she opened on Vanessa's vanity. She held up emeralds to Vanessa's neck, then sapphires, but in the end decided a necklace of opals would suit her and her gown better. She had a ring and bracelet to go with it and even a few matching pins that she tucked into Vanessa's coiffure.

"You're going to make me very, very proud tonight," Kathleen said, and gave her a hug.

Vanessa laughed, hearing an order in that remark rather than a prediction, but she allowed, "I intend to behave, even if I must bite my tongue until it bleeds."

Kathleen tsked. "Don't be dramatic."

"When I hate Albert Rathban above all people? But I will endeavor not to show it."

"I remember my first ball," Kathleen said with a smile. "It was the highlight of my youth. I hope you can relax and simply enjoy this one, Nessa."

Vanessa was surprised at how sincere Kathleen sounded. Maybe she was sincere. Circumstances had brought them both to this particular point in their relationship, but she had never doubted, at least, not in the past, that Kathleen wanted the best for her daughters. But how could she relax enough to enjoy herself tonight when she was about to meet her future husband, who Monty claimed was a rake of the worst sort? She still hoped he'd told her that only in an effort to talk her out of an arranged engagement. A shy, awkward boy becoming a philanderer seemed so improbable to her she doubted that it was true.

"I'm nervous about meeting Daniel," Vanessa admitted.

"Don't be. You are utterly exquisite tonight. I have no doubt a'tall that you will charm him right to the altar. It's time to go."

Kathleen left the room to gather the twins. Vanessa headed to the stairs. It was a lovely town house, beautifully appointed, but it felt cramped compared to Dawton Manor, where every room was large. She reminded herself that the cottage in Scotland had been tiny in comparison.

She looked for Monty below in the hall, but he wasn't there, nor was he in the parlor waiting. But he had mentioned that he would arrive at the ball separately. Or perhaps he'd changed his mind about going. That was a disappointing thought. While her purpose in attending this ball was to meet her future husband and get acquainted with him, she'd still thought she might have some fun if Monty were there.

It didn't take long to reach the Rathban residence in the northern part of Mayfair. It was a grand old mansion that had likely been built long before the many narrow town houses had gone up in this exclusive end of town. Vanessa was surprised to see so many people already in the ballroom, considering the reason for this ball.

Kathleen whispered to her on the way in, "You are to be a surprise for Daniel. Lord Albert doesn't want his son to think he organized this ball for the express purpose of introducing you to him, which is exactly what he did. But apparently the Rathbans haven't hosted a ball in over a decade, so everyone of note clamored for an invitation. And it appears that they were successful."

And to the twins she added, "The crème de la crème of young bachelors are in attendance, as well as your competition, though truly, my darlings, you will make the other young debutantes cry tonight."

Of course there was a receiving line to meet their host—and his wife. Somehow Vanessa hadn't expected such a vengeful man to have one. Nor did she expect him to look so normal when he ought to have horns. He was in his late fifties and had black hair with only a few streaks of gray, while his wife looked older, though that might be because of the very unfashionable white wig she was wearing. But then she had come of age at a time when everyone wore them, and it was rumored that most of the older crowd who had worn them the longest had actually lost their natural hair because of it.

"There he is! That's Daniel standing just behind his parents," Kathleen whispered to Vanessa before they reached their hosts.

Vanessa's eyes moved to the portly, plain-looking young man, although there was another young man who resembled him standing near him, so she wasn't sure which one Kathleen was referring to. Both of them looked so dull *and* bored. And neither one had a rakish air about him. If they chased women expressly to get them into bed, she couldn't imagine how they accomplished it. So Monty had lied to her just to keep her from getting married so quickly? She'd give him an earful about that the next time she saw him.

And then they were standing before the elderly Rathban couple. "You haven't aged a day, Lady Blackburn," Albert said cordially to Kathleen. "I find myself very pleased that you arrived in London with your family in time to join us. We have high hopes that our little gathering shall be a success."

Such innuendo, when he was so obviously referring to their bargain! But since he was giving Vanessa a very long look as he said it, she supposed he was patting himself on the back that she was prettier than he might have expected—pretty enough to get his son to the altar. But she said not one word to him, letting her mother handle the social niceties and introductions.

And Margaret Rathban leaned close to whisper to Vanessa, "You'll do fine, m'dear. Fine indeed."

So the wife knew about the bargain, too? Yes, of course she would. Daniel was her only son, too, who wouldn't do his duty to perpetuate the family line.

Then she heard her mother greet one of the younger men, "How do you do, Daniel?"

The young man looked behind him, while Albert gave Kathleen an odd look before saying, "That's my nephew Edward and his brother Charles, John's children." Then he added pointedly, "My brother Henry wasn't blessed with children."

Kathleen started to blush over her mistake, or more likely at Albert's mention of the brother who had died in a duel because of her.

But Albert's wife was quick to add, "Daniel isn't here yet, but he will be soon."

It was a rather tense moment for the four of them, or so Vanessa thought. And she was disappointed that neither of the two dullards was Daniel. They were nothing to look at, but she was sure she could have had them eating out of her hand. But Kathleen recovered enough to say, "We will all look forward to meeting him."

Vanessa would have preferred to head for the exit, but of course she couldn't. And as soon as the Blackburn women left the line, other guests converged on them. Kathleen was warmly greeted by old friends, and gentlemen surrounded the girls, requesting the first dance, even though the music hadn't begun yet. The twins happily made their choices while Vanessa declined. She needed to keep herself available to meet the Rathban heir as soon as he arrived.

But after the first dance began, she got her mother's attention long enough to ask, "Is the son here?"

"I would say, not yet, or he would have joined his parents to greet guests that are still arriving. I imagine he's making sure to avoid that very thing and waiting for the greeting duty to be over. But I don't doubt Lord Albert will bring him by to meet you once he does make an appearance. Feel free to dance in the meantime. The boy may be tardy deliberately."

Vanessa hoped not. She would prefer to get the meeting over with, then have a good cry if it didn't go well, or enjoy herself if it did. And then the music started again. The twins' second choices were back almost instantly to lead them to the large dance floor. She caught sight of a half dozen young men heading her way again to request a dance.

But a hand suddenly slipped over hers and tugged her toward the middle of the room, and while she could see only the back of him as he wove them through the crowd, she could think of only one person who would do that without asking first. He even stole her breath for a moment as soon as he began the waltz, giving her a frontal view of him. She'd never seen Monty done up this formally, with his cravat tied perfectly, his black jacket with tails, and his auburn hair tightly queued.

He appeared to be a little amazed himself, blurting out, "Good God, Nessi, you're beautiful tonight—not that you aren't always, but tonight you take my breath. I wish you didn't. Bloody hell, did you have to primp so much?"

She burst out laughing at the complaint. "No more than you did. I suppose you feel our friendship allows you to get a dance without asking for it?" she teased.

"Of course it does, since I'm the one who taught you how to waltz." But he amended with a grin that belied the words, "I saw you shake your head at nine others and couldn't bear the thought of a similar refusal."

"Did you get here before we did?"

"I've been lurking in the shadows."

She grinned. "You snuck in uninvited?"

"Not exactly, but now it's my turn to ask a question. Why do your sisters continue to think you were in the West Indies? You've had time to tell them where you really were these last years."

She frowned. "When did that subject come up again?"

"Today during the park ride. And don't think you can't satisfy my curiosity this time."

"Actually, I must think that because I can't. It's not my secret to divulge."

"Whose, then? Your father's?" And then he laughed. "Has he been hiding from his wife? She might be a dragon, but really, six years' absence likely won't make the heart grow fonder."

"Wrong and wrong, so do stop guessing," she said tersely, then suddenly had a good reason to change the subject. "Oh, my, was that Charley who just waltzed by? His new dark hair color certainly helps him blend in."

Monty raised a skeptical brow. "In that gold brocade jacket?" But he wasn't letting the previous subject go, remarking, "George mentioned my hostess's husband was in the West Indies. Two to one in favor of the Caribbean, as it were, or does everyone think he's been in the West Indies all these years?"

"My mother knows he's not there. They just agreed to tell people that's where he went. But she doesn't know where he really is, and he doesn't want her to know."

"And you don't trust me enough to explain, when I am your favorite confidant? Dashed if I'm not wounded."

"You don't look wounded."

"Would it change your mind if I did?"

"No."

"Didn't think so."

After a few more twirls, her annoyance with him faded and her nervousness returned. "Is he here?"

He guessed whom she meant. "The lucky cur? No, I haven't seen him yet."

"Perhaps he won't show up?"

"Was that a hopeful note I just heard? Alas, I must disappoint you. I believe he lives in this residence permanently, while his parents spend most of the year in the country."

And then the cur was there, at least, she guessed as much when she saw a tall, formally dressed man kiss Lady Rathban's cheek and the lady hooked her arm through his and started leading him around for introductions.

"I think you need to return me to my mother's side," she said in a nervous tone.

"Yes, I can see that," he fairly growled, confirming her guess that Daniel had arrived.

He did return her to Kathleen, who stood with two other ladies, and he immediately slipped away, but not far. And after Kathleen introduced Vanessa to her friends, she pulled her aside. "Are you ready?"

"You know the heir is here?"

"Yes, Lord Albert just caught my eye and nodded toward his son. Smart of him to let his wife do the introductions. Apparently the boy goes out of his way to do exactly the opposite of what his father wants him to do—sound familiar?"

"Not now, Mother," Vanessa hissed in response to the slipped-in scold. "And if you spotted him, you know bloody well he's no boy, so stop calling him that. You lied to me."

"Don't be obtuse, you must know it was an honest mistake. I was sure the boy with Albert that day at the races was his son. Without actually speaking to them, I couldn't know Albert was there with his nephew. But at least the real Daniel is handsome."

Too handsome. Vanessa wouldn't be wrapping this man around her little finger. And she had agreed to the match because she thought she could!

"He's too old," Vanessa said, wishing she didn't sound apprehensive.

"Don't be absurd. He doesn't look a day over thirty. And you have nothing to be nervous about, darling. You're bound to win him instantly."

Vanessa had no such confidence, but too much was riding on Kathleen's being right. And then the two Rathbans were there before her, giving her a close-up view of the man she was engaged to, although he didn't know it yet.

He had drooping eyelids as if he'd just awoken from slumber that gave him an aura of sensuality. He was older than she would have liked, no longer a young buck exactly, and older than most of the other gentlemen who frequented debutante balls, but he certainly wasn't too old to join the marriage mart. Because of his family's wealth and titles, and his looks, he would actually be considered a prime catch. But he was also imposing, a big handsome bear of a man, with black hair in the short, wind-blown fashion, and light brown eyes that were almost amber.

His drooping eyelids suddenly made her think of snake eyes, and she choked back a nervous giggle as they were introduced to each other by his mother. But he looked so bored as Lady Margaret said all the right things and he said not a word! He couldn't be bothered to be the least bit cordial. In fact, with a rude flick of his hand he walked away after the introductions, apparently concluding that he'd met enough guests for the night. He left his mother red-cheeked and uttering apologies. Vanessa, despite her hopes that she'd find her fiancé tolerable, couldn't deny to herself that what she felt at that moment was relief. She was still going to have to do something to win him, but apparently, not tonight.

Chapter Thirty-one

"I SEE THAT WENT WELL."

Monty said it so drolly Vanessa rolled her eyes. They were dancing again, and again, Monty had stolen her away right before a number of hopefuls converged on her.

"It appears he's not interested a'tall," she remarked candidly, then sighed.

"You're disappointed?"

"Not yet, though I don't doubt I will be."

"Why?"

"Because the match still needs to happen."

"The devil it does, and besides, now you know he's too bloody old for you."

Monty's sudden outrage made her want to smile, but she didn't. He seemed jealous.

"Are you incensed on my behalf because he snubbed me? Yes, I do realize that's what he did."

"No, I'm incensed that you would still consider him as

a marital prospect *after* he snubbed you. I assumed you would come to your senses once you met him."

"I believe I mentioned that I want this match for more than the usual reasons?"

"Which are?" When she didn't answer, he growled, "I've a mind to call him out for the insult he just dealt you. You can't marry a corpse!"

She was alarmed that he would suggest a duel and appear utterly serious about it. The man *was* jealous. Maybe he had deeper feelings for her than she realized. Or maybe her interest in a match with Rathban had aroused his ridiculous male competitive instincts. In either case, she felt compelled to say, "It will bring my father back," but that was all she was going to admit.

"To walk you down the aisle?"

She jumped on that excuse, lying, "Yes," when she knew very well that Rathban would insist on the wedding taking place before he relinquished his grudge.

"And marriage to a decent chap won't do?"

"No, and stop trying to figure out why. At least Daniel isn't ugly," she added.

"Just in spirit."

"It still may not come to pass," she said, hoping the subject could be dropped. "You saw how thoroughly he dismissed me with a bloody flick of his hand."

"You bore him."

She gasped, even sputtered, "How—?"

"Oh, settle down," he cut in. "I warned you he was a

rake of the worst sort, while you're too typical, dressed and coiffed like every other young debutante here. You have to stand out from the pack if you want him to notice you. Sweetheart, your beauty already makes you a beacon to most men, but it's not enough to attract Daniel Rathban, who is jaded beyond redemption." Then he relented, giving her a half smile. "If you haven't noticed, the cur has left the room. So enjoy yourself, Nessi. This is your first ball, after all."

She intended to—if she could now, when none of what he'd just said reassured her. If anything, it brought on more worries. Monty was himself a professed rake, and he certainly didn't ignore her. Jaded? Did that imply nothing could pique Daniel's interest anymore?

ACROSS THE ROOM, KATHLEEN braced herself when she saw Lord Albert bearing down on her and quickly moved toward the terrace, hoping to prevent a scene. He looked angry enough not to care if he caused one. But he did follow her and, thankfully, it was too early in the evening for anyone else to be out there.

"Didn't you explain to your gel what would be necessary?" he demanded immediately.

She blushed. "You saw her, she's utterly dazzling—I thought that would be enough."

"It's obviously not enough, but I did warn you this would be difficult. He's thirty, for God's sake, and still refusing to marry, which is why he won't attend these affairs on his own and only showed up tonight because his mother asked him to." Albert suddenly looked exasperated. "He even swore to me that if he couldn't have who he picked, then he would die a bachelor. He proved that by continuing to shun my choices for him, and they were all nice gels from good families. And I have no idea if he's still adamant about it because he and I have been at odds for too many years to have simple conversations about anything, much less personal matters. Whenever I bring up marriage or duty, he just disappears for a few weeks."

Incredible, Kathleen thought, that he didn't even know if this marriage between their children was possible. And she was afraid that Vanessa would balk if she knew what she might have to do to win Daniel Rathban. Why couldn't this just be a normal courtship, albeit with Vanessa doing the courting?

Annoyed that the entire matter was being placed on her family, she reminded him, "You hold the purse strings. Are you worried he will hate you if you force the matter?"

"I already tried cutting him off. He found other rakehells to live with and embarrassed me further with his multiple mistresses, his drunken binges and brawls, the immoral clubs he frequents when he's not living here."

"Then promise him he doesn't need to change a'tall after the marriage. I doubt my daughter will mind if she rarely sees him."

His brows snapped together. "I need heirs from this union or there is no point."

"One heir may be all my girl will want to deliver," she warned.

"She'll bloody well do as she's told!"

"You haven't asked for a coward, Lord Albert, you asked for my heir. She's amenable to this arrangement but only to get her father home. She has a mind of her own and the courage to stand up for herself. She ended up leaving the country with her father and has been with him these past six years. I believe I told you that's why she didn't have her come-out last year. And William raised her differently than I would have."

"But she was charming, even in the face of Daniel's insulting manner."

"Because she wants this match as much as you do—for her father's sake. Why don't I bring her here tomorrow so she and Daniel can get further acquainted apart from the crowd? You may not need to force the issue. Vanessa is determined."

"I begin to wonder who is the lamb being brought to the slaughter. Fine. I will tell Margaret to expect you. I fear this marriage still must be Daniel's idea or it won't happen a'tall. And apparently it's going to take a little longer than I'd hoped. I will feign an illness so my wife can insist that Daniel escort her while she's in town. He's fond of her so won't refuse. So keep me apprised of your gel's agenda for the Season and I will obtain invitations for my wife if she doesn't already have them." After issuing that command, he turned and walked back into his mansion.

Kathleen stared after the man who had sundered her family. He was old-school and not the least bit sophisticated. But this arrangement with him made her feel like she was in bed with the devil. And if anyone was at odds with a child, it was she. So how was she going to have such an embarrassing, unmotherly talk with Vanessa about what might need to be done to win Daniel Rathban? But now that Vanessa had met the "boy" and seen that he was older than she'd expected, did she still want the marriage?

Kathleen suddenly felt like crying. The unpleasant conversation she'd just had with Rathban could be moot. Vanessa could have already decided not to go through with this arranged match. And she realized she was afraid to ask!

Chapter Thirty-two

Vanessa had hoped to sleep late but should have known her sisters wouldn't cooperate. They both barged in and woke her when they pounced on her bed the next morning. They were as excited as they'd been last night about all the charming young noblemen they'd danced with at the Rathban ball. Vanessa felt exhausted just looking at them.

Both girls had danced the entire night, and on the ride home, they had chattered on and on about their dance partners—who was the best dancer, who was the wittiest, who they hoped to see again. Vanessa had remained silent. Kathleen hadn't said much, either. But before Vanessa had opened her bedroom door last night, Kathleen had whispered to her, "We shall visit Daniel tomorrow—if you haven't changed your mind. Lord Albert expects us."

"I'll be ready," Vanessa had replied. "But you will need to excuse yourself after we arrive there so I can have a few minutes alone with him, or the visit might be pointless."

"We should discuss strategies."

Vanessa shook her head. "Not tonight, Mother. I'm tired."

The warning about visiting the Rathbans tomorrow could have waited until the morning. It had kept her awake much longer than she would have liked. If Daniel would even receive her. If Daniel would even be there. If it would accomplish anything other than her getting rebuffed again. And she was going to have to pretend to like him—bloody hell.

She sat up in bed and rubbed her eyes, but the twins were already firing off questions.

"Who did you favor last night?" Emily asked.

"Does it matter?" Vanessa replied.

"Certainly it does!" Layla exclaimed.

"We don't want to encourage the same gentlemen."

"Em and I have made lists!"

"Did you?" Emily asked her.

If she were more awake, she might have realized sooner that they both were assuming that she no longer wanted the fiancé who had been picked for her. "You forget I'm engaged."

"No!" they said in unison, though Emily added, "He's too old. You can't actually want him."

Of course she didn't, but she still had to give a reason why she might. "Not old a'tall, and I found him very handsome."

"Really?" Layla said. "From my viewpoint, and I was watching, it looked like he snubbed you. Did he?"

Vanessa managed a grin. "A good way to pique my interest by pretending he's not interested in me. I did find that intriguing."

"Or he snubbed you because he's already being lured by a duke's daughter," Emily rejoined. "So he won't waste his time on any other women. We heard one has set her cap for him and that she can be quite cutthroat."

"Not just her," Layla put in. "I heard a couple of other debutantes tittering about him last night."

"I can't see in him what they do, as conceited and arrogant as he is," Emily added. "You can do better, Nessa."

"Or I can give Daniel a chance," Vanessa countered. "While I already find him attractive, I don't know him yet. I need to spend some time finding out if he's of good character. Unlike you, I'm in no hurry to make any decisions on the matter."

Good grief, more lies, when she'd already been assured there was nothing to like about Daniel—well, in Monty's opinion. But at least it stopped the twins' complaints about the match.

After joining her sisters downstairs for breakfast, Vanessa escaped the anticipated morning callers by visiting Snow for the rest of the morning. But almost as soon as she got there, she heard a throat being cleared behind her and turned to see Monty sporting his usual "I'm doing something I ought not to" grin.

She laughed. "Did you follow me out of the house?"

"Of course I did, since it's difficult to speak with you privately now, and I do so like speaking with you privately. Anything special on your agenda today or can you join me for a ride?"

"Visiting my fiancé after lunch."

"What the devil for?"

"For the usual reasons, though I suppose you'll point out they don't apply yet? So more to the point, he was foxed last night," she said even though she had no idea if Daniel had been or not. "Which could explain his rudeness. But I need to at least give him another chance while he's sober."

"Do make sure, while he's sober, to find out if he even knows he's engaged to you," he suggested dryly. "Just don't cry over his answer."

She sighed in exasperation. Monty definitely wasn't making this ordeal any easier for her with his negative predictions. But how telling, that she thought of it as an ordeal.

She changed the subject, mentioning, "You and Charley have been conspicuously absent from some of our meals."

"We decided not to be as much of a nuisance while in London. Besides, you and your sisters will be waxing ecstatically over your conquests whether we're there or not, so I thought it better if Charley's hopes did not get so thoroughly dashed."

She grinned. "You just didn't want to be bored to tears yourself."

"Well, there is that—if it's only your sisters waxing. Did you?"

"Wax ecstatically? No, I restrained m'self."

"Good," he said with a satisfied smirk. "As for me waxing, I at least managed to escape notice last night, a definite boon, but then it was an unusual mix of people for a ball. At least Charley had a grand time last night, though now he's in love with two more women."

She chuckled. "Perhaps you should explain to your ward the difference between attraction and love?"

He feigned surprise. "You think *I* know?"

She tsked. "And perhaps you shouldn't encourage Emily, either. I don't doubt she has your name on her list of possibilities."

He frowned. "That won't do."

His reaction made her smile, as if she'd just heard delightful music, so she teased, "I thought you rakes were in the habit of spreading yourselves around."

He laughed. "Never heard it put that way, but I suppose we do—but not with innocents, at least, those of us with integrity refrain."

"I'm an innocent," she reminded him, then blushed furiously at having said it.

"But you, sweetheart, will always be to me the bold wench who threatened to shoot two men off their horses and charged her horse into another to prevent an abduction! You are quite the exception. But I should mention we were discussing more'n kissing."

But her mind was suddenly back in that meadow they had raced across, and tumbling with him on the ground. Laughter and passion was a heady mix, and too often she remembered that delightful day and wished she could have more like it. But these were not the thoughts she should be having when she would be seeing the Rathban scion later today!

Silence wouldn't do just then, might even tempt him to the same memory, so she broached a neutral topic, asking, "You mentioned it was a boon that you weren't recognized, but if you don't want it known that you're back in London, should you even have attended last night?"

"I'm not a well-known figure at such affairs," he replied. "But my name possibly is, which is why I snuck in to avoid being announced."

"Does your friend know you're back?" she asked.

"You mean George? Absolutely. I went straightaway for a visit the day we arrived. He thought it rather amusing that we are having a go at hiding in plain sight."

"Which could go awry?"

"It could, but in the meantime I shall continue to enjoy your company."

She blushed only slightly, more from the sensual look he cast at her than the words. Clearing her throat, she got back to that neutral topic, asking, "So what was unusual about the people invited last night?"

"None of the gossipy grand dames were present. You didn't notice the lack of older women? It's rare that most of the young debutantes arrive with brothers or fathers, rather than their female relatives. I wonder if the elder Rathban arranged the guest list specifically with his son in mind."

"Quite possibly. He may not have wanted Daniel distracted by any ex-mistresses."

Monty laughed. "You may be exactly right." And then he gave her a thoughtful look before adding, "You know, it may be that Albert Rathban will take what he can get for his son at this point, engagement or no, which is why he invited so many suitable debutantes last night. If any of those other young ladies caught Daniel's eye last night, his father will likely let that run its course. It's no secret he laments his son's unmarried state."

As if she hadn't thought of that? "Are you trying to make me feel desperate?"

"Absolutely not!" he rejoined. "Just prepared for disappointment."

Joining her family at luncheon, she heard all about the callers she'd deliberately missed. Kathleen said nothing about her absence, but Layla remarked, "You were missed."

"And asked for," Emily put in curtly. "I've removed Lord Danton from my list, since he appears to be more interested in you."

"Don't do that," Vanessa said. "I don't even recall dancing with Danton last night, so I wouldn't add him to my list if I had one, but you already know why I don't have one."

Emily merely allowed, "If you're not interested in receiving callers, far be it from us to insist, but I'm not interested in your leftovers."

"Emily!" Kathleen said sharply.

There it was again, that underlying anger in Emily that she seemed less able to control. But Vanessa decided not to put her sister on the spot by demanding why, not with their mother in the room.

Vanessa rolled her eyes instead, then glanced at Kathleen. "You might want to mention, Mother, that it's far too soon to be fighting over prospective suitors—or making firm decisions about them, for that matter. One ball does not a Season make."

"Indeed," Kathleen agreed with a pointed look at Emily.

But Emily had already backed down from the sharp rebuke, eyes directed on her plate now. And Vanessa escaped to her room soon after, though she was determined now to try to catch Emily alone later today, or at least come up with an excuse to tear her away from Layla.

But she had more pressing matters just now, deciding what to wear for what amounted to a very important second meeting with the Rathban scion. One of her prettiest day dresses that screamed "innocent" or her bolder riding habit that wouldn't? She decided on the dark blue habit that was more sophisticated, even if she would be riding in a carriage with her mother.

It was such a short trip to the Rathbans, more's the

pity, and nervousness washed over her in a wave when the carriage stopped.

As they alighted from the carriage, she said to her mother, "Go immediately to visit Lady Margaret. I'll wait in the parlor."

"And how does that put you in the same room with Daniel?"

"I'm going to ask their butler to fetch him."

"Highly inappropriate."

"I'm not going to leave it to chance that he will wander downstairs and give me a few minutes to talk privately with him. If other people are watching us, that might affect his behavior. That might have been why he was so rude last night."

Kathleen nodded, but stressed, "You have my permission to return to the carriage if he *is* rude again. Some things can't be countenanced."

Kathleen moved up to knock on the door. Vanessa mounted the steps with leaden feet. Far too much depended on this second meeting. She had no idea what she was going to say to Daniel, but whatever it was, she needed to consider it carefully.

Chapter Thirty-three

"GOD, ANOTHER TWIT OF a debutante?"

Vanessa braced herself when Daniel stopped in the parlor doorway to say that. Had she really expected there would be no more insults from him after last night? But she had to allow she might have surprised him by being in the parlor after asking the butler to fetch him for her and declining to give the servant her name or the reason why she was visiting.

He wasn't dressed to receive, no jacket, his lawn shirt half-open. She was struck again by how handsome he was and so glad of it because it was the only thing about him that could account for why she might want to marry him when her family could match his in wealth and prestige. She couldn't care less if he thought her that superficial, as long as he didn't think she had an ulterior motive.

She was seated demurely on the sofa and didn't stand up to offer her hand for a greeting when it would just give him another opportunity to snub her. Besides, she doubted there would be anything cordial about this meeting.

When she didn't get up to run out of the room crying as he'd probably hoped she would, he added, "If you're here to see my mother—"

She cut in. "You and I met last night."

"Did we? I don't recall, but my mother is receiving in her suite upstairs."

"I know. My mother is with her now."

"Then why aren't you?"

"I decided not to be bored by motherly chatter—besides, I came to see you."

"Whatever for?"

"As it happens, the young bachelors last night didn't impress me a'tall, but then they wouldn't—when I like older men."

"Then wait for my father. He's gone round to his club but should be back soon."

Was he being deliberately obtuse, or was that meant to be funny? In either case, she bluntly clarified, "Older *handsome* men."

Those amber eyes suddenly narrowed on her. She was reminded of a snake about to strike.

And yet she realized his anger wasn't actually directed at her when he snarled, "D'you know how bloody many of you he's trotted before me?"

It appeared he'd drawn some conclusions of his own, the very one she'd been warned to deny. She wondered if the animosity between father and son went so deep that Daniel would even spite himself just to thwart his father. Or if he'd rejected all the potential brides his father had brought him simply because he refused to be controlled. But did it even matter why he was so lacking in a sense of familial duty? It did if he actually liked her but would still refuse her if he knew Albert had arranged their meeting.

So she mustered a little indignation to say, "He? No one trots me."

"Don't lie," he retorted. "You're my father's idea, aren't you?"

"Actually, my own mother recommended you to me because she thinks so highly of your family. But Mother can only recommend, she can't control me. To be honest, I'm rather fascinated by you or I wouldn't be here."

"Fascinated why? Because I don't want you? Are you really that vain?"

"Are you really beyond redemption?" she countered.

"I bloody well don't need redeeming, and you're barking up the wrong tree if you want conformity," he retorted.

"Not a'tall. But I do so love a challenge."

He snorted. "You might be pretty, chit, but I'm already bored with you. Go away."

She stood up, close to tears. Daniel's stance, his expression, his every word, told her just how much he disdained her. She made one last attempt, but only because he was still standing there.

She smiled, though it was truly hard to do at that moment, and said wryly, "Benefit of the doubt, et cetera, that you might have been having a bad night—and possibly a bad day? I merely thought we might become better acquainted today—and so we have. You *are* still here talking to me, after all."

He glared. "You thought wrong. Get out."

He walked out of the parlor and disappeared into other regions of the mansion. Trying hard to hold back tears, Vanessa asked the butler to tell her mother she was ready to leave. Daniel was impossible. There was no getting around his complete lack of attraction to her, which left her with absolutely nothing to work with.

Kathleen arrived with Lady Margaret, who was wearing that old-fashioned wig again. But they both looked so concerned she started crying.

"He was rude again?" Kathleen guessed as she put an arm around Vanessa's shoulders.

"Not so much rude as not cordial, but the exact moment he suspected his father had arranged my visit, he got very angry."

"I was afraid of that," Margaret said with a frown.

"You were supposed to deny it," Kathleen reminded her.

"I did. I said it was your idea. But the maggot had still got in his head, so there was no reasoning with him after that and he left."

Lady Margaret sighed. "I will try to salvage the situation

and confirm that your mother dropped the hint to me today that she wouldn't be opposed to a possible match between our families. It should defuse Daniel's anger at least."

Kathleen continued to console her on the ride back to the town house. "If you can get beyond his rudeness and if anger doesn't get in the way again, there still might be a chance, darling."

When he simply wasn't attracted to her? There was no getting around that. Kathleen merely dropped her back at the town house because she had an appointment to meet her friends. But at least the tears had dried by then and her eyes might have stayed dry if Monty weren't leaving the parlor when she walked in.

He saw her defeated expression and demanded, "What did he do?"

In answer she burst into tears again. He immediately pulled her into the parlor and closed the door before leading her to the sofa. Sitting down next to her, he drew her close to offer his chest to cry on. She took immediate advantage. Just being this close to him was soothing.

"Tell me what that cur said to you and I'll go throttle him."

He said it so calmly, gently, as if he were trying to console her or even make her laugh, but it alarmed her instead, and she leaned back from him. "No! I want to marry him." She railed at herself for being such a disastrous debutante. The one thing she wanted to accomplish this

Season she'd failed at—attracting Daniel Rathban. "I don't know what to do!"

"Nessi, do you really want to settle for a loveless marriage?"

"Yes, if it means my father can come back."

"What did you just say?"

"I— Nothing." She quickly wiped away her tears.

"That wasn't nothing, that was bloody well quite pertinent. What's keeping him away?"

She hadn't meant to mention her father again but she was so upset and Monty was looking at her with such concern, she admitted, "Albert Rathban is. Father went into exile six years ago at Rathban's insistence—or else our family name would have been dragged through the mud."

"That's blackmail. He doesn't have the power to exile anyone."

"When he holds all the cards he does—and did. It was my father's choice, ruination or leave England for good."

"Care to say how that came about?"

"No, I've said too much already."

"So this is why you've agreed to this match?" At her nod, he added, "And it's what you really want?"

"No, it's detestable!" she burst out. "But I came back to England to find a way to free my father from his exile in Scotland, and this marriage will do that. And that's what I really want."

Monty stared at her thoughtfully before he said, "I can

show you how to bring Rathban to the altar—with your permission, of course."

"Permission for what?"

"To teach you the sort of sophistication that appeals to Daniel. He takes his pleasures where he finds them, but he has to be tempted first, and not much does that anymore. So now he thrives on shocking others with his proclivities. So you may need to shock him to get his attention."

"What do you mean?"

"You will need to appeal to his prurient interests, and to top it off, he needs to think he can't have you, that you are utterly interested in another and that there are others determined to have you. We'll give him both barrels, so to speak, the lure first, then competition. Are you game?"

"You would do that for me?"

"With the utmost reluctance, when I want you for m'self. But if this means so much to you, Nessi, of course I'll help you. We are friends, after all."

She was amazed by what he was suggesting right up until he said *he* wanted her, then she could think about nothing else. She knew he was just teasing, but she wished he weren't!

He was waiting for her answer. However, it was clear to her that the last thing he wanted to do was help her into the arms of Daniel Rathban. And she didn't know if she could bring herself to take advantage of him, so she said, "I—need time to think. . . ."

"Certainly."

Chapter Thirty-four

VANESSA WISHED SHE HAD jumped at the excuse Monty had offered her to spend more private time with him. She still might, especially since it had sounded like it would be fun, but then again, it might be too much fun, and that wouldn't do. Did she really want her feelings for him to grow even stronger while he advised her on how to win the interest of another man? More to the point, was it already too late?

He wanted her for himself! She couldn't get that out of her mind even though she knew, rake that he was, that he didn't mean for marriage. She was still thrilled by that knowledge, so she was disappointed when he didn't join them for the dinner they attended that night. But imagining everyone seated at a long table, she guessed why—he couldn't avoid being noticed in such a small group.

Yet it wasn't actually a small group, and a buffet was offered because of the numerous guests. At least thirty people of assorted ages were in attendance that night, and at least half of them asked Vanessa if her father would be returning to England for her Season. And why wouldn't they wonder about it when it was where a father should be? She was afraid she might burst into tears if she was asked that question one more time, so she tried to avoid further conversation by staying by her mother's side and letting Kathleen fend off that question.

But Lady Roberts joined them on the way to the dining room, though not to ask after William. The elder lady was a little loud, a little rotund, and had a very annoying, high-pitched tittering laugh. Vanessa guessed as soon as the lady started sharing the current on-dits that she was one of the grand dames Monty had mentioned.

She found out who was in love with someone they could never have, who was nearing financial ruin, who had caused a sordid scandal by getting caught sneaking into a servant's bedroom—not in his own house! The lady described these people so well, without actually mentioning names other than using the occasional initial, like Lady C or Lord G, that Vanessa guessed Lady Roberts assumed that she and her mother must know who she was talking about. She didn't, of course, at least not until Lady Roberts ended her tittle-tattle with a mention of a lord who had been seen escaping an angry mob armed with axes. It was the mention of axes, after she'd seen one embedded in the door to their room at the inn, that made her think of Monty and wonder if this was what he might be hiding from?

"How do they get away with spreading rumors that might not be true?" Vanessa asked Kathleen after Lady Roberts moved on to another couple in the buffet line to impart her rumors to fresh ears.

"It's a pastime. For some, their only pastime."

"Unconscionable."

"Yes, scandal—and attempts to avoid it—can certainly alter people's lives." Kathleen gave her a meaningful look as they entered the dining room.

"Did you know who Lady Roberts was talking about?"

"Mostly. My London friends do keep me apprised by writing to me. But by the end of the Season, you'll likely know as well. Not all the gossips are as discreet as Lady Roberts. Most don't bother to conceal actual names."

She ate with her family, standing up, which was fine, since this was one of those times when they were supposed to only pick at their plates. Even Kathleen only picked. But it was easily done after they had shared a hearty meal before getting ready for—a dinner!

After dinner she met one of those less discreet gossips. The Honorable Mavis Collicot could also be called blatantly nosy and had cornered Vanessa because she was searching for new gossip. "You were seen visiting the Rathbans this morning, and dare I guess, you were at their exclusive ball last night?"

There was umbrage in that question. Albert had apparently insulted a lot of people by not including them in his ball. "I was there with my family," Vanessa said carefully.

Mavis waited avidly for Vanessa to say more, but when she didn't, the woman began guessing. "Albert is no doubt trying once again to pressure his heir into marrying someone of his choice. Daniel will refuse, of course. He despises his father too much to do what Albert wants, understandable when the women Daniel was in love with were both rejected by his father."

"Two women?"

"It might be more. I know only about two—are you next? Actually, Albert would find you more than acceptable, which means Daniel won't like you a'tall. What a shame! That boy needs a wife to put an end to his libertine ways, but he has atrocious taste in women to keep picking unsuitable gels."

Vanessa was wide-eyed, and before she could elicit any details from the lady, Mavis moved off, obviously more interested in picking up new gossip than in imparting old news. But what she'd just heard was rather far-fetched and unsubstantiated. Mavis Collicot seemed more interested in creating her own rumors than verifying others. But if she heard that story again . . .

Kathleen came to her and warned, "Don't believe a word Mavis Collicot said. She's a known liar."

"Is Lady Roberts?"

"No, that grand dame usually has the right of it, which is why she delights in not being explicit. Did Mavis tell you something unpleasant?"

"Something I wish Daniel was here to deny." And then she complained, "I would have thought you and your good friend would have arranged for his son to be here tonight."

"You make us sound like partners in a conspiracy."

"Aren't you?"

"Aren't you forgetting to include yourself in that number?" Kathleen rejoined.

She was, actually, so she sighed. "I just think it's a waste of my time to go to any parties that he will not be attending."

"Perhaps you can go just to have fun like your sisters?"

"My sisters are having a normal Season, I'm already engaged, so I'm not. But am I really engaged when my fiancé can't know about it?"

"You will be, once he proposes. But you already know why it has to be his idea. Five jilted brides is a daunting number to overcome."

"They weren't jilted, he simply snubbed them just as he snubbed me."

"I know you will wear down his resistance."

Vanessa snorted. "You make it sound like a bloody military campaign."

"Because it is."

"Well, I can't fight another skirmish if he doesn't show up for the battle."

"I didn't expect him tonight. I did send Lord Albert a copy of our agenda for the next two weeks, but he would have received it too late today to arrange for an invitation for tonight. I expect he will do better with the ball tomorrow night."

"I have to go into battle that soon?"

"Yes, and you have to win!"

"Mother, I'm beginning to think you want Father home as much as I do."

"I've never stopped loving your father."

"He won't take you back."

"I didn't think he would," Kathleen replied sadly. "But if he returns to England, I can at least see him occasionally when he visits you girls."

"That would be enough?"

"Ask me that after you've fallen in love with someone you can't have. Which, if you continue on this path I've opened for you, may be sooner than you think. Are you still sure you want to help your father this way?"

This way was a loveless marriage. But did it have to remain that way? Since it couldn't happen unless Daniel did the proposing, that alone would require his feelings about her to change. She might be able to work with that after the marriage was a fait accompli, maybe even find out what made him the way he was and help him back to a path of decency. Anything was possible. Wasn't it?

"Win or fail, this is still the only way, isn't it—for him to come back?" Vanessa said.

"Short of murdering Lord Albert and taking the chance that the rest of his family isn't aware of his nasty vendetta and thus, will not continue it, yes."

She actually laughed that that thought had even entered her mother's head. "Then I'm sure."

Chapter Thirty-five

"Ye've had nine offers for yer beastie, lass."

Vanessa was visiting Snow while she waited for a groom to saddle the gentle mare for her this morning. She turned to see Donnan peering into Snow's stall and asked in surprise, "How did that come about?"

"I've been taking him for a turn in that big park near here. It's become vera vexing. We canna get up tae a guid pace withoot being hailed by some laird tae stop and converse—aboot yer Snow."

That was exciting news, but it made her impatient to get her breeding stable started. She certainly hadn't expected members of the *ton* to be interested in Snow. Though why not? One of his offspring would look magnificent pulling a town carriage.

"I hope you asked for their cards so I can contact them later? I do intend to breed Snow eventually."

"Nay, I just glowered at them for disturbing me."

"Donnan!"

Yet he handed over a little stack of cards, making her grin.

"Thank you."

"Have ye decided on a groom yet? While this town is interesting and has muir taverns than we can count, Calum and I were wondering aboot the sassenach process o' getting yerself wed."

"A minimum of three weeks for the banns to be posted—at the very least."

"Or ye can hie yerself back tae Scotland where there's no waiting. So who's the lucky lad, then?"

She laughed. "I haven't settled on one yet."

That was only half a lie, and she felt no shame in telling it. She couldn't exactly share her goal to win the Rathban scion with the MacCabe brothers. Donnan, at least, might get it into his head to let her father know that she wanted to marry a man by the name of Rathban, and she wasn't about to let William risk coming home to dissuade her.

"Are you that eager, then, to return home? You could, you know. I'm perfectly safe here."

"Did I no' just mention muir taverns than we'll ever get tae?" He grinned. "We were just curious if yer pleased with the pickings so far. We ken ye dinna have the whole o' the town tae choose from, only a handful o' young lairds."

She chuckled. "More'n a handful, and I haven't even seen them all yet. It's too soon to fret over choices."

Her two escorts arrived with a mare for her. Monty

wasn't one of them. She'd left the house for this ride long before the calling hour, so she would have an excuse to miss it. There was no point for her to court boredom in that parlor, whether her mother wanted her there or not. But if she was going to be honest with herself, she'd hoped Monty would join her for the ride. Her sisters weren't with her, so she could have him to herself this time. She kept glancing behind her on the way to Hyde Park but was disappointed each time because she didn't see him.

It was only when she gave up looking that he arrived. She wished it didn't please her quite as much as it did. She wished her smile wasn't as wide as it was, too. Did she have to be so bloody obvious that she craved his company?

"How is it that you know when I'm going for a ride? Are you spending all your time lurking in the stable waiting for me?"

"I would like to say yes—sounds rather romantic, doesn't it? But no, I'm giving coin to a few members of your household staff to keep me apprised of your comings and goings. I was just caught unprepared this time, still abed, actually, or I would have been here sooner. And why aren't you observing the social niceties with your sisters this morning?"

She shrugged, saying lightly, "They are being courted while I'm doing my own courting—which won't happen in my mother's parlor."

"Getting yourself back into britches, are you?"

She chuckled. "I didn't mean changing roles, only that I have my target and intend to ignore all other Romeos."

"You wound me."

"You aren't a Romeo."

"I could be, with a little encouragement."

"Don't tease."

"You're asking me to surrender half my arsenal!"

She laughed. He was often endearingly silly. And she loved his teasing, just not when it implied he might be available, which he wasn't.

But then he said, "Since you haven't mentioned it, dare I hope you are declining my offer of lessons?"

She raised a brow. "I thought you were sincere in wanting to help?"

"Oh, I was, but I can still hope you'll come to your senses and leave this path you're—"

She interrupted him. "If you are about to repeat your prediction that misery and other forms of unhappiness await me, don't. Nothing is absolutely certain, and anything can change—and I am still considering your offer."

"Then forgive my momentary morbidity," he said, and offered a conciliatory grin. "Ride with me?"

She was about to say they were already riding together when she saw him pat his lap and her eyes flared wide. "Whatever for?"

"Because I long to touch you again."

Hot color rose up her cheeks as quickly as her pulse

now raced. He was doing it again, provoking her passion with mere words, and so easily! She quickly glanced ahead and cleared her throat to say, "There's nothing wrong with my mare to require the necessity."

"She's lost a shoe."

Her eyes came back to him. "No, she hasn't."

"Give me a moment and I'll show you."

She burst out laughing, amused that he would actually pry off a horseshoe just to prove his statement was true.

Chapter Thirty-six

VANESSA EXTENDED HER RIDE much longer than she meant to, but how could she not with such charming company? She was almost late for lunch because of it, so she didn't bother to change clothes first, just removed her riding jacket. Monty couldn't be as quick, since he didn't dare appear at the table in his borrowed groom's attire. And Charley arrived just after her and, in his usual chipper way, complimented everyone, even Kathleen.

It was a pleasant lunch inasmuch as Kathleen didn't need to scold anyone. While Layla was delighted that Lord Harris had called today and she couldn't say enough nice things about him, Emily was mostly silent, broodingly so. But Vanessa caught not one but two frowns cast her way, which made her decide to have a talk with Emily right away.

Before Vanessa left the dining room she whispered to Emily that she would like a private word, but her sister didn't follow her out. She waited for Emily across the hallway in Kathleen's study. And waited. Everyone except Emily had left the dining room.

Vanessa returned to the dining room, but Emily immediately said, "I'm not done eating."

Vanessa considered that an absurd statement when only a single small slice of sausage was left on Emily's plate and she was moving it around with her fork in a desultory manner rather than eating it. Vanessa took the seat next to her sister, saying, "We'll talk here, then." But when she saw a single tear slip down Emily's cheek, Vanessa gasped. "Em, what is troubling you?"

Emily's pale blue eyes, so like her own, glared at her. "*You* are! I hate you! But I hate hating you!" Great sobs arrived with that confession. "And it's tearing me to pieces—just go away."

Vanessa was taken aback, but she certainly couldn't leave her sister like this. "No, we're going to discuss this until you feel better."

"How typical of you," Emily sneered. "Dearest Vanessa to the rescue as usual. But I won't be feeling any better, how can I when you've ruined everything? Why did you have to come home?"

"I always intended to," Vanessa said carefully. "Did you actually think I wouldn't?"

"No, but you weren't supposed to return this year. I was to have all the eligible bachelors to myself. You were supposed to have your Season before us, so we wouldn't have to fight over our choices. But then you didn't come home, and we didn't know when you would."

"I really don't understand, Em. You would still have to share the crop of eligibles with Layla."

"That's different. Of course I would, but she'd defer to me. You, on the other hand, are entitled to first choice since you're older. It's not fair! You shouldn't be here this year. *My* year."

Vanessa wasn't sure how to respond. She'd never guessed that she would come home to this sort of sibling rivalry. Had Emily been dealing with these conflicting feelings ever since she returned?

"And it's already happening!" Emily suddenly added accusingly. "I want Monty, but he sees no one else in the room when you're there."

Vanessa frowned. "I suppose he's at the top of your list?"

"He was the only one on it before we got here."

"Of course he was, there are so few eligible gentlemen at home. And now? Is he still the only one on it?"

"Well, no—"

"Well, what I'm gathering from what you're saying is that you want them all for yourself, leaving none for me and Layla?"

Emily's cheeks blossomed with color. But Vanessa hadn't meant to go on the offensive like that. Bloody hell, she'd just displayed the same jealousy Emily had—over the same man.

"I'm sorry. It appears you aren't the only one who can be bitten in the arse by jealousy. Yes, I also like Monty. He's a charming flirt, very amusing, but I'm aware he isn't serious. He's a rake, Em. Marriage isn't what rakes have on their minds. Besides, if a man hasn't shown interest in you, then he's not worth having."

Good Lord, was she remarking on her own situation with Daniel? But she couldn't back away or her goal of bringing her father home would be out of reach again. And yet it was such good advice—except when a vendetta was involved.

"Easy for you to say when you're the one he's smitten with," Emily snapped.

"But he's not! That's the point I'm making. It's just fun and games for him, nothing more. And since I know that, I'm not going to get hurt by getting my hopes up over a man who isn't eligible. And I'm already engaged, which you keep discounting. So answer me this, why would you waste your time and thoughts on someone who isn't captivated by you, when so many others already are?"

Emily shot to her feet. "D'you think I haven't tried to squelch this jealousy?! I told you I hate hating you!" The tears were back to prove it. "And you haven't been the least bit helpful!"

Emily ran out of the room.

Exasperated, Vanessa yelled after her, "If logic won't work, we can revert to hierarchy. I'm older and I met him first!"

Angry at herself for getting into a childish tug-of-war,

she hit the table with her fist—and barely heard the tsk behind her. But she did hear it and glanced around to see
Kathleen standing in the doorway with her arms crossed—
and braced herself for a reprimand.

"Was it necessary to stir up all that nasty emotion?"
Kathleen asked. "She's going to have red eyes now for the
ball tonight."

Kathleen had pretty much just admitted to eavesdropping, though she didn't appear the least bit contrite about
it. "How much did you hear?" Vanessa asked.

"Just the end."

"Were you aware that Emily is jealous of me? She
thinks I came home just to ruin her Season."

"The twins don't confide in me, only each other," Kathleen said. "But it does explain her quarrelsome behavior
since your arrival."

"She's very conflicted. She doesn't think I should marry
Rathban, not only because he's a little older than we expected but also because you picked him for me. Yet she
doesn't want me casting even a glance at any of the men
on her list."

"Do I need to be concerned about our houseguest's
attention to you?"

"Not in the least. Monty is charming but not serious.
He's amusing himself with what I believe you would call 'a
harmless flirtation.'"

Only a smidgen of a blush colored Kathleen's cheeks.
"I should still have a word—"

"No," Vanessa cut in. "There is no point in embarrassing all three of us when he knows I'm already engaged. Perhaps Emily will be relieved once the engagement is official, since talking to her didn't do a bloody bit of good."

"Perhaps. And I've had word from Lord Albert this morning. Daniel will be escorting his mother to the ball tonight, so you will have another opportunity to advance the campaign, as you termed it."

Vanessa nodded. "Good. And I meant to ask you if you know why Daniel hates his father?"

"That's a strong word."

"Not really, not when the mere mention of his father yesterday enraged him, and Mavis Collicot also said as much and blamed their animosity on two lost loves that Albert rejected," Vanessa said.

"I warned you not to believe that woman. She fabricates most of her rumors. But I suppose something like that could explain Daniel's obnoxious behavior."

"And also why he does just the opposite of what his father would want."

"Then we shall find out if it is true. Lady Roberts might know. I'll broach the subject subtly tonight if she attends the ball and let you know."

Chapter Thirty-seven

It was a large town house, but the small back garden and terrace were completely walled in. Montgomery stared at the wall he was considering climbing. Six bloody feet tall! He should have just dyed his hair like Charley, then they both could have gone through the front door with their fake names as part of the countess's party. He could have averted his face during the announcement. Charley didn't need to worry about being discovered here, but Montgomery's face had recently been seen in London, so his false credentials wouldn't necessarily keep him from being noticed by the wrong people, though he didn't expect the noblemen he'd supposedly cuckolded to attend a debutante ball. Not that he cared if he moved back to the top of the gossip lists—well, actually, he did. He'd rather Vanessa not hear about those sordid affairs, fake or not.

"Your ancient bones can't manage it?" Charley said as

he leapt up to snag the top edge of the wall, pulled himself up, and climbed over it.

The boy obviously considered this a fun adventure, which is why he had declined entering the house with the countess. Montgomery certainly didn't. He should have stayed in the Blackburn house. He didn't have to attend every ball Vanessa went to.

At least Rathban's ball had been a much smaller affair with a carefully selected guest list. From the very long line of coaches out front, he knew this ball was far more grand and would include a fair number of crashers like himself—and too many gossips. He could still turn about, but it was too late to drag Charley away with him. The boy was already on the other side of the wall. And he told himself the only reason he was going over that wall was because he still had to keep an eye on Charley.

But it was Vanessa he looked for as soon as they entered the house. He saw her on the dance floor with a young man, resplendent in her pale yellow gown, too damn beautiful again. She appeared bored, which shouldn't delight him but it did.

Charley had already gone off to ask one of the debutantes for a dance, leaving him to get ambushed, which is what it felt like when he heard, "Father is in town. Have you visited?"

That took his eyes off Vanessa. His sister Claire looked

lovely tonight in a dark emerald gown that complemented her auburn hair and green eyes so like his own. She gave him a kiss on the cheek before he could reply, "No, and try to restrain yourself from sharing the news that I'm back in London."

"I didn't know you'd left. Where are you staying? A new flat?"

"With friends."

"You ought to ask me to dance while we catch up."

"We can catch up another time. I am otherwise occupied tonight."

She glanced back to find out who he was looking at, but her eyes stopped on another lady. "Ah, her, your mistress."

He followed Claire's gaze and groaned when he saw Lady Halstead. "Don't start, Claire. You know nothing about it."

"But I do—Lady Halstead is not the only one. From what I heard, you were on your way to filling your stable with old mares." And having gotten that nasty tease in, she patted his cheek. "Maybe now you'll dance with me?"

"Maybe now I'll throttle you. What are you even doing here?"

"Giving my husband a reason to divorce me."

"He's here with you?"

Her mouth turned pouty. "No, but several of his friends

are and will surely tell him what a wonderful time I'm having—without him."

"Why don't you just get it over with and forgive him. You know you will in the end."

"I will not! He cheated on me. He's lucky I didn't try to cut off—"

"Bite your tongue. If I didn't sympathize with him before, I certainly do now. Will dancing shut you up?"

She smiled. "It might."

He started to lead her onto the dance floor, but she paused to whisper, "Find me after you've dispatched this fellow. I don't think he needs to be introduced to me."

Montgomery didn't recognize the older man who was walking straight toward him until he said, "I've sent for my seconds."

"Lord Halstead, I presume?"

A curt nod. "We shall settle this tonight."

The man was in his fifties and of diminutive stature, at least a half foot shorter than Montgomery. There was no anger in his expression, just deadly resolve. After four written demands for a duel and now this fifth one, Halstead obviously felt a duel was mandatory given the situation, whether the reason for it was true or not.

But Montgomery's resolve hadn't changed, either. He wouldn't kill a man over something he had only pretended to do. And yet he still couldn't give up the absolute truth to the fellow.

So he said in a low tone, "Let me propose this instead,

a test of marksmanship tomorrow. You can even bring your seconds, and we will shoot at targets, rather than each other. If you win, I'll agree to a true duel then and there. If I win, we can put this nonsense behind us."

Halstead hadn't looked angry before but he certainly did now. "You want me to audition for a duel with you? By God, I should challenge you again for that slur on my marksmanship!"

"You can kill me only once."

"To my regret, but I'll have my once. You'll be hearing from me—"

"Can we not do this again?" Monty said in an earnest whisper before the older man marched off. "I didn't bed your wife, man. I only tried to. What a man does when he's foxed shouldn't lead to anyone dying. And I do vaguely recall being rebuffed by her." And then with a note of regret in his voice, he added, "But if you insist—?"

There was a very long pause before Halstead said, "Perhaps not."

Montgomery was a little incredulous as the man walked away from him. Bloody hell, it was that easy? Maybe he should try that excuse on Lord Chanders tomorrow as well and see if his luck held. It still wasn't the truth, but it preserved George's supposed innocence, and the respective wives' fidelity. Drink was the scoundrel instead of himself!

He caught up to his sister and whirled her onto the

dance floor. "I'm feeling much better," he said with a grin.

"Nasty business all solved?"

"Very likely."

"How many more must be placated?"

"Just one. But don't believe a word you're hearing, Claire—just don't defend me, either."

"We thought you were more discreet," she huffed.

"We?"

"Father has been in London all this time since you and I last spoke. D'you think he's gone deaf and wouldn't hear these rumors?"

"How angry is he?"

"Very."

He sighed. "You were correct, I am discreet—unless there's a reason I ought not to be. Trust me. You will laugh about this nonsense someday."

She raised a brow. "That's it? I'm to make do with a promise of an explanation—someday?"

"You could remember that I'm your favorite brother—"

"Who says you are?"

"And you know me very well, so you must have already concluded that there is more to this than silly rumors."

"Who says I have?"

He gave her a tender look before kissing her cheek. "I do, because I know you very well, too—except when it comes to your husband. Shall we discuss him again?"

"I think we're done talking," she said, and left him there in the middle of the dancers.

But the music had stopped, and as Vanessa passed him, he pulled her away from the fellow escorting her back to her mother. She gave him an inscrutable look, but he didn't have time to wonder why when the orchestra started playing and he began to dance with her.

"Again you don't ask?" she said curtly.

"Again I don't want to cry if you rebuff me."

That should have gotten a smile from her, but her expression didn't change. She was definitely annoyed about something.

"I was wondering if you would come tonight, Montgomery Townsend."

And there it was. If she'd heard his real name here, he didn't doubt she'd heard a great deal more.

Which she confirmed when she nodded toward Lady Halstead. "Really? Her? She's old enough to be—"

"Yes, yes, so people keep telling me," he cut in, then added drolly, "I must not have noticed."

"Too foxed at the time?"

"Or it was too dark." He didn't want her to think badly of him, so he leaned closer to whisper, "Some things are not what they seem."

She gave him a skeptical look before glancing away. He was struck with an odd frustration because she was displeased with him and he couldn't say anything that would get him back in her good graces. But he couldn't believe that she was jealous over rumors about affairs that had supposedly occurred before they'd even met. Was she just very disappointed in his choice of paramours?

And then he noticed who Vanessa was suddenly glaring at and laughed. "My sister Claire is here. She's going to wonder why you're casting daggers at her."

Chapter Thirty-eight

VANESSA ROLLED HER EYES. She did *not* just get jealous over his sister. Embarrassed that he knew she'd done exactly that, she started to leave the dance floor. But Monty—*Montgomery*—followed her. "Don't blush, it clashes with your glorious hair. Would you like to meet Claire?"

"No." She said it too soon, when she realized she would like to. So she stopped so he could come abreast of her.

"Dare I guess you won't be glaring at her anymore?" he asked.

"You have another life. I've known that from the beginning." And then she grinned. "I'll keep my daggers sheathed. It won't happen again."

"Well that's a shame. Other than being briefly confused by your jealousy, now that I'm not, I—"

"Talk too much."

"—find it a delightful surprise," he finished.

"*Really* talk too much," she repeated. "And that's

enough amusement for you tonight. Besides, I've changed my mind. I'd like to meet your sister."

"By all means," he said, and walked her over to Claire to make the introductions.

Same hair, same eyes, why couldn't she just have noticed the resemblance immediately? She couldn't believe she'd gotten jealous, and over nothing. That silly rumor about him and older women she hadn't credited in the least and would have only teased him about it. But a woman as lovely as Claire was another matter.

And she was charming—and a teaser like her brother. "A pleasure, Vanessa, and you're so young!"

Vanessa laughed. Monty was the one glaring daggers now, because that was a direct hit about the rumors about him that were circulating through the *ton*, and she wasn't clueless, having just heard them tonight herself.

But Claire didn't overdo the dig, she politely went neutral in asking, "Where did you two meet?"

Vanessa wasn't about to answer that, pistols and rebels and—no, not a word. But Monty apparently didn't want any of that known, either, because he went for an even bigger whopper. "At the Rathban ball the other night."

"Is it true the parents are determined to get their errant son leg-shackled this Season?"

"Was their throwing a ball for him that obvious?"

"Oh, indeed. So many mothers were chirping about it today. He is quite a catch, and it's such a surprise that he's finally putting himself on the marriage block."

Monty looked at Vanessa before he replied, "I'd say he'll fight it tooth and nail, but don't repeat that. Merely my opinion."

Claire snorted delicately. "Don't think I don't know you're talking about yourself, brother, not Daniel Rathban."

Vanessa waited for Monty to deny that teasing charge, but he didn't, merely said, "Give it a rest, Claire. There's nothing left of that bone to gnaw on."

It was a disquieting moment to have his aversion to marriage confirmed by a member of his own family. After the siblings hugged and parted, Vanessa moved ahead of him to return to her mother and stick close to her, determined to ignore that *confirmed* bachelor for the rest of the night.

Her mother was standing with Lady Roberts and another old dame, and she heard Lady Roberts say, "Silly boy fancied himself in love with a housemaid. It was barely a tidbit, when so many young men get their first taste of amour with servants who are conveniently under their roof. Always underfoot, available, et cetera. It was never confirmed, but the consensus was that his father paid the gel to leave England. But it was all rather typical, so it wasn't noteworthy gossip at the time. But why the interest in such a lothario, Kathy? D'you want him for one of your gels?"

Kathleen smiled. "As you know, I've been away from London for a few years. And who better than you to tell me about the current eligibles."

Lady Roberts shook her head. "I'm not so sure our

Danny is all that eligible. He keeps three mistresses, you know, yes, I did say three, and they even like each other! And he still philanders on the side. But his father obviously thinks this is the year to change all that. Hope springs eternal!"

The other matronly woman standing next to Lady Roberts finally piped up. "It won't happen."

"We don't know that, Gerty," Lady Roberts disagreed.

"Of course we do. That rift 'tween father and son is so wide now, all of England could fit in it! The boy went from gloomy to enraged, that his father would do it again!"

Vanessa almost intruded to ask "Do what?" but she really didn't want to draw attention to herself and have the two gossips tone down what they were saying, which was far too pertinent to her ears.

"That was a low blow," Lady Roberts agreed, "though it's been several years now since Danny fell in love with that second gel. And what else was Lord A to do after he heard she didn't have a spotless reputation?"

"It was more likely that he felt she didn't have sufficiently distinguished bloodlines to enter his family," Gerty said. "You know how snobbish he can be."

"Well, it's too late now for Lord A to figure out that might have been his last chance to get his boy wed. She's living up north now with the minor noble she married instead. But obviously he must think there's still a chance. Why else would he host a ball, which he's never done before?"

"That family has had its share of trials and tribulations with brothers dying too young and recalcitrant sons. So dreary!"

"Indeed," Lady Roberts concurred.

Vanessa wondered if the already-agreed-upon engagement to her might have had something to do with Albert's refusing that second woman Daniel had loved. But it was daunting, knowing what else she was up against. Not once, but twice Lord Albert had ruined his son's chances for romantic happiness. No wonder Daniel hated his father so much that he would do exactly the opposite of what Albert wanted.

"However, young Montgomery Townsend is a prime subject!" Lady Roberts added. "If that boy really has developed a taste for maturity—I think I'll go flirt with him m'self."

There was that high tittering laugh again before the lady moved off with her friend. And Kathleen remarked in a low tone, "I can see now why Lord Monty wanted a sojourn in the country, which makes me wonder what brought him back to London. Why set all these tongues wagging again?"

Her mother was giving her a pointed look, pretty much accusing her of encouraging him, but Vanessa managed a disinterested shrug. "Of course I like him. How could I not, as amusing as he is?"

"Not too much, I hope."

No, they couldn't have that. Fall in love with the wrong

man? Not a wrinkle either of them wanted. But she dismissed the subject when she asked, "I take it you actually asked Lady Roberts about Daniel?"

"Of course. And I noticed your arrival. You heard the gist of it. I'm sorry their gossip wasn't more useful to your campaign."

It wasn't, but then what had she expected? To learn something that would help her to mend the fence between father and son? "I'm not so sure it was entirely useless. It was a little encouraging to know that Daniel *can* fall in love."

"Or just the opposite, that after two heartbreaks he won't be willing to risk a third. I hope I'm wrong and you're right, but he's here if you'd like to test which of our theories is correct."

Vanessa immediately looked about the room until she spotted Daniel standing with his mother near the ballroom entrance, but her eyes didn't stay on him. She continued looking until she found Monty at the refreshment table talking to a pretty woman. Up went the bristles again. What the devil? She had no right to get jealous. He wasn't hers, would never be hers, so—*what* the devil?

"He's coming," Kathleen whispered.

Vanessa's eyes flew back to Daniel. She noted again how handsome he was, imposing in size, and looking bored again. She could definitely harp on about his jaded reputation. Three mistresses! She still mustered a smile when their eyes met across the room.

She didn't offer a hand when moments later he bowed curtly before her because she was absolutely certain that he would ignore it. So she was quite surprised when he simply grasped her elbow to lead her out to the dance floor. Without asking!

And he quickly warned, "Don't mistake this, it was my mother's idea."

She almost laughed. Having a soft spot for his mother wasn't a bad thing. "At least you like one of your parents," she remarked. "How ironic that we have that in common."

He wasn't curious enough to ask for an explanation but said in a blasé tone, "For some reason, you impressed her the other night."

"Perhaps because I didn't swoon over your rude snub?" she guessed.

His eyes narrowed at the criticism. "For whatever bloody reason. I need to show her that I'm utterly uninterested in you."

She refused to let his insult offend her this time. She even smiled. "By all means, snub me again. That should do it."

"Not if you don't swoon this time."

Had the odious man made a joke? But if he meant to be humorous, he must have regretted it because he immediately went on the attack, adding, "I should be dancing with one of your sisters instead. An unusual pair, pretty *and* identical. It would be interesting to have them both in my bed."

She was so shocked she couldn't even attempt to reply. Unfortunately, she didn't think he was joking now. Not lambasting him for his salacious remark about her sisters was likely the most difficult thing she'd ever done. Instead, she did her best to project an air of nonchalance. And, thankfully, he said no more. But he did go straight from dancing with her to asking Layla to dance. And Vanessa's protective instincts shot to the fore. She wasn't about to let either of her innocent sisters get involved with any member of that family.

She immediately looked for Monty and was glad to see him walking toward her, so she met him halfway and guided him onto the dance floor. He obliged.

As soon as they began dancing he mentioned, "Now that the hordes know I've returned to London, people might remark on my dancing with you more than once this evening—which could be to your benefit—depending."

"Oh?"

He didn't elaborate but instead asked, "You're still annoyed with me?"

She realized she must still look perturbed from her unpleasant encounter with Daniel, so she smiled at him. "No, not a'tall."

"A wonderful trait, not to pout."

"Oh, be quiet. What benefit?"

"You haven't accepted my offer of lessons yet."

"Oh, but I am now, most definitely. What do your lessons entail?"

"Are you absolutely sure you want to do this?"

She'd rarely seen him look so serious. "He's showing an interest in the twins. I can't allow that."

"Ah, mother hen has arrived."

"Don't joke, not about this. When do we begin?"

"Immediately—one of the two barrels I mentioned, remember? I will dance us close to him. You're going to laugh with me, give me a few adoring looks—if you see that he's watching us. And should you speak with him again tonight, make sure to tell him you have other options, or at least, mention me."

"But I told him I like older men."

"I'm twenty-six, old enough for our purpose and still younger than he is, which will bite all the harder if he does get jealous."

"If? There's no guarantee?"

"He has to at least have some interest first for it to annoy him. So we will likely only be planting the seed tonight."

"And the other barrel you mentioned?"

"Mothers teach their daughters only what they were taught—prior to marriage. They don't teach what they gain in experience and sophistication after marriage. We need to arm you with the latter, in point, step up your flirting techniques to a more worldly approach—we're close to him."

She panicked. "I'm not good at faking laughter!"

"Do I need to step on your toes tonight?"

She laughed. "Not if you value your life."

"That will do. And keep looking into your target's eyes, mine in this case. Especially in conversation, don't look away. Keep your eyes on his and try to smile, a more mysterious one as if you are having improper thoughts."

She demonstrated how easy that would be—with him. She only had to remember that day in the meadow and how hotly they'd kissed, or when they'd ridden together on Snow and his hands had been all over her . . .

But he drew in his breath. "Good God, woman, what the devil are you thinking about?"

She laughed in delight. "I take it I just passed your test?"

"It wasn't a test, just one of many lessons, but yes, you've definitely got the hang of that one. Now let's make sure Daniel is paying attention."

Monty danced closer to the target and bumped into him, though he immediately apologized before he added, "Wasn't watching where I was going, but can you blame me?"

Vanessa got one of Monty's more potent smiles, but Daniel remarked, "I've heard you've been keeping yourself busy, Townsend. Isn't the Blackburn girl a little too young for you?"

Vanessa wondered how many of those "rumor" digs Monty could stomach, but this time it didn't seem to faze him, because he grinned before countering, "Aren't you a little too old for your partner, old boy?"

Monty immediately whisked Vanessa back toward the

center of the dance floor before saying, "First mission accomplished. And don't decline a dance from Charley when I send him over. He won't need to pretend he adores you, and we want Daniel to notice that you attract gentlemen of all ages. For the rest, we will need privacy, which we don't get much of at your mother's house. Any suggestions?"

"I'll come to your room tonight."

"You would do that?"

"Why not? Or will I have reason to yell or throw things at you? That will certainly give us away."

"Not a'tall. It's just highly improper, and I thought you had fully donned proper."

"Exceptions must be made. And I don't think my mother would object if she knew. She wants this match as much as I do and has implied that I will need to do more'n just bat my eyes at Rathban to succeed."

"Now that just—infuriates me."

"Why?"

"Because she should be your stalwart protector, not your pander."

She chuckled but caught Daniel's eyes on her, so she patted Monty's cheek, whispering, "He's watching."

He sighed. "I should have known."

The music ended. Daniel returned Layla to Kathleen and caught Emily on her way back. She certainly didn't look pleased by Daniel's dance request, but she still agreed, probably with the thought that he might end up a member of the family. But Daniel was definitely making a point of his own—to Vanessa. But what? That he was serious about his preference for the twins, or was he only trying to make her furious enough to end her own pursuit of him?

Chapter Thirty-nine

"Take every opportunity that avails itself to touch him—discreetly, of course. On his hand, his arm, even his chest, anywhere you can reach and pretend, slyly of course, that it was an accident."

As Vanessa listened to Monty, she tried to concentrate on what he was saying, not on the excitement that had started bubbling up inside her when she'd knocked on his door and entered his bedroom, anticipating that some of his lessons might involve touching, not just the mention of it.

Monty had taken off his jacket but otherwise was quite properly dressed. As was she, though not in her ball gown, and she hadn't tied her hair back, had left it loose as she would for bed. She wasn't wearing shoes because she'd had to tiptoe down the corridor to his room. And he'd offered her a chair while he paced in front of it, gathering his thoughts, just like a teacher. Frankly, she was disappointed. He hadn't told her anything yet that he couldn't have told her while they'd danced at the ball.

"His neck, for example," he continued. "Perhaps he has a lock of hair out of place you can push back and graze the side of his neck with your knuckles as you do."

"He has short hair," she reminded him.

"So he does," he said. "I suppose I was imagining m'self."

She laughed, feeling a trifle more interested, and suggested, "Shall I try it now?"

"No, no, a few more instructions first before you practice—if I can survive the practice."

She grinned and twirled a lock of her hair around her finger in a coy manner. "If you keep saying things like that, I might think you've lured me here for other reasons."

He smiled. "Now *that* is a perfect remark for your target. Remember it when you have him at your mercy again."

Was he joking? "I wasn't thinking about him."

He ran a hand through his loose hair in a frustrated manner before giving her a pointed look. "Yes, you were. You don't want me to think otherwise or we won't accomplish a bloody thing tonight."

Her pulse began to race. He was doing it again, implying that she tempted him, yet keeping his distance. He didn't really want to give these lessons, not when he continued to say or show that he wanted her for himself. He was being so utterly magnanimous in offering to help her in this way. She shouldn't be making it harder for him.

She pursed her lips and sat back in her chair. "Do continue."

He nodded. "Now if you find yourself alone with your reluctant fiancé, perhaps on a terrace, you can be bolder, move in close and give him that suggestive smile you demonstrated earlier. And remember to keep gazing into his eyes as you do it. Debutantes will look away, blush, display their nervousness in obvious ways, but you won't be doing any of that, at least not with him."

She chuckled. "I'm not sure I've ever done any of that."

"No, you are certainly not the typical debutante. I suppose you have Nestor to thank for that?"

"My father," she corrected.

"Really?"

She shrugged. "He allowed me to behave as I liked, not as I ought to."

He smiled. "I'm not sure he did you a favor in that—well, as far as preparing you for normal situations. However, for your particular purpose, you are lucky to be accustomed to boldness and daring. You can be assured that Daniel might be beyond the pale in boldness, so you need to be prepared for that, which we shall address in a moment. For the last minor lessons, always modulate your voice when you're with him. No matter how angry he might make you, don't join the fight."

"I've already been practicing that."

"I'm sure you have. And you could compliment him if the opportunity arises, merely to disconcert him, but as it happens, women aren't the only ones who like to be told how nice they look. Oh, and end your encounter before he does, just walk away from him without looking back. If he wants you, that will leave him wanting you more."

"That's the problem, he doesn't want me."

"Yet. But don't leave if it will make him think you're angry or shocked by him. That will just make him assume he's won the 'you can't have me' game."

"Is it a game to him?"

"Probably not. As I said, by all accounts, he's too jaded."

"Are you?"

He grinned. "Not in the least."

"Do you know why he is?"

"Not exactly, but it would be my guess that over a decade of debauchery has something to do with it."

She frowned thoughtfully. "But that can't be the only reason why he steadfastly refuses to marry when he is his father's only legitimate heir."

"If there is a deeper reason you will need to ask him, but I wouldn't advise doing so when it could backfire and incite his rage—and I really don't think you want to deal with an enraged Rathban."

She had to agree because her family had been sundered by an enraged Rathban. But Monty added, "There is actually another factor that might account for his confirmed bachelorhood, one similar to my own."

"Oh?"

"An abundance of heirs, well, at least in my case. My

siblings have already given my parents a number of grand-children, giving me the perfect excuse to steer clear of a wife."

Lucky you, she almost said sarcastically, but the last thing she wanted to do was show disappointment in regard to his own confirmed state of bachelorhood. So she merely rejoined, "But Daniel doesn't have siblings, does he?"

"Not that I know of, but he has first cousins, the children of his uncle John Rathban, two of them male, one already married with children."

"Yes, I met them at the Rathban ball."

"For pride's sake, Lord Albert undoubtedly still wants his own son to be his heir, but the word around town is that after his brother's death, he became a second father to his nephews, so he most certainly does have other options."

"Well, that's interesting. So I am not really Albert's last resort."

Monty laughed. "You could never be a last resort, sweetheart."

He did it again. She was sure he didn't even mean to do it, the flattering words just tumbled out of his mouth.

And he continued, "Now for the lessons that require privacy . . ."

Chapter Forty

As MONTY TOOK VANESSA'S hand and pulled her to her feet, the palm of his other hand landed perfectly on her right breast. He even squeezed slightly to let her know his touch was no accident. She tried desperately to ignore the sudden flutters in her belly. She ignored the racing of her pulse and the delightful scent of him, which she couldn't help but notice now that he was so close to her. Somehow, she managed to just raise a brow at him.

He burst out laughing. "Well, I didn't expect you to already be immune to this brash sort of fondling. This is a demonstration of what Daniel *might* do in his effort to scare you away. And I don't mean in the course of an embrace, when a caress of this kind would be natural, but for no apparent reason."

"I'm not in the least immune—to your touch."

He drew in his breath. "*Please* imagine I am Daniel for this lesson."

She could never do that. There was utterly no comparison

between the two men. But she could see she'd disconcerted him again, so she said, "Sorry, I thought a little levity might be in order."

"So you were joking?"

She ignored the question and just said, "Do continue the lesson."

He nodded. "If he touches you like that or even more intimately—"

She cut in. "Are you going to demonstrate what could be more intimate than his putting his hand on my breast?"

He removed his hand, but he did so very slowly, as if he didn't really want to. "No. You will certainly know if it happens. The point I am making is that no matter where he touches you, don't look shocked, angry, or otherwise insulted. You want to intrigue him instead by responding in a way he doesn't expect."

"Like I did with you?"

He shook his head. "Raising a brow at him could have an adverse effect, even mortify him, resulting in his walking away and your not getting another chance to belittle him."

"That's too bad." She grinned. "He could use a little mortifying."

"Not if you still want him to join you at the altar," he warned.

She sighed. "Then intrigue him how?"

"You could lean in and whisper something in his ear, even if it's only a light scold for his effrontery."

She leaned closer to him and whispered in his ear, "I want you."

He took a step back from her. "No, no, no, no."

She laughed. "One was enough."

"Nessi, are you going to take this seriously or not?"

She managed not to sigh again. "Certainly."

"Then remember, you want to conduct yourself with a degree of sophistication, in that you can imply, just never deliver. That is paramount. Delivering will end the game for him. He will have his momentary satisfaction and go back to being bored with you."

She was disappointed. "Does that apply to every man?"

"Gads, no, only someone as jaded as Rathban. I, for one, don't think I could ever have enough of you."

He did it again! And he didn't even notice what those words did to her, he went right on with his lesson, saying, "Keep in mind that if he does resort to crudeness, it could well be his defense, an effort to shock you into retreating from your pursuit of him. So you will want to ascertain whether it is a defense or an actual overture, albeit a clumsy one, before you respond."

"How can I tell the difference?"

"You could try kissing him at that point."

"I'd rather not."

"If he's to be your husband, you may want to get used to it."

"Shall we practice kissing, then?"

She wasn't really teasing, and he didn't react with

annoyance this time. With one step he gathered her in his arms and was kissing her. If this was just practice, she would clobber him. But she felt as if she were in the meadow again, this was hot passion springing up wildly between them.

"I thought I could manage this, but I want you too much," he said against her lips. "Tell me to leave."

"This is your room."

"Then get out."

But he didn't stop kissing her! She felt like laughing, but she wanted to kiss him more so she wrapped her arms tightly around his neck. He wouldn't be able to stop what he was doing even if he tried, but he didn't. He put a hand at the back of each of her thighs and lifted her legs off the floor, placing them around his hips. So she wrapped those tightly around him, too, and he carried her to his bed. It wasn't far.

On the bed, with him! The fluttering inside her went a little crazy as he settled himself mostly on top of her because his position assured her that this wasn't part of any lesson, this was him giving in to his desire for her and her feeling thrilled that he was.

She groaned as his lips moved across her cheek, then the side of her neck, his warm breath near her ears tantalizing her not once, but several times. And when he finished kissing one side of her face and neck, he moved to the other. But his mouth kept coming back to hers. And he must have been lifting her skirt so slowly that she didn't notice until his hand brushed over her mound, paused, and came back to it.

"Good God, sweetheart, do you always flit about without your drawers?"

She chuckled at his surprise. "No, of course not, but I donned my nightgown so I would look prepared for bed in case my sisters paid a late-night visit. When I was certain everyone else was abed, I dressed rather quickly and snuck over to your room."

"I'm afraid it's too late for an explanation. I'm always going to imagine you without them now, no matter what you're wearing."

"No you won't, that's just silly."

"Men can be silly—especially when they're thinking about women."

"If you imagine I'm not wearing any, I promise I'll imagine the same about you."

He groaned and kissed her deeply again. She plucked at the back of his shirt to get it out of his trousers. He wouldn't pause long enough to help. It was utterly frustrating because she so wanted to touch his bare skin but didn't actually want to stop kissing him, either. Time seemed crucial, fleeting, and yet, good God, she wanted this night to last forever.

And then he rolled over on his back, taking her with him, lifting her on top of him. Now she had access! She settled herself on his hips and sat up to pull the rest of his shirt loose, then quickly unbuttoned it and ran her hands slowly up his chest.

She grinned when she saw him avidly watching her. "Your shirt was a nuisance."

"Was it? So is this," he said, and pulled her dress up and over her head. Then he groaned once again. "No chemise, either?!"

"I told you I was rushed in the matter of dressing," she said, and leaned down to embrace him, pressing her bare skin against his. "Ohh," she sighed blissfully against his lips. "Much better kissing this way, don't you think?"

"I think you're going to be the death of me—and we've gone too far in these lessons."

"The lesson ended a while ago," she said, kissing his neck, then nibbling on his ear. "I wasn't teasing earlier." And then in the softest voice, "I do want you."

He rolled over again, this time so fast she couldn't help laughing. And she didn't need to mention his pants. He rolled to the side and disposed of them so quickly, she barely got to watch. But then he was back, covering her with his long body, and she savored every inch of him.

"I must have died. This can only be heaven."

He was kissing her again, slowly, exquisitely. If he thought to take his time again, she'd be the one dying. "Is it always so frustrating?"

"That's anticipation."

"No, it's bloody well frustration."

"Does this help?"

This was him entering her, not far, just the tip. "Yes! No-o!"

"Now?"

He'd buried himself deeper. The pressure was so brief and painless, she was surprised enough to ask, "Why didn't that hurt?"

He grinned. "I think your ah—frustration—took care of that. You were eager to 'break.'"

She lifted her hips to test his theory. What she felt was sublime, exquisite, a tremor starting, growing, teasing deep inside her. "Don't move," she gasped.

"Have I hurt you?"

"No! It just feels so, so—oh!"

She held on so tightly she might have choked him, but she couldn't help it. The pleasure that peaked and burst so unexpectedly was beyond words, beyond anything she could have imagined. And he must have known she wouldn't mind if he started moving again, because when he did, thrusting deeply inside her, that amazing feeling stayed with her, prolonging the ecstasy.

She caressed him so gently when he lay heavily on top of her. For this one night Montgomery Townsend was hers and she felt very possessive. She didn't want him to move, to speak, to do anything except breathe heavily by her ear. She'd worn him out? It certainly seemed so, until he raised his head and she saw him grinning at her.

"Who warned you it was going to hurt? You spent your formative years away from your mother."

"Actually, my mother was the culprit. She was eager to get that particular conversation over with. I think I was only eleven, the twins only ten, when she sat us down to explain the most gruesome aspects of a wedding night."

"Gruesome?"

She laughed. "At that age, we found any mention of blood gruesome. I recall Layla even cried at the thought of it. Why do you think Kathleen lied to us about it?"

"She didn't, sweetheart. There usually is a degree of pain the first time, or so I've been told."

"So you're special?"

"No, you are. But believe me, I had no idea that your own—eagerness—could assuage it. You are, after all, my first virgin."

Her eyes widened. "Am I really?"

"Yes, and now you have to marry me."

"No, I don't."

"Don't say I didn't ask."

"That wasn't a question, it was an absurd statement. But I must say you are a superb teacher."

He caressed her cheek. "As you so brazenly pointed out, that wasn't a lesson."

Chapter Forty-one

VANESSA COULDN'T BRING HERSELF to abandon Monty and the delightful way they were cuddling each other. And every time she sat up, Monty tugged her back down, so he seemed as reluctant to part as she was.

She truly didn't want this wonderful night to end. But the moment she started feeling drowsy she hurried back to her room. She might not have the least regret about getting carried away by passion, but she wouldn't foolishly allow herself to be caught in his room come morning.

Their parting kiss was bittersweet. At least it was for her, because now that she'd learned Monty's lessons, she didn't dare dally with him like this again. She had a Rathban to marry.

Of course she overslept to an appallingly late hour. She barely made it downstairs in time to join the family for lunch. Kathleen raised a brow at her the moment she entered the room, but she didn't offer an excuse for her tardiness. But Emily pressed her for one.

So she shrugged. "I kept thinking about my fiancé, which kept me awake half the night."

"Because he showed so much interest in me?" Emily said with a coy smile.

What a little cat! Vanessa thought. And she couldn't even tell if Emily was serious or just trying to get even after their fight yesterday. Daniel had left the ball last night directly after returning Emily to Kathleen. He may have thought his mother couldn't complain after he'd danced with all three Blackburn sisters. But Vanessa had been disappointed that she hadn't gotten a second go at him.

"We had a little spat," she told Emily. "I assumed he danced with you merely to make me jealous, but if not, do feel free to add him to your list, since you apparently want every bloody man in London on it."

Emily's cheeks turned red, even more so when Kathleen exclaimed, "Good God, I am appalled by such bickering! You three will not leave this room until you patch up whatever has turned you into vixens. I expect you to be on your best behavior at the dinner party I'm giving tomorrow night. The Rathbans and the Harris family are coming among others—yes, I know you favor the Harris boy, Layla," she added when Layla smiled, but she was still angry enough to add, "This bickering will *not* be in attendance."

Kathleen marched out of the room to show just how displeased she was. Silence followed her departure. Emily pouted. Layla glanced anxiously between them. Vanessa wasn't sure anything could mend this fence.

And then the innocent in their little feud said, "Emily met someone new last night that she likes better'n Monty."

"Monty shouldn't be on anyone's list," Vanessa reminded them. "He's not looking for a wife."

Annoyingly, Emily said, "I'd like to keep him on mine anyway. I have a long list."

Vanessa rolled her eyes. "Exactly the problem, Em. How many of those men did Layla like more'n you? Or does she continue to only be allowed your leftovers?"

"I made a concession!"

"That you like someone better than Monty? D'you really call that a concession? Take a good look at how selfish you are and fix it, before you end up ruining your twin's Season."

Emily glared at Vanessa. And then incredibly, Layla remarked, "I suppose she did deserve that."

"Indeed," Vanessa said, and as if Emily were no longer there, added, "But you can tell her I'm inviting you both to join me for a ride after lunch."

"So you are forgiving her?"

"You can imply as much, though she won't hear it from my lips."

Layla grinned. Emily suddenly giggled. It was an old tactic the girls had used growing up, when one of them was annoyed with another. And it was a nice reminder that they had always settled their disagreements.

Having had her say and feeling much better for it, Vanessa picked up a sausage from the platter, stood, and pointed it to the door. "I'm not actually hungry. Shall we?"

They left the dining room together just as Mr. Rickles was letting someone in. The twins squealed in delight and greeted the man with hugs. Vanessa approached more slowly when she saw it was an old family friend, Peter Wright, but also greeted him warmly. His presence and the twins' reaction to him made her guess that he'd kept up his visits with the family over the years, perhaps as a favor to William. Many letters from Peter had been delivered to her father in Scotland, forwarded by William's solicitor.

He seemed surprised to see her there. "How lovely you turned out, Nessa. I'm not sure I would recognize you if I saw you somewhere other than here. Are the three of you enjoying your long-awaited Season?"

"It's been wonderful so far," Layla said.

"So many young men in attendance," Emily added.

"More than enough to go around I hope?" he teased.

What a touchy subject! Yet Vanessa grinned. "Possibly."

But Emily added, "With Nessa already engaged to Daniel Rathban, there are."

Emily wasn't being catty this time, Vanessa realized. Still she groaned to herself, well aware that Peter had been William's second at that fateful duel with the youngest Rathban brother.

He looked displeased by the news and baldly stated, "Whatever for?"

Vanessa pretended to be surprised by his reaction. "You must be joking. He's a very handsome man."

That didn't change his expression and he said to her, "Might we have a word?"

"We'll go change for our ride, Nessa," Layla said, and pulled Emily with her up the stairs.

Momentarily alone in the hall with her father's best friend, Vanessa braced herself, and Peter didn't tackle the subject delicately, asking her pointedly, albeit in a whisper, "Are you unaware that his father is directly responsible for William's absence?"

She didn't want to tell him that a bargain had been struck. There were already two opposing opinions of her agreement to the bargain, one from her mother, one from Monty. She didn't want Peter's opinion to tip the scale. And she'd prefer for Peter to think the marriage was her idea.

So she answered the question by pointing out, "How better to soften someone's feelings than by becoming a member of his family?"

"But still—does your mother actually approve?"

She grinned. "Mother doesn't quite know what to make of me. She has found, to her annoyance, of course, that ordering me around just doesn't work."

He rolled his eyes. "I am aware that Will gave you free rein, as it were."

"But as it happens," she continued, "Mother holds that family in high regard, so yes, I have her approval."

"Are you *both* forgetting the vendetta?"

Must he be so persistent? "A grieving brother, a bad decision made." She shrugged nonchalantly. "I place the blame where it belongs, as my father did. And one heart-sick old man doesn't blacken the whole Rathban family. Besides, all that matters is I am enamored of the son. I am quite pleased by the match."

Already wearing her riding habit, she headed to the front door before she blushed over that lie, but then something alarming occurred to her and she turned back to Peter. "If you write to my father, please don't tell him. That should be my happy news to deliver."

"Certainly. I won't spoil your surprise."

Chapter Forty-two

"How the deuce did you hear about that?"

Vanessa had come to visit Snow while she waited for the twins to join her and had found Donnan grooming her horse. And he'd immediately told her that there was a stable near London that was for sale.

He laughed at her surprise. "Ye'd be amazed what ye hear in taverns, lass. The owner seems a wee bit desperate tae sell, so ye could probably get a guid price, which is why I mention it—actually . . ." He seemed a little abashed before he admitted, "Calum and me, we've taken a liking tae this town. We wouldna half mind running a stable for ye if yer going tae breed these big beasties."

Vanessa was delighted that the MacCabe brothers were willing to do that. It solved one of the immediate concerns of owning a stable, finding men she could trust to run it for her.

"My schedule is full for today, but tomorrow morning when I escape all the daily callers would be a good time for you to show it to me."

"So yer still being kept busy?"

She nodded. "I expected it to be a whirlwind. Tonight we're going to the theater and I believe Mother has arranged a large dinner party for tomorrow night. I confess, looking further ahead than that is a little daunting."

The twins arrived, the grooms were waiting. Monty wasn't among them today, but she smiled as she imagined him still abed. But there was a little nervousness mixed into her anticipation of seeing him. If he teased her about last night, she wasn't sure how she would react. She hoped he simply wouldn't mention it, even though she knew that's all she'd be thinking about the next time she saw him.

She enjoyed the ride through the park with her sisters. She didn't even mind when they were stopped a few times by their favored gentlemen. The attention certainly kept Emily in a good mood.

Daniel attended the theater that night with his mother, though their seats were on the opposite side of the performance hall from where the Blackburns were sitting, which Vanessa didn't find helpful at all. If Lady Rathban was their partner in the engagement campaign, Vanessa wasn't impressed with her tactics, though to be fair, the seats surrounding the Blackburns had filled up rather quickly with the young men who were unofficially courting the twins.

Vanessa made her lack of interest in the present company clear, just as she'd done at the balls, just as she'd done by avoiding the callers who continued to knock on their door each day. She managed not to be rude about it; she just didn't want to encourage any of these young men when she was secretly courting another.

The twins were too busy whispering with the gentlemen to pay attention to the play being performed on the stage. And Vanessa made sure that if Daniel did happen to glance at her across the room, he would catch her smiling at him, so she wasn't actually watching the actors, either.

Kathleen assured her that she would take her over to Lady Rathban during the intermission and engage the lady in conversation so Vanessa could have a few minutes to flirt with Daniel. That word *flirt* had made her want to laugh. It wasn't exactly what she and Daniel did when they were together. Drawing invisible swords was far more apt.

But she got her chance to be with him for a few minutes in the lobby during the intermission where they were out of range of being overheard. Kathleen had immediately led Lady Rathban a few steps away and started a whispered conversation, and the twins were occupied with their own beaus, leaving her standing next to Daniel.

He looked very dashing tonight, despite his bored expression. But remembering Monty's lessons, she complimented him on his jacket and put her fingers on his lapel as if she were absentmindedly just feeling the fabric.

He responded to her touch by stepping back out of her reach! "You still haven't tired of irritating me?" he said cuttingly.

"I could never tire of you, Daniel. You make my heart flutter."

He snorted. "Rubbish."

She gave him that sexy smile that Monty had approved of. "My stomach, then?"

Any other man might have laughed, or at the very least, have had his lust provoked, but not this one. If looks could kill—was she getting to him? Or had she just gone too far? But then he mumbled, "Brazen," and looked away.

She had to choke back a laugh. *He* was suddenly behaving like a debutante. It made her wonder if he'd ever come to London during a high Season when he was young, or had he been too heartsick over his first lost love to do anything so festive? But he had risked his heart a second time, only to be thwarted by his father again. She would love to have the rumors confirmed by him, not that she actually doubted them, since it certainly explained his refusal to marry—and why he now hated his father.

But she held her tongue, remembering Monty's warning that that particular subject could incite Daniel's rage and that would ruin any progress she was making. If she was making any. Bloody hell, he certainly wasn't giving any clues one way or the other.

But to his accusation of being brazen, she grinned and pointed out, "We're two peas in a pod, aren't we?"

"We're nothing alike. You are daft to see any similarities between us."

"Well, it's true I am not rude, at least not intentionally—not that I really mind your being that way, if you haven't noticed. As for being bold, on the other hand, you might agree, I've got you matched there." And then she sighed. "You know, you really should take advantage of my eagerness to marry you while you can. Should your father disown you before the wedding, I'm afraid my mother will withdraw her approval of you."

"Your eagerness makes you rather pathetic," he said, cutting her to the quick, then confidently added, "There won't be any disowning."

She feigned incredulity. "D'you really not know how close you are to that very thing happening? You may think you can continue to defy your family indefinitely, but I was told confidentially that this is your last year to do your duty to the family—that is, according to your mother," she thought to add.

He deserved that, and it did turn his blasé tone acrimonious. "He's threatened again and again to disown me, but he never will. I'm his only son."

He seemed very confident of that, which might be why she wasn't making any progress with him. So she gambled with the information Monty had given her, saying candidly, "Actually—you aren't."

He snorted. "He wouldn't recognize my bastards, why would he recognize his own?" And then with more certainty, "He wouldn't!"

She shrugged. "Maybe not. But you do have a couple

of male cousins, don't you? You are merely the preferred choice, not his last resort, Daniel."

She felt a deep satisfaction when a smidgen of uncertainty showed up in his expression. Which was a good time to use another of Monty's lessons. She turned away from him, told her mother she was returning to her seat, and left the lobby.

Chapter Forty-three

THE NEXT MORNING AFTER breakfast Vanessa set out in the coach to visit the stable that was for sale. The Scots led the way, riding ahead of the vehicle. When they were a block away from her mother's house, she heard a thump, the door opened, and Monty slipped inside.

"Where are we going?" he asked as he sat down on the cushioned bench across from her.

Vanessa was too surprised to answer. He had actually made a running jump to get in the coach as it moved down the street! The Scots probably hadn't seen him do it. One or both of the two footmen on the perch might have, since the coach did rock a little from Monty's antics, but they must have recognized him.

And just as she'd feared would happen when she saw him again, she was assailed by nervousness, which made her tongue sharp. "I wonder about your sanity. You could have gotten hurt doing that."

"I recently vaulted over a high garden wall, a little coach step was nothing."

"What if my mother were with me?"

"I know exactly where the rest of your family is. The countess is guarding her chicks. She's not about to leave them alone in the parlor with so many young men visiting. And she also has to oversee preparations for her dinner party tonight, which, alas, I won't be attending, but Charley will happily take part. Does she even know you're running away?"

"Did you notice any trunks atop this vehicle?" she rejoined.

"I think if you ran, you wouldn't take them." And then with a very warm smile, he asked, "How are you, sweetheart? Miss me?"

"I might have noticed your absence yesterday," she said, trying to sound aloof. "I assumed you didn't have enough strength to get out of bed."

He laughed and pulled her across the way right onto his lap. "Why are you wounding me?"

Why indeed? And her main concern, that he would ignore her after bedding her, had been answered. Obviously no. But intimacy in a coach in the bright light of day was much too risky when one of the MacCabes might fall back to tell her something through the window.

She tried to get off his lap, but he held fast, so she distracted him by mentioning, "Donnan is taking me to a stable that's for sale not far from London."

"You mean to buy it for that breeding farm you told me you want to start?"

"If it's in good condition. You did tell me that Daniel lives permanently in London, rather than at his father's country estate, so this one is close enough for me to visit regularly, if I'm going to be living in town with him."

His hand was lazily moving up and down her back, but his fingers were getting a little too close to the back of her neck. She tried to ignore the shivers that ran through her. She tried to ignore the urge to caress him back. What had happened to her resolve to distract him?

He continued the conversation as if he weren't casually inciting her passions. "I have a feeling you won't want to spend the entire year with that particular husband, in fact, you'll more likely want to escape his presence as often as you can. So a breeding farm near London might not be ideal for you. Besides, the owner won't sell to a woman. I suppose I could buy it for you?"

"Thank you for the generous offer, but that won't be necessary. He'll sell to me when I tell him the stable is for my father, a surprise gift, so it will need to be put in his name. I already intended to do that, so the Rathbans can never touch it. I expect to get it for a good price, too, once I tell him I don't want his livestock, just the buildings. I'll be filling it with shire mares."

"All for your Snow King?"

It required a strong effort of will to focus on their conversation and not on his hand, which was slowly lifting her skirt. She slapped his hand away before she said, "Indeed, until he has sons to further his line. Now do let me up before anyone sees us like this."

"You're forgetting your lessons. Daniel won't care who might notice."

She narrowed her eyes on him. "This isn't that private. We could be interrupted at any moment by one of the Scots. Are you trying to compromise me?"

His hand was back on her skirt, and then under it. "Would it work?"

"The lessons . . ." She gasped as his hand crept up the inside of her leg. "Were finished."

"Practice makes perfect—drawers today? How utterly disappointing."

She gave in. "Do shut up and kiss me."

A good while later she heard, "Lass, we're being—"

She didn't catch the rest because Monty immediately dumped her on the floor. It was such a rude awakening she burst out laughing and didn't stop when she glanced back to see Monty's astonished expression.

"Sorry!" he said. Was he blushing? He helped her to the seat opposite his. "Bloody instant reflexes are my bane," he tried to explain.

"I'm sure they are lifesaving—or should I say, compromise-saving?"

"Men don't get compromised the way you mean—yes, I know, it's quite unfair. Shall I deal with your Scot?"

"You might as well. He'll know you're here when we

arrive at the stable, unless you intend to hide in the coach?"

He stuck his head out the window to ask Donnan, "Being what? Followed?"

"Aye, as it happens. They've had time and room tae go around us but dinna do so. And I'm thinking ye'll be riding my horse for the rest o' the trip."

Vanessa cringed at Donnan's disapproving tone, but Monty ignored it, saying, "I doubt they're foreigners, but it would be wise to find out. Ask them directions or something and make sure you hear each one of them speak decent English without an accent."

Donnan nodded, but warned, "Ye need tae stop visiting yer troubles on the lass, ye kin?"

"I don't think he likes you," Vanessa said when Donnan turned about to ride behind them.

"He's never hidden that fact."

"D'you really think this is Charley's trouble showing up again? When he's not even with us?"

"I do. They've obviously connected me to him and they keep showing up in too many places. I'm beginning to think they sent a bloody army after the boy, not just a handful of hounds."

Donnan returned and called for the coach to stop. Vanessa felt a moment of fear when Monty opened the door to find out why. "D'you at least have a pistol?"

"One," he said, and grinned at her. "I suppose I'll need to make good use of it."

But after he stepped outside, and before he even looked behind the coach, he was ambushed by a castigating remark. "You're like a runaway dog, Montgomery. Don't ever make me chase you down like this again."

"Good to see you, too, Father."

Chapter Forty-four

THIS REALLY WAS ONE conversation Montgomery shouldn't be having yet, since he couldn't address any of his father's concerns. But Brian Townsend, Earl of Marlham, wouldn't accept half-truths or evasions, which is why Montgomery had done his best to avoid him. At least he had time to think up a good excuse on the ride back to London, though not a single one had occurred to him yet.

"I think he's more angry at having to chase you down a road than he is about those silly rumors. They were dying down, you know, while you kept out of sight. And then you suddenly showed your face in London again and poked the hornet's nest."

Andrew was amused by the whole situation and had offered to share his horse with Montgomery for the ride back to town. Their elder brother, Weston, had made his displeasure clear with his typical condescending look rather than a greeting. But their father hadn't said another word after his warning, which Vanessa must have heard.

At least she had stayed hidden. He didn't need any further censure from his father about riding in a coach with a young debutante unaccompanied by a chaperone.

"How are you three even on this road?"

Andrew laughed. "We were on our way to the Blackburn residence to find out if that's where you've been hiding yourself, when Weston spotted you jumping into that coach."

"Why there?"

"Because Claire noticed the attention you were paying to the Blackburn ladies at a recent ball—you even introduced her to one of them—and mentioned it to Father. Despite his fury over those sordid rumors, he was actually intrigued by her news. I think he secretly hopes you are interested in one of them."

Montgomery didn't address that when he was more concerned about his father's anger. "Fury? Really?"

"I'm afraid so, at least, once he started getting ribbed at his club over it. Typical nonsense, although Weston was with him and repeated the one that lit the fire, 'Passing down old mistresses to your sons now?' Even Weston was furious over that one."

"No doubt," Montgomery mumbled. "But why are you and Weston with Father if he was only going to make an inquiry at the Blackburns' house?"

Andrew chuckled. "I wasn't invited, but once I knew where they were going, I insisted on joining them. I guess Weston went along in case you needed to be dragged home."

Montgomery snorted. "The last time I fought with our elder brother, I believe I won."

"Did you? Or did Claire's distraction let you get in that lucky punch? But in either case, I'm glad force wasn't necessary. I assure you I would have been quite annoyed if Father told me to pitch in."

"But you would have?"

"Of course! You might ignore Father's wishes, but none of the rest of us do. So will you tell me now why you were chasing old dames around London?"

"No."

"But you're going to tell Father?"

Montgomery groaned. "No."

"It's your funeral, Brother."

"I know, so give me a little peace so I can figure out how to keep him from shutting the lid on that coffin."

"Very well, but please, please don't hop off and run down one of these alleys we're passing. That would be the final straw, you know."

Montgomery laughed. He wasn't sure if Andrew was suggesting it or really trying to warn him not to. But they were back in London already, the family residence even in sight, so he said, "Relax. I've been caught. I'll shoulder the ceiling when it falls."

Inside the house, the earl went straight to his study. Weston gave Montgomery a little push in that direction. "I don't usually feel any sympathy for you, Brother, but for once I do. I believe you are supposed to follow him. Get it over with. You'll feel better."

That was quite possibly the nicest thing Weston had ever said to him. Montgomery nodded and entered the study, even closed the door behind him.

His father was already seated behind his large desk, arms crossed, brows furrowed by a daunting frown. There was a sprinkling of gray in his auburn hair, but his light green eyes were still crystal clear and sharp.

"Sit down," he said.

Montgomery ignored the two comfortable chairs in front of the desk other than to put his hands on the back of one of them. "I'd rather not."

"Sit!" Brian barked. "You're not going to stand there poised for flight."

"But I find comfort in having that option."

"Then let me make it easy for you."

Brian stood up, crossed the room, but it wasn't to leave, damnit. He leaned his back against the door, forming a stalwart barricade. "Well, when you put it like that," Montgomery mumbled, and sat in one of the chairs.

"Do you really intend to make light of this?" Brian said as he returned to his seat. "You've been to war, you've come back wounded, you're too bloody old to be flippant about your transgressions. Or have you really failed to comprehend the backlash this sordid gossip has had on your own family? Your mother was looking forward to this trip, but now she refuses to leave the house. I've been sub-jected to ridiculous ribbing m'self. Evelyn has even come home crying."

"Evelyn is always crying, which can be blamed on her husband, not me. She hates the man."

"She loves him too much, but they are both volatile in their emotions. They fight, they patch it up. Not all marriages are as peaceful as mine."

"I've heard Mother yell at you."

"Bloody hell, Montgomery, the only fighting your mother and I ever did was over you children. All of which is beside the point. Explain yourself. Why would you let such absurd gossip about you be spread throughout London?"

Montgomery sighed to himself, because the only thing he could say wasn't going to be enough for his father. He still had to try. "Have I ever lied to you?"

"Not that I'm aware of."

"I haven't, so believe me, everything you've heard was deliberately arranged and necessary, but unfortunately, it's a fire that needs to continue to smolder."

"What does that mean?"

"It means that while it's not a'tall what you think, I won't deny any of it—but you can if you feel inclined to. Say I was foxed."

Brian humphed but took the bone. "Claire said as much. So you were?"

"No, but it's as good an excuse as any. Drink can lead to stupidity, after all."

Brian gave him a hard look. "I expected a full denial, not this nonsense about necessity. How is scandal a necessary evil?"

"I would hardly call this sort of gossip a scandal. If anything, these rumors have merely made me a laughing-stock, which I'm willing to bear. And I did deny the truth of them to you, you just can't share with anyone else that I did." And then to distract his father from this distasteful subject, he told him what he was sure Brian would be pleased to hear. "By the by, I think I've fallen in love."

Momentary incredulity. "You think? That's not something you really need to wonder about, boy. You either are, or you aren't."

"I am."

But Brian's frown was back. "If it's one of those old dames—"

"Gads, no," Montgomery cut in. "Wasn't I clear? That is all an illusion, Father. I appeared to chase them, but never with the intention of catching any of them."

Brian tapped his fingers on the desk for a moment thoughtfully, before his expression turned somewhat hopeful. "She's of good breeding, the one you love?"

Montgomery rolled his eyes. "I highly doubt that would matter to me, but yes."

"Who is she? One of the Blackburns Claire saw you with?"

"I'm not sure I should mention names yet. The situation is rather complicated, seeing as how I'm helping her to win a different husband."

Brian shot to his feet. "The devil you are. Why would you?"

"Because it's what she really wants."

His father sat back down with a sigh. "So you finally fall in love but with a young woman who doesn't return your sentiments?"

"I didn't say that. Didn't I mention complicated? She doesn't love this other chap, but marrying him will help her father, and that's all she really cares about."

"A girl devoted to her family? Incredible. You settle on a good girl, one I might even like, and your solution is to help her win another man? You disappoint me."

That, unfortunately, was abundantly clear, but Montgomery pointed out, "If I lure her away from her goal, I would never forgive m'self. All I can do is hope she doesn't succeed, but then she likely won't forgive *her*self. It's— complicated."

"So you said. So uncomplicate it."

Chapter Forty-five

VANESSA COULDN'T STOP THINKING about the very close call that morning when Monty's family had stopped them on the road. What could be so important to cause them to come after him like that? Would they keep him from returning to her mother's house? Would he come back only to collect Charley? And there could have been consequences if they had thought to look inside the coach before hieing off with him. It made Vanessa realize she'd been taking far too many risks with Monty.

She hadn't done the instigating, but she hadn't tried to put a stop to his tagging along with her when he ought not to, either. Because she enjoyed his company too much! Even when he wasn't caressing her or trying to kiss her, she simply delighted in his presence, was loath to give it up. But she had to. She knew the rules and she'd been breaking too many of them. They could never be alone like that again. He'd understand. Of course he would. He knew the bloody rules, too.

Having made the decision, she fell into a dismal mood that bordered on tears. She'd been so excited about buying her own stable, but even securing an agreement from the owner didn't lift her spirits.

She stopped by the office of her father's solicitor to have him finalize the deal for her. She was glad to make his acquaintance because she would likely need his help in transferring her money back to William before her marriage—if there was going to be a marriage. But if there was, the Rathbans weren't going to get a single copper from her.

She received a surprise when she returned home. The twins heard her open the door to her bedroom and rushed out of theirs into hers before she could close the door.

"You will never guess!" Layla began.

"Why wouldn't she?" Emily said. "The real question is, why did it take so long?"

"I've no interest in guessing," Vanessa said wearily, and dropped down on her bed and closed her eyes.

"He called on you, your aloof fiancé," Emily spilled their news. "We were beginning to wonder why he wasn't more solicitous. Or does he think no further effort needs to be made because the engagement was arranged for him?"

Vanessa didn't want to try to defend a man who had no clue he was engaged because there was no bloody engagement yet, only the expectations of both families. "I have a dreadful headache. Go away."

They didn't leave.

"He departed the moment he was told you were not at home," Layla said.

"And where did you go?" Emily asked. "You not only missed Lord Daniel but also both breakfast and lunch."

Vanessa growled under her breath as she sat up again. "I raided the kitchen before I left. And you do not need to know how I spend my time when I'm avoiding that bloody parlor and all of *your* admirers. As for Daniel, did you not consider that he might feel out of his depth, competing with younger men? And why would he subject himself to niceties, inane conversation, and tea when he doesn't have to? We're already engaged! And we're getting to know each other quite well at the parties we attend, or haven't you noticed? So do not expect him to behave like your beaus when he's already won me."

She finally sighed over their surprised expressions and reminded them by way of an excuse, "The headache? It makes me snappish. I'm sorry."

"He shouldn't have won you, Nessa," Emily said stiffly, but in apparent concern.

"We just think you can do better with a man closer to your age," Layla added before taking her twin's hand and leading her out of the room.

Vanessa yelled, "He's not old!" before she lay back on the bed. Now she felt a headache coming on.

She was curious, though. She could even think of a number of reasons why Daniel had braved the lady's den, including his mother having made an emotional appeal for him to get married. However, if Lady Rathban were going to do that, she probably would have done it back when all those other brides had been offered. Or maybe what Vanessa had implied last night at the theater about his getting disowned had him worried and he wanted to know who gave her that information. Or maybe she was just getting to him. Could he actually want to start a real courtship? She supposed she would find out tonight.

THE TWINS CAME BY to collect Vanessa when the hour approached for Kathleen's party. They were wearing their usual colors, white for Layla, pink for Emily, but Vanessa was impressed and somewhat amused by how the dressmaker had managed to differentiate the twins' many white and pink gowns so that they didn't all look alike. Layla was so excited she seemed to be glowing tonight. Vanessa wondered if she was starting to fall in love with the Harris boy.

The guests had started to arrive, the girls saw as they reached the bottom of the stairs. Kathleen was there to greet them at the door and direct them to the parlor.

"The dining table has been extended to seat twenty, which I think is going to leave only one extra seat," Layla said. "Two from my list are coming."

"And two from mine," Emily added. "But two other debutantes as well, with their respective chaperones, since this is a social event, not a showcase for us, more's the pity.

A few of Mother's friends were invited, too. Oh, and the three Rathbans."

Vanessa frowned, aware that the only reason Kathleen was giving this dinner was specifically to get Daniel here for her. "Three? Daniel doesn't like his father. If Lord Albert shows up, his son won't."

Layla nodded. "Mother said as much, but etiquette, you know. She couldn't very well not put his name on the invitation."

"It doesn't sound like there is going to be room at the table for our own guests," Emily said.

Monty had told Vanessa he wouldn't be attending, and she wondered if he would even continue to reside with them after being dragged home today by his father, as it were. But she didn't mention this to the twins.

"That was discussed prior to the invitations being sent," Layla replied. "Charley will be attending, but Monty declined. Something about his not being able to shine when he's underfoot. He's so droll."

Vanessa grinned. He was certainly that. And she saw Charley leaning against the parlor doorway in a bored manner, though he perked up when she approached him.

"I know Monty has deserted you tonight, but is he even in the house?" she asked.

"I don't believe so, but I have my orders. I'm to continue to be your reluctant swain's rival, but only if needed, of course. Not that it isn't true! I do so adore you."

She grinned. "I think you adore all women."

"How can I not? There is only one of me and so many of you."

She laughed. He was such an outrageous flirt even at his young age. Heaven help women when he got older. But then she saw Daniel at the door with his mother. Of course Albert wasn't with them. She mustered up a wide smile for her supposed intended. He noticed because she saw him looking at her, but he didn't smile back. So much for her cracking that icy shell of his. Nonetheless, she moved over to the little group at the door and, after a slight curtsy for Lady Margaret, put her arm through Daniel's to lead him into the parlor.

"I was told you called today. Dare I guess you're ready to declare yourself?"

She led him to the small bar in the back corner of the room and took a glass of champagne from the servant manning it. Daniel requested brandy instead before he said, "Women shouldn't guess in regard to men's motives. They are never correct, so what is the point?"

"I'm *guessing* you don't know it can be fun to guess?" she rejoined. "Sort of like a treasure hunt. You never know what you'll discover. And you've avoided answering the question."

"I didn't hear a question, merely an inaccurate guess," he replied.

She chuckled. "If I didn't know better, I might think you have a sense of humor buried under that icy veneer. But I do happen to prefer frankness, so the question was and still is, why did you call on me today?"

He drained his snifter and requested another. She only sipped at her champagne while she waited for his answer. He was still looking away from her when he gave it.

"I wanted to see if you were merely toying with me while you entertained other prospects closer to your own age."

She hadn't thought of that reason! Had jealousy actually kicked in? Or was he overly aware that he was older than the Season's crop of bachelors? But why would he even admit it when it apparently embarrassed him, at least, he wouldn't meet her eyes now. But, ashamed or not, she wasn't going to let that subject go when she considered any expression of feeling from him as progress.

"So you thought you would catch me being duplicitous? I didn't think you would resort to spying, but how encouraging that you did!"

He snorted, but then his eyes were back on her, and he asked baldly, "Why do you persist?"

The obvious reason was love. It wasn't true, but he still ought to conclude the possibility and she probably should encourage him in that direction, so she countered, "Have you never been in love?"

The flicker of pain in his expression was so brief she might have missed it if she weren't staring at him. It suggested Lady Roberts's rumors about him were indeed true. Not once but twice thwarted in love—thanks to his father's interference.

But the most recent one must still be a raw subject, so she asked carefully, "D'you still love her?"

His reaction was frigid. "Mention her again and we speak no more—ever."

Her mistake brought a chill. She shouldn't be so bloody nosy, not with him. She tried to recover, saying, "I just wondered if you knew the feeling, since I have it—and it's why I won't give up on you."

He was back to snorting—and being crude. "It's not a lady I want in bed."

Such a bored tone! And boring him wasn't part of her lessons. "What about out of bed?"

"Meaning?"

"Would you like me to be as outrageous as you? Breaking with proper decorum? I assure you I wouldn't balk if that is your wish."

He gave her a blank look for a moment before he actually laughed. "You really are—different, aren't you?"

She smiled. "Have I swooned even once over your attempts to shock me?"

"No, you haven't, which was disappointing, but now it's rather intriguing. So you aren't a virgin?"

She didn't blush despite being mortified by that outrageous question, but she was now in a quandary. She had the distinct feeling that he wasn't interested in virgins other than to shock them with his rude and inappropriate behavior. A momentary satisfaction that would immediately dissipate into boredom. And yet, didn't every groom expect his bride to be a virgin? But there was nothing normal about this jaded man. And the conversation had turned a little too personal for them to continue it in a room that had quickly filled up with guests.

"A lady never tells," she whispered. "But—follow me."

She wasn't sure if he would. He wasn't smitten with her so was unlikely to jump at the crook of a finger like one of the twins' beaus would do. And not following her, despite his being a rake, would just reinforce his assertion that he wasn't interested in her. But she went to her mother's study and paused before entering it so Daniel would know where she went if he did follow. She really didn't want to be alone with him, even in her own house. But he obviously didn't care if they were overheard, even though their conversation could be considered scandalous, whereas she did.

"But?" Daniel said as he entered the small room.

She let out her breath and turned to close the door behind them. "But—are you hoping for tears and whimpers on the wedding night?"

"I don't want a wedding night—ever," he replied. "But I am suddenly tempted to change my mind. I think a sample is in order."

"As much as I would like to give you one, it will be in a wedding bed or no bed—my mother insists."

"To hell with your mother. This desk will do."

Vanessa sucked in her breath and panicked. He mistook her reason for wanting privacy! And he'd already lifted her to set her on the desk. Dare she allow him to at least kiss her before she reminded him about a wedding first? She might have, but he was too rough. She banged her head as he shoved her back on the desk, the inkwell stabbed her shoulder, his nail scratched her thigh as he yanked her skirt up. That was the last straw.

She clamped down on the scream that would have rescued her—and ruined her—and rescued herself, forcefully pushing him back before his large body could trap her there, and she rolled off the desk to get out of his way before she turned to snarl, "Was that another attempt to shock me into running away? Or have you never bedded a lady to know any better? Get rough with me again and I'll shoot your bloody arse. You won't be marrying a milksop in me. There will be passion in our bed, not war!"

And then she did exactly what Monty had warned her not to do, she walked out of the room, leaving Daniel certain that she was furious over his manhandling.

Chapter Forty-six

After Vanessa had stormed out of the study last night, she'd gone immediately upstairs to compose herself. She couldn't even say if that crude attempt at sex—she wouldn't call it lovemaking—had been deliberate on Daniel's part. Had it been a last attempt to ensure she would give up on him? Or was he just accustomed to women who didn't mind such clumsiness? Or—had he been so impassioned with her that he hadn't been aware he was being rough?

Whatever that had been about, she'd had the strongest urge to burst into Monty's room and cry on his shoulder, but she doubted he was there and resisted checking to see if he'd come back. But by the time she went back downstairs, the guests were all seated for dinner—and Daniel wasn't among them.

When she went downstairs for breakfast the next morning, Kathleen was just leaving her study. She beckoned to Vanessa to enter it, whispering, "He's annoyed."

He was Lord Albert Rathban, the bane of her family,

the last person alive she wanted to be in the same room with, let alone speak to. And he blasted her immediately. "Explain yourself!"

Vanessa slowly closed the door behind her. She would have so loved to revile him, but she was mindful that the man could end up being her father-in-law. He could also change his mind about wanting her in his family, which would negate their so-called bargain.

So she faced him and said carefully, "That implies you think I've done something wrong?"

"Didn't you? Why else would Daniel leave his mother here alone last night? And he didn't even tell her! She was mortified!"

So he'd slunk away after her stern rebuff so quickly he couldn't even give his mother an excuse for it? "Your son took liberties. I threatened to shoot him if he did so again. Or did you want me to give away the goods thereby removing all incentive for him to join me at the altar?"

That surprised him. "He wanted you?"

"Wasn't that the point? But I'm not sure he knows how to treat a lady when he's been steeped in lechery for so long—and that's your fault." And before he took umbrage, she gambled. "I don't think he's ever forgiven you for sending his true love away."

"That recent one? He didn't love her," Albert scoffed. "She was too slutty even for his tastes. He only wanted to marry her because he knew I wouldn't allow it—as if he needs excuses to continue to defy me."

"But he was in love with one of them, so I think you already gave him that excuse. Refusing to marry whom you want him to marry is his sort of revenge, as it were. You don't agree? Like father like son?"

"You're far too lippy, gel."

"But it's true, isn't it?"

"Nonsense. He was only eighteen at the time he first fell in love, but—" He frowned and nearly a full minute passed while he delved into his memories. "Now you mention it, there was a vow, something about going to his grave unwed if he couldn't have her. But she was a servant, utterly unacceptable, and he was still a child. It was absurd to think he could be that foolish, and it was forgotten."

"But because you got rid of her, he'll never marry. That is more acceptable?"

"I told you I didn't believe it, or even remember it until now!"

"Even when he started refusing the potential brides you introduced to him?"

His eyes narrowed on her. "He was still sowing his oats, reveling in his bachelorhood. No, I did *not* relate it to that damned servant wench. And it's moot. She ended up dying in childbirth."

"The child, too?"

"No, the infant survived," he said in a grumbling if slightly proud tone. "The man I sent the wench off with was to find her a husband in another country but she refused, then died. He didn't know what to do with the infant so he brought him home to me. I had him educated at boarding schools and he comes home to us on holidays."

Her eyes widened. "Why didn't you say Daniel knew she had given him a son?"

"Because he doesn't know and don't you dare tell him. He would legitimize him just to spite me! He and the boy both think he's an orphaned cousin of my wife's and that is how it will stay."

"He claims to have a lot of bastards. Are you secretly raising them, too?" she asked.

"They had mothers to see to them. I made sure they managed on their own, those I knew about."

She was incredulous that this vengeful old man had done that much. But then he added, "Now tell me why Daniel would even mention that woman to you?"

She thought about lying, or claiming intuition. She wasn't sure what she'd hoped to gain for sharing her suspicion. A reconciliation of father and son that would result in an end to the vendetta against her father as recompense for pointing out the reason why Daniel refused to marry? Or it could go the other way and he could end the marriage bargain because she'd interfered in his family's personal matters.

So she said simply, if rather evasively, "I asked him if he'd ever been in love before. His reaction was honest. But you must realize a son, the son of the woman he loved, could change everything. You should tell him!"

"To what point? He still needs a wife, still needs a son

of good breeding, not a servant's whelp. He needs *you*. So get him to the altar. Whatever you've been doing, it appears to be working."

He abruptly walked out of the room. Her shoulders drooped. She didn't want to pursue a marriage to Daniel, not when she had information that could turn him around, might even mend the rift with his father if he knew that Albert had done right by his first love's son. But what she knew wasn't going to get her father home. She would have to keep her enemy's secret.

Chapter Forty-seven

"I WAS BEGINNING TO THINK you'd abandoned Charley and moved to your family's residence in town," Vanessa said when Monty found her in the small garden behind the town house. Two days had passed since she had last seen him when he'd gone off with his father.

"Gads, no, not with my father in London. He's too nosy, too demanding, and too autocratic. He tends to still treat his children like children—and I've missed you."

She almost blushed when her heart skipped a beat, and his warm smile didn't help her get beyond the rush of excitement those words gave her. She took her eyes off him and continued walking to regain her composure, while he fell into step beside her.

"Was it painful, having to explain those tawdry rumors to him?" she teased.

He laughed. "A little."

"My mother is autocratic like your father. I'm glad I missed the worst of her regimen, and now it's too late for her to take control of my life again. My father, on the other hand, was just the opposite."

"And yet your mother arranged that engagement for you and you've allowed it."

"Because she did me a favor! And don't give me that look, Monty. I warned you, I've said all I'm going to say about my reasons."

He pulled her behind a bush and into his arms. "What if I could find another solution that doesn't involve you marrying a man you don't actually want?"

"You can't. And don't use unfair tactics, such as suggesting you can come up with miracles, to get me to confess all. Besides, I think I may have burned my bridge to Daniel. He didn't stay for the dinner the other night after I threatened to shoot him, and he didn't show up at either of the last two social events I attended, either."

"Are you exaggerating?"

"No."

He was too amused by that. "You give me such hope!"

"Oh, be quiet. I am devastated."

He raised a brow. "Not after only two days you aren't. But it does give me an excuse to distract you."

His distraction was to start kissing her. She groaned because she couldn't just enjoy it as she so wanted to. She stepped back to glower at him.

"No more rule breaking. Don't force me to never leave my room without a maid in tow."

He cringed and lamented, "The bane of most marriages.

How are couples supposed to actually find out if they are suitable for each other with a chaperone listening to every bloody word they say? They might as well be strangers at the altar."

She rolled her eyes at him. "Are those chaperones the reason you turned away from the marriage mart?"

"No, I was never tempted to join it when that particular family duty didn't fall on my shoulders. And then I went off to war."

"And then you became a rake."

"Guilty!" He grinned. "But let's not forget my offer to give all that up for—"

"Shh!" she cut in, but she felt tears forming in her eyes so hurried back to the house before he noticed. He tempted her in every way, including his gallant offer to marry her. Reminders just made the weight she was bearing all the heavier.

Five days and as many social events later, Vanessa was convinced that she'd failed with Daniel. She hoped his mother was to blame for his failure to attend any of those events. Perhaps she was taxed from so much socializing. He certainly wouldn't attend any parties without her. But for a whole week?! He'd even missed her third ball, but so had Monty—which had been even more disappointing.

But on the way home from the ball that night, Layla had remarked on Charley and Monty's absence, and Kathleen had replied nonchalantly, "Our guests are entertaining, but you girls have your own agenda that doesn't require their presence. I asked them not to attend tonight's ball."

Vanessa was infuriated but held her tongue until the coach stopped and the twins alighted first. Putting a hand on her mother's arm to stay her, she demanded, "Why would you do that?"

"Because you're smitten with Montgomery and he distracts you from your purpose. Daniel was jealous of him. I saw it at the second ball."

"That was a deliberate tactic that obviously worked. Monty does happen to be aware of my goal and offered to help me achieve it."

"Kind of him, but once was enough, darling," Kathleen replied. "Too much help of that sort is known to backfire. But if you've changed your mind about who you want to marry . . . ?"

"My target has been absent, if you haven't noticed, for a whole bloody week! Perhaps you should find out why."

"I believe you already know the answer to that. You can't threaten to shoot a man before he proposes. You could have at least waited until you'd married him. Instead, you have no doubt scared him off, that would be my guess."

"Who told—?"

"Lord Albert, of course. He mentioned it before he left that morning he came here for your explanation. What were you thinking, making a threat like that?"

"I was thinking that I didn't want to have sex on your desk, Mother," Vanessa replied sarcastically.

Kathleen's cheeks lit up. "Did he really try that?"

"Yes, so I let him know I was furious. But I did *not* imply I was done with him, only that there would be no sex until the wedding night. I'll handle this m'self and pay a visit to Lady Rathban tomorrow to find out why Daniel has been avoiding me. But he's not scared of me. That would be ridiculous. If anything, he's probably making me stew, to get even. That family is nothing if not vengeful— as you well know."

Chapter Forty-eight

V ANESSA HADN'T EVEN FINISHED dressing the next morning for her visit to the Rathbans when she received a summons to that very house. The note was simply signed "Rathban," so she guessed it was from Lord Albert. With eight days having passed since she'd seen his son and no further progress having been made in dragging Daniel to the altar, he was probably going to tell her that it was no use trying anymore, that Daniel was a lost cause.

She had mixed feelings about that. Should she accept defeat graciously or put up a fight? The possibility of defeat actually lifted her heart a little but not fully, not when her father would lose in the end. But the idea of putting up a fight didn't appeal to her, either. Hadn't she done enough fighting already? However, if Daniel had told his mother that he simply wouldn't have her and she had then told her husband, how could she get around that?

She reminded herself that she'd met Daniel only two weeks ago. Courtships tended to take longer than that.

And she had made progress, enough that he'd wanted her that night in Kathleen's study. What had gone wrong? Had her rebuff wounded his pride? Had the reluctant groom run off to hide somewhere to lick his wounds and neither parent knew where he was now?

It was infuriating that all she could do was guess, so with the answers only a few blocks away, she picked up her pace to get there. She took a maid with her this time so she wouldn't have to tell her mother about the summons yet. Not that the twins' maid could bolster her courage, timid girl that she was, but she wanted someone with her in case tempers flared. And they might. She would insist that Rathban make good on their bargain, even though it hadn't been completed, since she had made an effort, a great effort.

It was a gloomy house, too many grays, no bright colors other than a vase of flowers in the hall. Even the paintings were dull and uninteresting. Had she been too nervous her last time there to even notice how uninviting this mansion was in the daytime? It had been quite festive-looking the night of the ball with lots of flowers and candles lit everywhere. If she had married Daniel, she could have redecorated—and then gotten bored. What actually could she do with herself living with a man she didn't love? But she was doing it again, predicting doom and gloom when anything could have been possible if she hadn't burned that bridge.

She was shown to the parlor to wait, and that wait had

better not be too long, she thought, or she would work herself into a fine snit. He was lying on the sofa, arms crossed. Sleeping? She cleared her throat. He sat up, his expression inscrutable when his amber eyes rested on her. No surprise that she was there? Had *he* sent for her?

She turned to tell the maid, "Wait in the foyer for me, I won't be long." Then to Daniel as she took off her gloves, "If you're going to apologize you should have come to me, not asked me here."

Now he was surprised. "Apologize for what?"

"You were talking too freely in a crowded room on our last encounter. I only wanted privacy to finish our conversation, not for anything else."

He snorted, even waved a hand dismissively. "That was nothing."

Vanessa was trying to contain her own surprise. It hadn't occurred to her that the summons had been from him. And apparently, wounded pride didn't account for his conspicuous absence this past week. Was there some other reason Daniel had avoided her?

Carefully, she said, "I beg to differ."

Vexed, he stood up and grumbled, "Fine, apologies for whatever I did wrong."

She smiled. That was too easy. Daniel Rathban malleable? Why the devil had he invited her here?

She was too curious not to mention, "You have been noticeably absent from recent social events."

He shrugged. "I was washing my hands of this entire . . . confusing business. I even bought passage to leave the country. And visited the properties that were given to me the day I was born so I could arrange to sell them, only to find out I don't actually own them yet. I'd been given the incomes from those properties but the deeds won't be mine until I marry. My father has kept me on a rope from the day I was born, but I hadn't realized it until now."

There was the bitterness she was more accustomed to hearing from him. So she steered him away from the subject of his father and pretended nonchalance that he was leaving England. "When does your ship sail?"

"It did, yesterday."

Had he stayed because of her? Or had Albert done the right thing and told him about his son?

He disabused her of both notions when he continued. "I squandered away the fortune I had when I turned eighteen. Don't ask me on what, because I honestly don't remember those years. I was rarely sober. But I had depended on the fortune I would gain from the sale of those properties. Without them, I can't really afford to live anywhere else, so I'm still unable to cut that bloody rope my father tied on me." And then with a snarl he added, "I have often thought of killing him, I hate him that much. Do you find that strange?"

She would probably feel exactly the same if she had a father like his. "No, I confess, I don't like your father, either."

He snorted. "I still suspect my father's machinations have brought about your interest in me, though Mother swears it's not so."

"Didn't I tell you that as well?"

He ignored that and warned, "Don't expect me to be faithful."

Out of the blue! As if he'd asked her to marry him and she'd already accepted. But considering everything that had led to this moment, she wasn't going to insist he propose the normal way.

"Don't expect me to be, either."

He narrowed his eyes on her. "Do as you like after you produce a male heir. That is what this bloody marriage is about, after all, and it will get Father off my back for good. This is all so pointless! He could have acknowledged any one of the bastards I've produced—"

"Spare me the details," she said dryly. "I'm really not interested in how you've populated half of London. But I wasn't joking about shooting you. I'm not a scullery maid. You will deal with me gently or not at all." And having stressed that, she smiled and asked, "Shall the banns be read this Sunday? I'd rather not have a long engagement."

"No banns. Apparently, Father obtained a special license the very day I turned eighteen."

She laughed, though it sounded hollow. "That's definitely planning ahead. So you told him the good news?"

"I don't speak to him unless I'm forced to. I left it to

Mother. We will have a private ceremony here this weekend, only family invited. Don't worry about a wedding dress. My mother has offered hers if you don't have one."

This weekend! Her heart began to pound, not with happiness, but dread. And she didn't dare try to delay the inevitable. She'd put this marriage in motion herself.

Chapter Forty-nine

WHEN VANESSA ARRIVED HOME, she was only a little late for luncheon with her family. Even Charley and Monty were at the table today. Charley stood up to bow in greeting in his usual flamboyant fashion. She avoided Monty's eyes as she took her seat and tried to concentrate on the plate set before her—without much luck. She was too aware of Monty across from her, could feel the heat from his eyes without looking up to see it.

"I would like a word after you eat, darling," Kathleen said.

Rickles, that traitor! Of course he would have let Kathleen know about that summons. And of course she would be eager to know what Vanessa had found out this morning at the Rathban house. It didn't require a lengthy explanation, though she'd barely had time to digest it herself.

"I hope you weren't looking forward to planning a big wedding, Mother, at least not for me. I'm to be married in four days at the Rathbans' London residence. They have a special license to allow it."

How dull her voice sounded! Vanessa hadn't meant to just drop it out there like that, either, but was glad she did. Anything to do with this wedding couldn't be over and done with soon enough for her.

The twins squealed with excitement over her news and got up to hug her. Kathleen was more reticent, saying, "This weekend? Why so soon?"

"Less time for wedding jitters?" Vanessa suggested, adding, "The date wasn't my idea, though I'm not displeased by it. And they want a private ceremony, with only the immediate family present."

"Hiding it?" Kathleen said, clearly annoyed. "The Rathbans better have a good reason. Yes, I did expect you to have a grand wedding that I was looking forward to planning—not this!"

Vanessa chuckled wryly. "Considering jilted brides are the bane of that family, I would guess it's merely a precaution to ensure less embarrassment, should one of us end up being jilted."

Kathleen actually stood up. "He wouldn't dare—that is, he *did* ask you?"

"More accurately, he took it for granted that I would agree, but yes, this is his idea. Do sit down, Mother. We are getting exactly what we both wanted. But if you're worried about it, maybe you should hire someone to keep a pistol on his back until we're wed. Monty perhaps?"

Levity was so uncalled for, and Vanessa regretted it immediately. She had avoided glancing at Monty after her announcement, didn't want to see his reaction to it, might end up crying . . .

But Monty actually replied, "I would pull the trigger."

An embarrassing, telling, overly dramatic response that left an uncomfortable silence in its wake. Vanessa was likely the only one there who didn't think he was joking, in poor taste or not.

Kathleen took her seat again and cleared her throat before returning to the subject of the nuptials. "Since we didn't prepare *this* far ahead, I would be honored if you would wear my wedding dress, Vanessa. It is exquisite, inlaid with seed pearls. You will be pleased with it."

"Thank you," Vanessa replied. "Daniel offered his mother's gown, which is no doubt moldy by now, she's been married so long."

The twins giggled, though a little nervously, which didn't surprise her considering the mood at the table.

Vanessa still couldn't bring herself to look directly at Monty. Now she regretted having made her announcement with him in the room. But he would have found out, likely later today. Her family would no doubt be talking about nothing else for the next four days. And wasn't it better that he hear directly from her that she had attained her goal? Bloody hell, he'd even helped her attain it!

And then Charley lamented, "I confess I'm devastated you will wed another. I would have made you my queen."

Vanessa smiled at the boy. "Thank you, Charley, but you know that wouldn't happen."

"My mistress, then?"

She rolled her eyes. "Not bloody likely."

"I'm too young to have my heart broken."

"Young enough for it to heal quickly."

He sighed. "I suppose."

But Monty stood up and his remark broke *her* heart. "Don't do this."

Kathleen gasped at his temerity and said sternly, "Lord Monty, this is none of your concern."

To which he tossed his napkin down and left the room. A moment later the front door slammed shut behind him, leaving yet another pregnant silence.

Vanessa managed not to cry right there at the table. But she did cry, a lot, over the next three days, so her eyes were quite red and puffy on the day of the wedding. Thank goodness for wedding veils. And that day arrived far too quickly.

The twins had cornered her the night before. They had been her only source of comfort at this trying time. Monty hadn't returned after storming out. Emily and Layla knew she wasn't happy about the marriage she'd agreed to. They kept asking her why she was marrying Daniel when she so obviously didn't want to. She didn't even try to deny it at that point. She just told them that some things were more important than love, that they would understand one day. Very soon, she hoped.

"Can we even wish you happy?" Emily asked.

"Or is it pointless to?" Layla asked.

"I *am* going to find some happiness in this marriage," Vanessa assured them. One way or another she would.

But it was hard to keep that thought in mind when she stood at the improvised altar next to Daniel Rathban. They were being married in the mansion's music room only because it already had chairs in it. No decorations had been added, not even flowers, to brighten up the dreary room, which was mostly filled with Rathban relatives. Actually, there was one bright spot, Charley, who was wearing a lot of gaudy jewelry and a bright gold jacket. He'd been allowed in for the ceremony only because he was a guest at the bride's house. Monty could have gotten in, too, for the same reason, but he hadn't tried.

The handsome groom took her hand when she joined him and whispered to her, "We got here on an angry note, you and I, which I apologize for. I will try to make this work, Vanessa."

Which made her want to cry again! She would have rejoiced at the words if she'd heard them before she knew where her heart really belonged. So how could she make it work when she loved another? She could still run. The last words hadn't been spoken yet. But then her father would remain away from his family for the rest of his life.

And then the priest asked if anyone objected to the marriage and Vanessa held her breath. Only Monty would be bold enough to do that, but he'd given up! He hadn't tried again to dissuade her. She had the sinking feeling that she'd never see him again.

"I do," was said loudly at the back of the room.

Vanessa turned, eyes wide, but then another man said, "I do as well."

Vanessa saw only her father and immediately ran to him. Everyone else in the room saw only Prince George.

Chapter Fifty

"Why wasn't I invited, when I reside only a paltry few blocks from here?" George asked calmly.

The Prince Regent had availed himself of Albert's chair behind the desk in Albert's study.

But Albert was enraged and not hiding it very well because he had come so close to getting Daniel married, only to have those machinations ruined by an interfering royal. "If your objection to the wedding is because of that oversight, Highness, I assure you it wasn't intentional."

"Not a'tall. I confess I was merely curious. So the reason was?"

"My son wanted a small ceremony—"

"Or you did?" George cut in. "I've been apprised that it was a ceremony steeped in the distasteful business of blackmail."

"No! The marriage was arranged amicably."

"Your terminating an earlier blackmail scheme in

exchange for a wife for your son was the bargain, was it not? Amicable or not, that is still a new instance of black-mail. Are you beginning to see where you erred, dear Albert? What you did previously was to usurp a power that is only mine to wield. Only I can banish one of my lords from my kingdom. *Do* you deny it?"

Albert dropped into a chair in front of the desk. "He killed my youngest brother."

"So there was a duel?"

"Yes."

"Thank you," George said. "That was the missing piece of the puzzle."

"There was no puzzle. Blackburn was asked, begged, to stand down, and he wouldn't."

"Perhaps you aren't familiar with my father's chronicler? A strange fellow with an even stranger memory. He doesn't need to write down the facts he gathers from one end of the country to the other, though he still does, because everything he has heard, has been told, or has ferreted out as pertains to our kingdom stays in his head."

"What has that to do with any of this, Highness?" Albert demanded.

"Everything, since I had reason to summon him this week once I became aware of your distasteful dealings. He told me immediately why there could have been a duel the year of your brother Henry's death, though you managed to keep it quite secret, that your youngest brother had very obviously pursued Lady Blackburn that summer. So it would seem there was a reason for that duel, and it would seem you were less than honorable to blackmail Lord Blackburn because of it."

And then almost as an afterthought, George added with a tsk, "As for your recalcitrant son, you should have approached me with your worries, Albert. I could have found a suitable match for your boy without resorting to the unsavory business of blackmail."

"You don't understand—"

George cut in, "But I do, actually. Remember the chronicler? Five disappointed debutantes, wasn't it? I'm also aware that the gel has feelings for another and is only here to get her father home, which is redundant, since he now has my permission to return without consequences."

"My boy won't agree to this. He actually wants the chit."

"I will deal with your son. I can be very persuasive. Be assured, he will marry whom I tell him to marry. And you will consider the revenge you exacted on the Blackburns to have run its course and is now over." George stood, his affable manner gone. "You don't want to cross me on this, Albert. You have broken laws that could have serious consequences for your entire family if the courts are so informed. Do we understand each other?"

"Perfectly."

"Splendid. Now about your son . . ."

AT THE BACK OF the music room, even as she hugged her father fiercely, Vanessa exclaimed, "Why would you do this? You've exposed yourself!"

He hugged her just as fiercely, but in a calm whisper assured her, "It's all right. I had hoped to sneak into London and speak to you privately to forbid this, but I didn't get here in time, was almost too late to stop this nonsense that Peter informed me about."

"Peter! I asked him not to do that."

He smiled gently. "Don't be mad at my friend. He knew I would never allow this farce of a marriage. But it's still all right, Nessi. That was the Regent I came in with. He was also apprised of what was happening and why. He'll be wiping the slate clean for us, or the Rathbans will know royal vengeance. Well, that is the Regent's intention," he said with a laugh. "Whether Albert agrees or not, we will know soon enough."

There was no time to say more when the twins excitedly arrived for their reunion with their father. Vanessa laughed as she was pushed out of the way. She could never have imagined this wedding being aborted so—royally. And the relief she felt was so overwhelming she was afraid she was going to start giggling and not be able to stop.

"Is he really back? For good?" Kathleen asked behind her. "Without this wedding taking place?"

Vanessa moved to join her mother, who was nervously

hanging back from the reunion. "It would seem so— thanks to royal intervention."

"How did that come about?"

"I haven't a clue, but it's ironic that this day has turned out to be such a happy one after all. However, I have a feeling the twins will balk if they don't have full access to Father now, after all this time. So you might want to invite him to stay at your house for the duration of the Season at least, or they are likely to insist on moving to his house with him."

"Will you ask him?"

"You wanted him back, Mother. Now he is here. You aren't afraid of him, are you?"

Vanessa regretted the question immediately, when it was very obvious that Kathleen was experiencing some trepidation. "I just recall the last time we spoke. It was— difficult. And if he is still angry at me I'd prefer that you girls not witness it."

"Many things have changed in these last years, but he has his life back now—most of it, so he may not feel like fighting with you, may only want to get reacquainted with the twins. But of course, I'll ask him for you."

Most of the Rathbans had already moved past them to leave the room. The priest even walked by, but glancing to where she had almost married the wrong man she saw that Daniel hadn't left. He was standing exactly where she'd left him. And he was staring at her with—confusion? Or was that regret? She cringed inwardly. He wouldn't be there if she hadn't poked, prodded, seduced in her fashion, and lied. She had let him think she loved him, all for a good cause, but still, she felt bad about it now.

He did not deserve her pity, as nasty as he'd been about their courtship, so why did she pity him? She walked over to him and said, "I'm sorry. I can't marry you, but I can do you a good turn to maybe make amends. Your true love gave you a son before she died. Your father has cared for him very well, even made him a member of your family. You both know each other as cousins. Do with that knowledge what you will, but I hope it will lighten your heart, Daniel Rathban."

She had shocked him, perhaps twice. She hurried away before he recovered sufficiently to question her—and ran into the Prince Regent just outside the music room where her family was waiting for her. He appeared jovial. His meeting with Albert must have gone well! Her father's wide smile confirmed it.

After she curtsied to him, George said to her, "I'm glad not to be kissing a bride today, 'deed I am. You can thank your champion for my interference, m'dear."

She stared after the corpulent fellow as he sauntered toward the front door. William put his arm around her waist. "What did he mean by that?"

"I have only a slight idea, so I'm not going to say. Can we *please* leave this house? And you have been invited to stay at Mother's house, where you will have access to all three of your daughters. Don't refuse just because it's hers and not yours."

"I believe she and I are still married, on paper at least, which means . . ."

She laughed. "That it's yours, of course. How *male* of you, Father."

Chapter Fifty-one

VANESSA WAS LOOKING FOR William later that day and was about to check in the study for him when she heard her mother inside it saying in an accusing tone, "You did it deliberately, didn't you? Raised her to be exactly what she ought not to be just to spite me!"

"I did nothing of the sort," William replied. "But I wasn't going to treat her like a delicate flower in Scotland, and she was so happy doing the same things I did that I didn't have the heart to stop her and curtail her activities. I decided it wouldn't hurt to give at least one of our girls more options in life than being a wife and a mother. So yes, I raised her differently than you would have, gave her a more thorough education, prepared her for anything that might come her way, and I bloody well won't apologize for it."

Vanessa put her hand on the doorknob to interrupt them. Her parents couldn't even wait a single day before fighting with each other. But she paused when she heard

Kathleen say, "I hate to admit it, but she makes me so incredibly proud that she's mine."

"Then maybe you should thank me instead of complaining. And why are we rehashing the past?"

"Because you never listened to me when I explained what really happened! Henry set me up, Will. He had everything planned ahead of time, he showed up wherever I went, he made sure people saw us together and heard me laugh at his jokes. He made it appear as if we were already lovers when we weren't."

"Is that really your excuse, Kathy? It appeared so, so you might as well make it so? Was that your logic?"

"No, that was *his* logic, and his blackmail. He threatened to spread the rumor that we were lovers if I didn't agree to make it so. I did exactly what you did, William. I was willing to make a sacrifice to prevent a scandal. Why is it perfectly fine for you to protect our family that way, but not for me? But you stopped it from happening. It never happened!"

Vanessa wasn't interrupting *that*. She turned about and headed to the little garden behind the house. And stewed. Her parents still weren't going to tell the twins the whole story. She learned that from her father when she rode home with him on his horse, despite the wedding dress. "Perhaps when they are older. Perhaps never," William had said. Instead, he was going to give them a few dreadful details about the islands and nature's vengeance thwarting him again and again, and nothing more—other than the assurance he would never go back to the West Indies because he'd sold the bloody plantation.

She'd dealt with the truth fairly well—no she hadn't. She'd ended up hating her mother. Did she still hate her, when as Kathleen had just told William, Kathleen was only trying to protect her family from a scandal just as William had done, but in a different fashion? Maybe it was just as well that her parents were getting that fight over with, though she didn't think it would mend the boat, as it were.

"I heard it went well, that you're back on the marriage mart."

She turned about to see Monty approaching her with that heart-stirring smile he seemed to reserve just for her. "Heard from who?"

"George, of course."

"So you're my champion?"

He shrugged. "He owed me a favor. I gave up a promised property for it."

She chuckled. "No, you didn't. You're just good at fixing things."

"I'm better at it when the problem doesn't break my heart," he replied.

"Stop teasing. Have you met my father yet? The Prince Regent wasn't the only one who objected today to that wedding."

He laughed. "Your father was there? Was that your

doing, letting him know so he could arrive in time to save you?"

"No, of course not. That was the last thing I wanted, for him to endanger himself and provoke the very scandal he left England to prevent. An old friend of his found out about it and let him know, even though he promised me he wouldn't."

"I'm pleased for you, Nessi. I expected it to be another few weeks before your father returned to England, but now your every wish has been granted."

Not quite. Dare she tell him that she had no desire to get back on the marriage mart? That her heart was already his? She didn't really need to hide it anymore, did she? But he didn't want to marry. To push him into it would be the worst sort of manipulation after everything he'd done for her. But she didn't have to avoid his kisses anymore—if he still wanted hers.

She tested that thought and put a hand on his chest. He teased, "Still practicing seduction?"

"Is it working?"

He pulled her close and kissed her in answer. She wrapped her arms tightly around his neck, wondering if this might be the first time she happily swooned. It felt like she might. This was where she wanted to be. They should be painted like this. She could pose for hours pressed this closely to him. . . .

"Vanessa?" William called out.

She leapt back. Her father's voice was too close. Having both parents in the same house wasn't going to give her much privacy!

And then William appeared at the entrance to the garden. "Your mother is looking for—"

"I'll find her!" she cut in, and rushed past him into the house.

Chapter Fifty-two

"And who might you be?" William asked from the doorway.

Montgomery bowed slightly, uncomfortable with the frown forming on the older man's visage. "You would be William Blackburn, Earl of Ketterham, home from the war, as it were? I am Montgomery Townsend. My ward and I have been guests of your wife's for a few weeks now."

The frown deepened. "So my wife keeps her lovers under her roof now?"

Montgomery started to say he preferred younger women, but with William in London now—if he'd heard the rumors that Montgomery pursued older women, he just might try to kill him. So he stated the truth. "I'm in love with your daughter."

"I have three."

"Nessi."

"She told you my nickname for her?"

He was relieved that at least the earl's frown was gone.

"It was a mistake. She meant to say Nestor. She was wearing britches at the time—and brandishing pistols when we met."

William stared hard at him for a moment, but then laughed. "You'll have to tell me all about that—before you have my blessing to court my daughter."

Just court? He wanted more than that! "Well, Lord William, if you have a couple of hours I will tell you all about my acquaintance with Vanessa, recount every delightful hour I've spent with her. And by the by, I'll be happy to sign her contract."

But then Mr. Rickles appeared to announce, "You're needed on the third floor, my lord."

"Who is?" William asked.

"Our guest is," the butler replied.

"I'm also a bloody guest," William stated, a very clear complaint.

"My ward is on the third floor, so I think he means me," Montgomery said. "We'll talk again I'm sure, Lord William."

IT WAS BEDTIME, EARLIER than usual tonight because the day had been so thrilling, but exhausting, too, with so many emotional ups and downs. Vanessa had spent most of it with her father and her sisters, who were happy that she could enjoy the remainder of the Season with them and choose her own husband. William had gone to his own house because that's where his luggage was, but he planned to move in to Kathleen's house tomorrow to be with his daughters. After he left, Kathleen had mumbled about needing a sleeping draught tonight. She was obviously upset and disappointed over his cool reaction to her.

Vanessa was frustrated because she didn't get another chance to talk more with Monty after her father interrupted them. He and Charley had both stayed out of the way of the family reunion. It didn't take much mental arguing with herself to decide to seek him out now while the house was quiet. She even put her pants on for the visit, remembering the effect they usually had on him.

When he answered her knock on his door, his surprise was evident. He waved a hand for her to enter before he asked, "Should I be delighted—or wary?"

"I couldn't sleep. And I still have questions that I would have asked earlier if my father hadn't interrupted us in the garden."

"I seem to recall something else had already distracted you from whatever you intended to ask."

He grinned with the reminder of that wonderful kiss they'd shared in the garden. It was a good opening for why she was really there, but she suddenly got a little nervous. She might be bold, but not so much when it came to him.

So she asked, "Why did you use up one of your favors with the Prince Regent to get him to object to my wedding?"

"Because that wedding was a tragedy, and it occurred to me that George could stop it, since you wouldn't—yes,

I know, helping your father was more important, but George could and did negate all that. So can you tell me now what Rathban's blackmail was about?"

"Must you know?"

He smiled. "When you're ready will be soon enough."

"You're too accommodating."

"A flaw?"

"Not a'tall! So why did you come with us to London to risk stirring up that hornet's nest of rumors again?"

"There was a lure I tried to resist but, in the end, I couldn't."

She snorted. "You like this town that much?"

"London can be amusing, but I'm not that fond of it."

She realized he hadn't answered her. "So what was the lure?"

"You know."

It wasn't just that answer but the sensual look he was giving her when he said it that made her gasp softly. Yes, she did know. He was as strongly attracted to her as she was to him. She didn't care if he was a rake and passion was all he could offer her. He was her kind of rake and she loved him.

He suddenly asked, "Are these questions really why you came to me tonight?"

"No, with the tragedy—as you so aptly named it— averted, I have a strong urge to celebrate."

"What did you have in mind?"

Her boldness reared up. "You."

It was almost instant, the space between them disappeared as he wrapped his arms around her and started kissing her. Such a primal attraction they had for each other. Every time she was near him, this was what she wanted to do. Resisting these urges had been incredibly hard. Tonight she didn't have to.

"As much as I like seeing you in pants, I'd rather see you out of them right now," he said as he led her to his bed.

She stretched out on the bed as she watched him remove his shirt. He did so slowly, his eyes roving up and down her body. Did he really want to take his time when she was so eager for him to be inside her?

She harked back to their first time in a bed, giving him an alluring look and whispering, "I'm not wearing any drawers under these pants."

"Show me."

She drew in her breath, his look got so hot. He wasn't taking his time now! She quickly slipped out of her pants. He was quicker getting out of his. And then she felt his skin, all along her length. She felt a moment of blissful happiness. This was where she wanted to be for the rest of her life, next to him, touching him, feeling him, tasting him.

He was kissing her so ardently, stirring that chord deep inside her, then her neck, her breasts, all over, every single touch of his mouth heightening the urgency. "You're frustrating me again!"

He laughed. "There is much to be said for anticipation—but, perhaps not when you're so new to this. Shall we"—he paused to give her one more long kiss—"celebrate now?"

"Yes!"

He mounted her, slipped easily inside, then slowly turned over so she was lying fully on top of him. But she wasn't sure what to do up there so she sat up to have more options, at least gain some control, but that was a mistake—or perfect, because it put him even more deeply inside her and her eyes closed as the orgasm washed over her.

"You're amazing," he said, sounding a little awed. "Can you slow down now?"

"I can sleep now."

"Bite your tongue!"

She grinned and slowly rolled her hips. "I was teasing. You can proceed at your preferred pace."

"After that incentive, you must be joking."

He flipped her on her back and thrust only twice before he exhaled deeply and put his forehead to hers to whisper, "You surprise me at every turn."

"Is that why you think I'm amazing?"

"That and in so many other ways. I think it would take a lifetime to know them all."

She smiled dreamily as he rolled to her side then snuggled her against his side. She'd like to give him that lifetime, but that wasn't a subject to broach when they were both influenced by sublime bliss. Perhaps tomorrow, when logic and reason would prevail to ensure he had no regrets.

But it wasn't long before she heard a noise downstairs. He heard it, too. "The hour isn't that late. Perhaps your father is returning, after all?"

She nodded her agreement. He added, "I'll just check to be sure. If you fall asleep, I'll carry you back to your room."

How could she sleep after that thrilling experience they'd just shared? She did.

Chapter Fifty-three

BEFORE MONTGOMERY REACHED THE stairs he heard the clanging of swords downstairs. Practicing at this hour? But when he came around the corner for a full view of the hall below, two things caught his eye immediately. Rickles, the butler, was pressing his full weight against the front door as if he expected intruders to push their way in. And Charley was engaged in a sword fight with a stranger. Instead of helping, Arlo just stood back out of the way!

Montgomery bounded down the stairs, but before he could say anything, Charley knocked his opponent's weapon from his hand and pointed the tip of his sword at the man's throat. A lot of whispered gibberish spilled from the obviously terrified man's mouth, so Montgomery waited for it to end before demanding an explanation.

When Charley finally lowered his sword, he glanced back at Arlo and said quite drolly, "They wish to be forgiven before you go on a rampage of head chopping. They got word before we did that the uprising is over, the palace has been reclaimed for the monarchy. This one, seeing only one of us armed, made one last attempt to take a hostage so they wouldn't have to beg for their lives."

"I thought head chopping was your prerogative, Charley," Montgomery remarked dryly.

The boy turned with a grin. "That was just one of my many exaggerations, my friend, to embellish my role. But my king doesn't chop heads, either."

"Your king?" Montgomery said, and cast an incredulous look at Arlo, who gazed back at him with an inscrutable expression. He turned back to Charley. "Then who the hell are you?"

Charley bowed with his usual flourish. "Sebastian Bahmann, from a long line of Bahmanns whose sole duty has been to defend Feldland's royal house. I have spent all of my life training in the lethal means to perform that service, to protect my king at any cost."

Montgomery snorted. "Should I be impressed by all of seventeen years' training? Make that seven years, at the most, maybe nine—you know bloody well you weren't training as a child."

Charley chuckled. "If age matters, I'm actually twenty-seven, older than you, I believe? Seventeen was merely a number we determined would better match my pretty face—as you termed it. And it did, didn't it? Not once did you doubt seventeen was the age of this package," he added, waving a hand over his body.

Montgomery pinned Arlo—or was it Charles now?—with

an annoyed look. "I suppose you aren't seventeen, either?"

"Nineteen, and don't be angry with Sebastian. Swapping identities allowed us to come to England safely."

"I was charged with *your* care, not that of your bodyguard servant who apparently can protect himself. Can you?"

"He doesn't need to when I protect him," Sebastian said in a deadly serious tone Montgomery hadn't heard from him before. "You were charged with secreting us away, which was my idea, not you in particular, just someone of your caliber to help us deal with the riffraff."

"Let me guess, you annoyed the hell out of George deliberately to make that happen?"

Sebastian nodded. "It was necessary. Carlton House is too open. They even let in tradespeople! And it was utterly boring there. I was right to change our location. One of the rebels learned of our whereabouts from a servant at Carlton House after pretending to be a supporter of Charles's. The Prince should be warned his servants gossip too loosely."

"Were the golden locks an exaggeration, too?"

"Blond is my natural color," the king said. "Which I have sorely missed."

Sebastian added, "Mine, too, but I don't usually wear such fine attire and jewels. Our disguises began as soon as we were safely out of Feldland."

"I suppose this means you're going home now?"

Sebastian nodded. "Napoleon hasn't gained the support he needs to spread his wings across Europe again, so as you said, it won't be long before he is defeated again with the armies that did so previously gathering."

Montgomery glanced at Rickles, who was still guarding the door, before asking Sebastian, "Are there more rebels outside?"

"Quite a few, but I've warned this one." Sebastian thumbed the man who had surrendered. "They will never be forgiven; they will court death if they return home."

"We deal more harshly with assassins here," Montgomery said to Charles. "Is banishment enough punishment for you?"

"Sebastian knows my mind. For a Feldlander to lose his home is a grave punishment."

"Well, then! With my job apparently ended, I will say I'm glad your difficulties are over, but I won't say it's been a pleasure."

Sebastian jabbed his ribs. "You know you will miss us."

"Not a bit," Montgomery denied.

"And we shall miss you, Monty. You should visit us in Feldland someday, and bring your delightful wife."

"I don't have a wife."

"You will."

Montgomery wished he were as confident about that. But he glanced at the servant-turned-monarch again, annoyed that he'd been so perfectly fooled. "At least Feldland doesn't have a buffoon for a king."

Sebastian snorted. "It was a role!"

"One you played too easily, *boy*. I need a drink." And then his eyes widened. "Good God, you let your king drive a coach?! That's taking disguises a little too far, don't you think?"

Sebastian laughed. "He insisted. And we will return to Carlton House tomorrow to await passage home. I do owe Prince George an apology as well as an introduction to his actual ally. How do you think he will take the news that it wasn't actually Feldland's king who bedeviled him?"

"Depends on his mood, so I'll go with you to make light of it. If you want to leave here with your current disguises intact, it will avoid a lengthy explanation to the Blackburns, but that's up to you. In either case, I'll explain to Vanessa after you're gone."

"You ought to do more than that."

"Yes, I know. And matchmaking doesn't become you. Stick to bodyguarding."

Chapter Fifty-four

VANESSA WAS PLEASED WHEN she saw Monty at the bottom of the stairs. Waiting for her? She was smiling before she reached him.

"Thank you for getting me back to my room last night. I must have been very tired not to have woken up when you carried me there."

"It was an eventful day, but no need for thanks. It was my pleasure. I happen to like holding you in my arms."

She hoped that was why he was suddenly leading them toward the garden again. To continue where they'd left off yesterday, before her father had found them there?

"D'you know if my father has returned yet?"

"Hoping for another interruption?" he teased. "By the by, what did your mother want with you yesterday that was so pressing she sent your father to fetch you?"

She snorted delicately. "It wasn't pressing a'tall, she just needed someone to complain to about my father."

"She's not pleased that he's back?"

"Oh, she is, she just hoped for a different sort of re-union with him."

"I see," he said.

She smiled to herself. He didn't nor would he unless she finally told him the whole of it, but that still wasn't her secret to share.

And then he added with a sigh, "My guardianship has ended."

Her brows furrowed. "Why does that sound like you're leaving us?"

"Because my excuse to be here is leaving us."

He briefly explained that their companions had told the truth about royal blood, but not about who had it.

"Arlo is a king? Really? But he looks so unassuming!"

"That was the point."

"And you kept that secret all this time?"

"No, I bloody well didn't know, either, until last night," he grumbled.

She laughed. "It suddenly feels like we've been in a theater all this time. Charley—Sebastian is it?—even asked me for advice about how to act like a commoner! And he said it was to please you!"

"You know he was laughing at us all the while for fall-ing for his performance."

"I doubt that. If anything he was having fun being someone so different from who he really is. Don't begrudge him. I find it highly amusing now. But you don't need to leave when he does. Aren't you still avoiding duels here in the city—and axes?"

"Sebastian was able to hide in plain sight here, but I wasn't. However, I did straighten out that mess I had been avoiding, enough so that the respective husbands no longer think I'm quite the culprit and have backed off. So you see, my excuses really are gone to remain tucked away in your home. While I won't miss Charley, I will miss you. I can't imagine a better traveling companion on a lifelong journey."

It was the look he gave her when he picked a flower and handed it to her that made her heart race. Hope was a tricky thing, but in this case, it was suddenly soaring.

Until he asked her, "So you're going to finish off the Season and find another groom?"

There was hesitancy in that question. And she wasn't letting go of her hope yet. She moved a little closer to him until their shoulders brushed as they walked.

"No, someone else has already proposed," she said.

He stopped abruptly and demanded, "Who?"

"You did," she replied nonchalantly, and then put it out there to win her dream or lose it. "So you're going to marry me."

"I am?" he said with a very big smile.

"Yes, you did actually ask, twice I believe, so don't even think of wiggling out of it."

"Don't know how to wiggle. I suppose you could teach me, but I'd rather you didn't."

She shoved him back when he started to lean closer. "That wasn't an answer."

"Of course it was. I love you, sweetheart, so much that I nearly lost you. I accept your proposal."

"But I didn't propose, you did. I was the one accepting."

"If you say so."

She pulled him back to her, put her arms around him. "One of these days I might not think you're teasing and then you'll be in a pickle."

"That will never happen, because you know me too well, as I do you, which is why I know you love me, too, Nessi. I don't need to hear it."

"But you want to, so I'm saying it. I do love you."

"Thank God!" he exclaimed.

"You weren't in doubt," she reminded.

"No, I wasn't. But it was still an excruciating wait at Carlton House yesterday for George to return when I'd wanted to go with him. It should have been my voice objecting to that wedding so you'd know bloody well that I *did* object to your marrying another man. But George insisted I not muck up the intervention with unnecessary complications, which a declaration of love certainly would have done. As for now, you'll be pleased to know that I already have your father's permission to court you."

Her eyes widened. "How the deuce does he know before I do?"

"He mentioned it when I met him yesterday."

"Just out of the blue?"

"I might have confessed to loving you."

"Smart of you to get one parent on your side."

"Do I need to worry about the other one?"

"My mother? Not in the least. But I think we've already done sufficient courting. You and I are going straight to the altar."

"I couldn't agree more. I'll arrange for the first bann to be announced today, then we will only have to wait two weeks."

"It's only a couple days' ride to Gretna Green, where we don't have to wait a'tall," she pointed out.

"No, we'll let your mother do her planning, and my mother will be ecstatic to help, and you'll have time to order a new wedding dress of your own design, and *then* we'll escape to the estate my parents are giving me as a wedding gift, for at least several years of seclusion with parents not invited."

She laughed. "You're marrying me just for property?!"

"No, bliss first, then property," he teased back. "At least I'll forgo a dowry!"

IT HAPPENED JUST AS they'd planned, they were married two weeks later directly after the third bann was announced at Sunday service. It had been an excruciating wait, especially because Monty had indeed returned to his parents' town house. He still called daily, though her parents wouldn't leave them alone together, one or the other always present, never both together. But whenever they were in the same room they treated each other like strangers, or got into whispered arguments, none of which they wanted to visit on the happy couple. At least at meals the twins kept them distracted from each other.

But the wedding must have softened their hearts, because when Vanessa and Montgomery turned to leave the church as man and wife, she saw her parents kissing, rather hotly, too, and on either side of them, the twins giggling about it.

Vanessa shook her head. After only two weeks her father had forgiven her? William must have realized he still loved her, after all. But she wasn't annoyed about it. Hadn't she hoped, deep down, that her parents would get back together?

But at the wedding party that afternoon, she pulled her father aside to ask, "Has Mother blackmailed you into her bed?"

He laughed. "You need to strike that word from your vocabulary, Daughter."

"So you're happy about it?"

"I believe I am."

She humphed. "Then take Mother home to Cheshire and keep her out of London."

He laughed. "Good advice." But then seriously, "I don't need to ask if you're happy, when it's so obvious. But don't let him change you, Nessi. You are perfect as you are."

"He happens to agree with you, Father, and wouldn't have me any other way!"

And Emily teased her a while later, "You said he would never marry."

"I didn't think he would. I'm pleased to be wrong."

"I can see that. I knew he wasn't interested in me, so I'm glad you won him. Really, I'm happy for you."

She hugged the twin who waxed hot and cold. "I know you are. And I'll be happy for you when you make up your mind about a husband. You really don't need to rush it, Em. Be sure first. It's so much better when you're sure."

"Are we going to cry?" Layla asked as she hugged them both.

"We might," Emily mumbled. "We only just got you back, Nessa, and now you're leaving again."

"But I've been told I'll only be a day or two away."

"Then we'll both visit you."

"Not until you're invited," Vanessa replied, but softened her words with a grin.

"Of course not, you'll be on your honeymoon," Layla agreed.

"Which could last a year or more."

"Nonsense, we'll see you soon."

She was hoping that she and Monty could escape soon when she was besieged by his family, en masse. She'd already met the lot of them, even the nieces and nephews, when her family had been invited to dine at their town house.

Angela Townsend hugged her warmly today and whispered, "His father and I despaired that this day would ever come. It's such a joy to welcome you to our family."

And Weston said to Monty, "I suppose I'll have to tolerate you now. You're too bloody happy to get annoyed at my jibes anymore."

It was a complaint and yet it wasn't. Weston even smiled as he said it. But Andrew still poked him in the ribs, saying, "You still have me, Brother. I promise to take the bait when you feel inclined to boorishness—oh, wait, you always are!"

Weston snorted, but Monty's eldest sister, Evelyn, put her arm through his and warned Andrew, "Leave him alone. Today is a day for cheer. Baby Boy has joined our ranks."

"Let's hope without our trials and tribulations," Claire put in with a grumble.

Vanessa might have been confused if Monty hadn't already told her that Evelyn wasn't talking to her husband and Claire wanted a divorce from hers because she believed he'd cheated on her, even though her entire family had assured her it wasn't so.

But then Evelyn said to Claire, "Speak for yourself, darling. I'm talking to my husband again."

Vanessa whispered to Monty, who had just put his arm around her waist, "Did she really call you Baby Boy?"

"They all did for a while. It's hell being the youngest." But then before the tiff between his sisters escalated, he grinned at Evelyn. "I think I'm a little too old for that nickname, Evy."

But Claire, still smarting over Evelyn's remark, turned to her older sister. "At least he didn't use his old nickname for you, Evil."

At which point Brian Townsend said in a warning tone, "The lot of you will remember that this is a gloriously happy day for our family."

"Of course!" more than one of them said in unison.

But then even he ribbed the groom a little. "The rake never did become you, Montgomery, but I always knew it would only take the right woman to help you to figure that out. Wasn't so complicated after all, was it?"

Monty laughed. Vanessa guessed what his father was referring to, though she doubted Monty would tell his family it had required royal intervention to free her to marry him. She was so pleased that his parents appeared to like her so much, but now they wanted more grandchildren! When that subject was mentioned, Vanessa extricated herself without blushing.

"WE SHOULD ARRIVE BEFORE evening tomorrow. The property is near Harwich on the Essex coast. Your father mentioned that you like a view of the sea, so I'm quite pleased with the location. And Mother assured me the staff she hired has the manor cleaned and stocked."

"Just hired?"

"The house has been empty for a good number of years.

And you can pick your own staff if you'd prefer. She just wanted the place ready for us."

"To be dealt with as needed. Just now, you've a wife to be dealt with."

He rolled her over in the large bed. "Like this?"

He entered her for the second time that night. "Exactly like that," she said before she gasped, and held on tight.

This was their wedding night, and a nice enough inn to be having it in. And she reminded herself that she could sleep in the coach tomorrow. . . .

"You . . . do that . . . splendidly."

He threw back his head and laughed. "You spoil me."

"You object?"

"God, no."

She drew her nails up his back lightly, then down to grip his buttocks. He surprised her by climaxing with a loud groan, but it was a deep enough plunge that she joined him. She smiled in delight to have caused it.

He rolled to her side then pulled her close. "How did I get so lucky?"

"You got attacked by two Feldland rebels. That started it all."

"Well, if we want to be precise, George started it all by offering his friendship, which led to this and that and then two Feldland rebels."

"I'd rather not thank George."

"I'd rather not thank the rebels."

"Then you can thank my Snow for shaking me off his back just as you were passing by."

"I have a feeling your Snow is going to be thanking me."

She was too tired to ask what he meant, but when they reached his property the next day, he didn't take her directly into the very large house. He took her straight to the stable, and it only took a moment for her to notice a large area filled with shire horses in assorted colors.

"They're all mares," Monty told her. "My wedding gift to you."

She turned around and hugged him tightly before she cried.

"So you'll be happy here?"

"Did you really have any doubt?"